MURDER OR SUICIDE

— The Missing Link —

A Nick Edwards Novel
By Allen E. Boekeloo

Order this book online at www.trafford.com
or email orders@trafford.com

Most Trafford titles are also available at major online book retailers.

Note for Librarians: A cataloguing record for this book is available from Library
and Archives Canada at www.collectionscanada.ca/amicus/index-e.html

Printed in Victoria, BC, Canada.

ISBN: 978-1-4269-0735-7 (sc)

*Our mission is to efficiently provide the world's finest, most comprehensive book publishing
service, enabling every author to experience success. To find out how to publish your book, your
way, and have it available worldwide, visit us online at www.trafford.com*

Trafford rev. 9/14/2009

 www.trafford.com

North America & international
toll-free: 1 888 232 4444 (USA & Canada)
phone: 250 383 6864 ♦ fax: 812 355 4082

<u>Summary</u>

MURDER OR SUICIDE
THE
MISSING
LINK

Nick Edwards tries to solve two murder cases from Chicago. First case; a twenty-year old murder or suicide never been resolved. Mr. Edwards client . . . a twenty-five year old woman, the daughter of the victim, Sheryl Boehlis, does not believe her mother, Sandy Boehlis, committed suicide. The 1977 case wil re-hash a lot of agony and pain, but she is prepared for the worst. Sheryl wants justice and closure, but the lack of truth from her Uncle Dale, Auntie 'Bee' and her Grandmother Barryhill, and the lack of clues from the police department, Miss Boehlis had no one to turn to, but Nick Edwards . . . .

. . . . Second case; a twelve-year old murder that involves the mafia and the Chicago Police Department. Mr. Edwards client; Lisa Murray, which is Nick's girlfriend. Lisa thinks and truly believes there is a connection between her father, Donald Murray; a homicide detective, who was short of two months from retiring, dying and the mafia. Her belief; the mafia planted a bomb in her father's vehicle, which also cost her mother's life, Katie Murray. Lisa's father put two brothers from the mafia in prison for ten years for murder. After serving their time, the brothers, Rudy and Ruby Balesteri sought revenge. But the police files had little, if any, clues to go on, proving the Balesteri Brothers were involved. Nick Edwards will try to prove if there was a cover-up . . . . and why. Nick's cohorts and some of his friends had been involved in solving this mystery. Which will call for an explosive conclusion.

<u>SALUTE</u>

Chapter One

I T WAS A late February afternoon in Tomah, Wisconsin. I had hot chocolate from the coffee shop next door. I would've had coffee, but hot chocolate was more appropriate this time of year. I sat back in my high-back swivel chair with my feet resting on top of my desk. Over- head lights were on in our office. I glanced at the desk calendar, which I picked up from FirstStar Bank. The year; '1997' was sparkling in gold on top of it. I had the calendar at close range, so I wouldn't forget my birthday. I'd even circled the date in red. I aged another year. So I am forty-eight and still going strong. Except my right leg when I had a bul- let shatter my knee-cap last year during a drug bust.

Clint had a client sitting on the right side of his desk with his back toward me. They were whispering. Top Secret, I guess. Lisa, my girl- friend, sat across from Clint's client, cleaning her weapon, a .38 Smith and Wesson Chief Special. His client had his head turned slightly and faced Lisa while she had the barrel toward his direction. He seemed uncomfortable. Lisa and Clint didn't notice. Maybe they didn't care.

I looked out my picture window and studied people coming and going from Wal-Mart Department store. A young woman walked slow- ly and carefully on the snow covered parking lot. While she passed by my window, she smiled and waved at me. I waved back with my finger- tips. She dressed for the weather. Outside the temperature was 35 de- grees. The clouds were low and gray. The snow had dimenished to flurries, leaving a fresh blanket of sparkling snow under the parking lot lights. Beautiful. A minute later, the front door to our office opened.

It was the same young woman who had waved and smiled at me. May- be the wave of my fingertips were not enough. Maybe she needed a kiss and a hug, too. By golly. Lisa glared at her as she walked by her desk. But Clint didn't notice her. Again, maybe he didn't care. Clint's client stood and they shook hands. Then his client went.

The young woman walked confidently to my desk, and stood erect with her right hand extended. "Mr. Edwards, I'm Sheryl Boehlis."

I shook her hand, and gestured with my left hand to sit in my client's chair. She did.

"How is your right leg, Mr. Edwards?" She asked politely.

1

"Fine, thank-you. It only hurts when I laugh. But it could have been worse. Lisa, my girlfriend got shot, too." I said nodding in Lisa's direction.

Sheryl turned around and faced Lisa. But Lisa was too busy cleaning her gun to notice. So Sheryl turned around and faced me again.

"Sorry, Miss Boehlis." I said.

"About what?"

"I didn't recognize you at first. It must be all the layer of clothing.you have on." I got Lisa's attention when I said that. I waved at Lisa with a grin.

She returned my grin. Then she went back cleaning her .38 Special.

"I guess I do look different, don't I." She crossed her left leg over her her right. She seemed comfortable.

"Coffee?" I asked. She glanced at my foam cup.

"I'll have what you are having."

"Hot chocolate." I said.

"Okay. Hot chocolate it is." Sheryl smiled and winked.

I stood and bended readily on my right leg.

"How did you and Lisa get shot anyway, Mr. Edwards?"

"We were on a drug case not too far from here. Lisa and I were blind- sided. It was dark. Lisa received a flesh wound in her shoulder. But healed very well. I also got shot near my left ear. I'm thirty-percent deaf." Sheryl nodded with no further comment or concern.

When I walked by Lisa, I gave her a comforting pat on her left should- er. We smiled at each other. I hobbled outside and turned right, and right again. I went inside the coffee shop. A few minutes later I'd returned with two hot chocolates. One for Lisa, the other for my client. Clint doesn't like chocolate. Or coffee, for that matter. So I didn't buy him anything. When I had returned to my office, Sheryl was holding a picture in her right hand of

Lisa. She was standing near my file cabinets. I didn't realize how tall she was. Slender too. Sheryl wore a blue knitted cap with tie strings at the ends.

Tassels were white. The down ski jacket was off-white. It had soft brown leathered but- tons. Her jacket was unbuttoned. It revealed her blue, but styl- ish turtle-neck sweater. Her black tight slacks overwhelmed me. Her white boots came over her shins. White fur spilled out of them.

I stepped in closer to my desk with the two steaming cups of cocoa.

I'd startled Sheryl when I placed the cups down on my desk. She turned suddenly and faced me.

"Oh, you scared me. I was just admiring this woman's photo. Is this Lisa?"

"Yes, it is. That was taken a few years ago." I said.

"Well, I must say, you do have good taste in woman." Sheryl winked.

"Thanks." I called over to Lisa to meet my client, Sheryl. But before Lisa agreed, she wanted to finish maintaining her weapon.

Sheryl and I blew in our cups before we sipped. Hot. I took a care- ful sip. Swallowed. She continued to blow in hers. She finally sipped, and swallowed. She placed her drink on my desk and looked up at me.

"What is your price again, Mr. Edwards?" She leaned over and took another sip of her hot chocolate. But it wasn't as hot as it was earlier. I could tell by the way she gulped instead of sipped.

"1,000 . . . 400 as a retainer." I smiled.

While Sheryl was getting the money, Lisa walked that special walk to- ward my desk. Her walk always turned me on. But before Lisa approached my office, Sheryl handed me a white envelope from the inside of her ski- jacket pocket.

"I have 500 in there, Mr. Edwards." She handed it to me gracefully, like she was pleased with herself. I gracefully took it out of her hand. I was pleased. I unsealed it, and pulled out five one-hundred dollar bills. Crispy. I even sniffed them. Fresh.

"Do you always do that, Mr. Edwards?" She slightly grinned.

"Yep. Tells me if it is counterfeit." I sniffed again.

"Really?" Her eyebrows were raised with little wrinkles on her fore- head. I shook my head and waved my left hand in the air. "Nah, I just like the smell of money"

"Don't us all." She finished her cocoa. She seemed satisfied.

Lisa walked in my office quietly, but not intentionally. We had very thick carpet throughout our office space. An elephant could have snuck in. I slid the money in its envelope, and dropped it in my desk drawer.

"Lisa," I said. "Meet my client, Sheryl." They shook hands. Sheryl seemed taller than Lisa. Maybe by three inches. Maybe it's the boots.

"Please to meet you, Lisa."

"You, too."

Lisa glanced at me nervously. Speechless. She waited for me to say something. I did.

"Lisa, Miss Boehlis is the client I was telling you about last year. Do you remember?"

"Oh yeah. Chicago, Illinois. Right?"

Sheryl nodded. "Yeah. That's correct. My mother's name was Sandy.

I was five years old when she passed on." Suddenly, my office became quiet. Sheryl had tears flowing slowly down her smooth facial skin. Lisa held her for a while.

Clint had left the office. Then returned a few minutes later with a cup of ice tea. He'd lit a cigar. Smoke hovered above his head. I'd noticed him staring out his front office window, smoking his cigar, and drinking his ice tea. It was dark outside. Highway 21 and Highway 12 intersected near our office building, and the rush hour traffic had de- minished. He'd stood and stared outside for a long while. Tough, but a quiet man. The stillness was interrupted by my phone ringing.

"C-N-L Detective Agency, Nick speaking. May I help you?"

"Just me, Mr. Nick. Mr. Wu from the pizza parlor next door."

"Good-evening, Mr. Wu. How can I help you?"

"Have pizza cancelled. Party didn't answer door when delivered. Do you want it. It's on house."

"Great! Thanks Mr. Wu."

"Be right over." We hung up. Mr. Wu came and went. He didn't want to disturb my meeting with my client. The deluxe pizza was mmm . . . . good!

Sheryl regained her composure, and sat back down in my client chair.

Lisa slid another client chair next to her and sat on her right. We'd ate the pizza and discussed Sheryl's case.

"Sheryl, do you have an old picture of your mother?" I asked.

"Sure." She picked up her purse from the floor, next to her left foot, and thumbed for the picture. She pulled out a black wallet and searched through that. After a few minutes, maybe three minutes, she delicately slid out a faded yellow-edged photo from one of the plastic windows that was made for identification and photo's, such as the one she had given me.

"Please be careful with it, Mr. Edwards. That's the only one I have."

"You bet." I inserted it in the envelope carefully.

"I also have the police report and death certificate." Sheryl said.

She handed it to me with tears in her eyes. Lisa wrapped her left arm around my clients shoulders. I folded the documents, and tucked them neat- ly in the envelope, carefully not to damage her mother's picture.

"Miss Boehlis, I need to ask you a few questions. Maybe a lot of questions."

"Um-Umm. Sure, yeah. I understand." Sheryl wiped her tears on the tissue I had given her. She wiggled her lower-half of her body into the chair and got comfortable. Lisa had this concern look while she continued to console Sheryl. Lisa can relate with Sheryl. Lisa also lost both of her parents about twelve years ago in a car bombing. That's my next case. Chicago, here I come.

"You were very young when your mother passed."

"Yeah, five years old. Why?"

"Anything you can tell me makes you believe your mother did not com- mit suicide."

"Well, when I got older, in my early teens, I'd asked questions to peo- ple who knew her. I was told she wasn't the type."

"Do you think there are special types?" I chewed my lower lip.

"Maybe . . . Maybe not. But I was told my mother was happy and content with her life. No signs of depression." She turned to Lisa. Then back to me.

"These people you asked; were they close friends of your mother's, or relatives, or both?"

"Relatives. Relatives, you say." I nodded. "Hell no. My mother's side of the family didn't tell me anything." She paused. I waited. Her lips moved again.

"My dad was killed in Viet Nam. 1971." Tears formed again. Lisa did her thing, and handed her another handful of tissues.

"So you became an orphan when your mother passed." That statement didn't need a response. And I did not get one, either. "So, who took care of you?"

"My Gram'." Her lips became tight when she said ' "Gram" '.

"Your mother's mother?" I asked.

Nod. And a sniffle.

Sheryl blew her nose and wiped her tears once again. Her eyes were red and puffy. Her beautiful soft eyes became hard and stern. "Damn it, Nick. I believe she was murdered, and I want them found. I want justice done."

I nodded. Lisa just sat there next to Sheryl and had her arm draped a- round the back of the chair.

"Sheryl, you said '**THEM**'. You think there might be more than one?"

"Figure of speech, I guess. But it could be."

"More than one?" I said.

"Maybe. How should I know? Figure of speech. Let's leave it at that.
Okay?"

"O-kee-doke," I said. "You don't think your mother was depressed over your father being killed in Viet Nam, and maybe killed herself for that reason?"

"She was probably depressed for a while, I guess. But she got over it, I was told."

"Of course." I sat back in my chair. And thought. Pause for silence. I leaned forward again. "I don't blame you for having, uh, the murderer or murderers found, if it was mur- der. But why now, Sheryl, after twenty years?"

"I was hoping my Uncle, Aunt and Gram' would have showed some concern how my mother died. As I got older, I was trying to convince them that my mother would not have committed suicide. But they didn't budge. So, when they didn't have it investigated, I looked you up. Heard you were good."

"Thanks, but people exaggerate." Lisa looked at me. Sheryl seemed to be disappointed when I said that remark.

"Don't mind him, Sheryl," Lisa said. "He's too modest. He is good . . .
Great, a matter of fact." I just sat back, and let Lisa tell her story about us.

"That is how we met, Sheryl. About two years ago, he was investigat- ing an arsonist. I was his witness. He protected me. Within five days, he had the suspect arrested. And she was on the 'Ten Most Wanted'."

Sheryl's eyes gleamed. "Really? Jeez. That makes me feel very confident in you, Mr. Edwards." I nodded modestly.

Chapter Two

I SAT BACK IN my high-back, and my hands laced behind my head. Sheryl changed position. Her right leg over her left. Lisa still had her left arm over Sheryl's shoulders. And Clint smoked his Ashton Cabinet Belicoso cigar. He was writing something on his legal pad. I didn't need to know. None of my business. He took a sip of his ice-tea from the clear plastic straw and looked at me from across the room. He had a very serious look. I turned toward Lisa and then glared at Sheryl.

"I need some more questions answered before I pursue your case. Okay with you, Miss Boehlis?"

"Sure, of course."

"Some of these questions I'll be asking, will be harsh and personnel."

"Sure, I understand, Mr. Edwards." Her eyes shifted toward Lisa. She squeezed my client's hand. Sheryl seemed ready, but nervous.

I slid my legal pad toward me, and was ready to jot down any valuable information with my shiny new pen. It was silver coated. Click. "Do you remember anything about your mother's life?"

"Such as?"

"Such as; your mother's occupation, love life, habits. Good or bad. Even her physical profile, uh, appearance."

"You do understand I was only five years old. Not too much to remember. But, I'll try."

I nodded. And clicked my pen again. I was ready to write. I think.

"What I do remember was my mother worked at a corner bar near our house where she had died." Sheryl paused. Held back tears. Lisa was ready to assist with kleenex tissues. But didn't need to. Yet. "She also worked at a grocery store. I think she worked at the store during the day, the bar at night."

"Um. What did she do in the store?"

"Worked in the deli. Made sandwiches and such."

"The bar?" I asked. I shifted my blue eyes toward Lisa. Then Back at Sheryl.

"Bartender, I guess."

"Remember the names of those places?" I had pen in hand . . . . Click.

"The store was A and P Foods. I remember that, because my Gram' and I walked there everyday to see my mother, and buy sanwiches and meat."

"The bar?" I asked

"Uh . . . . 'Peanut . . . . uh . . . something . . . . Something peanut." Sheryl tapped her temple a few times. "Damn. Think, Sheryl." She said to herself. "Got it" She was relieved. I was ready to write. I think. Click. "Bowl . . . . That's it, 'Peanut

Bowl'." I finally got to use my shiny new pen. Hurray!

I asked. "Location and address?"

"Come on, Nick. Pete-sake. I was only a little kid. Give me a break."

"Sorry. Thought I ask. It's my job to ask questions."

"Yeah, I know. Sorry." She crossed her legs again. She grinned a shy and girlish grin.

I patiently waited for her answer to my last question. I just smiled. Waited.

I tapped my new pen a few times on my desk pad. I cleared my throat. She got the hint, finally.

"I do not remember the location or address." I smiled and thanked her politely.

"Okay. Love life?"

"Excuse me?" Sheryl's face became tight. Winkles formed on her fore- head and her eyebrows were lifted high.

"Your mothers love life."

"Oh. She dated this guy as long as I can remember. Maybe when I was a baby, or a little older. All I can remember she dated him 'til she died."

"Name?"

"Mike . . . something. Last name I don't recall. Sorry."

I nodded

"Her habits?" I asked.

"My mother worked all the time. I didn't see much of her."

"But when you did see her, what did the two of you do together?"

"Nothing to brag about, I guess. We just sat around the house watching television."

"Sheryl, this is where I'll be asking personnel questions. They might be a little harsh. Understand?"

"I guess." She wiggled in my client chair. She crossed her legs again. And smiled child- ishly. Lisa had laid her hands in her lap, folded. And intently listened. Her feet flat on our thick carpet.

"Did she drink, ah, smoke pot, ah, have crazy sex in front of you with Mike, or any other guy you can recall?"

"Nick Edwards." Lisa raised her voice, just a tad. Well, maybe more than just a tad. "Please! Aren't you being *more* than just a little harsh?"

"Maybe. But I'm trying to get a feel of her mother's life and habits. I do not want to take this case with my eyes closed."

Lisa's tone came down a notch. "I understand you have to ask ques-tions, honey, but less harsh. Okay?"

"Alright, sweetie. I'll try."

I studied Sheryl's eyes for a-while, just to be sure she wasn't lying.

"You're not holding anything back, are you?"

She shrugged.

"Miss Boehlis, I am a professional investigator. I will find out sooner or later, but I prefer sooner, so this case will be solved sooner. Understand?"

Nod.

Sheryl seemed nervous. Her eyes began to shift. I was losing faith and trust in her. "Relax, Miss. You came to me, remember? To solve this case, you must be one-hundred percent honest with me. You got it?"

She took a deep breath. Her hands were trembling. And her left eye twitched. Lisa turned and looked at her. She grabbed and held her hands again.

Sheryl said. "May I smoke?"

"Sure. Knock yourself out." She pulled a menthol cigarette out of her black purse, which was sitting near her left foot on the thick carpet. She lit it. Inhaled. Exhaled. The smoke streamed out of her nostrils. She seem to relax.

"Damn it, anyway, Nick. Yes, my mother had wild sex and parties in my presence. She even had me sleep on the floor so she can have her fun with whoever in my own bed-room. But, mainly with her boyfriend, Mike.

Micheal, ah, Micheal Barton. They also had drug parties. Mike hits us and beats us, whenever he felt like it. The bastard."

"Sorry to hear that, Miss Boehlis." But saying "Sorry" didn't relieve her pain.

"Well, at least we're getting somewhere with this interview. Do you know where he is, or what happened to him?"

"Who gives a rats-ass. He's out of my life. Thank God." She sat and re- composed her-self. She took another pull of her cigarette.

Well, I must say, my new silvery and shiny pen got its work out for the day.

I said. "Did he go to your mother's funeral?"

"I don't know. I wasn't allowed to go to the funeral. My Gram' told me it wasn't a place for little children."

I glanced over to my desk calendar. Happy birthday, I thought.

"She also told me," Sheryl said. "the casket was closed. It didn't mat- ter if I went to her funeral or not. Couldn't see my mother anyway."

I said. "Closed casket?" Lisa just sat there and shook her beautiful head. I believed I'd seen tears slowly running down Lisa's rosy cheeks.

Sheryl said. "Yeah, that's what she'd told me. A closed casket. Doesn't make any sense, does it, Nick . . . . Lisa?" Lisa and I shook our heads and agreed. No it didn't make any sense.

I opened my desk drawer and pulled out the white envelope with the money and documents that Sheryl gave me. From the envelope, I pulled out the Death Certificate, and studied it carefully. I looked up at Sheryl and Lisa.

Put my head down, again. I studied it some more.

"It says here," I said, not looking up, "Your mother died of toxic poison- ing."

"Yeah." Sheryl lifted her shoulders and then relaxed them. "So. What does that mean?"

"My question is; why a closed casket?"

"I don't know that, either. Maybe my Gram' lied about that, too."

"Maybe." I said.

I put the document back in the envelope and placed it neatly in my desk drawer. I folded my hands in front of me, and shook my head disgustedly.

"Anything else, Mr. Edwards?" Sheryl said. Her eyes were puffy and red. And her nose reminded me of 'Rudolph'.

"Yes. I need your mother's and father's birth certificate, your birth cer- tificate, and their marriage license."

"Why?" Sheryl's ash was long and bended. I quickly grabbed an ashtray from my bottom desk draw, and slid it across my desk toward her. She miss- ed. It fell into her lap. She moved so fast, the ashtray went flying against my side wall, and almost went through my picture window. She brushed the ashes from her tight slacks.

"Shit." She jumped away from my client chair. " Damn it." After she'd cleaned her mess, she sat back down. I stared at Sheryl and grinned. Lisa moved her chair somewhat away from Sheryl's. Lisa probably didn't feel safe near Sheryl anymore. Smart.

"Relax, Miss Boehlis. I have fire insurance." She grinned. One big hap—py family.

"Why do you want the certificates, Mr. Edwards?"

"Because your mother's death certificate that you gave me is stamped *PENDING* on it. Where is the Medical Examiner's final analysis?"

"How in the hell should I know. All I know, I went downtown in Chicago a few years ago, and that is what they handed me."

"What was the name of the place where you went?" I gave her a stern and hard look.

"I don't remember. Why?" Her eyes shifted and twitched again. A sign of nervousness and dishonesty.

"Vital Statistics ring a bell, Miss Boehlis?"

She shrugged.

"You are not telling me the truth. Are you?" I sat back in my chair, and pulled on my suit jacket and inserted my shiny pen in my inside pocket. I wasn't writing anyway.

"Yes, I am. Seriously." I looked into her hazel eyes. She seemed to be telling the truth. But she couldn't pull the wool over my eyes. Nick Edwards, trained investigator.

"The reason I need those documents is because I need something official and com- plete. As far as I'm concerned, this certificate is bogus." I picked the certificate from the desk blotter, and waved it, flapping it in the air. Lisa's and Sheryl's jaw line dropped way down.

"Explain that, Mr. Edwards." Sheryl said, as she went in her purse for another smoke.

"Yes, please, honey. Explain that." I was beginning to doubt who's the boss of this investigation.

"It's inconclusive. It doesn't tell me anything. I need something solid.

Substantial. You know what I mean." I glanced down at the document, a-gain. "And who is Dale Nowak, Miss Boehlis?"

"My uncle. Why?"

"Why did he sign the certificate as the next of kin?"

"I don't know that either. I told you before. My mother's family was very secretive. They had kept everything from me that pertained to my mother's death. I need your help, Mr. Edwards. Please!" She had put her cigarette out in the ashtray without any disasters. Whew.

I nodded. "You got my help, Miss. But I am still confused about the signing. Your grandmother, or grandfather, even siblings are the next of kin.

Not uncles. Unless they're the only ones living, or Mr. Nowak was her brother." She nodded and had crossed her legs. If she kept crossing her legs, she just might put a hole in her knee of her pants. Friction.

"My grandfather died before I was born." Suddenly she raised her hands to her face and cried extremely into them. Her voice muffled. "Everyone's dying around me. As far as I know, my Uncle Dale and Auntie 'Bee' are alive."

I waited for Sheryl to calm her tears before my next question. Lisa left my office to get more tissues from her desk. Clint had left the building. Maybe couldn't take the crying anymore. I had my new pen in my left hand again. Ready to write.

Lisa had returned with a fresh box of Kleenex. Sheryl pulled a few out and blew her nose. She'd wiped her tears with the back of her hands. She wiggled in my client chair again. She seemed comfortable. Lisa sat down next to Sheryl. We were ready.

"Your Auntie 'Bee' . . . . What was the relationship between your mother and aunt?"

"My aunt was my mother's sister." Sheryl stood and walked around my cubicle/office. "I can probably get most of those documents you asked for, Nick, but not all of them. Alright?"

"Oke-kee-do-kee. I'll do my foot-work, which I do best and see what we can come up with. Fair enough?"

She nodded. We shook hands. Then she left.

Whew! What a day . . . . .

Chapter Three

I INVITED LISA TO my apartment. It was smaller than her condo suite, but I'd missed my apartment too much to stay another month while my right leg was healing. It had been four months already I'd stayed with Lisa. But it was convenient. She had an elevator. I didn't.

She'd made my meals, cleaned my clothes. She'd even cleaned my own apartment and checked my mail. What a sweetheart. But I was going crazy.

Stir crazy. I wasn't used to be waited on and spoiled. I felt my leg was cape- able to climb my own stairs today. Of course, with Lisa's assistance.

"Well, Nick, are you ready to climb fifty stairs to the third level?" We were standing downstairs in my hallway, my left leg on the very first step. I was not ready for my right leg to give me the first boost. So, the left leg it is. Up-sa daisy. "Yes, sweetie, I am." Left leg, right leg. Lisa stood behind me as we climbed. I would've felt awful if I had lost my balance, and rolled my body over Lisa and had crushed her. So we took one step at a time. Slowly.

Lisa cleaned my apartment to perfection. I was impressed. But she did re-arrange some of my furniture. When I felt up to it, later, I'll re-rearrange my apartment when she wouldn't be here. My front window faced Superior

Avenue, where my futon used to be. Now the futon was in the center of my living room, surrounded by my recliner, T.V., and coffee table. I liked the futon by the window. Not much to see, but it was home. And cozy.

Since it was my birthday, Lisa decided to cook dinner for us. I hobbl- ed to the kitchen, opened the refrigerator door, and grabbed a MGD beer.

I leaned over the stove.

"What's cooking, blondie?"

"I'm cooking something different. It's called 'Lemon Vodka Shrimp'.

And I am making it special just for you, big boy."

"Because I like shrimp?"

"Yep."

" Can I pour beer in there, too?" I had my bottle tilted over the shrimp, about to pour.

"No, silly. It'll ruin it." I kissed Lisa on the neck. I went to the living room and sat on my futon, which was in the center of the living room away from the window. I took a sip of my beer. Ummm . . . Good.

I noticed how fast and graceful Lisa was. She seemed to be gliding from the kitchen to the dining room.

I yelled from the living room. "Anything I can help you with, honey?"

She screamed from the kitchen. "No thank-you, sweet patootie." She came gliding toward me and sat next to me on my right.

"You were hard on Sheryl, Tex. Why?" Her bright blue eyes were wide and gleamful. I loved her eyes. It made me see deep into her soul. And she had a lot of it, too.

"I had to be. I knew she wasn't telling me the truth. I had to make her open up to me on my terms, not on hers. Otherwise, this case probably wouldn't get off the ground. I just gave her a little push."

"Did you realize Sheryl was trying to save face and protect her moth- er's reputation."

"Yes I did realize that. But that wouldn't help me solve this case."

"Yes. I understand that, Nick. Also she wanted to keep her hurt and pain buried within herself."

"Right." I said. Lisa stood and walked back to the kitchen. But not without a love tap on her butt. She turned and blew me a kiss. "Sweet patootie?" I said. "Sweet patootie." She said and smiled. Mmmm.

In the kitchen, Lisa was making music with the pots and pans. Stir here, and a rattle there. She combined cream, coconut milk, lemon juice, two teaspoons lemon zest, two tablespoons of vodka, a teaspoon salt and sugar, white pepper, one half of teaspoon gin- ger paste, one yellow, one red bell pepper, seeded and sliced. Lisa topped it off with one zucchini and one and one-half of jumbo shrimp, peeled. Before she'd put it on sim- mer, she added a half-a-shot more of vodka. She loves her vodka. Then she put it on simmer. She came gliding toward me and sat on the futon next to me. She said. "Happy Birthday, tough guy." She'd undressed in front of me slowly, and hummed something sensual. It dazzled my cloth- es right off. Fortunately, the dinner was on slow simmer. So were we, but not that slow, but slow enough. Within the hour the Lemon Vodka Shrimp was ready for eating. I poured the white wine in our glasses, Kendall Jack- son. Lisa liked hers on the rocks. She sipped some and eyed me over the rim of her glass.

She said. "Nick, why do you want all those documents from Sheryl.

What good will they do?" She sipped some wine.

I took a drink, and thought about Lisa's question. I set my drink down and set it on my right of my plate. I rested my chin on the right heel of my hand. Then looked up at Lisa.

"Well, Sheryl's birth certificate will prove to me who the father is. Sandy's certificate will tell me where she was born, and any birth defects.

Sheryl's father's birth certificate will tell me who his parents are. It will also tell me where he was born."

Lisa nodded. She seemed impressed. She took a small bite of shrimp, and swallowed slowly, taking in all the flavor. Maybe the vodka. Maybe the shrimp. I bet on the vodka.

I said, still looking at Lisa's chewing-style. "I feel that her grandmother kept her from reality, almost a recluse, so to speak. I also feel Sheryl was kept from her dad's parents, for whatever reason."

Lisa said. "Maybe Sandy's mother was afraid Sheryl's father's family would've taken her away from her. Sheryl's father being dead, it made it easier for 'Gram-ma'." The last syllable, 'Gram-ma' was extended and emphasized.

"Yeah, honey. I suppose you're right." I took a bite of my shrimp and chased it with Mr. Kendall Jackson.

Lisa said. "Why the marriage license?" She had her chin supported on her knuckles.

I said. "Nothing else to ask." We grinned at each other and winked.

We ate without another word.

Chapter Four

IT WAS EARLY Monday morning and still dark when I woke up with a sore neck on the futon in the center of my living room. I reluctantly pushed my- self up and away from my bed. I hobbled to the front window, and peeked through my blinds. It was raining with snow mixed. It was four-thirty. I had the shower running until it was the right temperature. Luke-warm. Took my shower, and got dressed. At five-o-five, I care- fully descended the fifty stairs and went to my garage, opened the garage door with my blonde hair and lea- ther coat soaked from the rain and snow. I climbed in my 1995 Chevy coupe and started it up, slowly backed-up into the alleyway, closing the door with my remote control. I put the car in gear and sped off fish-tailing.

I took Superior Avenue heading north with my tires spinning. The trac-tion was lousy. I was the only one on the road. Stupid me. I could be sleep- ing, but I had a big case to solve. The early bird catches the worm.

From Superior Avenue, I turned west on highway 12 and drove a-quar- ter mile and turned left into the parking lot. Put my shift in to park, got out, and unlocked the build-ing door to my office and went in, closing the door quietly behind me. I sat behind my over-sized mahogany desk. I turned my chair toward the picture window. I looked out at the darkness. If it wasn't for the parking lot lights, it would've been pitch black. I switched my desk light on, and went to work.

But before I went to Sheryl's case to investigate, I decided to get myself a cup of coffee and a jelly doughnut next door. I sometimes have hot choco- late, but this is one of the times I didn't. So hot coffee it is. It was six o clock and the coffee shop next door was open and ready for my money. It was still dark and the neon lights from the coffee shop reflected brightly on the wet blacktop. I went in and ordered a small regular coffee. I had two sugars and two packets of powdered cream. I also ordered a jelly doughnut, apple-cent- ered. I paid the dish-water blonde haired waitress. She smiled when she took my money. I smiled back when she gave me my items and change.

When I stepped out of the coffee shop, the rain and snow had subsided.

It was seven in the morning and the sun peeked through the dark and gray clouds. I noticed some blue sky trying to peek through also. It seemed to be a promising day. The temperature was forty-eight degrees. Three more weeks, it'll be Spring. Hurray!

It had been a week now since Sheryl came to me with her case. She did not call. Neither did I. I gave her enough time to collect the documents I had requested. It was quiet in my office. Lisa and Clint were on separate cases.

I took advantage of the quietness. I lifted my legs and stretched them on top of my desk, and started my day out slowly. I sipped my coffee and took the last bite of my jelly doughnut. Sipped again. I was ready for the day.

I studied the death certificate that Sheryl gave me last week. I couldn't figure out why it took me this long to notice an error, or lie, or whatever. I must be slipping. I turned 48 years old, and I'm already losing it. Damn. I flipped the document over on the back-side. It had a date coded in red. She had informed me the death certificate was given to her a few years ago. Liar.

But, the stamp on the back-side said differently. This document was released and given to someone on February 1, 1978. It was a year after her mother's death. Sheryl was too young to get it herself. So, who gave it to her? Why did she lie to me? Who is she protecting . . . ? Herself? Or someone else?

Maybe her mother did commit suicide, but, Sheryl couldn't accept it. I'm on a wild goose chase. And for what? Just to satisfy her beliefs? Mmmm. I decided to call Sheryl Boehlis. Her phone rang a few times. The answering machine clicked on. A male's voice came on the other end. The voice said.

"This is Art's and Sheryl's pad. Please leave a message after the beep." The 'Beep' had sounded. So, I left a message to call ASAP. I hung up . . . Pad?

I swiveled my chair toward my cubicle window and observed the Wal-Mart employees parking their vehicles in their selected stalls. A few climbed out of their cars at rapid speed and ran. Some others got out of their vehicles at slow a rate, and walked. The rest didn't seem to care. Some bundled up like it was thirty-below-zero, others had their jackets and coats wide opened and flapping in the breeze. Different strokes for different folks. Heard that from somewhere before.

I waited for Sheryl to call, or better yet, report to my office. Or cubicle.

I like it, no matter what size it is. And it's mine. I'm happy with it.

The time on my eagle clock, which sat dead center on the front edge of my desk, read seventeen-after-nine. The front door opened and let some air, actually, cool air in. The door closed softly. I turned my chair to the left, and looked up. It was Sheryl.

"Well . . . . Well . . . . Well. Look what the March air blew in."

"What's with the attitude, Mr. Edwards?" She sat without permission. What nerve.

"Cut the bull, Missy. I'm not too happy with you and your lies."

"What are you talking about?" She threw her black fur gloves on to my desk, and sat there in my client chair, sternly. Her back stiff against the back and her feet firmly planted on the thick carpet. She didn't seem comfortable.

Good. I threw the death certificate at her. She gave me a devilish stare. Then looked at the front of the document. Sheryl briefly looked at me. She gave me that look again. "What is wrong with this?" She was shaking the docu—ment in the air violently. Temper. Temper.

I said. "Look on the back of it, Miss Temper-mental." I sat back with my arms folded over my chest. She turned it over. Her mouth dropped.

She said. "Oh. That." She froze her eyes to the year coded in red. And then looked down toward the floor for a few long minutes.

"Well," I said. "I need an explanation. And if I am not satisfied with it,

I'll kick you out of here, and then drop you as my client." Tears had formed on her cheeks and rolled down her ski jacket. I slid a tissue box toward her.

She took a few and wiped her eyes and nose.

"Okay . . . . Okay . . . . No more fricking lies." She had sniffled her last snif—fle. She looked up and faced me.

"I'm listening." I said. I leaned forward and rested my arms on my over- sized desk. I felt like the President of the United States.

"A neighbor friend of the family's tried to help out after this person had heard about my mother's death. This person took me to the courthouse in the

City of Chicago. It was downtown." I nodded. She said. "This person gave it to me in secret. I didn't tell a soul. I was told not to tell anyone whatsoever.

My grandmother, and everyone else kept it a secret, why not me? Huh?"

"So, who was this person?" I said.

"I'm not saying." She said with a firm lip. Tough broad. Maybe stupid.

"Okay." I said. "It's your prerogative. But, the less people I know who knew about your mother's death, the longer it will take to solve this mystery of her passing. Ca-peesh?"

She nodded. But she didn't care.

"So you haven't been back to the courthouse since?" I said.

She shook her head. "No. But I brought the certificates you asked for."

I grunted. "Well, that is very mighty kind of you. I was beginning to think you didn't care about finding your mother's killer. You being so secre- tive. In fact I was even think-ing about dropping your case and serve my next client. But we'll see what these certifi-cates will tell us."

Sheryl didn't show expression. Her face was blank. Not even a tear. A- mazing. She just sat in my client chair, stiffly.

I said. "Where are these certificates you claim you have, missy?"

She unzipped her ski jacket and pulled out a large brown sealed enve- lope. She handed me the envelope, I took it from her right hand, opened it with my letter opener, which I had in my left hand, and slid out the contents with my right. I looked up at Sheryl and asked sarcastically if these docu—ments were real or official. She gave me that look again, which she was good at. It must have taken her a lot of practice. Or did it come naturally?

She said. "Yes, of course they are." She made a clicking sound with her tongue. I laid the three certificates evenly on my desk. Side by side. I'd studied them for five, maybe ten minutes. The first one I studied, I studied very closely. In fact I studied all three very closely. Checking for errors, lies or whatever. The first Birth Certificate was Sheryl's dad:

John Boehlis; Born April 15, 1953. Chicago, Illinois. Roseland Community Hospital. Father's Name; Patrick Boehlis. Occupation; Truck Driver. Mother's Name; Barbra Boehlis; Maiden Name; Fargo. Scars Or/And Deformities: None
Both Parents From Chicago, Illinois.

The Second Certificate Was Sheryl's Mother: *Sandy Barryhill; Born: January 2, 1954. Chicago, Illinois. Cook County Hospital. Father's Name: Joseph Barryhill. Occupation: Steel Worker. Mother's Name: Grace Barryhill. Maiden Name: Clark. Scars Or/And DeFormities: 4 Fingers/2 Thumbs, L/H.*
Both Of Her Parents Were From Chicago, Illinois.

The Third And Last Certificate Was Sheryl's Herself: *Sheryl Boehlis: Born: March 9, 1972. Chicago, Illinois. Cook County Hospital. Father's Name: John Boehlis. Occupation: U.S. Marines/Deceased. Mother's Name: Sandy Boehlis. Maiden Name: Barryhill. Scars Or/And Deformities:none.*
Both Parents Were Also From Chicago, Illinois.

These documents were official. I noticed the 'certified seal' stamped and impressed in the lower right hand corner. I was satisfied. I made copies and gave the originals back to Sheryl. Then I inserted them in my white manila folder and filed it away in my lower right hand desk drawer.

I settled in to my chair, and rested my right foot on the bottom drawer of my desk. I looked up at Sheryl and she seemed to be asleep. Maybe I took too long reviewing the birth certificates. Oh well. I closed my bottom desk draw with a **BANG**. She jumped awake.

"Sorry." She said, as she stretched and rubbed her eyes with the back of her hands. "I must've dozed off. So, how did it turn out, Mr. Edwards?"

"What?"

"The review, examination, searching, looking for clues, or whatever you sleuth's call it." She shifted her body and crossed her legs.

"Oh. The certificates?" She nodded. "Very well, I must say. While you were in la la land, I made copies for myself and inserted your originals in the brown envelope."

"Thanks. So, are we through here, or what?"

"Nope. I need to ask more questions. Do you have time?"

She nodded.

I said. "How long did you live in Chicago?" I opened my desk draw a-gain and re-sumed with my right foot resting on it.

"Until I was eighteen. After my Gram' passed away, I'd moved in with my Uncle Dale and Auntie 'Bee'."

"Where was that?"

"Florida."

"Where in Florida?"

She pleaded. "Please don't bother my aunt and uncle. Please. I beg of you, Mr. Edwards." She had her hands together, folded, as if she was pray- ing. Maybe she was.

"Why? Or why not. They might have the answers we're seeking."

"They didn't tell me anything. Why should they tell you?"

"Good point, Sheryl. But I could be persuasive, if need be."

She suddenly said, surprisingly, "Orlando . . . . Orlando, Florida."

"Thanks. Thank-you very much." I wrote that information on my legal pad. My new silvery and shiny pen worked very well. Very smooth. I gazed in Sheryl's eyes. I just was double checking to see if she wasn't lying again.

She's good. "When was the last time you have heard from your Uncle Dale
And Aunt 'Bee'?"

Sheryl said. "Two years ago. That is when I'd received the certificates I just handed you. My auntie mailed me things I didn't even know she had about my mother and father."

I said. "But she never sent you, or even discussed the original death certificate . . . and you haven't called her or your uncle in two years. Correct?"

"Un-huh. That is correct, Mr. Edwards. But I do have a full bag of let- ters and Christmas cards and birthday cards my aunt sent me two years ago.

I had forgotten them when I had moved away from Florida. I was little at the time when I got 'em."

"The cards and letters . . . . From your mother?" I said. "Yep. Of course mother was still alive back then. Auntie 'Bee' stashed the cards and letters in a huge laundry bag, the size of Santa's bag, if you know what I mean." I nodded. "Well, anyway, my auntie kept them for remem- brance, after her passing."

"Huge, Santa-like bag, huh?" I asked interestingly, scratching the back of my head.

"Did I give you a clue, or something, Mr. Edwards?"

"Maybe. Maybe not. But the laundry bag seems to be a little too big for only being five years of your life. Why a large bag, Sheryl?"

"I don't know." I squinted my eyes and glared into hers. Was she lying to me again? Maybe. Nick Edwards, master sleuth.

"What I need from you is a list of names of your old neighborhood co- horts . . . you know, friends, associates, partners, etc. Okay, Missy?"

"What good will it do?" She stood up and walked to my mirror I had hanging on the partition, bended her knees to catch her reflection, and had tightened her ponytail with two sharp tugs of her blond hair. She returned to my client chair and smiled a nervous smile. She seemed content with her hair and make-up. Party. Party.

"Well, you get me those names and maybe we'll just see what good it will do. Ca-peesh?"

"Sure, I guess. But they might have moved by now."

"Yeah. I am aware of that, Miss Boehlis. Got to start somewhere." I had my mouth par- tially opened, and was ready to say "Ca-peesh" again, but she'd seemed confused when I said it. So I decided not to confuse my client anymore . . . . ."Ca-peesh?"

Sheryl shrugged and nodded doubtfully. She was confused. And I did not even say the word "Ca-peesh." Oh boy!

I said. "The address on the pending death certificate and police report, were they far from your grandmother's house?"

She said. "About a half-a-mile, maybe."

"Your aunt's and uncle's house?" She cocked her head to the right. Confused. "Did they live far from that address which was stated on the po-lice report and death certificate? . . . . Ca-peesh?"

"Same-o Same-o. My Gram' and auntie and my uncle all lived in one big house together. Ca-peesh?" She said with a cocky grin. Smart-ass. I did not answer her. I ignored her.

"Did you ever return to that house, uh, your own house where you had lived or uncle's house?"

"Why should I?"

"Curiosity, uh, memories. Even maybe, uh, school buddies." I said.

"You keep forgetting I was only five years old when my mother died."

"Stupid me. Old age. I turned forty-eight, and I'm already senile."

She grinned.

"Do you know when your dad got killed in 'Nam'?"

"I told you." She looked at the ceiling, and rolled her eyes again. At me again. "1971"

"What month?"

"I don't know. Why?"

"Curious." She had a puzzled expression. She shrugged, and grabbed her pack of cigarettes from her purse, took one out with her lips and lit it and casually blew the smoke in the air. The bluish smoke lingered for a moment, and then floated over our heads.

"Don't burn yourself, Miss."

"You are not senile." She smiled.

"Nah. I guess not . . . One more question." I took an ashtray from my big desk drawer and handed it to her this time. She took it and held it in her hand carefully. Safe and secure.

"Okay, one more question."

"Do you remember noticing your mother's two thumbs on her left hand?"

"Yeah, I guess. It was gross. I tried not to think about it."

"She never had it removed?" Traffic on highway 21 and 12 near my office was loud. Horns were blaring, loud voices cussing at each other and tires screeching. People are just impatient anymore. My philosophy on the matter, get up early enough so you won't be rushing on our busy high-ways and expressways. Common sense? I think so. Road rage! . . . Who needs it.

"No. She never had it removed. I always wondered why not. It must've gotten in her way many times at the deli. Cutting meat, and such."

I nodded. "I suppose it would have . . . What do you think of Mike Bar- ton?"

"I don't want to talk about him. I hate him. Besides, you said one ques- tion." Her cheeks flushed a little. It blended with her make-up. Nice.

"Yeah, I know. But we should discuss him."

"Why?" She snuffed her half-smoked cigarette in the glass ashtray, as if snuffing out Micheal Barton. She set the ashtray down on my desk rather loudly. She sat back and crossed her legs. Her left foot dangling and shaking in the air. "Well, did you, or did you not say, Barton had beaten you and your mother anytime he wanted to?"

"Yeah. So." She sat there with her arms folded over her breasts. And her left leg and foot still shaking in the air.

"Did he ever threaten your mother? Remember?"

She thought for a moment or two. "Yeah. When he got drunk. Or when he was high on crack. The son-of-a-bitch. Do you think . . . . .?" The question was left hanging. But I knew what she was about to say. Mr. Nick Edwards,

Psychic Detective.

"Possibility. Another reason I need the list of names from your neigh- borhood, north-side of Chicago. They might know his where-abouts."

"I know what neighborhood you meant, Mr. Edwards. I'm not stupid like you think I am."

"Was it 'Ca-peesh'?" I said.

"Huh?" She said with a look I couldn't describe.

"Never mind," I said. "What about your grandfather?"

"What about him?" Before I answered the question, she said. "Which grandfather anyway?"

"Your mother's father. When did he die?"

"I told you that, too. Jeez. Maybe you are going senile . . . . Before I was born." The ceiling was sure getting a work-out with her devilish eyes. If she had rolled her eyes one more time, her eyes would had frozen in that posi-tion. My God. "Anymore questions, Mr. Edwards?" She pulled another cig- arête from her pack, but hesitated, and had put it back. Good.

"Not for now, Missy. I'll call you. And keep me informed of anything new you think of. Understand?"

She nodded. She was about to leave my office when she pivoted on her left foot. She glared at me and said. "You forgot to say Ca-peesh, Nick."

She pivoted again, facing away from me, and left the building. She left me smelling her stale cigarette smoke. Cough . . . . Phewey.

Chapter Five

I T WAS HALF-PAST—NOON, an hour after Sheryl had left my office. I had ordered pizza from Mr. Wu's Pizza Parlor next door. I sat back in my high back chair with my semi-healed right leg resting on my desk. I had a slice of pizza; green pepper, pepperoni and mushrooms with extra cheese in my left hand, the police report Sheryl had given me, in my right. The front off- ice door opened and closed. I didn't pay much attention to it. Too busy en- joying my pizza and reading the police report.

"Mr. Edwards?" I slowly relaxed my right arm and let the police report uncover my face. A tall and husky young man, shaggy blonde hair, early thirties, my guess, leaned over slightly with the palms of his hands resting on the front corner edge of my desk for support.

"It all depends who's asking." I said.

He remained his position on the corner of my desk. "Sheryl's friend.

Actually, her boyfriend."

I lowered my right leg to the floor. "Is she all right, Arty, my boy?"

He had this look like a sad and confused puppy. "How did you know my name?"

"I'm a detective. I am supposed to know these things." He was silent.

I repeated the question.

"She was before she came here this morning." Arty said. "You upset her. And I am pissed."

"She's good at getting people pissed-off." I said. "Welcome to the complaint depart-ment." He walked around my huge mahogany desk and stood erect on my left. I looked up at him, straining my muscles in my neck.

"WOW! You're a big boy. Aren't you? Six-five?"

"Six-six."

"WOW, again. But good guess on my part. Whaddaya think? Should I join the carnie and guess height and weight, huh?" I rolled my chair back slightly and stood up. He had two-and-a-half inches on me. Maybe fifty pounds heavier. He gazed down on me.

"Look, butt-face." He pressed his right index finger in to my chest. "I'm only telling you just once. Back off." Then he began jabbing his finger on my chest. Didn't care for that too much. I pulled his finger and held it, tightly. He grimaced."From what?" I shifted a little to my left, out of range from his breath, still squeezing his finger. He didn't even try to move.

"Whew! Bad breath . . . . Whew! Your mouthwash just isn't making it."

"The murder case. I came to get her money." If he was in pain, he wasn't letting on.

"Sorry, big boy. No-can-do. You see, she had signed a contract. And if she wants to reclaim her money, she needs to come down herself. Does she know you are here?"

"It doesn't matter."

"Matters to me." His finger was turning blue. Nice guy, as I am, I had released his finger. He seemed relieved. "If she tells me in person she wants me to back off, I'll be more than happy to tear her contract and return her money. But not until then. Now take your sorry-ass out of here. I have a piz- za to eat."

He appeared to leave, but the stupid jerk took a swing at me. His right fist came at me, I pulled back, but not enough. His fist grazed my lower left chin. My right leg almost gave-way, but I held my balance. I rolled with the punch. He swung at me again with his right . . . . Fool me once, shame on you, Fool me twice, shame on me . . . This time I wasn't the fool. I blocked his arm with my left forearm. My right fist slid over his left shoulder and made con- tact with his jaw. He stumbled back and braced himself against my gray cab- inet. The cabinet rocked slightly, and my Mr. Coffee pot went crashing to the floor. Damn. He repeated the swing with his right fist. I blocked it. I went for his groin area with my right hand, squeezed and held it. Vise-like grip. The pain . . . The pain. His face turned fire-engine red and gasping for his breath. I walked him through my office building door that way. I tossed him in to the parking lot. He fell and rolled over, holding himself between his thick legs. A car came from nowhere blowing his horn at Arty. I had put my hands over my eyes with two of my fingers separated, so I could peek through them. The driver turned his wheel sharply to the right and came to a screeching halt, just barely missing my Chevy Coupe. The driver looked at me and flipped me 'The Bird'.

Mr. Wu was standing outside of his shop shaking and scratching his head. I said. "Great pizza, Mr. Wu." He nodded and went back in his pizza parlor.

I stepped back into my building and sat behind my desk. I nearly got comfortable in my high-back chair when I heard tires squeal. I quickly got up and looked out the picture window of my office and had seen a black

Trans Am fish-tailed from Wal-Mart's parking lot. The car turned left on

Highway 21, driving toward the Town of Sparta. Then disappeared among a line of tall pine trees. I guessed big boy was pissed. Oh well.

I resumed position with my legs on top of my desk, crossed. I had piz-za in one hand, the police report in the other. I carefully read every word on the report. The police report had a flaw, or maybe two. Or maybe the death certificate had a flaw or two. Which one, I did not know. The address was correct on both of them, but the apartment number differed.

The police report said **4600 N. Lawrence Avenue**, *Apt# 103*. The cert- ificate said **4600 N. Lawrence Avenu**e, *Apt# 105*.

According to Mike Barton's statement, Sandy's boyfriend, he lived with his girlfriend, Sandy, in Apartment 105. He had also stated he had to force himself in because Sandy did not answer the door. He stated he was concerned. So he didn't have a choice, but to break-in . . . .

I paused for a moment, and had wondered about his force entry . . . . Why didn't he have a key? Maybe Sandy didn't trust him. Then again, maybe he'd lost it somewhere. Or maybe Sandy took from him, thinking he had lost the key. I read further . . . .

The reporting officer stated he had discovered a female body in Apart- ment-number-one-zero-three, lying on her back, on the living room floor. No sign of blood or weapon. No force entry. No sign of a struggle. Whatsoever.

Apartment-number-one-zero-five was vacant. Mr. Barton was taken in for question- ing. Later, was released. His alibi agreed with the witnesses, which were the bartenders, Mr. and Mrs Polycheck. Mr. Barton stated he and his girlfriend, Sandy, were celebrating Valentine's Day at the Peanut Bowl club.

After a few drinks, Sandy Boehlis had left and went home alone without Mr.

Barton. The time approximately, 10:15 P.M, Thursday night . . . . .

I paused again . . . Why did she leave the Peanut Bowl alone? Did Sandy

Boehlis and Mike Barton have a lover's quarrel? Maybe then she grabbed his house keys from the bar. Ummm. Or . . . Or . . . Maybe, just maybe, he had poisoned her drink at the bar. But when? And with what? Maybe when she went to the lady's room, huh? Or she made a call to a taxi service. I read further . . . .

According to Mr. Polycheck's statement, Mr. Barton stayed until clos- ing. Which was 2 A.M., Friday morning. I had stayed late in my office . . . . cubicle. It was midnight. I missed din- ner. I missed sleep. But most of all, I missed Lisa. She had to process/serve summons in Milwaukee, Wisconsin. She might be gone a while. Unless she locates the person or persons quickly. It might take her one day, two days, or a whole week. But she is dedicated. Knowing Lisa as I do, she will stick to it until the subject be served. But I will still miss her.

My mind had drifted back to the police report and certificate. I com- pared them over and over again. Maybe it was nothing. Maybe it was some- thing. It is worth looking into. I sat back in my swivel chair and lit a cigar- ette, contemplating on the report. I read it again. No change. Words were the same. I reviewed the death certificate again, too. For the tenth time. The time of death was between 11 P.M, Thursday night and 1 A.M., Friday morning.

Well. I thought some more. I guess there wasn't a need to pursue Mr. Barton. His alibi stuck. 'Less the Polycheck's had lied to protect him. Why?

I need, I must find Mr. and Mrs. Polycheck and interview them. That is if they are still around. They have to be. There is a piece to the puzzle missing.

And I have to find it. Maybe several pieces to the puzzle. And they might be the ones to help me find the pieces. They might be the *missing link*. Maybe they can help me solve this mystery.

Chapter Six

A TWENTY YEAR OLD murder case was difficult to locate witnesses and clues. But not impossible. I carefully slid Sheryl's mother's photo from the envelope. I studied it for a while. She had dark brown hair, maybe au- burn color, her face was perfectly round and soft-looking, pale blue eyes, and a pug-nose. Attractive. Just like her daughter, Sheryl. But Sheryl had dish-water blond hair and hazel eyes. Maybe she got them from her dad.

Sandy's second thumb on her left hand was prominent. It stood out like a sore thumb. No pun intended. I had made a memo to myself to call

Sheryl's dad's parents, visit Tomah Library, call the Chicago Police De- partment and ask for the reporting officer, Dave Cole. I looked at my desk clock. The cherry colored eagle chimed at 1:15 A.M.

I smashed my cigarette in the clear glass ashtray, wrapped my tan trench-coat around my squared shoulders and let it hang loosely. I switched my desk lamp off. It matched with my eagle clock. I slowly walked, trying not to damage my right knee, to the front of the office building and pushed the toggle switch down. The interior went black. Then I left closing the off- ice building door quietly behind me, 'til the lock clicked into place. I rattled the door once. It was secured. I went to my car, still smelling the aroma of

Mr. Wu's pizza parlor. It made me hungry. Unfortunately, he was closed. I climbed into my car and drove home.

The following morning I reported to work early. Lisa and Clint were already typing their reports from yesterday's cases. I gave Lisa a peck on her lips and told her I missed her. She said. "I was only away for a day." I said. "Didn't you miss me?" She nodded. Her eyes smiled when her lips had widened. Beautiful smile. She said. "Yeah, Tex, I missed you." I gave her another quick kiss on her cherry red lips. I would've given her a longer kiss, but Clint had been watching us. Lisa was still looking up at me. She said.

"Your phone had been ringing since six-thirty this morning. Many clients do like you."

"Yeah. Like me dead." Nobody asked why. It wasn't worth discussing.

I listened to my messages. Every message was from Sheryl. I called her im- mediately. Her phone rang twice.

"Hell-o." Sheryl's boyfriend answered.

"I need to speak to Sheryl" I said.

"Who is this?" I told him.

"She doesn't want to talk to you."

"Yes she does. Or do you want your groin stretched out some more?"

Art was quick calling out Sheryl's name. I grinned to myself. Clint and Lisa looked up at me and away from their typing when I said that. They calmly shook their heads. They resumed their typing. Sheryl came to the phone.

"Miss Boehlis speaking."

"Aren't we formal." I said.

"Huh?"

"Never mind."

"Well, good-morning, anyway, Mr. Edwards. Thank God I got hold of you."

"Yeah. What's up?"

"Sorry about my irate boyfriend yesterday. He gets upset quite easily."

I can nearly imagine her pout face.

"Don't we all, Miss Boehlis. Don't we all. What is the message that was so important?"

"I just want to tell you, I do not want you to drop my case. It was my boyfriend speak- ing. Not me."

"I gathered. Will you be able to come to my office ASAP?"

She agreed. I felt her smile.

When she'd entered my office, I could smell her clean soap. I couldn't smell perfume. Miss Boehlis sat in front of my desk in my client chair. Her legs crossed as usual. Her blond silky hair was up in a ponytail, and held back in a pale green rubber-band. Her hands folded in her lap, as if she was patiently waiting for the school's principal. She was alone. Thank goodness.

"I wrote the list of names you asked for, Mr. Edwards." Her politeness was sickening me. I think I'll puke on her ski boots. Nah. Maybe not.

"Thanks." She extended her arm across my desk, and my hand reached hers. Then I took the 'post-it' and set it in my desk with her files.

"I might have something for you, too, Sheryl." I said. But not as polite.

"Great! What is it?" She grinned from ear to ear.

"Let's not get too excited just yet. But I think it's something that might help." I handed her the police report and death certificate. They both were highlighted in yellow, the discrepancies I had found. She studied the docu- ments carefully with piercing eyes. I sat back and patiently waited. I mused myself with my new shiny pen. When she was finally done examining them, her eyes were slightly over the top edge of the police report, and said to me.

"My mother's body was found in my godmother's apartment?" Her eyes be- came swelled with tears again. Oh my. I handed her a handful of tissues. My Lisa should be here. She blew her nose and wiped her eyes. She looked up and seen me through red and blurry eyes. "What was she doing in her apart- ment anyway. My godmother never stayed up that late. The latest she ever stayed up, is when she talked to her parents. And that is at midnight. Maybe shortly after. It was a weird thing with her and her family." Sheryl uncrossed her legs, leaned toward my desk and placed the documents neatly on my desk blotter in front of me. She sat back and crossed her legs again.

"Visiting, I guess." I said. "But the point is, and the question remains, why kill herself in someone else's apartment, when she could have been by herself in her own apartment. Suicidals usually are alone and leave notes. Odd. Isn't it?"

"I guess. But where was she when the police found my mother?"

I shrugged. "Your godmother?" She nodded. "I really don't know. The last time you had seen her, was when, Sheryl?"

"Two days before my mother died. She took me shopping for cards.

"Valentine cards?" I said.

"Yeah. Valentine cards. The cards were for my mother, auntie and my Gram'. I stayed with my Gram' for three or four days while ass-hole Mike and my mother partied for Valentine's Day. I haven't seen or heard from my godmother since. I often wondered what had happened to her. I asked, when I got older, the people who knew her. But nobody seemed to know where she vanished to. Just another mystery."

"Yeah. Sure is." I said. I leaned forward on my desk with my arms ex- tended and pen in hand. "What is your godmother's name?"

"Clara Rueton." I asked her to spell it. She did. I wrote it on yellow le- gal pad with blue lines. I was creative with my new pen. Fancy.

"What did Clara look like?"

"Like my mother. Except, slightly heavier."

"Define; " 'like your mother'." I said. Pen in my left hand. Click.

"Same color hair. Same style. Same height. Could pass for sisters. They even competed with each other." Sheryl took in a deep breath and let it out. She seemed to lose ten pounds.

"How?" I said.

"Who can pick up most guys. That sort of thing, you know."

I nodded. "I guess. Was your mother 'picking up guys' when she was dating Mr. Barton.?"

"Yes. She sure was. Which caused most of their arguments and their fights."

"Dangerous, but adventurous. You do realize, Miss Boehlis, after read- ing the police report, Mr. Barton was cleared of any wrong-doing. Don't you?"

Nod. But, doubtful. She said. "I believe he might've killed her, but if not him, then who, Mr. Edwards. Who?"

"I was hoping it was Mr. Barton, too. Well, one . . . he had motive, and two . . . oppor- tunity." I had two fingers up, then, relaxed them. Picked up my pen again. I love my pen. "But," I said. "I have to dig deeper. Once I speak with Officer Cole, from Chicago Police Department, and some of the wit- nesses, if they are still available, then maybe I will have positive results. The Medical Examiner is also a great source of information."

She nodded again. When she did nod, I wasn't too sure if she was doz- ing into la-la-land, or if she was agreeing with me. She held her head down longer than need to. Oh well.

I said. "Sheryl, are you telling me the truth about Mr. Barton?"

She said. "Whaddya mean?"

"You haven't seen or heard from him since your mother's passing?"

"No more lies, Mr. Edwards. Straight up, from now on. Okay?"

I nodded. But she reminded me of my lawyer back east. But, just the same, I took it as a 'no'. Sheryl hesitated and had a deep wonder in her hazel eyes. "Nick?" She said.

"Yes."

"Do you think the puke and my godmother had anything to do with her death?" She sat back down in my client chair. Crossed her legs. "I had thought about it briefly. I played it around in my mind and it is possible, if not probable, that the ' "puke" ', as you put it, and Clara had the hots for each other, and rode off in the sunset together. You even said your mother and Clara competed with each other and picking up other men. May- be Clara competed to win . . . uh . . . Mr. Barton's heart. Maybe she poisoned your mother in her apartment, the night in question."

"Well, that would explain why I haven't seen either of them since my mother's death."

I nodded. "Good deduction, Miss Boehlis. Great point."

Sheryl glanced at her 'Betty Boop' watch. She said. "Sorry. But I have to run. I have a customer at noon. She'll freak-out if she doesn't get her hair done on time." She quickly slipped into her ski jacket, and nervously push- ing her long, thin fingers into her fur gloves. She tried to button her jacket with her gloves on. Difficult. She gave up on the second try. She held her right-gloved hand in front of me. I shook her gloved-hand.

"Good-day, Mr. Edwards. And thanks."

I stood up. I said. "For what? Doing my job."

"Well that, and keeping me as a client." She grinned a half-grin.

"I nearly did give up on you." She nodded and walked out of my cub- icle. I watched her as she was swaying her hips. Nice. But before she had reached the front door, I called out her name. "Miss . . . Miss Boehlis." I had to call out twice, just in case her hooded-jacket was tight on her ears. She turned around gracefully and her eyes gleamed at me. She didn't say any- thing. But then again, she didn't have to. She waited for me to speak. I did.

"You really haven't read those reports before, have you?"

"No. No I haven't, Nick. I was too confused and upset to read them. I thought I should just let go of the past and go ahead with my life. As much as I tried, I just couldn't." She looked down at the thick carpet, and did small circles on it with her pointed high-heeled shoes. Then she raised her head and our eyes met. She said. "But now, after being intro- duced to you, I'm glad, no, grateful . . . yes grateful that we met and you are pursuing the case."

She looked down again, and was still doing circles, but bigger ones.

"Sheryl," I said. "we're pursuing the case. You and I." She looked up again, but this time she had a smile and her eyes swelled with tears. Without another word, she turned and faced the door, opened it, and then she went. The door quietly shut. And I stood in the middle of the office, staring out the front picture window watching her drive off in her Gremlin. You don't see those anymore. WOW!

Chapter Seven

AFTER SHERYL HAD left, Mr. Wu walked in when I was pouring my coffee in my Elvis mug. I took in some coffee. Added more cream and sugar. I'd turned away from Mr. Coffee, and faced Mr. Wu. Today he wore black and creased slacks. Fact of the matter, Mr Wu always wore creased black slacks.

His crisp white chef's jacket was heavily starched. His black shoes highly shined. Very sharp. He was of average height and weight. As average he could be. Especially someone from the orient. He resembled Bruce Lee and had an accent like Charlie Chan. He nodded to Lisa and Clint. He gazed in my direction and grinned.

"Nick, what happened yesterday afternoon with oversize, uh, gorilla? I was impressed." Lisa and Clint stretched their necks and listened in.

"Ah, nothing really. He just wanted to take a bite of my pizza. I would not let him. His feelings were hurt. He swung at me. Well. You saw what happened."

"Yeah. Sure did. You won. But don't believe one word said about pizza." We smiled.

"Maybe that wasn't the way it actually went down, Mr. Wu, but your pizza is worth fighting for."

"Ah, big thanks, Mr. Edwards. Big thanks. Next pizza you want, be on house." He bowed several bows and walked backwards out the door. "Ah-so Mr. Nick . . . Ah-so, Mr. Clint . . . Ah-so, pretty one, Miss Lisa."

"Ah-so, Mr. Wu." Clint, Lisa and I said in unison.

Lisa and Clint looked curiously at me. Lisa said. "What did happen yesterday, Nick?" She had her chin resting on her knuckles. Clint drew in some smoke from his cigar. His dark brown eyes squinting through the gray smoke.

"Sheryl, my client, well, her boyfriend was pissed about something. He wanted me to drop the case and back-off. We rumbled in my office, and then I tossed him on his funky-ass onto the parking lot."

Clint said. "You didn't, did you?" Smoke was flowing from his wide nostrils, nearly enclosing his face.

"Drop Sheryl's case?" I shook my head once to the left, and once to the right. "Nah. But almost did, Clint. But now I am on to something with this case. It's worth looking into. Besides, Sheryl has money, unlike my other clients."

Lisa said. "That's a good thing." She was silent for a moment. Then said. "When are we going to Chicago and start investigating my parents mysterious death?"

I said. "Few more days. I need to make a few phone calls to Chicago and get more information on Sheryl's case. Okay, sweetie?" She seemed to pout. But she agreed to wait a few more days. I hugged her and gave a kiss on her cheekbone. That didn't seem to help. She still exposed a pout face.

"I also need to call Eagle and his wife Pam and give them heads-up we're going to Chicago." I said.

"Good." Lisa said. "With all of us on my parent's case, we're bound to solve it. Clint and I agreed.

I dialed 302-555-1212 and got hold of Information in Chicago. I asked for Mr. and Mrs. Patrick Boehlis. She said there weren't any Boehlis's under Patrick. But there was a Barbra Boehlis in Cicero, on Austin Court. I wrote the number in my note-pad. She also gave the numbers to Chicago P.D., District-Five. But when I had asked for the Peanut Bowl Lounge, North-side of Chicago, I was informed it wasn't listed in their system. Damn. I thanked her, and we hung up. It was getting late, and the Registrar of Deeds office were closed. I'll call them tomorrow.

We closed our office, and went next door to Mr. Wu's Pizza Parlor and ordered our free pizza as Mr. Wu had promised. The inside was elegant, as elegant as it could get, for being dainty. But it was cute. The parlor held twenty-five people. If it was full. But now, there were only five, including us three. There were five wrought-ironed rounded tables with matching chairs. Four per table. The tables were made with glass-tops, chairs were crafted with red leather seats. The wrought-iron was curly-cued designed. They were evenly centered on the red carpet. And one booth near the window. We sat in the booth. The two love birds sat two tables away from us, closest to the front entrance. Centered on our table were a crystal vase with a rose in it. I leaned over to smell. I was fooled. It was only plastic. Our Asian waitress came over to the booth, leaned over carefully and set our pizza and drinks down in front of us. Then she went away.

After a few bites and swallows of my sliced pizza, and a few gulps of my MGD beer, I had asked Lisa if her father had any close friends that we could trust on the police force.

"Peter Dillman. Sergeant Peter Dillman, to be exact. He was my dad's partner."

"Is he still with the Detectives'?"

"As far as I know. At least he was two years ago when I moved here. I could call him for you. He was the only one seemed concerned about my parents' death. You could say; he was part of the family." Today Lisa wore a dark blue dress with a wrap-around leathered belt. With matching high heels. She had a white silk scarf around her neck. She reminded me of Real Estate Broker. Her blonde hair, evenly trimmed, and curling underneath, barely touched the back of her collar. Her make-up was moderate. As usual. I went back eating my slice of pizza. Lisa took a sip of her wine. She normally drank Vodka and Tonic, but Mr. Wu didn't have that on his menu.

Well, what do you expect from a small, dainty pizza parlor anyway. I was happy he served MGD beer. Clint had no worries. He drank iced-tea with a mint leaf floating on top. He sipped through the clear plastic straw, swal- lowed and said to me.

"I spoke with my wife, Julie. She wanted me to tell you she is considering the trip to Chicago. But she isn't quite sure when Tomah High School will be closed for Spring-Break. She just might have to meet us down there. When are you planning to go, Nick.?"

"Another week, or so. I already spoke with Eagle and Pam. Eagle said they're on stand-by. Whenever we're ready, they're ready."

"Great!" Lisa and Clint said in harmony. We finished our pizza and drinks. We paid for the drinks, left a decent tip and we went.

Chapter Eight

"REGISTRAR OF DEEDS, may I help you?" It was a bright morning. The weather seemed promising. Fifty-degrees and clear blue skies. I had my right foot resting on the bottom of my opened desk drawer. The phone in my right ear, my pen in my left hand, with the note-pad at an angle. I was ready for the day.

"Yes. I hope so. What can you give me on "The Peanut Bowl?"

"Is it a bar, restaurant, or a bowling establishment?"

"I guess a bar. It might even be a restaurant-slash-bar." I said.

"Okay. I'll be right back." The Registrar Clerk did some tapping on a typewriter, or a keyboard. I was on hold for more than my ear could take. I kept rotating from right ear to left, and back to right ear again. I even had time to doodle on my yellow legal-pad. Oh joy. The clerk's voice appeared from the other end. "Here's what I got. You ready to write?"

"Um-hum."

"*Peanut Bowl* was located on Sheridan Boulevard . . . . *Peanut Bowl Club* is still in operation. That is located on Lawrence Avenue, 4800 North. And *Peanut Bowl Lounge* is located on Broadway Avenue. They are owned by a Mr. and Mrs Robert B. Polycheck."

"All of them?"

"All of them, except the one on Sheridan Boulevard. He sold that back in . . . . uh . . . ." The clerk tapped a key from the computer's keyboard, my guess.

"1985." The clerk said. He seemed satisfied with himself.

"What is the name of it now?" I said.

"The one on Sheridan Boulevard?"

"Um-hum."

The clerk tapped a few more keys. He cleared his throat. His voice was loud and clear.

"Its name is *"THE COVE"*

"Could I have the address . . . uh . . . the complete address?"

"Sure." He gave it to me gladly. He was nice enough to give me the phone numbers as a bonus. Sweet. I thanked him. We hung up. I called the 'COVE'. A gruff voice came over the line. "The Cove." I waited for the voice to say something else. But, he didn't.

"Hell-o . . . Is someone there?" The gruff-voice said.

"Yes, I'm here. I thought you were going to say something further."

"Yeah, like what?"

" . . . . .May I help you, or, maybe, something like this . . . . ,What can I do for you' . . . . Here's one more I think you might like. 'Hell-o, Sweetheart.' Maybe, this one . . . . 'Make my day, punk.' " I paused and waited for his response.

"Are you being a smart-ass, or what?" Mr. Gruff said.

"Just trying to help."

"Well, what do you want?"

"I was wondering if you had seen a blonde fella' named Micheal Barton in the last twenty years. Or a Mr. Polycheck . . . Robert B., to be accurate, the last twelve years?"

"Are you being a smart-ass again?"

"On the level."

"No' Mr. Barton. But Yes' Mr. Polycheck.. Robert B., to be exact, sold this place to me, 1985. He bought another place called Saxony's Family Restaurant on Kenmore Avenue. You can reach 'em there."

I said thanks. And Mr. Gruff told me not to call back again. Mean bastard. But easy. I called Saxony's Family Restaurant. Someone answered in Spanish and said something like, "Call back at 'seex.' "

It was nearly noon when I made contact with the Boehlis residence. A young, male voice answered.

"Hell-o." "Good-afternoon." I said. "I would like to speak to either Mr. Patrick Boehlis, or Barbara Boehlis, please."

"Patrick Junior, or Senior?"

"The father."

"Well, my father died recently. But my mother is home. Do you want to speak with her?"

"Sure. Sorry about your dad."

"Thanks." In the background, I had heard "Mom" called out.

Tapping of shoes on the bare-wooden floor got closer. A few seconds later, a woman answered. "Hell-o." Her voice was raspy, but sweet.

"Hell-o. My name is Nick Edwards from the C-N-L Detective Agency, and I am calling from Tomah, Wisconsin."

"Oh, are you soliciting something. I'm not interested."

"Wait a minute, ma'am. I'm investigating a murder."

"What? Oh, no. Who was murdered?" But before I could answer the question, Lisa had stepped into my office. She leaned over and whispered in- to my ear. Mrs. Boehlis kept asking about "Who was murdered?" It wasn't easy to speak with two people at the same time. Lisa said."I got hold of Dill- man. He's Lieutenant now. He will be expecting us." I winked at Lisa and gave her thumb-up with my left thumb, and patted her on the butt as she turned and left. "Who was murdered" was ringing in my ear when I put the ear-piece back into my ear.

"Sorry about that, Mrs. Boehlis. Something came up all of a sudden." I believe she didn't hear me.

"Well, damn it. Who was murdered?" Mrs. Boehlis screamed.

"I am not quite sure if it was murder or suicide. But it has to do with your daughter-in-law, Sandy."

"The slut. That promiscuous slut of a bitch. Is she the one dead?"

"Yes, ma'am. I'm afraid so. Bad terms, huh?"

"Yes, damn straight. And that is saying it mildly." She took in a deep breath of air. "How long had she been dead?"

"Twenty years. Around Valentine's Day."

"Twenty years, huh? Never heard anything about it. We weren't close anyway."

"I gathered. But the actual reason I am calling, I'm curious about your Grand-daughter, Sheryl. What can you . . . . ."

"I don't have a Grand-daughter named Sheryl."

"Excuse me , ma'am. Just to be sure I have the right Boehlis resident, and I believe I do; Sandy was married to a John Boehlis, and he was a U.S.

Marine, and served in 'Nam'. Am I correct?"

"Yes, unfortunately, you are. But no grand-daughter."

"You sure. Or did you disown Sheryl out of anger toward Sandy?"

"Of course, I am sure. What do you take me for?"

"I don't know, ma'am. I hardly know you."

"Are you being a poop?"

"A 'poop?' No ma'am. Sorry if I was offensive. Please continue."

"I don't have a grand-daughter. But if I did, I surely wouldn't have dis- owned her. Doesn't matter if I was angry at her mother. Children are the in- nocent victims, aren't they." I agreed.

"Oke-kee-doke." I said. "Can you tell me anything about Sandy's and John's relationship?"

"What do you want to know, besides Sandy was a whore and a thief.

And they got married too soon, I might add." I agreed to that, too. "She took my son for a ride, and married him on the re-bound."

"Re-bound? From who?" I said.

"A guy named Mike, Michael, Mick, or whoever."

"Barton . . . Mike Barton?"

"Yeah, him. The dope addict."

"I'm sorry if I am re-hashing dark memories, ma'am, but, unfortun—ately, that is part of my job asking hurtful questions. Sometimes I have to."

"Yeah, sure."

"I am more interested in Sandy's daughter, Sheryl."

"I don't know if I can help you in that area."

"Maybe you can."

"Okay. I'll try."

"When was your son in Viet Nam?"

"Before my son, John, turned seventeen, he was always talking about joining the Marines. My husband, Patrick, and I, tried to discourage him. But since the draft was in effect, we wanted to be proud of our son. We would rather have him enlist than being drafted. So he volunteered in 1970 on his seventeenth birthday."

"April fifteenth." Right?" I said.

"Yeah. How do you know?"

"Sheryl had his birth certificate. She gave it to me."

"What? What is going on here? What is your name again?"

"Nick Edwards, ma'am. I'm a private investigator for C-N-L Detective Agency from Tomah, Wisconsin."

"Oh yeah. Right. So what is going on, Mr. Edwards?"

"I was hoping you would tell me."

"I don't know what to say?"

"Okay, ma'am. I'll tell you what I know, or what I think I know. We'll take it from there." She agreed.

"Sheryl Boehlis, as far as I know, but I am confused at the moment, is an orphan.

She hired me to investigate her mother's death. Sandy's family had been very secretive about her death. So secretive, Sheryl couldn't even attend her funeral. Sheryl was born March 9, 1972. She will be twenty-five next week

Thursday. On her birth certificate it has John Boehlis stated as her father.

When Sheryl informed me her father was killed in 'Nam', the year of '71',

I was curious about when Sheryl was conceived. This is the purpose of this phone call. What can you tell me, ma'am?"

"What I can tell you is, Mr. Edwards, that is B-U-L-L-S-H-I-T. Buull- shit. My son was killed in the month of January 1971. No way in hell he was the father. And if my calculations are correct, Mr. Edwards, Sheryl was . . . . .

. . . . .conceived, either late June, or early July of 1971. Do you agree?"

"Yes, ma'am. Absolutely. That is all I needed to know. Thanks. I'll be in Chicago about a week from now. If you have anything you want to talk a- bout on this matter, please feel free to call." I gave her my number and con- dolence's on her loss.

"Thanks." She said.

Thinking the conversation was over, I was just about to hang up the phone when Mrs Boehlis said, "And if you call me 'ma'am' one more time,

I'll track you down and knock your block clean off your shoulders. Unner- stand?"

I said. "Yes, ma'am." Then I hung up. Poop.

Chapter Nine

CLINT, LISA AND I were discussing our current cases and eating Chinese food from Mr. Wu's, sitting around my over-sized mahogany desk.

"So, honey, how is your case going with Sheryl?"

"It's going. I'm waiting for Detective Cole to return my call. And the Medical Examiner from Cook County Hospital Coroner's Office, who's on vacation until next Monday. David Stack is a good friend of mine."

"David Stack is the M.E.?" Lisa said, wanting confirmation.

"Yes. Also, I have to call Mr. Polycheck on the North side of Chicago.

He probably was the last person to see Sandy alive. He owns several family restaurants. I need to call him at six tonight."

I studied Lisa and Clint. They were so talented, they ate their dinner with chopsticks. But I was special. I ate mine with a plastic fork. Yum.

"Lisa. What about your case?" I said.

"You mean the American Furniture and Appliances in Madison."

"Yep. That's the one." I said. I took a forkful of Chinese noodles and slurped it in between my lips and swallowed. I looked down at my white, pressed shirt. Gravy stains. Damn.

Lisa said. "I probably have another week or so. Then I think I'll have the internal theft wrapped up."

"Great." I said. I cocked my head toward Clint. "And what about you, Clint?" He inserted the chopsticks in his mouth with ease, as if he was fed that way since infancy.

"Fine. I'm waiting for the bozo's to slip-up. And when they do, WHAM . . . ! I got em' " He pounded so hard on my desk, he made my egg noodles scrambled. "If we get this gang of druggies, it might be the biggest bust yet, Nick . . . Lisa." He looked at us. Then he realized what he had just said. He shrugged. "Well, outside of your big bust last year, I just might come close." We grinned at each other.

I said. "And where's this undercover operation taken place again, sir?"

"Green Bay's Carpet Cleaning." Clint said. He sipped his iced-tea.

"Oh, yeah." I said, looking at Lisa. Then back at Clint. "If I remember correctly, Clint, that factory only employs six men."

"So, what's your point, Nick?"

I shrugged and grinned. I didn't say anything. I guess I wanted to stay employed as a P.I. I glanced at my watch. Cole hasn't called yet. I was go- ing to visit the Tomah Library, but I didn't want to miss Cole's call. So I waited. After we ate our fabulous lunch, and Lisa and Clint returned to the cases they were hired to do, I did what I do best, sit in my recliner with my feet resting on top of my desk and study people coming and going from Wal-Mart, wait for information. Or wait for clients. Wait. Wait. Wait.

It was nearing dinner-time, 4:24 P.M. And still no call from Cole. I had hoped he would call by 5 P.M. Clint and his wife, Julie, invited Lisa and I to their Condo Suite for dinner. We're expected to be there at 6 P.M.

I was just finished putting my final ingredients into my coffee when Lisa walked in. She came to me and rubbed her hands on my lower back and upper back. Then she worked her way up to my shoulders. She turned me around slowly and looked into my eyes.

"What's wrong, honey. You look so . . . so depressed." I just shrugged. I usually hide my emotions very well. And there are things I don't reveal very often. My anxiety. "Want to go outside, Nick, get a breath of fresh cool air.

We could talk about it. Alright?" I grinned and put my arm around her waist. Gave her a kiss on her right cheek.

"You think you know me, huh, blondie?" I said.

"Yep. You have a problem with that?" She grabbed both of my hands into hers, and squeezed them gently.

"Nope. Kinda like it. Let's go outside." We left the office door slightly opened just in case the phone will ring. Who knows, it just might be Detec-tive Cole calling me. Or Maybe a new client. Well, that'll be great. I would rather have something like that, than telling Lisa my inner-most feelings, which I'm not too good at anyway. I just have a dif-ficult time with it. That's all.

Lisa said. "This case is getting to you." It was a statement. We sat closely together on a bench in front of the coffee shop next door. She had put her right hand on my left knee and rubbed it slowly, making small circles with her index finger.

I didn't immediately answer. We sat in silence for a while. Maybe a long while, I don't know. She continued doing circles on my left knee. Then I said. "Maybe." I paused. "I spoke with Mrs. Boehlis. The person who was supposed to be Sheryl's grandmother . . . . ." I paused again. Lisa continued to listen patiently and intently. She was very good at that listening stuff. She should've been a psychoanalyst, or some sort of counselor. Not saying she isn't a great detective. She is . . . One of the best. Well, of course there is Clint and I . . . .

"Well, Nick. Please continue. Tell me." She moved her hand from my knee to my lower back, and rubbed that all-so gently. Umm. "Well . . . she isn't."

"Oh, no! What are you going to tell Sheryl, honey." Lisa had her hand over her mouth.

"The truth. It'll hurt. She'll cry. Maybe even run away from me and fire my ass." I combed my hair with my opened fingers. Disgusted and up- set. Lisa said. "There are truths which are not for all men, nor for all times."

"Alfred Adler?" I said.

"Some letter it was written in a long time ago. Don't remember." Lisa put her hand on top of mine. Very consoling. Then she said. "Do you want me be there with you when you tell her?"

"I was hoping you will suggest that. I didn't want to ask you."

"Yes. I do know you, don't I, Tex. I nodded and patted her right knee.

The phone rang. Lisa walked in. I hobbled in. I picked up the phone on the fourth ring.

"C-N-L Detective Agency, Nick speaking." It was Detective Cole.

"Mr. Edwards. Detective David Cole from Homicide, District Five."

His voice reminded me of Sergeant Friday on Dragnet. He probably had his haircut just like him, too.

"Please to hear from you, sir." I said.

"Yep. Sure you are. How can I help you?"

I cut to the chase.

"In the year 1977, February fourteen, a woman named Sandy Boehlis was found lying on the living room floor, Apartment 103. According to the police report, you were the first one on the scene. What can you tell me, sir?" I took a sip of coffee . . . Memo to self; Add more sugar to coffee.

"How did you get sucked in with this case?" I told him about my client.

"Yeah. I can tell you everything, like it was yesterday. Crazy, and most unusual case I was involved with. First, let's get the facts straight, okay?"

"Sure, sir. What are the facts?"

"It wasn't the fourteenth, Valentine's Day, as you mentioned. It was two days before that special day."

"The twelfth?"

"Great, Mr. Edwards. Least I know you can subtract."

"I had an excellent math teacher."

"It was the twelfth, Friday morning. I came on duty at midnight. It was quiet that night. Maybe, too quiet. If you know what I mean, Mr. Edwards?"

"Yes, sir. I know exactly what you mean."

"Well, as I was saying, it was quiet for a Friday morning. It was a tail end of the full moon. And believe you me crime is higher around the full moon."

"Yes, sir. I can relate with that on many occasions." I took another sip of my not-so-sweetened-coffee.

"Mr. Edwards?" Cole said. I detected a different voice-tone.

"Yes, sir?" I said.

"Before we go any further, please do me a favor, will ya'?"

"And what's that, sir?"

"Please . . . Please quit calling me 'sir'. Will that be alright with you, Mr. Edwards?"

"Sure. What shall I call you? . . . . uh . . . Jack Webb, Or, Sergeant Friday?"

"What? Not you, too. My partner says I sound like him. Damn."

"Your partner, Harry?" I said.

"Shut-up. Just call me by my first name. That will suffice."

"Only if you call me by my first name." He agreed. Then I agreed.

"Well, where were we . . . oh yes. As I was saying, while I was patrol-ling the North-side of Chicago, I had a call to report to 4600 Lawrence Avenue, Apartment 103, about a concerned friend to check on the person in question. When I pulled my cruiser in front of the apartment building, I had clear view through the glass lobby door where I could view the entire first floor, right to the end of the hallway. A man tried to break-in in one of the units, which he claimed was his and his girlfriend's, I had found out later."

"May I interrupt for a minute and ask you several questions, Dave?"

"David. Please call me David. Okay, Nicholos?"

"Only if you call me Nick. Okay?" He agreed. And then I agreed.

"Where were we?" I said "You wanted to interrupt me and ask several questions." David said. "Oh yeah, right." I said.

"What time did you receive that call, David?" I stressed his name.

"Well, it was around bar-closing-time. I would say between 2 and 2:30 A.M. What's the next question, Nick?"

I said thanks for saying my name properly. He grunted.

"Yeah, sure." David said.

"What apartment number was this guy trying to force his way into?"

"Good question."

"I try." I sipped my coffee. I wheeled my chair close to the window, opened it, and tossed my coffee into the parking lot. Bad coffee.

"Hope so. Well, back to your question, if I remember correctly, I believe it was a few doors from the lobby door. Yeah, that's right. I remem- ber now. The corpse was found in Apartment 103, and the apartment in question, was one door over, further away from the lobby door entrance. It was 105, Apartment 105. That's it." David seemed pleased with himself. "Any more questions, Nick?"

"Yep. I do. What did this guy look like?"

"Can't forget his ugly puss. He was always in trouble, it seemed. The law would be happy to put him in the slammer, only if we can find him."

"The description, please, David."

"Sorry. He had dirty blonde hair, and I mean dirty blonde hair. Prob- ably six-footer. 175 pounds. Busted him on regular occasions for drugs. And DWI."

"Hazel eyes by any chance, David?" I stressed his name again.

"I know what you're trying to do, Nicky baby. It isn't working. But I would still ap-preciate if you cut the crap. Got it?" I agreed. But not without a cocky grin.

"Sure. Sorry."

"You said, hazel eyes. Why? Do you know this creep."

"No. Just curious."

"If you know anything, let me hear it. This pot-head is a big time deal-er. He hasn't been seen since the Boehlis case. Have anything you want to tell me?"

"Not actually. 'Cept he could be my client's father. My client was told from her mother and other relatives, her father was killed in Viet Nam ..'71'.

But found out today, he wasn't her father."

"Man, I surely don't want to be in your shoes when you tell her. You are planning to tell her. Aren't you?"

"Yeah . . . . Yeah, I am."

"Anything else, Nick?"

"Yes, David. This caller; was it a female or male?"

"It was anonymous caller. According to the dispatcher, the call came from a local payphone."

"Couple more questions. You have the time?" I said.

"Yep. But that is it. I gotta get going. I have family waiting for me."

"Thanks. I'll try to make it snappy."

"Snappy?" David said. "I haven't heard that word since my police off- icer days."

"Nostalgic." I said.

"Yeah, I guess. Please continue, Nick."

"Why did the investigation take so long to determine the cause of death? I had homi-cide, suicide and natural death cases, but never in my pri-vate investigator career did it take this long. Any idea why."

"Whaddya mean?"

"The death certificate I have in my possession, was typed *pending* in the block *Cause of Death*, as of February 1, 1978. My client told me a friend from her old neighborhood had picked-up the certificate from the Vital Statistics office on that date. That was a year later. The results should've been in and the case closed way before that date."

"I agree up to a point, Nick. It shouldn't have taken that long, unless the detectives had a difficult time with it. What did she die from?"

"Toxic Poisoning."

"Umm . . . ." I can imagine him scratching his chin and thinking deeply.

"That is a tough case to solve. It could go either way. Murder or suicide."

"What about accidental poisoning, David?"

"Accidental poisoning, huh? Maybe. But then again, I'm no doctor. Accidental poison-ing could only be determined if the victim had loss of her or his memory. Hell, I don't know, Nick. It's a toughie. I just cannot honest-ly define it. Need to talk to the M.E. He or she could tell you better than I can . . . You said couple of questions."

"Did you notice anything unusual about her hands?"

"Hands? Again, whaddya mean?"

"Extra fingers or thumbs. Or even, maybe, scar tissue where the extra finger or thumb could have been removed?"

"No. Nothing unusual. The corpse had all natural count of digits on both hands. Back then my eyes were twenty-twenty without glasses. I would have noticed something that unusual. And most definitely, no scar."

"Dave, can you describe the surroundings of the crime scene before or when you went inside her apartment?"

"Sure. The apartment door was closed, but unlocked. The inside of the apartment was immaculate. You can even eat off the floor . . . the kitchen, and living-room."

"Blood?" I said.

"No."

"Bruises on the body?"

"Nope."

"Force entry?" I said.

"No. Not even a trace of a struggle. Like I said earlier, most unusual case I was ever involved in."

"Just a corpse lying on the living room floor, huh?" I said.

"Yep. She was lying flat on her back with her left leg cocked, the right leg stretched out before her. Oh. Just for the record. And no weapon."

"Shoes?"

"What? Where are you going with that?"

"Running out of questions to ask, I guess."

"Well, in that case, I'll hang up and get re-acquainted with my family. I have been working long hours lately, I believe I forgot what my family even looks like. I hope I can find my house."

"Wait a minute. I got a great question for ya'." I said.

"It better be good, Nick."

"I said *great*, David. Great question for ya'. Not good."

"Okay . . . Okay already. What is it?"

"How about the renter?"

"The renter? What are you talking about?"

"The actual person who was renting that apartment."

"Yeah, what about it?"

"Was she ever notified that a body was found in her apartment?"

"Have a name?"

"Yes. My client's god-mother, Clara Rueton. Was she ever questioned?"

"Man. Are you getting yourself in deep with this investigation."

"How?" I said.

"Clara Rueton had been on the 'Missing Persons Report' shortly after the Boehlis case. You're onto something big, Nick. Be careful. Keep me in- formed on your findings. Got it?"

"Yep. Got it. I will need a copy of any flyers that you have on file on Miss Rueton."

"Sure. But why?"

"I would like a picture of her and see what she'd looked like. Is that possible?"

"Of course, Nick. If you crack this case, I'm sure everyone concerned will be over glorious."

"It's all part of my goal. I like cracking cases wide open. It's good for my reputation."

"Anything else, Nick? Or am I sorry I had asked?"

"Maybe. It all depends."

"On what?"

"I don't know. I haven't thought that far ahead yet. But I do have some more questions to ask you."

"That's what I was afraid of."

"Was Clara into drugs or trouble with the law in any way?"

"Nah. Just your ole' town drunk. Hardly any trouble."

"No drug-gangs, gangs in general, that sort of thing."

"Nope. But as I told you, Whatsis name, always trouble with gang- lords. We need him off the streets. I believe he's in hiding somewhere, or had moved to another locale. I know we haven't seen him since Sandy's death."

"Whatsis' is Mike Barton, David." I said just to clarify.

"Yeah. That's his name. Big time pusher and dealer to the max. Well,

Nick, gotta go. I'll send you flyers on Clara. ASAP."

"Thanks, sir. Oops . . . David."

"How soon we forget, huh, Nicky baby?"

"Well, anyway, thanks for your help, David."

"Yeah, anytime, kid. Just do your self a favor, though."

"Yeah. And what is that?" I said.

"Keep your head low, and your ass tucked in. You got that, Nick?"

"I got it." We disconnected. The office was totally quiet. Except the humming from the central heat, and Lisa snoring. I swiveled my chair around and discovered Lisa sleeping with her head resting on her arms on her desk. Clint went home to help his wife, Julie, for our dinner date tonight.

Well, that wasn't happening. Not tonight anyway. I sat back in my chair with my feet resting on top of my desk, my fingers laced behind my head and watched Lisa sleep. I smiled at myself . . . *Great job, Nick. Great job.*

Nicky baby?

Chapter Ten

AFTER I HAD spoken with Detective Cole, Homicide Division, I decided to call Saxony's Family Restaurant on Kenmore Avenue, North side of Chicago. It was 6:15 P.M. And it was still Wednesday. A very long day. I punched the last number on my phone key pad. It immediately put me through. A Spanish-accented female with a smooth and sexy voice, had answered the phone on the first ring. Quick. She must've had her hand rest-ing on the phone. Sufficient.

"Saxony's Family Restaurant on Kenmore Avenue, how may I assist you?"

I told her she could assist me by letting me speak with Mr. or Mrs. Polycheck, the owners of the restaurant. Her smooth and sexy tone faded a- way.

"I know who the Polychecks' are. I also know they own theese place. You do not have to tell me, meester." Her Spanish accent was emphasized.

There was a long pause.

I said. "You feel better, miss." Still a pause. I continued to speak.

"Well, if you do feel better, I will like to speak to the Polychecks', the own-ers of Saxony's, just in case you had forgotten who the owner's were."

She said something like 'you-ass'. A few moments had passed. I had heard pots and pans clanging loudly, and sometimes humming of distance voices over the phone in the background. The loud-speaker was very loud. I guess that was why it was called the "loud-speaker." Duh. " 'Mr. Polycheck, telephone, line one'. " She came back on the phone, and said. "I had Mr. Polycheck paged." I said, "I heard."

"Mr. Polycheck, may I help you?"

"Yes, sir. I surely hope so." I identified myself, and the reason of the call.

"It's about time somebody looked into this matter." He said.

"Wasn't there an on-going investigation?" I said.

"Only two of our finest in blue. They only came to my bar on Sheridan just once. And that was the night of the eleventh, I mean, the morning of the twelfth of February. They were mainly concerned about Mr. Barton's alibi, you know, his whereabouts. Well, I told them he was here until closing time. Which was the truth. They left, and I never saw them again. Not even one measly detective. Case closed, I thought."

"How much do you remember of that night, Mr. Polycheck?"

"Well, some things are a little sketchy, but I'll manage. Now, let's see, Sandy and Mike came in peaceably and sat down at the bar. He ordered a beer, I forget what brand, and she ordered a Brandy and Coke, or maybe it was Rum and Coke, well, either way it started off peaceful. Then Sandy said something that pissed Mike off."

"Like what?" I said.

"I'm getting to that. Now, let me think. She said something like 'Let's move away, or she wanted to move away. Well, something liked that."

"Maybe," I said, "Sandy meant breaking-up with Mike."

"It could be. Whatever it was, he was ticked . . . big time." He paused to take in a breath or two. "Did you know she worked for me, Mr. Edwards?"

"Um-hum."

"She was a very good employee, too. But a huge flirt." He stressed 'huge'. "The male customers just loved her. But Mike was another story. He was so jealous, I thought he might kill her one of those times. I didn't really care if she was flirting with them. It brought in the moo-la, you know, the green stuff."

"Yeah, I do know what the green and moola stuff is, Mr. Polycheck."

"Well, I didn't really care for Mike, you know, Mr. Barton, and his wild ways. He had tried to sell crack and weed at my old bar I used to own. It turned out to be a rat-hole and a troubled place. So I sold it for cheap, just to get out of there. And I bought this beautiful palace of a restaurant. It's on the better side of the city." He finally took in another lungful of air. I took advantage of it. So I asked again about the night of the quarrel.

"Oh yeah. Well, Sandy left her Brandy and Coke on the bar while she used the lady's room, or wherever she went to. Well, she never even took a sip of it. She came out of, wherever, and grabbed her purse off of the top of the bar, and stormed out. And she left a very good drink, too. Mike was so angry, I thought he'd might chase her down the street, and beat her up again.

"Again?" I said.

"Yeah. Again. That was what I said. Again. She came to work many of times with bruises on her face. But I had stayed out of it. But, if you want my opinion, she was stupid for staying with that prick. Somebody should have taught him a lesson."

"So, what happened after that episode?" I said.

"Well, after Sandy had left, I went over to where she sat, proceeded to take her full drink off of the bar and dump it. But, no, prick-face had to get violent. He grabbed my wrist and said; 'Don't touch that drink, or I'll break it'."

"Break it?" I said. "Break what? Your wrist, or the glass?"

"I assumed he meant my wrist. So, I pulled back and served my other customers."

"Is that it?"

"Well, not all of it."

"Well . . . And . . ."Getting information from Mr. Polycheck sure wasn't easy. But I patiently listened. For how long, I had no clue.

"Well, the town drunk walked in very shortly after Sandy had went home, I would say, about ten, maybe, fifteen minutes. Anyway, she stag—gered in and sat down next to Barton, you know, Mike. They sat at the bar real close-like, if you know what I mean, Mr. Edwards."

"Um-hum." I was getting sleepy, but that information was very import-ant to the case. So I succeeded to stay awake.

"The next thing I knew the town drunk and Mike lip-locked right there in front of me and several of my customers. It was embarrassing. They acted more like lovers than Mike and Sandy ever did. And they dated a hell of a long time, too."

"Maybe Sandy and Mike didn't love each other."

"Well, maybe or maybe not. I'm no Ann Landers, but I don't think Sandy and Mike should ever been matched together."

I didn't know what to say to that. So I let it pass. So I went to the next question.

"Who was this town drunk?"

"A friend of Sandy's and Mike's."

"What's her name? Remember?" I had inhaled in deep. Exhaled and relaxed.

"Funny name, sort of . . . um . . . . uh . . . . Rooty . . . Rudy, or Rueden, or some- thing liked that."

"Clara Rueton?"

"Yeah, that's it. Clara Rueton. Great woman, but she drank too much."

"Anything else you might remember?" I said.

"Yeah, and this beats the cake. Mike went nuts, you know, bezerk, crazy, bonkers. Well, you get the picture." I grunted. But I don't think he had heard me.

Mr. Polycheck continued his long and detailed story. I took in another deep breath. Oh..hum.

"I nearly kicked him out. But he apologized, and calmed down."

"What happened?" I said. I looked at my watch. It was nearing nine-thirty in the eve-ning. I wondered if Clint and Julie were enjoying their din-ner. Work. Work. Work.

"You know the drink that Sandy left behind, and nearly got my wrist broken over?"

"Yeah, I'm listening."

"Well, the town drunk . . ." I interrupted.

"You mean Clara Rueton. Call her Clara Rueton."

"What's with you, pal. You sensitive?"

"Yeah. Sensitive."

"All right. Clara it is. Well, Clara Rueton drank it in one gulp. And she was hammered when she came in earlier. When she finished the drink, Mike went bezerk. He yelled at Clara and said; 'That was Sandy's drink. She was supposed to drink it. Not you. Damn you, Clara'. Then he had this look on his face as if he was going to pass out. He turned pale as Casper the Friendly Ghost . . . He said; 'Oh-my-God, Clara, Oh-my-God'. Then he ordered her to go home and make herself vomit. So she staggered out of the bar, and was never seen again. Just like Sandy. Poof! Vanished. Both gone. Just like if the earth swallowed them up. Shortly after, maybe a week or so later, Mike had vanished without a trace. Vanished. Poof! Gone."

I didn't know what to say to that, either. These might be good clues. Another day in my thinking room. I said. "Did Mike ever leave the bar?"

He said. "Yeah. Several times to use the john and phone."

"What I meant to say," I said. "did he ever leave the building at any time?"

"No. I think so." He hesitated and thought. "No. He stayed the whole time 'til closing."

"Which was?"

"Two-thirty in the A.M."

"You said he used the phone."

"Yeah, I did say that. Why?"

"Was it a pay-phone, or house-phone?"

"You sure ask a lot of questions, don't you?"

"Yep. It's my job. Please answer the question. It's very important."

"What happened to Sandy and the rest of them? Do you know, Mr. Ed- wards? Something terrible happened to them. Didn't it?"

"I don't know yet. But I'm working on it. My client hired me to find out what had happened."

"Who's your client?"

"Can't say. It's confidential. Now, answer the damn question, Mr. Poly -check."

"Alright, alright, already. Mike used the pay-phone several times after Clara left. I guess he was worried about her."

"What makes you think he was calling her?" I said.

"Just an assumption."

"Assumptions could make an ass out of you sometimes."

"Yeah. I suppose. You assume a lot. How do you feel, Mr. Edwards?"

"An ass."

"Anything else, Mr. Edwards?"

"Yeah . . . What time were these phone calls made?"

"First call was made just before Midnight. The second call around twelve-thirty. Third call, just before closing. Maybe two, or two-fifteen."

"Did he ever get an answer from any of those calls?"

"I'm not into eaves-dropping, man. I don't make it a habit to listen in on my customers conversations, pal. I gotta get going."

I ignored him and continued my interview.

"Did Mike tamper with her drink. Such as; dropping tablets, capsules, or any type of powdered form substance into her Brandy and Coke?"

"No. But I can't say for sure. I was getting pretty busy."

"Did you see anything of the sort when Sandy went to the bathroom, or wherever she went?"

"Well, that would have been around ten or ten-fifteen, just before she left. I was really busy then. For sure."

"A few more questions, alright?" I said.

"Man. I gotta go." I ignored him again. Hope he doesn't hang up on me.

"Did Sandy still have her two left thumbs that night?"

"Yep. She did. And we'll never know how she managed like that. But she did."

"Yes, Mr. Polycheck. You might be right about that."

"About what?"

"We might never know how she managed."

"If I remember anything else, Mr. Edwards, I will give you a jingle."

"Please do, Mr. Polycheck. Thanks again for your time." I gave him my phone number. Then we hung up. I had stared at my phone for a long while. I had asked myself . . . What did I just learn here? Not much. Just more questions to deeply think about . . . . Why did Mike get so defensive and upset about Sandy's drink? Did he put something in Sandy's drink. And who was he calling those three times on the pay-phone? Was it Sandy, or was it Clara? Was it Mike who'd called the police between 2 and 2:25 A.M.? If he had, did he assume that Sandy was visiting Clara at that time? According to the police report and Detective Cole, the caller wanted the police to check on Apartment 103, and to see if Sandy Boehlis was alright. Not Clara. Or may-be Sandy called from a payphone and wanted to throw the police off by ask- ing them to check on *Sandy Boehlis*, in Apartment 103. So when Detective Cole and other officials arrived, they would've been looking for a Sandy Boehlis. This will definitely give Sandy a big break to fake her own death.

Therefore, Clara would've been found dead by Sandy. Maybe Sandy had overheard Clara heaving her guts out, like Mike told her to, and Sandy came to her rescue, or tried to rescue her. Maybe by that time Sandy checked on Clara, she was already dead. I reviewed some things over in my head . . . . . The time of death was between 11 P.M., Thursday night, and 1 A.M., Friday morning. Supposedly, Clara walked in the bar, lip-locked with Mike, drunk Sandy's drink, and all of this had taken place between 10:15 and maybe, 10:45 Thursday night. Their apartment building was only a block and a half away from Peanut Bowl Lounge. The status, or condition Clara was in, it probably would have taken her maybe twenty minutes to get into her apart-ment. So, at 11:05, or thereabouts, she probably was in the bathroom with her head buried into the commode, puking. She probably had ridden the substance from her system, assuming Mike had dropped or poured some—thing into Miss Boehlis's drink, or most of it out of her system. But was it enough? Maybe it was, just to stay alive a little longer. Could she have lived up to 1 A.M. like the *time of death* report had stated? Maybe, or maybe not. I have been wrong before on such cases. So, I might be wrong again. Nothing appears as it seems. That is why I keep on searching, digging and turn over every rock, until it appears truthfully correct.

I stood and walked toward my dream girl, who was snoring pretty damn good now. I gently kissed the back of her soft and kissable neck. Her perfume had slightly faded away, but still enough to get a good whiff. Nice.

She slowly awoke from her deep, deep slumber. Her eyes squinted against the over-head lights as she tried to look up at me. She said. "What time is it?" I said. "It's late, honey. It's time to go home." I'd followed her in my car to her Condo, in Tomah, not too far from my three story apartment, and spent the night lying in each other's arms.

Chapter Eleven

It was Friday morning, March 3rd and Spring was moving in quickly. Can't wait. Today, the temperature was holding fifty degrees. But, much warmer inside, 'cause I had Lisa lying next to me in her doubled-size bed.

Lisa had the day off, so we took advantage of it. Today was the day we'll be speaking with Sheryl about how not John Boehlis was her father. Lisa had promised, or suggested, she will be with me when I would tell Sheryl the very sad news. I had spent another night at Lisa's Condo. Two nights in a row. How lucky can a guy get? The appointment was set for 9 A.M.

We had little over an hour to kill. Lisa and I made passionate love, and still had time for a quick breakfast. We had breakfast in bed.

"Do you ever think of moving in with me, Tex?" Lisa said.

"Sometimes."

"When are those 'sometimes'." I took a spoonful of my bran-flakes, wiped my lips with a soft white napkin, and swallowed.

"When I am alone at night, and I don't have any cases to attend to."

She looked at me with those bright blue eyes with her head cocked slightly to her left.

"Well, then, in that case, maybe you will be able to move in with me when the case with my father and mother is over."

"Maybe. Only if I don't get any lengthy cases after that."

"Well, me to, I guess. We'll discuss this matter after we return from Chicago. Alright with you, honey bunny?" Lisa smiled that special smile.

I melted.

"You bet." I leaned to my right and kissed her naked body. We quick-ly got dressed and quickly did the dishes. Lisa washed, I'd dried and put a- way. We both were dressed casual. Lisa had faded blue jeans with a 'Betty Boop' tee-shirt, over-lapping her thighs, just above her knees. Since I had to work, I wore dress casual slacks, perfectly creased and a powdered-blue dress shirt, no tie. A black wind-breaker to hide my .38 Police Special, snub—nose, Smith and Wesson.

Lisa and I drove from her Condo Suite, which was on Ellison Road. I turned right on Superior Avenue, going north toward Highway 21. We drove about ten miles. We intersected with '21', turned left, heading west and drove directly past our detective agency, which was on our left. Another nine miles further, we drove by Lisa's last place of employment; 'The Bar & Grill'. It was surrounded with humongous pine trees. And very tall, too. Probably had been around for hundreds of years. I'd heard somewhere if you count the rings in the center of the cut-ed wood, it'll tell you the age of the tree. Maybe I should cut one down sometime. Nick Edwards the lumberjack.

"Remember that place, Tex?"

"Yep, pard'ner. Sho' do. If it wasn't for the arson case, we would have never met. Can you imagine it had been two years since we'd met." She had no comment to that latter statement.

"Maybe, maybe not. But we don't have to think about that now, do we?" Lisa said. "You know, since we met and all."

I didn't comment on that. Why comment on the obvious anyway? But my thoughts went back to the arson killing. Bethany Miller is still serving time up north Wisconsin somewhere, where she definitely belongs. I'd won-dered if Lisa was thinking about it. I shouldn't even think about it. It's very depressing.

"Five more miles, Blondie," I said. We'll be there."

No comment again. She was just concentrating on the drive through the country. Sheryl lived in the better part of town in Sparta, Wisconsin. The apartments were named Candlewick Apartments. It was structured with red brick. And it was in a sub-division. The oak, maple and birch trees were lined evenly around the circle where we had parked. We parked right in front of Sheryl's apartment building. Her address was 5005 W. Park Place. I thought it should have been 'Circle Drive'. Well, we were *parked* in front of the *place*. 'Park Place' it is. The neighborhood was surrounded with public parks and fields. About a mile back, there was also a small airfield. Private planes mostly. It's a very quiet neighborhood. And she lived on the second floor too. Damn. No elevator. I managed to climb the two flight of stairs with Lisa's help, though.

We took a break now and again. I glanced through the stairwell's window and admired the two vehicles in Sheryl's driveway. They were parked side by side. The vehicle closest to the building, was a beautiful black Trans AM.

It was freshly painted, maybe two or three days old. The gold eagle centered on the hood was prominent. I was a little envious. But not much. It was a 1976 model. "Knight Rider", here I come. But I had to wait 'til my right leg healed completely. The second car was parked next to the Trans AM's pass- enger's side. It was a cute, 1973 AMC Gremlin. You sure don't see those anymore. By golly. It was painted light purple and with a wide white stripe from the rear to the front frame of the headlamp. The interior had the Levi's trim package, completed with denim seats, orange stitching, copper rivets. Far out. I was envious again. But I was still happy with my '95' Corvette Coupe. After I thought about it, I wasn't envious after all. Thinking is good.

Lisa and I stood in front of Sheryl's apartment door. I knocked with my knuckles, as 'The Three Stooges' would've done. (5 rapid taps . . . . .then a pause . . . two more rapid taps). Lisa turned her head at me and shook it. And clicked her tongue. I grinned and shrugged. Then she'd turned away and faced the door again. The door opened. Lo and behold, Mr. Big Boy stood before us. He was wearing blue sweat pants with white stripes along its sides, and a white tee-shirt. White socks. No shoes.

"What the hell do you want?" Lisa and I ignored him and brushed him aside.

"Well, good-morning, Nick . . . . . Lisa." Sheryl got up from the sofa and greeted us. Mr. Big Boy just stood there with his left hand still on the door- knob with the door still wide open.

"Morning, Sheryl." I said. I was still ignoring Big Boy.

"Good-morning, Sheryl," Lisa said. "Beautiful place you have here."

Lisa looked around in awe. She left me standing alone facing Sheryl and Big

Boy holding the door open, while she decided to tour the apartment, un- guided.

"Honey, you can close the door, now." Big Boy did. He obeyed. Good boy. Sheryl set her eyes on me again. "Have a seat, Mr. Edwards . . . Coffee?" I nodded and thanked her.

Today, Sheryl was wearing gray sweat pants, a gray tee-shirt with 'Betty Boop' logo on the shirt pocket and white socks. Also, no shoes.

"Help yourself to the cream and sugar, if you use it." Sheryl smiled her childish smile and sat down on the sofa. After I made my coffee to perfec-tion, I sat across from her on the love seat. I sipped my coffee. Yummy.

Lisa returned to the living-room.

The apartment was colorful with bright white walls in the dinette area and sky-blue walls in the living room. The spacious floor plan was very stylish in every room with solid oak flooring. The structure had high ceilings with sky-light features. The deep bronzed-color ceiling fans were in every room.

Even the long hallway had two fans. Cool. And I mean cool. The cherry colored di-nette set matched the wall cabinets.

Lisa said again, "Beautiful. Just beautiful," when she had completed her tour. Then Lisa sat down next to Sheryl on the six-foot, powdered-blue sofa and helped herself to coffee. She added two sugars and several drops of real cream. Big Boy then slowly walked across the oak floor from the front door to the wall that divided the living room and dinette area. He sternly eyed us and let his body rest firmly against the edge of the dividing wall. He glared strongly on me. Was it love? I surely had hoped not. We'll never survive the rela-tionship on the first date. I turned away from lover boy and rested my eyes on Sheryl.

"Speaking of beautiful," I said. "The two cars in the driveway are just wild. Yours?" Sheryl set her 'Betty Boop' coffee mug on the blonde coffee table. I looked at her deco-rative mug and thought. 'Betty Boop' must've had a big pro-mo. 'Betty Boop' watches, tee-shirts, socks and coffee mugs. I probably should have worn my 'Goofy' tee-shirt for competition.

"Yes," Sheryl said. "The Gremlin is mine, the Trans AM is Art's." She briefly looked at Art, then turned her eyes on me.

"Yeah. The Gremlin was bought for me on my first birthday. My Uncle Dale preserved it for me until I turned eighteen. Unusual gift."

"I'll say." Lisa said. "The Trans AM?" Big Boy Art spoke gruffly.

"I bought that car out of my own pocket." Ego freak. I thought.

"That's nice." Lisa said, without looking up at him. We still had ignored him.

"How can you afford something this elegant, Miss Boehlis?" I said.

"I do well as a beautician. The extra bedroom in the rear is my beauty parlor."

"Is Art employed?" I asked. Art moved. By golly.

"That, my friend, isn't any of your fucking business." Art clenched his fist. Lisa looked at me. So did Sheryl.

"Art is right, Mr. Edwards. It isn't your business."

"Sorry. I guess I don't know when to stop asking questions." Art relaxed and resumed his position against the wall. Arms folded.

"I was just curious about how you can afford this apartment."

"Okay . . . Okay . . . . Mr. Edwards. If you truly must know." She took in a deep breath. Exhaled. "I received a lump sum, which I refuse to reveal to you the amount, when I turned eighteen. My mother came into some money before she'd died. She opened a trust fund in my name. Of course I couldn't withdrawal any of it until I was eighteen. My mother wasn't the greatest, but she wanted me to have a future. You know, security. It seems to me she knew she wouldn't be around to support me, morally, financially, and emotionally. Satisfied now, Mr. Edwards?"

I shook my head. "No, I am not at all satisfied." Sheryl was set back a ways by my remark. But remained silent. "Where in the hell did your mother get the money? That's what I like to know." I glanced at Big Boy. He didn't move. Good. I probably couldn't get up fast enough anyway. I noticed from the corner of my right eye, Big Art was changing colors in the face. If I was not mistaken, his face turned rainbow colors. I believed he was pissed off, again.

"Miss Boehlis, I am not employed by your boyfriend. Does he have to be in the same room with us? I'm getting annoyed with him. It interferes with my concentration." I stared at him for a time. Sheryl didn't say anything to him. I maintained my gaze. Big Art got the hint. He pushed himself away from the wall, turned right, and walked away to some room and played with his toys. After I heard the door slamming, I turned my eyes on Sheryl.

"Do you really need that information, Mr. Edwards?" I looked at Lisa She sat silently next to Sheryl on the sofa. Her hands clasped in her lap. I sat across from them with my eyes bouncing back and forth from Lisa to Sheryl, Sheryl to Lisa, and back to Sheryl. I was getting dizzy. Lisa should be with me. I thought. She should sit next to me on the love seat and take advantage of it. But I understood. When the time was right, I'll tell Sheryl about her father, whoever he was. Then Lisa would jump in, and console her.

"Yes, I think I do, Miss Boehlis." She lit a cigarette with a butane lighter, which was sitting on the blonde coffee table in front of her. She set it back down, sat back against the cushions, crossed her legs, which she was good at, blew smoke from her nostrils, and got comfortable. Then she turned to Lisa.

"Lisa, do I have to answer his question?"

"Sorry, Sheryl. I'm not in the position to answer that. You hired Nick. You didn't hire me. If he needs to know something, there as to be a good reason for it."

"Oh. Yeah. Just like he needed to know about Art's employment status."

"Okay, Sheryl," I said, as I was trying to get up from the love seat. I hob- bled to my feet and stood as straight as my right leg would let me. I heard the slamming of a door. Lisa and Sheryl jumped a foot. I turned around, and there was Art. He came out of his playroom, and seemed flushed around the gills. He just stood there in the hallway, near the living room and waited. For what, I didn't know. But Lisa and Sheryl were very tense. Time will tell, I guess. "Let me ask you a question you probably can answer." I said.

"What question is that, Mr. Edwards?" Sheryl said.

"What caused you to move here, near Tomah, Wisconsin, and settle in this small Town of Sparta?"

"Art and I met in Orlando, Florida in 1993. He was just discharged from the Navy. Then, when he walked into my beauty salon for a haircut, the love light came on. Love at first sight, you know." I nodded. "Since he had fam-ily here in Sparta, he wanted to be closer to them. So, about a year later, late 1994, maybe early 1995, I followed him up here from Orlando. I found this lovely place and opened my salon here in this apartment. So far, it has all seemed to work out. Happy now, Mr. Edwards?"

I shrugged. Then I said, "Was Art discharged from the U.S. Navy for being stupid?" Lisa smiled. I believe Sheryl had a grin. Art didn't show a smile. I don't think he ever smiled.

"Enough is enough, Asshole." He came at me full force.

"Big Boy, don't be stupid." He came at me like a steamroller. Lisa and Sheryl both jumped on the sofa, out of the way of two strong males em-bracing each other. We went down and crashed our weight on the blonde coffee table. Splinters of wood went every-where. We rolled on the oak floor and our bodies made connection with several floor lamps. The lamps fell over, like a pine tree falling after being cut by a lumberjack, then a big sounding crash followed. Broken glass from the bulbs slid across the waxed oak-wood flooring. The lamp-shades blown out and ripped. Lisa and Sheryl had their hands over their mouths and shaking their heads. I had a difficult time getting on my feet. Between my injured right leg, and the waxed floor, I just couldn't get up.

I had vision myself as Curley Link from the 'Three Stooges', rotating in circles on the floor. Maybe if we did this for awhile Big Boy will get dizzy and roll off of me. But that wasn't going to happen. So, I took my right hand and locked on a crop of his hair and pulled his head back as far as it would go. A few more centimeters of his neck, it would have snapped. His face grimaced showing his yellow teeth and his last meal he ate. His tongue was hanging out, and his mouth was drooling.

My leg was in pain, but I held my own. The ladies were screaming and tried to main-tain their balance on the sofa. I felt like I was in a wrestling arena. I had hoped Lisa was cheering me on. Maybe Sheryl and Lisa had made some popcorn and enjoyed the enter-tainment with a few glasses of alcohol. Suddenly, I heard something snap close to my ear. Was it me? Was it Big Boy? His pressure of his weight had been released from me. I felt his weight leaving my chest. He rolled off and away from me and sprawled flat- ly on his back on the not-so-beautiful waxed floor. I slowly rolled my legs behind me, and braced myself with my left hand, and stood up. Big Boy did not. He just laid there in a full daze. Lisa jumped from the sofa and ran up to me and hugged me tightly.

"Hey, tough guy, are you alright?" I nodded and gasped for air. I turned around to see Big Boy, but Sheryl was blocking my view. She was leaning over his body, crying.

"Sheryl," I said. "He is . . . only . . . passed out . . . . from lack . . . of air. His muscle . . . was pulled . . . . ,.but he'll be okay. Get a . . . cold glass of . . . water and a clean cloth and dab water on his neck and forehead and face. He will wakeup eventually." She got up and ran into the kitchen, and few seconds she'd returned. Then Lisa and I helped Sheryl lift Art's dead weight to the sofa. Lisa and I sat down in the love seat with my left arm around her.

Dreams do come true . . . Yes.

Chapter Twelve

SHERYL AND HER boyfriend Art were sitting across from us in the living room on the multiple-colored sofa. She had Art's head in her lap, and his body stretched out with his feet hanging over the arm of the sofa. Lisa and I were still romantically holding each other . . . uh . . . well, maybe not roman-tically, but we were embraced. Art was returning to reality. I'd observed his dark-ring eyes fluttering. Lisa and I were just sitting in the love seat, watch-ing. No words were spoken, but if eyes could kill . . . .

Lisa and I removed our bodies from the loveable love seat and casually walked to the door. I turned around, Lisa continued to the door, and I faced Sheryl's angry facial expression and Art's fluttering eyes.

I said. "Remember what I'd asked for, Sheryl. You tell me where your mother got the money, then I'll tell you about your father. If you decide not to tell me what I need to know, I'm afraid I will have to resign myself from this case. You have seventy-two hours to make up your mind." I was about to leave, then I turned around again facing Art and Sheryl. "And keep your not-so-bright of a boyfriend out of my face. Or he will find himself in the hospital . . . or worse." Sheryl looked up at me and gazed silently.

Lisa and I left, closing the door softly behind us.

"Well . . . Well . . . Well . . . All in a days work. Where do you want to go to eat, Blondie?" We were sitting in front of Sheryl's apartment building in my car, trying to de-cide if we should get drunk, or find a decent restaurant to fill our emptiness. Lisa decided it would be wiser to eat a good balanced meal.

Party Pooper.

"Let's head out to Mr. Tee Pee, in Tomah. Good idea?" She said.

"Yep. After we eat Indian corn, then I'll get blitzed. Good Idea?"

"Nope."

"Oke-kee-doke-kee. The 'nopes' have it." I put my car in gear and went.

I couldn't wait to meet Chief Hiawatha and smoke his peace pipe. HOW!

Maybe Art should have come along. He can smoke the peace pipe and choke on it. I was tempted to turn the car around and pick him up and take him with us. And let the Indians tie him to a tree and burn his funky ass.

The waiter took our order and went away. He didn't look Indian. I thought. Ugh!

"Tex, what do you think of this crazy situation?" Lisa said.

"Sucks. I hate the idea knowing I'm onto something, and to think, I might have to close the door on this opportunity and miss out solving this case. But it isn't my problem, is it."

"No. No, it is not. Don't forget, though, she came to you. If Sheryl doesn't want to co-operate with you, then she cannot be very serious finding her mother's killer." The imitated Indian reappeared and set my MGD beer and Lisa's wine in front of us. She had Chardonnay White wine. Let's get drunk together. I thought.

"With the information that was compiled thus far, I don't think that was her mother lying on the living room floor in Apartment 103." I said, sipping my beer.

"Do you think she planned on faking her death?"

"Maybe," I said. "And maybe the whole Barryhill family were involved.

Faking ones death, just makes me ill inside. And this case is headed in that direction. Why? I just don't know. But hope to find out."

Lisa said. "It does explain the closed casket, unknown money Sheryl has, and the bogus death certificate. Most of all, the secret of Sandy's death."

I said. "There was a body found in Apartment 103. Who do you think it could be?"

Lisa thought for a moment. "Her Godmother?"

"Bingo. My thoughts exactly." I gulped my first glass of beer.

"Easy, Nick. You're driving, don't forget."

"Just a few more glasses like that, then, I'll slow down . . . . Please?"

"I'm watching you." Lisa said. She leaned toward the table, picked up her wine glass, and took a lengthy sip.

"I love it when you're aggressive, sweetie. But I'm watching you, too."

She ignored me.

The Chief Waiter brought our dinner and set it down carefully. Steam arose from our plates. I quickly gulped another glass of beer. Yum. Yum.

Lisa's face was pointing at her steaming plate, but her blue gaze was on me.

Shit.

"Mike Barton," Lisa said, as she swallowed her mashed potatoes. "What about him?"

"Barton probably ran off with Sandy, but doubtful. Or the underground caught up with him. Most logical."

"You mean, killed him?" Lisa took in some of her wine.

"Yep."

"The money. What do you think about that?"

"Part of it is probably John's insurance from the Marine Corp."

"The other part?" Lisa said. She pushed her plate aside, and rested her elbows on the edge of the table, and focused on my eyes.

"What do you think, Blondie?"

"Drug money." It was a statement. I nodded aggressively.

Chapter Thirteen

A FTER LISA FINISHED her baby back ribs and her dinner salad, and I took in the last forkful of my homemade chicken pot pie, and paid the bill with a decent tip, we drove back to our office. The time; 3:20 P.M. Clint was just touching up his typing on his 'drug' case report, when we strolled in. He looked at Lisa, then, stared at me for a time.

"Nick, where did you get that mouse? You look like a half-a-raccoon."

"Fun-ny" I said, as I walked to the Fax Machine.

"Ah, let me guess, from Sheryl's irate jackass of a boyfriend." Clint said with a wide grin.

"Yep," Lisa said. "But you should've seen Sheryl's boyfriend."

"Yeah. I can imagine." Clint said. He seemed pleased.

I stood near the Fax and studied the flier that Detective Cole had sent me on Clara Rueton. He also included a second page, which proved interesting to my swollen eyes. The second page had a note written by Sandy Boehlis. At least, I thought it was her handwriting. It read:

> *I'm tired of life and Mike's bullshit*
> *I'm sorry to end it this way. I love*
> all of you in my special way. Good-
> *bye to my friends and my family and*
> *this sick and cruel, cruel world.*
>
> *Love,*
> *Sandy Boehlis*

Every word was printed neatly, and her name signed artistically. Wasn't sloppy, or written speedily. It didn't seem to me like a person was contemp- lating suicide. It was too damn neat. The 'Missing Person's' flier of Clara's picture, was like staring at Mrs. Boehlis. Sheryl was right. Pass as sisters.

The only difference, Clara wore glasses on the flier. Sandy's photo had not. I Xeroxed a copy of Sandy's picture. I returned to my desk, set the pic- tures side by side, then, I studied the resemblance. I snatched a magic mark- er from my desk drawer and drew circles around each eye of Sandy's copied picture. I studied the two some more and carefully compared. The 'Magic Marker' glasses on Sandy's photo and the real picture of Clara's can pass as twins.

I glanced at Lisa and Clint and gestured with my forefinger. "Come here, guys." Lisa resented the 'guy' thing. "You need to see this." They both looked over my shoulder, eyes shifting back and forth for a few moments. I turned my head and looked up. "So, what do you think, Lisa . . . . Clint?"

"Well, I'll be damned." This could be a case of switchy-switchy." Clint said. "Sandy could've wrote the note and planted it on Clara, as Detective Cole pointed out on the fax coversheet. She could very well easily replaced Clara's identifications with her own. Such as; DL, Social Security card, checkbook, or whatever and placed them into Clara's purse."

Lisa said. "That doesn't explain Clara's death. Did Sandy kill her? Or by chance, Clara had killed herself and Sandy took advantage of the situation so she could escape from Mike Barton's clinches." Lisa walked around me and sat her left cheek of her buttocks on my desk, turned, and faced me.

"Well, Nick?" Lisa said.

I said. "I'll have to probe further into that before I can answer that honestly. I will need to call the five people on the list that Sheryl had given me and have a talk with them. If the five knew Sandy, chances are, they knew Clara as well. But the question still holds . . . Is Sheryl willing to cooper- ate and let me continue with her case?" Clint, Lisa and I pondered that thought for a long, long while.

Chapter Fourteen

I WAS SITTING IN my office on a very bright, sunny Sunday morning. The time; 10 A.M. I had collected six phone numbers to Chicago. And I was still patiently waiting for Sheryl's phone call . . . . time was running out. I had given her until Monday Noon, March 6th, to reconsider the information I'd needed about the inheritance she received from her 'late' mother.

I'd studied the list of names on my legal pad. I could call them in alpha- betical or- der . . . . or call them randomly. I have choices. As I mused myself on which order I was going to call, the phone rang. I picked it up.

"C-N-L Detective Agency, may I help you?" It was Sheryl.

"Is this Nick?"

"Yes it is . . . Sheryl?" My eyes protruded from my eye-sockets.

"Good. I thought it over about the money thing."

"That's good." I said, as I sipped my cold coffee.

"Yeah. I need you on this case. And sorry again about Art."

"Yep. Me too. Are you going to release the information to me, or are we going to chit-chat about how sorry we are about your lover-boy?"

"Alright, already. This isn't easy for me to disclose this sort of informa-tion to you, or anyone else. Bear with me, Nick. I hope you'll understand."

"Un-huh."

"I understand you're upset with me, Mr. Edwards, but please don't be cold toward me. Alright?"

"Un-huh."

"You're doing that, again."

"What?"

"The 'Un-huh' thing. Cut it out. You sound so cold and distant. Stop it."

Sheryl had sounded as if she was going to burst into tears.

"Un-huh. Maybe I am cold and distant. And why shouldn't I? For a per-son who wants her mother's killer found and punished, you're not very co-operative."

"I am sorry, Nick. Quit torturing me."

"Torture! You haven't seen torture. This is my good side. Now, tell me."

"Okay . . . Here it goes." She took in a deep breath, and slowly exhaled. Her voice sounded shaky. "The money . . . the money . . . is . . . uh . . . is dirty." It came out forcefully.

"Yeah, okay. I'm listening." I said.

"I found out that the money was dirty from my auntie and uncle. I had promised them I would never, ever, mention this to anyone. Under any cir- cumstances. Telling you this is very difficult."

"Yep. We already had determined that. Spit it out, Child."

"Don't call me that. I am not a fucking child."

"Then, grow up. Learn to speak your mind. And grow a spine."

"Alright . . . Alright. The money, or most of it, is drug money my mother stole from Mike Barton."

"You mean the underground, drug dealers, or whoever. But before you go any further, Sheryl, let me point out to you that your life could be in grave danger."

"How? What do you mean by that?"

"The underground, or drug dealers never quit looking for what's theirs. They might be searching you out, or your aunt and uncle. And they might be in danger too."

"Whatever. But what does matter, Nick, my mother was trying to make a life for me. You can believe that or not. I don't care a rats-ass. And you can take that to the bank."

"So the money was put in a trust fund in your name, in care of your aunt and uncle. Right?"

"Well, not exactly. Just my Uncle Dale. The rest of it was from my mother's life insur- ance policy, and my father's insurance from the Marine Corp."

"But your mother committed suicide. Did the insurance cover that?"

"I'm not quite sure. That was what my Auntie 'Bee' told me." I sat silent-ly for a time, and soaked this all in. My eyes shifted from my desk pad, to the outside parking lot, then back to the phone. Sheryl broke the silence.

"Don't you have something to tell me, Mr. Edwards." I was still silent. I knew I had to tell her the truth about her father, whoever he was. But this would be the best time then any. I did bargain with her. I thought. Tit for Tat. So, this is it.

I wasn't very good at this. So, I asked the first question that came to mind.

"Do you have any children, Miss Boehlis?"

"Well . . . No . . . Yes . . . But not really."

"Explain that, Miss."

"I have to?"

"Nope. My point being is, since you have-slash-had children, you do know human nature allows the seed to grow inside the mothers-to-be womb for nine months. At least, that is the average time. Right?"

"Yeah, I guess. I hope I'd understood the question."

"Okay. With that in mind, I spoke with a woman named Barbra Boehlis who lives in Cicero, Illinois. Her son, John Boehlis, was killed in Viet Nam.

The month, January. The year, 1971." I hesitated to speak. I wanted this info to sink in Sheryl's head before I'd said anything else.

"Your speaking about my grandmother and father. Correct?" This was more difficult that I thought it would be.

"When were you born, Miss Boehlis?"

"March 9th, 1972. Why?"

"You weren't very swift in math, were you? Figure it out."

"You don't have to get so sarcastic, Mr. Edwards."

"I'm trying my best to make this simple for you without hurting your feelings more than they are now." Suddenly, silence came over the other end of the phone. I'd waited for a short time.

"He's not my father," she said, sniffling. "And she's not my grand-mother. Is that what you're telling me?"

"I'm afraid so, Sheryl. I'm afraid so. The facts have it. Do you want to come to my office?"

"Yes. Yes, I would like that very much. Give me an hour to freshen up and change clothes."

"Come alone. Understand. We don't need Art to interfere again."

I said.

"Alone. You got it." I believed I heard a small chuckle.

Chapter Fifteen

I WAS ON MY third call when Sheryl walked in. I gestured with my left hand to sit. She did. When she had crossed her legs, her red dress crept up slightly, showing her kneecaps and thighs. And waited patiently while I was on the phone speaking with one of her old neighbors from Chicago.

Sheryl ran her long fingers through her shoulder-length blonde hair, then, she shook her head, straightening her loose crop. She seemed satisfied.

"Thank-you very much, Miss Dirken." We hung up. Sheryl stood up, walked around my desk, leaned over to me, and gave me a hug and a kiss. I returned the hug lightly. Her perfumed had a great smell of a rose garden. I inhaled deeply. As she was returning to the client chair, I'd wiped the lipstick from my left cheek with a white Kleenex tissue.

"What was that for?" I asked.

"For keeping me as your client."

"I know. I know. We'd been through this once before. Anymore inform- ation you keep from me pertaining to this case, out the door you go. Do I make myself perfectly clear, Miss Boehlis?"

"Perfectly." She said with a pout face. "What do you have for me, Mr. Edwards?"

"Detective Cole from Chicago, told me some information about the body found in Clara's apartment."

Sheryl leaned over and rested her elbows on the edge of my desk, and listened intently. Her eyes gleamed, momentarily.

"Are you positive about your mother's extra left thumb not being re- moved?" I said.

"Yes. I am very positive."

"Okay, as long as you are sure of yourself." I studied her eyes for a short time, being confident she was telling the truth. "You know, Sheryl, this case might take a three-hundred-sixty-degree turn."

"What do you mean, Mr. Edwards?"

"The body that was found didn't have an extra thumb on the left hand." I said, as I took in a swallow of my coffee.

"Are you absolutely sure?" Her eyes seemed to gleam, again.

"That's what the detective and other people I spoke with informed me. They sounded positive. Instead of your mother being murdered, she might have just went into hiding to get away from Mike Barton."

"Be alive somewhere?" Sheryl smiled ear to ear, and had tears streaming from her hazel eyes onto her flushed cheeks. I slid the box of Kleenex to-ward her. She snatched a handful.

"Maybe. But I have plenty of questions that need to be asked before we jump to that conclusion. But I must admit, it's heading in that direction." I sipped, then, gulped the remaining portion of my coffee. I stood and went over to Mr. Coffee and poured another cup. I gestured, with pot in hand, at Sheryl. She shook her head, and waved it off. "I heard when I'd walked in, Mr. Edwards, you were speaking with a Ms. Dirken." She dabbed her cheeks and eyes with the white tissue I had slid to her. Then, she rested her hands on her lap.

"Yes, Sheryl, you'd heard correctly. She told me, and some others I had interviewed, your mother was planning to escape from Mr. Barton's mean- ness and evil ways. She was fed-up with Mike beating on you. I was told she had this planned a week before her al-leged death." I showed Sheryl the sui- cide note. Then, I asked her for the bag of birthday and Christmas cards, so I can compare the handwriting for myself. After she'd studied the note, she slid it toward me across the desk, and asked her if she recognized the writ-ing? She nodded positively.

"Why did the police think it was my mother in the first place?"

"Firstly, the suicide note. Secondly, there was a great resemblance be-tween your mother and godmother."

"That was my godmother the police found dead in the apartment?"

"It sure seemed that way." She covered her face with her hands and just bawled. It was my turn to hug her. I held her until she'd stopped crying. She snatched another handful of tissues. I made a mental note: Buy several boxes of Kleenex.

"How did all of this happen, Mr. Edwards?" Sheryl said, still crying, and pressing the Kleenex against her left cheek. "What I mean is, how did the police screw-up the evi-dence? All these years my life was nothing but lies.

Who can I trust? Who can I believe?" Sheryl still had her face in her hands, and rock-ing back and forth in the client chair. I held her tighter, with my chin resting on the crown of her head.

"The police didn't screw-up, honey. They just went with what they'd had found."

"Whaddya mean?" She was still talking into her hands, sobbing.

"I don't have the full details yet. Maybe never will. But it seems to me that the evidence was planted on your godmother to throw the police detect-ives off your mother's trail." Sheryl thought about that for a time. Then she said.

"Did my mother kill my godmother so she could escape from Barton?"

"I don't know if your mother killed Clara. Clara was a heavy drinker ac- cording to Detective Cole. And she was also consuming heavy medication.

Mrs. Dirken advised me of that. But, I do need more information before I can honestly answer your questions." Was she murdered? Did she commit suicide? Or, was it just an accidental-death? These questions I had pondered since this case had begun. Sheryl had legitimate questions that needed to be addressed and answered. Poor girl. I'll do the best I can.

I focused on Sheryl, and noticed she had lifted her head away from her hands and looked right me.

"If my mother is alive, and you happen to find her, would my mother go to prison?"

I tried to answer that cleverly, and carefully.

"That is a possibility, honey. That would depend on the judge."

"Do you think others are involved?"

I looked at her awkwardly. She was reading my mind. I thought.

"Funny you asked, Sheryl. Because I do think others were involved in your mother's disappearance."

"Who?" Her tears subsided. She seemed to be calm. Thank God.

"Maybe your Uncle Dale and your Aunt 'Bee'. Maybe your Gram' too."

"My Gram'? She's dead. So, she probably took this to her grave."

I nodded solemnly and held her cold and very tense hand in mine.

We were silent for a moment or two. We meditated on our thoughts and shifted our eyes back and forth at one another. Sheryl broke the silence.

"My uncle and aunt, huh? Why them?"

"The secrets of your mother's death, the signing of the death certificate, and lack of concern. Like they knew she was alive and where she was at, but too afraid to tell you." I studied her hazel eyes as she sat silently. "And another thing, and this might be hard for you to understand, Sheryl, I really think your mother loved you enough to do something like this. That is, if it happened this way."

"That's crazy, Mr. Edwards. And you know it. If my mother really and truly loved me, she wouldn't have left me to begin with. Damn it."

She stood and paced nervously around my small space, which is called my office/cubicle.

"Let me explain my feelings and thoughts on this matter, okay?"

I said.

She turned and faced me with her arms folded across her chest. She gazed and twitched her right eye, and then slowly nodded once.

"Well, okay . . . . Mike Barton seemed to be a very possessive type of a guy, and he probably didn't want your mother to leave him. Maybe she tried over the years to leave him, but too afraid to follow through. Until now, maybe . . .

She got fed-up with his abusiveness toward you. She probably mustered enough courage to fulfill her wants and needs for your own protection. And hers, of course.

"And the only way she could have protected you from his anger, drugs and violence, is to have your Gram', your aunt, and uncle take care of you.

She knew very well she couldn't drag you around everywhere she needed to go. She probably even protected herself by changing her name and appear-ance. And if she did, it will be very difficult for me to locate her. You do un-derstand this is all under assumption she is alive and well, don't you?"

Sheryl nodded, again. Then, she slowly walked toward me and gave me a tight hug. I gently pushed her away from her embrace with my arms extend-ed and my hands resting on her shoulders. I looked into her angry, but sad eyes, and I said.

"Tell you what, since I have a few more calls to make why don't you go home, get your bag of cards your aunt sent you, bring them here to me, and I'll treat you on a late lunch. What do you say?"

Her eyes brightened big. She blinked, and her eyes welled up. "It's a deal."

Chapter Sixteen

I CALLED LISA, INVITED her to lunch with Sheryl and me. Told her to meet us at my office within an hour, or so. She accepted gladly. I then called Clara's parents; Gregg and Tiffany Rueton.

"Hell-o, Rueton residence." A foreign voice answered. The woman's voice sounded Spanish, or maybe Cuban.

"Good-afternoon, ma'am. My name is Nick Edwards. I'm calling from Tomah, Wisconsin. And I am trying to track down the parents of a Clara Rueton. Is this the correct number?"

"Si. Who do you which to speak? The Papa . . . Or Mama?"

"Either one will do. Are they both at the house?"

"Si. They are here. I get Mama Rueton, now. Moment, please."

As I waited, the sound of Spanish music came from the background. It was so soothing, I found myself swaying in my chair. I waited awhile longer looking out my window. Wal-Mart must had some kind of a 'blue-light' special. Every parking stall was filled with a variety of different colored ve- hicle shining in the sunlight. If I had time I might consider shopping today.

Not my best past-time, but I'll accept the challenge. Suddenly, my thoughts were interrupted from background noise, like someone tap-dancing. It was getting closer, and closer. Then, a voice appeared over the phone.

"Tiffany Rueton speaking, may I help you?"

"Mrs. Rueton. I'm Nick Edwards from Tomah, Wisconsin."

"Yes, yes. The maid told me you mentioned my daughters' name. What do you know about her? Did you find her?" Her voice sounded thrilled with excitement, it shrieked. I ignored her questions.

"I need information from you that goes back twenty years."

"Yes, yes, of course. Let me get my husband. He'll be listening on the other extension. Please . . . One minute." After a short time of Spanish music,

Mr. and Mrs. Rueton's voice crackled on the other end.

"Are you ready, Gregg, honey? Can you hear me?" A deep, shaky voice appeared into my ear piece.

"Yes, Tiff, I got it."

"Mr. Edards, is it?" Mrs. Rueton said.

"No, ma'am. My name is; Edwards . . . Mr. Nick Edwards. But please, call me Nick."

"You'll have to excuse both of us, Nick. Our hearing isn't what it used to be."

"Yes, ma'am. I understand perfectly."

"Nick, is this a prank? We had a lot of those over the past twenty years, you know. You tell Gregg and I what you think you know, then we'll decide if this is a prank. Fair enough?"

"Sure, of course." I said, as I sipped a bad cup of coffee. Mental note: Change coffee brand. "I am an investigator for C-N-L Detective Agency, here, in Tomah, Wisconsin. My client had hired me to investigate a Sandy Boehlis . . . ." I was cut off.

"What! Did you here that, honey? Nick is investigating a Sandy Boehlis.

She's the drug addict who corrupted our daughter." I sat back in my high-back swivel chair, and listened to their comments. Then, Gregg spoke.

"Yes, yes. I heard. Dick, is it?"

"No, sir. It's Nick. Nick with an 'N'.

"Okay, Mick." Jeez. I rolled my eyes and stared at the phone. I guess I'll be 'Mick' for awhile. I shrugged. I put the phone piece back into my ear.

"We told Clara over and over not to get hooked-up with Sandy and her male friend Mike."

"Mike Barton?" I asked.

"Yes. Mike Barton. He was always in trouble with the law. Selling, and buying drugs. But when Clara turned twenty-one, she moved out, and moved next door to Sandy. We asked her to call us everyday, just to be sure she was alright."

"Did she call you everyday?" I asked.

"Yes." Tiffany said. "When she didn't call us, we'd called her."

"When was the last time you have heard from her?"

"The twelfth of February." Gregg said. "Just a few minutes after mid- night."

"1977?" I asked. They both answered in unison. "Yes."

"When she didn't call you, what did you two do?"

"We called her. But she didn't answer. So we gave her the benefit of the doubt. We thought maybe she visited one of her other friends. Or met a male friend and went on a date. Since it was around Valentine's Day, there would have been a good chance of it. When she didn't call Monday, the day after

Valentine's Day, we became concerned. We called the Chicago Police that day, hoping they would check on her. But we were told to wait since she was an adult. There wasn't anything they could do.

"So we waited until Thursday, the eighteenth. When she still didn't call, Gregg and I drove over to her apartment."

"Did you continue to call her in the meantime?" I asked.

"Oh. Sure we did. But there was still no answer."

"The apartment she'd lived in, was Apartment 103, wasn't it?"

"Pardon me?" Tiffany said.

"Apartment 103. That was her apartment, correct?"

"Oh, yes." Gregg said. "This isn't a prank call, Tiff. He knows too much about her. I'm convinced Mick is telling the truth. You, Tiff, honey?"

"Yes Dear. I certainly agree."

Gregg said. "Well, Mick. Did you find her?"

I didn't know what to say. I couldn't tell them she was dead. 'Cause I did not know at this point. I could tell them what I thought had happened, given them closure. But they might give up hope. I decided to ask more questions.

Maybe I should call Gregg . . . . Fred, or Sue, just to get even. Nah!

"Mr. and Mrs. Rueton, may I ask you more questions?"

"Of course, dear," Tiffany said with delight.

"Certainly," Gregg said. "Ask away." I cleared my throat, and took in a sip of coffee.

"Was Clara on any medication?"

"Yes," Tiffany answered confidently. "High blood pressure pills, uh, in- sulin and high cholesterol medication . . . . Why?"

Ignoring her 'Why' question, I went on to my next question.

"Did you know she had a reputation of being a town drunk?"

"No. We don't believe that." Tiffany said. Gregg agreed. "We admit she drank wine a great deal."

"Was she on Codeine?"

"That's funny that you should ask, Nick." Tiffany said. "She had rot—ten teeth, and complained of toothaches quite a bit. She had to go to the local dentist many of times."

"When was the last time she'd seen the dentist?"

"Few days before Valentine's Day. I remember, because she said some-thing about chocolate candy. Oh yeah, I remember now. She said: 'There goes my Valentine's Day present to myself.'

"She just loved candy, which explains her bad teeth. Why all these ques- tions about medication, Nick?"

"Yeah, Mick, why?" Grrr! I was really tempted to call him *Sue*. But I had thought against that.

"I don't quite know how to tell you this. I don't have all the facts in, just yet. But the Chicago Police pulled a body from your daughter's apartment on the twelfth, Friday morning between 1:30 A.M. and 2 A.M. The Medical Examiner from the County Hospital had claimed the cause of death was toxic poisoning. If Clara was on Codeine and drink-ing wine she could have had a reaction from it . . . And died."

"No way," Gregg said angrily. "They would have notified us. What is this? What are you trying to pull here, Mick?" This wasn't the time to call him 'Fred' or 'Sue'.

"I believe Sandy Boehlis had faked her death. I also believe Clara died an accidental death. Sandy wanted to get away from Mr. Barton. She had prob- ably even wanted to say good-bye to Clara in person. When Sandy walked in Clara's apartment, Sandy found her dead on the living room floor.

"Sandy had opportunity to replace all of her identification with Clara's, and when the police arrived, they found a suicide note clipped to her blouse signed by Sandy Boehlis."

"Do you know who'd called the police?" Tiffany asked.

"I was told by Detective Cole it was an anonymous caller. Again, I be-lieve it was Sandy. Cole had told me the call came from a local payphone." My arm was tingling from talking on the phone so long. So I switched it to my other hand. "When you spoke with your daughter shortly after midnight on the 12th, how did she sound?"

"Fine, I guess. She sounded as if she'd been drinking, you know, slurring her words. Stuff like that." Gregg said. "But she had sounded fine."

"Did she sound sick? Or complain of being sick?"

"Just her stomach had bothered her. She did say, though, she had to vomit just before we had called her. But she felt fine after that. Except for the pain in her mouth from her decaying teeth. Maybe that was why she was drinking so much. Kill the pain. You think, Mr. Edwards?" Tiff said.

"Maybe," I said. *Or to kill herself, or Mike had killed her . . .*

"One more question," I said. "What makes you so sure you spoke with your daughter shortly after midnight?"

Gregg said. "Few minutes after midnight, Mick. What makes me so sure, well, let me tell you. We agreed to call each other when the old day ends and the new day begins. It was one of our quirks we had among each other."

"Interesting," I said. "But before we end this interview, let me give you the phone number of Detective David Cole. He works out of District Five. He was a police officer at the time when the incident occurred. He was the first one on the scene. Matter of fact, he received the call to report to Clara's apartment. He is also the person who sent me a flyer of your missing daugh-ter. That is how I got your name."

"Oh. We were wondering about that, Nick." Tiffany said.

"Thanks for the information, Mick," Gregg said. "But I surely hope you are mistaken about our daughter's death."

"Me too, Sue . . . Me too." Our conversation was concluded. So I went on to the next person from my list. I tried to call a Becky Hartwig, but the Infor- mation Operator told me it was unlisted. No further information followed.

The last name on my list was a Tom Keenas. Within five minutes of the interview, I'd had found out that Mike Barton was found floating in Lake Michigan not too far from Lake Shore Drive by a female jogger. His body was washed ashore with a knife in his back. No witnesses. No suspects. Mr. Keenas told me he read the article in the Chicago Tribune a week after Valentine's Day. 1977. I thanked him kindly. We hung up.

Chapter Seventeen

LISA AND SHERYL and I were sitting in a cherry-red booth near a big win-dow facing Superior, not too far from my apartment. Sheryl sat across from Lisa and I. The Carlton Lounge wasn't very busy this time of day. The time was 3:30 P.M., still Sunday, March 5th. I told Sheryl what I'd had learned about Mike Barton floating in Lake Michigan.

The waitress brought us our drinks. Lisa had her normal refreshment; vodka and tonic with a lime twist. I had MGD beer. Sheryl didn't drink alco-hol of any kind. She had a tall Diet Coke with a slice of lime floating on top and resting on the crushed ice. She stirred it slowly with a clear plastic straw. Her hazel eyes planted on mine.

"Do you think Mike Barton was my father, Nick?" She sipped her coke.

"That is a difficult question, Sheryl. I guess it's possible. Your mother was involved with him for a very long time." But what did I know. I'm only a PI. Sheryl shook her head, disgustedly. Lisa touched my hand gently.

"What about Clara, honey?" Lisa played with the rim of her glass with her left forefin-ger. Our dinner arrived.

The waitress placed our plates in front of us carefully. Lisa and Sheryl had opened-face meatloaf. I had jumbo shrimp with a salad on the side. It was covered with Ranch and Bacon bits. Mmm . . . Good. With my beer, I washed it down. Double . . . Mmmm.

"Well, Lisa. I think my theory is correct. She probably died an accidental death. But that will be hard to determine from the autopsy report. The ME had determined to be suicide. There just isn't enough evidence to prove homicide." Lisa nodded. Again, Sheryl shook her head.

The waitress returned and asked how everything was. We nodded and smiled politely with a mouthful of food. She pointed at our empty glasses. We nodded and smiled po-litely, again. I just hate it when they do that . . . Ask you questions with a mouthful of food. Don't you? G-r-r-r!

The lovely waitress took our plates away and she went. We had another round of drinks. I poured beer into my glass and watched the foam overflow, and run down onto my napkin. It soaked it up really good, too. Lisa and my client, Sheryl, shook their heads. I grinned. Then I rested my eyes on Sheryl.

"The Gremlin was your mother's, right?"

"Maybe . . . Why?"

"Do you remember the odometer reading when your uncle gave it to you on your eighteenth birthday?"

"Little over fifty-thousand miles. What's your point, Mr. Edwards?" She said, squinting her eyes, as if she was in deep thought.

The sunlight had been replaced with the moonlight, shooting pale-yellow rays over the town of Tomah. The brightness was soothing. With the lack of people walking the streets, the town had seemed deserted.

"That sounds about right. My point, as farfetched as it may seem, Sheryl, there just might be something in the car that might tell us where your mother had been last before she gave it to your uncle to save it for you."

"Good point," Sheryl said. "I guess that is why people say you are a great detective."

I bowed my head modestly.

"Okay. I'll check that out tomorrow." Sheryl curled her lower lip, nod- ding. Lisa was doing something next to me, Sheryl or I hadn't paid much at- tention to.

"Tex. You have the suicide note with you?" I looked down on Lisa's lap.

She was rummaging through the huge bag of cards. Lisa had an off-white envelope in her left hand. In her right hand, a brightly colored card, which seemed to be of Christmas decoration.

"I left it at the office in Sheryl's file. Why? What do you have?"

Lisa handed the off-white envelope to me. I studied it for a few seconds.

Sheryl half-stood from her booth and leaned over the table to sneak-a—peek. It didn't have a returned address, but the postage stamp that was encircled in the left hand corner of the envelope read: **Dec-1,-1978** . . . Tallahassee, Florida.

I snapped my head toward Sheryl. Sheryl was gazing at Lisa. Lisa looked at me. Then we'd looked at each other. My hair stood up from the clue we had.

Sheryl's face seemed a bright pale, ghostly-like. She fell in her seat, weakly.

Lisa took in a few large gulps from her drink. I downed my beer. When the waitress had returned, Sheryl had ordered a stiff drink for the very first time tonight. She told us she had never drunk before. This should prove interest- ing.

The Christmas card Lisa was holding had Sandy's handwriting on it. I wasn't defi- nitely positive without comparing it with the suicide note, but I'd had leaned toward the positive.

The salutation read: *'Dear Sheryl, My beautiful daughter . . . . !'* It was en- dorsed: *'Love, Mom . . . P.S. Be good . . . . And have a Merry Christmas . . . '*

We ordered another round of drinks. Sheryl did too. I glared at her.

"Did you ever see this card before tonight?"

"No . . . ! My God! I'm just as surprised and shocked as you two are." She shifted her eyes back and forth several times from me to Lisa and back to me.

"If you *are* telling the truth . . ." Sheryl interrupted me.

"I am telling the truth, Mr. Edwards. I really am. Honest."

"Maybe you just don't remember seeing the card. You kept so much in- formation from me already, and lied to me more than several times . . . Why should I believe you?"

"Because it's the truth. Why would I spend a lot of money finding her killer if I knew she was alive all this time. Huh?"

"I don't know, Miss Boehlis. I just don't know. But, for the sake of it, I'll give you the benefit of the doubt and assume your aunt kept this from you until recently. Or at least two years ago, hoping you'll find this card and maybe pursue your mother's whereabouts on your own accord."

Lisa tapped my knee.

"Nick, look at these." Lisa handed me nearly two dozen cards. To be fact- ual, there were eleven birthday cards and nine Christmas cards. Lisa and I studied and took in a closer look. The post-stamp was dated from the years 1979-1990. The cards were mailed from Tallahassee, Florida. There weren't anymore after 1990. These cards were the ones sent to Sheryl's Gram's' house in Chicago before her Gram' had died. Her Gram' had de- ceived her own granddaughter for all those years.

From the huge bag, Lisa had pulled out pictures of Sandy, Christmas gifts, and birth- day presents. They were still wrapped with colorful ribbons and bows. I shall assume, which I don't like assuming, but I shall assume the presents were for Sheryl . . . From her mother. Which I believed her Gram' kept from her all these years. What a bitch!

I looked up at Sheryl. Her face was red and her eyes were glassy. She couldn't handle her drinks very well. I thought.

"Are you all right, Sheryl?" Lisa set her eyes on Sheryl. Lisa began to laugh. "You're drunk, Miss Boehlis. You are absolutely drunk." Lisa cover-ed her mouth with both hands and muffled her laughter. Sheryl smiled a crooked smile, which defined her drunkenness. The waitress returned to our table. She pointed to our glasses. I ordered two more drinks for Lisa and me.

Sheryl got black coffee.

"Can you answer anymore questions, Miss Boehlis?" I asked. Her head wobbled. I took that as a 'yes'. I asked a few more questions. Maybe two, or three. I had to be careful. Didn't want to overload her brain in her condition.

"When did you move to Orlando, Florida with your aunt and uncle?"

"When I was eighteen." 'Was' came out as 'wuzch'.

"That would be 1990." The calculation wasn't difficult. Nick Edwards, wizard detective.

She nodded. It was a half-a-wobble.

"That is when the cards and presents had stopped coming to you." I said.

"I guess." Sheryl said. She shrugged loosely.

"What do you think, Nick?" Lisa asked.

"I don't know. Maybe something happened to her."

"Or maybe, either she moved in with Sheryl's aunt and uncle, or she visited her on Christmas and on her birthdays." Lisa said.

"That's a thought. If that will be the case, obviously Sandy had to dis-guise herself. Otherwise, Sheryl would've known she was alive. But why?"

"Yeah, Nick. Why would Sandy disguise herself? Unless she had some- thing to hide, and she didn't want Sheryl to know." Lisa and I glanced over and noticed Sheryl leaning to one side, as if she was sleeping.

"Are you okay, Sheryl?" Lisa asked.

Sheryl shrugged and nodded with drool from the corner of the right side of her mouth.

I said. "Sheryl, while you were living in Florida with your aunt and uncle, do you remember seeing a woman visiting the house, or maybe staying there for a length of time, like a-live-in nanny or something?" She shrugged. Her concentration wasn't up to par. Then suddenly, Sheryl pushed herself away from the booth and rushed clumsy-like toward the bath-rooms, to release her meatloaf dinner down the commode, no doubt.

I paid the bill, left a decent tip, and we went. Lisa and I waited about fif-teen minutes for Sheryl in front of the Carlton's. Losing patience, Lisa fin-ally went back into the restaurant to check on Sheryl. Sure as shoot'n, Lisa found Sheryl hugging the toilet, fast asleep.

Chapter Eighteen

I T WAS MONDAY morning, March 6th, I was sitting at my desk and waited for the Medical Examiner from Cook County Hospital to return my call. In the meantime, I'd faxed the suicide note and several copies of the cards to a friend of mine in Madison. He was a Handwriting Analyst. His name: Joe Carlson. Nothing else to do, but wait. Lisa and Sheryl walked in. Sheryl was too drunk to drive home last-night, so Lisa was kind enough to let her sleep at her condo. Sheryl appeared to be herself again. No hangover. Amazing. "Good-morning, Mr. Edwards." I nodded and shook her hand. She sat in my client chair. Legs crossed. Lisa came over to me and gave me a hug and a kiss. Clint didn't arrive, yet. Probably pissed-off from screwing up our dinner date plans last Thursday. Work . . . Work . . . Work.

"Is your car here, Sheryl?"

"Yes." She nodded.

"Let's all go outside and search your vehicle for any evidence on your mother." They agreed.

I searched the trunk, while Lisa and Sheryl searched the interior. We went over everything. From the glove-box, to the seats, from the ashtrays to the trunk. Nothing, but old matchbooks from the Peanut Bowl Lounge where Sandy was last employed as a bartender before she had disappeared . . . . or . . . . . died. It was worth the try to search Sheryl's/ Sandy's Gremlin. I try not to leave any stone unturned, if I could help it.

I still thought I had enough evidence to prove she wasn't dead. Well, may be not dead on February 12th, 1977, anyway.

I went back into our office building, strolled the length of the plush carpet and went into my cubicle/office, and sat behind my desk. Lisa and Sheryl went to the coffee shop next-door. My message light was flashing on my tele phone. It was from the Medical Examiner. I returned his call. Phone tag. What a bummer.

I left David Stack another message, and apologized for missing his call.

The time was 10:30 A.M. I sat with my feet on my desk and stared out the window. A Brink Armor truck pulled up and parked and a gray uniformed guard got out with a big gray bag with brown handles. He briskly walked into Wal-Mart. Two other guards in gray uniforms stood outside near the the armor vehicle with their 9mm automatics in their hands. Barrels facing downward toward the blacktop of the parking lot. After a few minutes had past, the guard with the gray bag, came out as fast as he went in. The bag folded under his right armpit. He jumped in from the side of the truck, with the two other guards following suit. They sped off with white smoke trailing from the vehicle's tailpipe. My phone rang.

It was the ME.

I quickly dropped my feet to the floor and swiveled my chair into the leg opening of my desk. I picked up the receiver and announced myself.

"Yes, Mr. Edwards, I vaguely remember the case. Twenty years ago, huh?"

"Yes sir. The female victim probably had bad teeth. You'd had deter- mined the cause of death toxic poisoning. It was under investigation for a year, or so. Now, do you remember?"

"What's the victim's name again?"

"Clara Rueton. She went under another name . . . uh . . . Miss, or should I say, Mrs. Sandy Boehlis."

"Spell that, please." I did. I heard click-clack over the phone. Maybe a type- writer. Or keyboard. Then he returned to the phone.

"Oh yes. Now I remember. Her brother came in and identified her as his sister, uh, Sandy Boehlis. After inspecting her driver's license he had given me I was satisfied he had made a positive I.D. I just needed someone from her family to confirm it."

"Do you have her files handy?" I asked.

"It's in the computer system. Technology. Isn't it great."

"Un-huh. The files. Are they available?"

"Let me check the computer again." Click-clack . . . Clack-click. A minute or two later his voice re-appeared on the phone.

"Oh. Oh." He said.

"Oh? Oh?" I said.

"Yeah. Now I know why it was pending for so long."

"Why?"

"Every corpse comes in here, get their fingerprints taken. Of course back then, the investigative system was slow in the process. It took months later before the prints came back. And when it did, it came back as Clara R. Rueton. Not Sandy Boehlis. A major discrepancy in our findings."

"I'll say." As I was speaking to the ME, Sheryl and Lisa walked in from the café. "Can you hold on a minute, Doc?"

"Sure." I asked Sheryl if her mother had a brother. Her eyes squinted, froze in place, as if she was thinking deeply. Then she shook her head.

"Okay, sir. I'm back. You said 'Brother', not brother-in-law. Correct?"

"Yeah. Brother. Why?"

"My client is standing right here and she just shook her head when I'd asked her if Sandy Boehlis had a brother."

"Ask your client if she knew a Dale Barryhill. I wrote his name in my notes. He's the one ID'd her. Ask her."

I did. Then returned to the phone.

"She only knows a Dale Nowak. He is her uncle. Sandy's brother-in-law."

"I'm getting confused by the minute, Mr. Edwards. What's going on here?"

"It's called faking ones death. Better term, fraudulent death. Clara's body was used to cover up Sandy's disappearance."

"This is outrageous. This is a federal offense that was commited."

"Yes, sir. I agree."

"Would you know where this Mr. Nowak lives?"

"The last word I had heard, he was living in Orlando, Florida. Let me ask my client."

After I had asked Sheryl for her uncle's address, she shook her head again and ran out the door. Lisa gave chase. But it was too late. Sheryl sped off in her Gremlin, leaving smoked rubber clinging to the cool March air.

"Sorry, sir. My client just left. I'll get back to you on that."

"I should hope so, Mr. Edwards. I should hope so."

"Yeah. Also, can you send me copies on whatever you have on the corpse?"

"Sure. No problem."

I gave him my fax number. We hung up.

Lisa stood in my cubicle entranceway, and just stared at me. She shook her head in disgust. "Honey, this is your case, but I believe at this point, you should let it go. Sheryl had been lying and keeping important in—formation from you that is relevant to your case. Besides, you were hired to find her mother's killer . . . . ."

"You are so right, my dear. I guess I should let it go. Nothing else to resolve, but Sandy's whereabouts. I wasn't hired to find her mother. I was hired to find her mother's killer."

"I wish I had said that." Lisa said with her arms folded over her sexy breast.

"Yeah. It did have a nice ring to it, didn't it." Lisa jerked her body disgustedly. But I really didn't know why. My eyes remained on her sexy breast. Mmmm! I asked Lisa if she wanted to make love in my high-back chair. But before she could answer, the phone rang. I answered. It was Sheryl. "You're fired." She hung up, left me holding the receiver to my ear for a moment. I shrugged and set the phone in its cradle quietly. Then Lisa and I made love in my favorite chair. I was happy.

Chapter Nineteen

LISA AND I just completed out afternoon delight when the phone rang again. I was half-naked in my chair, wearing nothing but my white shirt and blue tie with small yellow specks. Lisa pulled up her pantyhose and pulled down her long black dress. Buttoned up her silk and sexy sky-blue blouse. Very sexy. I like sexy. I pushed the green button on the speaker phone so I could pull up my pants and zip it.

"Hell-o. Nick speaking. May I help you?"

"Is this C-N-L Detective Agency?"

"Yes it is."

"Good. This is Joe Carlson from Madison. I'm looking for Mr. Nick Edwards."

"This is he." I said.

"Oh. Good-afternoon, buddy. I got the results on Sandy Boehlis's hand- writing."

"Great. Is it hers?"

"Yep. But there is something peculiar about the last three cards you sent me."

"Yeah. What's that?" I buckled my belt and sat down behind my desk.

"The last three cards dated from 1988 through 1990 were handwritten with the left hand."

"Aha."

"Aha?"

"Oh never mind. I just felt like saying 'Aha'. Detective stuff, you know."

Joe was silent for a time.

"Okay, Nick. Whatever you say. The handwriting probably was changed to, I believe, to change her identity. Or something had happened to her right hand."

Clint had walked in and stood for a moment in the doorway of our build-ing. He put his nose in the air and sniffed. He looked at Lisa. Then at me. He smiled and shook his head. He pulled his high-back chair away from his mahogany desk and got comfortable. He sniffed again. I think he knew Lisa and I just had satisfied our lust for each other. I smiled and swiveled my chair toward the window. Lisa's face had turned tomato red. She grinned and put her head into her desk, as if she was looking for something.

"Why you say that, Joe?" I stretched my legs on my desk, looked out my window and waved at a woman walking her Irish Setter through Wal-Mart's parking lot. She didn't wave. Neither did her dog. Unfriendly neighborhood.

"Think about it, Nick. If she sprained or even broken her right hand, it wouldn't have taken two years to heal."

"No. Unless she is a slow healer."

"Well, you know and I know that isn't likely."

"Yeah. I know. So you think it is permanent."

"Uh-huh. Don't you?" Joe said.

"Yeah. I guess." I said. "The mafia." I mumbled. Maybe even drug dealers. I thought.

"What did you say, Nick? I didn't hear ya'."

"Oh. Nothing. Thanks, Joe. I owe you one."

"Yep. You sure do. Two-hundred dollars and a six pack."

"Can we negotiate on the six pack, Joe?" There was silence for a minute.

"Sure. Have a good day and good-luck."

"Thanks. You too." We hung up. I leaned back in my chair and pondered about Sandy's hand. Or, maybe, her missing hand.

Chapter Twenty

AFTER THINKING A lot about Sandy's quandary, I decided to call the Rueton's and inform them of the bizarre news of their daughter Clara. This wouldn't be easy over the phone, nor in person. But in person, it would've been less cold.

"Hell-o." A man's voice answered. I guess the maid had the day off to—day. I played with the name of the voice that said 'Hell-o'.

"Sue. Sue Rueton?" I tried not to laugh.

"Yes. Who's this?"

"Mick. Mick Edwards from Tomah, Wisconsin."

"Oh yeah. I remember you, Nick." I choked. He pronounced my name correctly. I'll be damned. "Let me get the Misses. Okay?" Gregg said.

"Sure, Gregg. I'll wait." I figured he got my name correct, I just might be nice. I heard a click on the other end of the phone.

"Hell-o, Mr. Edwards. Tiffany speaking. Dear, can you hear me alright?"

"Yes, Tiff. I can hear perfectly. I got the volume on ten."

"Wow!" I said. "Not too loud, I hope."

"Nope. Just perfect. What do you have for us, Mr. Edards?" Jeez. Now he had my last name screwed up. Damn.

"Not good news, I'm afraid, sir." I said.

"Nick . . . Is she dead? Oh . . . My . . . God. My beloved Clara is gone." Tiff's voice had faded in the background. I believe I heard the phone crash to the floor.

"Are you there, Mr. Rueton?" He was crying, loudly. But he spoke between sobs.

"Yeah. I'm here. I am so sorry I am crying like a big baby, Nick. Forgive me. Please."

"No need, Mr. Rueton. Quite understandable." I let him cry in silence. I lit a cigarette. My first one in seventy-two hours. Not bad, I guess.

Tiffany's cry came closer to the phone and picked it up.

"What happened, Nick? Why weren't we notified? Why?..Why? . . . Why?"

"Ma'am. Sandy and her brother-in-law are at fault here. They were in a major cover-up."

"Whaddya mean? What cover-up." Gregg was still crying. He couldn't even speak between tears.

"It seems to me, but you need to confirm this with the Medical Examiner, but to me, I feel and believe Clara died an accidental death. Maybe Mr. Bar- ton killed her unintentionally. At least that is what I gathered after speaking to the bartender, Mr. Polycheck."

"Maybe so. Maybe her death was accidental. But still no excuse. We still should've been notified."

"Yes, ma'am. I agree wholeheartedly. But the evidence the police had, constantly pointed to Sandy. The officials thought they had the right corpse.

After all the evidence was collected, they closed the case as suicide. I'll give you and your husband the ME's phone number. His name his David Stack. He'll explain everything to you in depth." I don't think she had heard me.

"What cover-up?" Tiff said. "Well. What cover-up?"

"That's not your worry, ma'am. Just that Sandy had big problems and she used your daughter to solve them."

"Did Sandy solve her problem, Mr. Edwards?"

"No, ma'am. No . . . I do not think so."

"All in vain, huh?"

"Vanity, like murder, will out."

"Yep. Cowley . . . something."

"Something . . . Cowley." I gave them the ME's number and wished them the best.

Chapter Twenty-One

I STARED OUT THE picture window from my desk. People were walking by carrying Wal-Mart bags, overflowing with goodies. But I didn't really notice them. I didn't even pay much attention to Wal-Mart's store at all. I just stared into space. I stared at nothing. My eyes were damp. I had cried sound- lessly. I'd wiped my tears on the back of my hand and stared at my phone.

I gently grabbed it and put it in to my ear, unaware what I was doing. Be- fore I knew what I was doing, Detective Cole's voice appeared on the other end of the line.

"Homicide." He repeated it. "Homicide. Anyone there?"

"Oh. I'm sorry, Detective Cole."

"Is this Nick?"

"Yep."

"You don't sound very well. Are you alright? Is your ass still intact?"

"So far. But this isn't over yet. By a long shot."

"Whaddya got?"

"Fraudulent death."

"Interesting. Tell me more, Mr. Edwards."

"The body you found in Apartment 103 belonged to a woman named Clara R. Rueton. She probably died accidentally. But between you and me, Detective, I believe Mr. Mike Barton tried to poison his girlfriend, Sandy Boehlis at the Peanut Bowl. But she didn't drink it. A few minutes later Clara walked in and sat next to Mike. I was told she was heavily intoxicated with, whatever. God only knows. I was also told Clara chug-a-lugged Sandy's drink. Then Mike ordered her to go home immediately and force herself to vomit."

"Don't surprise me any, Detective Edwards. Anything else you have?"

"Yep. My client's mother, Sandy Boehlis, is probably somewhere in Tallahassee, Florida. Maybe the drug dealers caught up with her by now. I don't know for sure. Her sister and brother-in-law are probably somewhere in Orlando, Florida. And Mike Barton is dead. He was found floating in Lake Michigan with nine or more stab wounds in his back. No witnesses. No suspects. Must've been out of your jurisdiction twenty years ago. Otherwise, you would've known about that." I said. "Yeah, I guess. Anything else?"

"Yeah."

"What?"

"I'm going to that hot tourist state and pluck them out." I guess my voice had carried over to Lisa's ears. She looked at me, and her eyes froze. I know she knew I got fired. The question in her eyes now lies heavily on my mind. Why am I continuing with this crazy case? I really don't know. Maybe I just need to finish what had started. I'll do pro-bono. I did it before. I'll probably do it again. I have to. Its part of me. Its what I do. Investigate. Client or no client. I need to find the Nowaks' and Sandy Boehlis and bring them in.

Maybe, just maybe, I can bring Sheryl and Sandy back together again. Maybe they can work out their differences. It would not be easy. But who said life was easy.

Detective Cole said. "Hope you know what you are doing, Mr. Edwards.

Do you know what you are up against? And what about back-up? You can't do this alone."

"I'm not alone, Detective Cole. And I do know what I am doing. I've been doing this line of work for twenty years."

"Okay, tough guy. But be careful."

"When I find them, I'll drop them off at your front door of your head—quarters."

"Whaaa?" It seemed Cole was lost for words.

"Well. Did it or did it not happen in your parts of Chicago?" I said.

"Good point, Nick. Good point. See ya' when you bring them in."

"You betcha'." We hung up. Even though I felt Lisa's staring eyes on me, I tried to ignore it. Instead I glared out the window again. I still didn't see anything. But red and deep anger. Not hate. I don't have the capability to hate. How could anyone desert a child, as Sandy did? And why was it a big fucking secret? Why didn't Sheryl's relatives tell her the truth? What were they afraid of? Damn . . . Damn . . . Damn sonavabitches!

I suddenly turned my chair around. And there she was . . . My sunshine of my life. She had a smile on her pretty face that melted my heart. She stood in front of me with tears in her compassionate blue eyes looking down at mine. Words were not spoken. Our eyes were doing a great job all by them- selves. She let her well-shaped body fall into my lap. Her warm arms around me, and her head resting on my right shoulder. Mine in hers. I had closed my eyes and let the teardrops trickle slowly on Lisa's black dress. The office door opened. But not a client. Not even Sheryl to hire me back. It was Clint.

Our boss. He was smiling. Why? I didn't know. He just gave Lisa and I thumbs up. The door closed softly. Lisa and I were alone once again. We didn't make love. Just holding each other is just as important. We'll make love later. I can feel it.

Chapter Twenty-Two

LISA AND I lay in bed in her condominium, this Monday night, 6 of March. The moon was bright outside her window, and it looked like it was cold. I glanced at the bedside clock. 9:35. The room was whitewashed and furn-ished with colonial pine. The moonlight flooded her room and it made it al- most dazzling in its simple brightness.

Lisa said, "Since you're fired, maybe we can concentrate finding my par- ent's murderers."

"Yes. I already had made plans with Eagle and his wife Pam to meet us at our office on March 9th, Thursday morning. Clint will be making reserva-tions at Grand Milwaukee Hotel in Milwaukee for that date. Our arrival time will be approximately noon-time. After visiting my friends in Milwaukee, we'll then head to Chicago and investigate your parents death."

Lisa took my hand under the quilt and we lay silently on our backs on top of patterned sheets and pillows.

"Even though Sheryl had fired you," Lisa said. "You still plan to look for her mother in Florida."

"Yep." I said.

"Why?"

"This is what I do. I investigate."

"But, you've been fired. Why continue?"

"I don't like starting something and not able to finish it. I will finish it, if I have to do pro-bono."

"You are a package, you know that." Lisa said.

"A loveable and sensitive package, and just for you."

We continued staring up at the ceiling under the covers and holding hands in silence.

➤ ◄

Today is March 9th, 1997, and the weather was very windy, but warm. Winds had gusted over fifty miles an hour. The temperature was seventy-degrees on this Thursday morning. The digital clock read 7:00 A.M.

Bright yellow and blue trash barrels that belonged to the City of Tomah, were rolling and bouncing across the parking lots and highways. The sea-gulls and pigeons didn't seem to mind the wind. Their little twig-formed legs held firmly to the ground. Amazing. But in flight, well, that was another matter all together differently. The fowls had realized it was safer to be grounded.

The sixty-foot pine trees were bending in the wind, as if bowing to us as we'd past by them. The debris of trash was blowing loosely from the hard winds, and were being caught up and clinging to cyclone fences and high weeds and tree branches alongside the highway and the interstate.

Above us, the sky's color was ocean-blue with slightly gray clouds. But no sign of rain threatened us. Yet. Traveling was extremely dangerous, but Clint's '94 Olds Bravada SUV held its own on Interstate 90/94 to our surprise. At this time of day we were heading east toward Milwaukee. But before we had met the bend in the road heading toward Milwaukee, we exited off I-90/94 in Portage and ate break-fast at Country Kitchen.

At 10:30 A.M., we were back on the 'I' continuing east to Milwaukee to introduce Lisa, Clint, Eagle and Pam to my other friends in Milwaukee. I haven't seen them since I moved to Tomah and worked for Clint Douglas, my boss, who owns C-N-L Detective Agency.

We'd had only planned to stay for one night, and then head for Chicago to investigate the murder of Lisa's parents that had happened twelve years a- go. Lisa is my girlfriend, and also is employed with our detective agency. She's been a private investigator little over-a-year now. And a damn good detective, I might add. Before Lisa came on board, our agency was named C-N-N Detective Agency. The letter 'L' now, stands for Lisa.

Eagle and Pam Neuman had been friends of mine since Desert Shield/ Desert Storm in 1990-1992. They had helped us in a few investigations last year. *The Big Bust* I had called it. After we'd had caught the suspects, I guess you could say . . . it *was* a big bust.

Upon our arrival in Milwaukee the winds had strengthened to 70 mph. On Howell Avenue, we were driving north toward Layton Avenue, which was the cross-roads leading to General Mitchell International airport. At this time, approximately 12 Noon, the gray clouds had covered the ocean-blue entirely. Still no rain in the forecast. The temperature had climbed to seventy eight degrees. Suddenly, Clint swerved and dodged several heavy broken branches that had laid across our left lane. He regained control, expertly.

Whew!

We were less than a mile away from our destination; The Grand Milwau-kee Hotel. The hotel was directly across the airport eastside of Howell Avenue. As we approached the hotel, which was on our left, a huge Boeing 747 roared over Clint's Bravada, vibrat-ing the SUV. I didn't know which was worse; being blown around by heavy winds, or a Boeing 747.

Clint flipped his turn signal downward, signaling a left-turn. The left turn led us into the hotel's parking lot. Safe and sound . . . We had hoped. We con- tinued into the half-circled driveway where passengers are picked up and dropped off, and parked directly in front of the automatic-glass-doubled slid- ing doors. The time: 12:15 P.M., Thursday afternoon.

We quickly unloaded the SUV, strolled into the lobby, and admired the interior of the hotel. The line to the front desk was a ten minute wait. Busy day. When we'd walked in, I noticed they had a lounge downstairs named; Down-Under. But it was closed at this time. The sign in front of the lounge door read: 'OPEN AT 4 P.M. KARAOKE TONIGHT' To the left of the lounge, and across the hall, Harold's Restaurant. The connecting lounge from Harold's was named BJ's, which was now open. Very good . . . BEER!

The line in front of us disappeared. We were next. We checked in under our detective agency, Clint as the responsible party. Surely, he loved that idea. Our rooms were located in French Quarters, the first floor and around the bend near the game room and the gift shop. Marvelous.

If my understanding was correct, we were told the Grand Milwaukee Ho-tel was one of the largest in Wisconsin. The hotel had several ballrooms; The Grand Ballroom, Baton Rouge Hall, and New Orleans. Some others, too, I was told. But it had failed my memory.

Ten years ago, the Grand Ballroom used to be a bowling alley. And the hotel's name was Red Carpet Inn. What an awesome improvement. The hotel also had several wings for different guests . . . The Presidential Wing, In- ternational Wing, and I believe, the Tourist Wing. And of course, The French Quarters where we were staying, (even though we weren't French).

After we'd settled into our rooms, showered and changed clothes; Clint, Eagle, Pam, Lisa and I casually walked into BJ's Lounge, happily.

Chapter Twenty-Three

Bob, also a friend of mine, was bartending today. The time: 2 P.M. There were eight people in the place sitting around several round tables and drink-ing beer mostly, though one guy appeared to be drinking a martini with sev- eral olives in it.

Even inside the lounge you could hear the winds slapping against the out- side walls of the hotel's structure.

Bob the bartender was wearing a handsomely white shirt with a black vest that was unbuttoned and hung open loosely. He always reminded me of an educator, maybe a professor of some kind. Awhile back, when I started coming to the hotel, it took me some time to get to know Bob. But once the ice was broken, we learned to share a few laughs. Either together, or at ourselves. He's a great guy to know. And a very good friend of mine. I am sure he had missed me. After all, it had been a few years.

"Oh no! What the hell do you want now," Bob said with a serious expres-sion. "You're not going to borrow any money from me, are you?" He seemed worried.

"No, Bob. Not today, anyway. But when I did I always paid you back. So don't worry," I said smiling. "Good seeing you, too." I said.

"What brings you back here after two years disappearing?" Bob said.

"Just passing through." I shifted my body to my friends and introduced them to Bob. They shook hands with a nod and a smile.

"I'll buy the first round," Bob said with a half-moon smile.

We smiled and thanked him.

Bob stood about six foot, maybe six foot-two with broad shoulders. His salt and pep-per hair was neatly trimmed around the ears and neck. His age, my guess, was nearing middle fifties. And approximately 200 pounds. Fin-gernails manicured evenly. His hands were the size of a sledge hammer.

Nice guy, but don't get him angry.

Clint said, "The truth of the matter, Bob, we are on our way to Chicago on business. Nick, here, decided to stop here and rest for the night. It also gave us a chance to meet you and the rest of his friends."

Bob nodded, then, looked at me. "So you are still detecting, huh?"

"Yep," I said. "Probably 'til I die."

"Do you think you'll ever move back to Milwaukee, Nick?" Bob said, as he was leaning on the edge of the bar. "We have plenty of suspicious charac- ters walking around the hotel, you know. We could use you again."

"Maybe I just might move back here, Bob . . . . Someday." I sipped my Red Lager from my glass and set it down.

Lisa and Pam drank Vodka and Tonic, and Eagle drank MGD beer. And, of course, Clint enjoys his Scotch on the rocks. Bob served us several bowls of nuts and cashews. I took a handful of cashews, popped a few in my mouth and chewed, then swallowed with a few sips of my beer. Tasty. As we were enjoying our nuts and cashews, Bob de- cided to walk away and leaned against the other end of the bar. He leaned, and stared at nothing.

Suddenly, the martini drinker who was sitting at a round table directly be- hind us, yelled loudly in German. All of us turned around and noticed him holding one of the beer drinkers, the table next to his, by the coat lapels.

I said, "Clint, you speak and understand German. What is he saying?"

Clint said, "He thinks the beer drinker is a gay person. And told him to quit staring at him."

I nodded.

Bob swiftly walked around the bar and went toward the two men. He tightly grabbed the German guy by the neck of his collar, opened the hall-way door leading to the park- ing lot, and threw him out. Bob then closed the door and slowly walked back around the bar, as if nothing had happened.

"Good job, Bob. I'm impressed," I said, as both my thumbs went up. "Al- right. Way to go!"

Bob nodded glumly, and flipped me the 'bird'. I said, "Did you ever see the doctor about that twitch you have with your middle finger, Bob?" His middle finger twitched again. I shrugged. I then took in some beer.

Bob resumed his stare at nothing.

Lisa said, "I thought you said this lounge was a friendly and quiet place, honey."

I gulped my beer, chewed some cashews, and gulped some more. I turned to Lisa. "I lied."

Chapter Twenty-Four

THE TIME WAS 3:30 P.M., and we were still enjoying the company of my friend Bob. He didn't talk much, but his expressions amused us.

Eagle and Pam had their backs against the bar and were watching some educational game show on the wide T.V. screen. Pam and Eagle always competed with each other when it comes to these type of shows. They were fun to watch, especially when they tried to guess the answers correctly.

Pam had a habit sticking her tongue out at Eagle when he'd guessed the correct answers. And Eagle would slap the back of Pam's head when she'd guessed the correct answers. Gently, of course.

It was approaching 3:45 when Kim walked through the kitchen's swing- ing doors. She had grabbed some keys from the beer cabinet's handles that was hanging on a brass key ring. Kim had this habit studying people, espec-ially new faces. And she smiled a lot. But when her eyes met mine for the first time, after not seeing each other for several years, her hazel eyes widely gleamed. She smiled at me from ear to ear.

"Nick, is that you?" Her eyes strained against the dim lighting above the marble bar. Then her eyes focused. "It is you. Well, I'll be damned."

She grabbed the keys to the Down Under lounge, briskly walked through the kitchen's swinging doors, and a few seconds had elapsed. Suddenly, she had her arms around my neck and gave me a quick kiss on my right cheek. She stared into my eyes.

"Where have you been, Nick," Kim said, "It must've been two, maybe three years last time I had seen you."

"I moved near Fort McCoy, Wisconsin. I live and work in Tomah now."

I gestured with my head. "Meet my crime fighting friends." After introduc- ing every-one, Kim rushed downstairs and opened the Down Under Lounge.

The time was four-o-five. Late again. Thanks to me.

After Bob took our order from the bar menu, another very good friend of mine ap-peared before us. She was very sweet and very intelligent with words. I think she had missed me, too. Her name is Belle. And she had a lot of respect for me.

"Well, Alley-cat, you ole' sonavabitch. What brings you back here again?

. . . You . . . You, troublemaker. Where have you been? In prison? Or some-thing?" Belle said.

Belle was young in spirit and had this beautiful features about her. She might've been fifteen or twenty years older than me, but that didn't stop her from looking younger than her age. She was slender build, had an oval face, and pure white short hair. She stood about five-four. And friendly. But she spoke her mind. I respect that.

The time was getting closer to five. Belle was pleased to meet my friends.

So, with that, she bought us around of drinks. She clocked in.

Few moments later, Bob came through the kitchen doors with our food order. He set it down, expertly. If I'd remembered correctly, Bob had been bartending over twenty years, or so. He's good at what he does.

I took a bite of my Milwaukee Sausage and Cheese with Brats, and savored every chew. The taste was just as good, if not better, as it were two years ago. I looked up at Bob, after I washed down my sausage with the Red Lager.

I said, "When are you getting off from work, Bob?"

He said, "Seven."

"What then?"

"I'm going Down Under and maybe sing a song or two."

"Great! We'll probably join you downstairs. What do you sing?"

"I like the song 'Mack the Knife'." He smiled nicely.

"Bobby Darin, isn't it?" Lisa asked.

"Yeah, I think so." Bob said, flirting with his eyes at my girlfriend Lisa.

Lisa, Pam and Eagle were slowly enjoying their nacho basket, while Clint had his All-American-cheeseburger. You can always tell Clint enjoyed his meal. He closes his eyes as he chews, as if he was meditating on some-thing serious.

At 5:30 in the afternoon, Greg, who works room service, walked in through the kitch-en's swinging doors displaying a wide smile. His wide brown eyes focused in the dim-light and noticed me sitting at the bar sip-ping my Red Lager. His smile had widened.

"Nick, you old son-of-a-gun. How in the hell are you doing?" His eyes scanned over the marble bar. "Are these your friends?"

"They sure are." As I introduced my friends to Greg, Belle and Bob cleaned our mess from the bar. We then ordered another round of refresh-ments. This round of drinks were on Greg. Before this night would be over, I thought, we would all need guidance to our rooms. But I didn't think the ho-tel had escort service, though. What I meant, escort us to our room safely.

Greg said, still smiling. "When did you and your friends arrive?"

I think Greg likes to smile, or he was well trained.

I glanced at my watch. "Five hours ago."

Greg said, "Can you believe this weather, Nick. The wind . . . It's mad out there."

Clint said, after taking in a sip of his drink, and swallowed. "My Bravada was rocking most of the way down here, but it kept on rolling. I admit; I was holding my breath a few times on Interstate 90/94."

"I can imagine." Greg said. His smile was fading slowly. Maybe he was getting sore cheeks from smiling too much.

"Is there a storm in the forecast for tonight, Greg?" Clint said. He took a- nother sip of his Scotch.

"I didn't hear anything on the news." Greg turned toward Bob. "Hey, Bob, is there a storm in the forecast for tonight?"

Bob shrugged and shook his head. Then he turned left and waited on an im- patient customer.

Belle was in the kitchen momentarily, and as she returned to the bar, Greg approached her. He asked her about the weather.

"How in the hell should I know. What do I look like? Malan, the meteor-ologist?" The two bottles of wine in Belle's hands were stacked neatly in the liquor cabinet. Greg looked at me and Clint and shrugged with his palms facing up toward the bar's low ceiling. Then he picked up a large oval serv—ing tray, brown in color, and balanced it perfectly and evenly next to his head. He walked away smiling. Amazing. Lisa said, as Greg returned to the kitchen. "How does he do that? I could never do that for the life of me when I was employed as a barmaid at the Bar and Grill in Sparta. And I'm a girl."

"Pretty one at that, little lady." I said. She smiled and sipped her drink.

Clint slid off his stool and studied the display of cigars near the corner of the marble bar. The cigars were protected and secured in a wired cherry cab-inet. The cabinet was tightly secured with large screws and nails. Very expensive cigars, I guessed. Maybe it had an security alarm attached to it, too.

Eagle and Pam were quiet, but amused themselves with another game show. It had something to do with spinning the wheel and solving a puzzle.

They were married for a long time, but still acted like newlyweds.

Sweet. Clint returned to his stool with four fresh cigars standing up in his breast suit pocket. He seemed happy and content.

From the corner of my right eye, I believed Eagle answered the puzzle correctly. Or, maybe Pam had difficulty keeping her tongue in her mouth. I shrugged and turned to-ward my beer. And drank a few gulps.

Yum. Yum.

Chapter Twenty-Five

THE TIME WAS five-fifty-three, late afternoon. At this time, BJ's Lounge was at its full capacity. According to the safety law, 75 people was full cap-acity, but the look of things, I would estimate 80 people. It was wall to wall with more than several people standing shoulder to shoulder. Every stool, chair, and booth were filled with chatty people. The chatting turned into humming. Our ears adjusted to the sound. The humming voices made me think of swam of hundred bees circling around your head.

Eagle and Pam were still quiet. Obviously, very shy in a strange environ- ment. We couldn't hear each other speaking, anyway. So it didn't really mat- ter.

The loudness became overbearingly disturbing. But somehow we were tolerating the noise.

Through the crowd of well-dressed customers, probably here for a major convention, I'd noticed two females I had recognized. It had been a while, but I was positive I had seen Dena and Carina heading toward Down-Under. I had not seen them in two years either. They were dressed with white shirts, black slacks and black vests. Carina had her dishwater blonde hair into a ponytail that was swaying with every step she took. Dena had her jet black hair combed back behind her ears and cut evenly. It barely caressed her shoulders. Both were attractive. Dena had beautiful smooth dark skin and shiny. Cairna's skin was cream, slightly off-white. Both had that young look. Very nice.

But, as I was fighting the crowd to get to the two female friends of mine, both were swallowed up from the mob of high-classed customers, and dis- appeared downstairs. I'll catch up to them later. I thought. So I returned to my stool at the bar and drunk my beer.

By the time the clock struck six, our eyes were watery and bloodshot. And not from drinking too much alcohol either. But from the blue-gray smoke drifting toward our direction. I'd asked Belle if she could adjust the speed to 'HI' on the ceiling fans. But she just gave me this certain look.

She said. "Screw you, Alley-cat. Suffer with the rest of us."

I knew she was joking with me when I had noticed the fans rotating in a faster circular motion. Nick, the observer, never sleeps.

Suddenly, the kitchen's swinging doors abruptly flew open, and a male face peeked into the bar. Just as suddenly, he disappeared back into the kitchen. Lisa, Clint, and I couldn't focus rapidly enough to get a good des-cription of him. But he was male. We knew that positively.

Bob quickly approached us and asked if we needed another round. We a- greed. I wanted to ask Bob who was the new face in the kitchen, the male we'd just seen, but he was too damn busy with the convention personnel. So I let the question pass.

A few moments later our drinks arrived. Then the five of us decided to fight the crowd and take our drinks downstairs and visit Kim, who was bar-tending Down Under. As we were descending the curvy and carpeted stairs, we had studied the surrounding walls of the interior of the lounge. The walls were decorated with baby Kangas, Mama and Papa Kangaroos, and a few Croc's were poised near a thick-green swamp that was painted on the far side of the lounge. I was expecting Crocodile Dun-Dee to jump out at us at any moment caring his double-edged hunting knife between his teeth. The art of the 'Out-Back' was just awesome.

Down Under wasn't as busy as it was upstairs in BJ's Lounge, so our ears adjusted eas-ily to the quietness. What a reprieve.

As we approached the 'J'-shaped bar, I noticed Kim preparing a drink for a thin and frail looking man with dark frame glasses, the kind of eyeglasses you might've seen from the military point of view. They weren't very styl-ish. The better definition; Gaudy and ugly. The thin dark man made me think of Saddam, the Iraqi President from the Middle East.

We found five empty stools at the bar and sat near Mr. Ugly. Kim glanc-ed at us pleas-ingly as we settled into our seats. Her smile brightened up the lounge so much, even the Kangaroos jumped.

Mr. Ugly sat at the very end near the swimming pool. Which was near the glass-dou-bled doors. If you went through the doors, you'll be in the swim-ming pool area, which was on the left of the glass doors. We can smell the chlorine from where we were sitting. That'll clear the sinuses.

We took our seats with me sitting in the middle. Lisa was sitting next to Mister Ugly. The rest of the gang sat on my left.

The two lovebirds, (Eagle and Pam), were getting kinky. Pam sat on Eagle's lap, but I didn't think that wasn't allowed. Behaving herself, Pam decided to sit on her own stool next to Eagle.

They both shrugged embarrassingly.

Mr. Ugly dressed nicely, even though it didn't do anything for his body features. He wore a glossy dark blue three piece suit, a flashy Elvis Presley tie, and supremely-polished black oxfords.

The drink Kim had prepared for Mr. Ugly, appeared to be a coke, probab-ly laced with rum or dark brandy. It had a small green straw standing up in it. He was stirring the plastic straw carefully, as if he was worried the glass would shatter. With his pinky finger raised slightly as he stirred his drink, he decided to strike-up a conversation with my girlfriend Lisa. Um. I turned to Clint, and he was conversing with Eagle. I had a choice, either strike-up a conversation with Pam, or with Kim. Maybe I could converse with the two females I had seen earlier; Dena and Carina. But they seemed very busy set- ting up the tables for the busy night to come.

So, I flipped a coin. Heads: Pam . . . Tails: Kim. I flipped and caught the coin in my left hand and slapped it on the top of my right hand. I took a peek. I took another peek. Have to be positive about these things, you know.

Tails it was. Kim's it.

Suddenly, the unidentified male whom we had seen earlier upstairs in BJ's lounge, stormed through the glass-doubled-doors near the swimming pool. Mr. Ugly jumped. The Kangaroos did not.

As Kim and I were talking, he simply slipped behind the bar and brushed purposely against Kim's backside. She gave me this look as if she wanted to kill him. Kim quickly stood from her leaning position and gave him that kil-ler's look. But he only displayed a shrewd and untrusting grin. At this point, I was positive he was employed at this estab-lishment. He also wore a white shirt and a black vest. His long sleeves were rolled up to his elbows. There were entwined rattlesnakes tattooed on the man's forearm's.

The unidentified pervert grabbed a bottle of red wine from the top shelf. He snatched the corkscrew from the bar, jammed the point of the corkscrew into the cork, unscrewed it until it made this loud popping sound . . . Very good wine. I thought. And he started to drink it right from the bottle.

Kim gave him that look again. Then, said. "Why don't you just crawl un-derneath the rock you came from, sleaze-ball. Who in the hell hired you any- way." Then she turned to me, and we continued our talk.

Mr. Sleaze-ball was silent. He just grinned, that shrewd and untrusting grin, and cocked his left eyebrow. He picked up the wine bottle and gulped a quarter of it. As he was gulping, I had noticed a scar from the tip of his left earlobe to the edge of his lower left side lip. He wore mean, hollow brown eyes, as if he didn't have a heart pumping blood to his brain. Zombie-like.

Lisa, for some odd reason, looked away from Mr. Ugly and froze her blue eyes on Mr. Zombie/Sleaze-ball "Honey, are you alright?" I asked. She was silent.

But, she kept her hard gaze on Mr. Zombie/Sleaze-ball. He saw her blue gaze on him.

"What are you staring at, bitch?" Zombie said.

With that, I stood up quickly. So quickly, my wooden stool fell over, hit- ting the hard floor. Kim tried to stop me.

"Nick, please don't." Kim pleaded. "It isn't worth it. Okay? I'll apologize for him. He's a new employee."

"Nobody calls my woman a 'bitch'." I said, controlling my tone.

Kim pleaded me with her eyes. I nodded. For Kim's and Lisa's welfare, I regained composure.

I picked up the fallen stool and set it near the bar. But I didn't sit. I stood.

I'd realized he had an inch or two of height on me, and solid. As if he lifted weights and worked out everyday. But he appeared slightly older than me. I noticed a few streaks of gray pushing through his jet black wavy hair.

Lisa slid from her stool and walked dizzily to the ladies room. She didn't look so good.

Chapter Twenty-Six

THE TIME: 6:56 P.M., Thursday night.

Blake, the Karaoke and Dee-Jay Host, and also Hotel Security, all for the Grand Milwaukee Hotel, was just finished connecting the coaxial cable to the monitor when Lisa returned to the bar.

"Nick, honey, can we sit near Blake. This creep is freaking me out." She carefully pointed her forefinger at Zombie where he couldn't really see it.

"Yeah, I noticed, babe. But, why? Do you know him from somewhere?" I said.

"I don't know. I think I do. But where . . . ? I just cannot put my finger on it." She tugged on my sleeve. "Let's talk about this later, okay? I might be mistaking, anyway. Let's go see Blake." She tugged on my sleeve again.

Eagle said. "Nick. When are we leaving for Chicago? Tomorrow?"

I said. "That's the plan. Why?"

"I'm willing to leave right now. We need to escape the storm that's brew-ing here. Besides, I'm getting jittery and very anxious to catch the people re- sponsible for killing your girlfriend's parents."

"Me, too, Eagle. Me, too. But not tonight . . . tomorrow." I said sternly.

"Okay. But the high winds are frightening Pam. Something is telling me,

Nick, we should leave now. Tonight."

I rested my hand on his shoulder, glared into his eyes and shook my head.

"Tomorrow," I said. Eagle shrugged, tensely.

We grabbed our drinks from the bar and went to a high legged table with high legged stools near Blake's Karaoke equipment. And also where he Dee-Jays. There weren't enough room for us at one table, so Eagle and Clint pul-led another high legged table and set it evenly near us. I found some more high legged stools and brought them over. Then I set them around the sec-ond table. Comfy.

At seven-fifteen, Karaoke started. Just in time, too. Bob came toward us with Pam, a singer and a good friend of mine, walking side by side.

Cool.

While Blake played a few introduction songs from his CD's, which he does normally before the first Karaoke singer appears in front of the micro- phone, I introduced him to my friends. Blake and I shook hands, strongly. Then he continued shaking hands with my other friends.

We spoke of the past-times; Halloween parties the hotel had years ago, five days a week Karaoke, which, now is down to one night a week. Phew-ey. Approaching our table, Pam was introduced to my friends. She sat with us and fitted right in, as if she knew my friends a lifetime. One big happy family. I'd asked Blake what he knew about the bar- tender working alongside of Kim. Mr. Zombie.

"Not much," Blake said, "I think he just been hired not long ago. I was a- way for a week. But when I had returned, he was already working here. I do not know much about him now, but I will very, very soon. I assure you, Nick." I also told Blake about the earlier incident I had with Mr. Zombie. Blake said, "Yeah. I know, buddy. His manners suck. But if he gives you or your friends anymore trouble, please let me know immediately."

I nodded. "Are you still with hotel security, Blake?" I asked.

"You bet I am. For ten years now. And loving it." Blake smiled, as if he didn't mean it. Loving it?

The CD of Diana Ross came to its completion. And Blake announced his first singer. *"Pam, come on down . . . Pam will be singing for us, 'Save a horse, Ride a cowboy'"*

We applauded. Pam was a sweetheart. Not only when she sings, but when she con- verses, her eyes showed a lot of expression. She's a wit. A laugh a minute. We just sat back, sipped our drinks and listened to Pam's strong singing voice. Great voice! Great entertainer! Boy! She can sing. When she ended her song, we applauded again. The audi- ence loved her. Encore.

Blake spoke. *"Before you sit down, Pam, we have you up for one more song . . . . And that song is . . . uh . . . , 'It's Raining Men'"*.

We applauded again. Carina the cocktail waitress came to our table. She was young and attending college . . . Business Management, I believe she told me. She was of aver- age height and weight and intelligent. She also received her bartending license, recently. Something to be proud of. Yeah.

I really didn't know Carina very well, but what I did know of her, she'll be going places. She's dedicated to her job and education with a lot of de-termination going for her. I introduced her to my friends, they shook hands.

Then, she took our order. She went away.

As Pam returned to the table, Blake announced Bob the bartender to step up to the microphone.

"Bob will be singing for us," Blake announced, *"'Mack the Knife'."*

We applauded for him, encouragingly.

The time: 8:05 P.M. The wind was horrific. The huge plate window, that was to our rear and next to the rear exit door, was vibrating rapidly. Paper and foam cups swirled in circles. Around . . . Around . . . Around . . . Like a dog chasing its tail.

While Bob sang, a news flash streamed across the bottom of the tele—vision screen above the bar . . . *A tornado has been spotted near Waukesha County, and heading for Milwaukee/*

Milwaukee County. The force of wind and speed is approximately 70 to 80 miles an hour. It will entail hail and extremely damaging winds. Please take cover ASAP! The news flash repeat-ed.

"I told you, Nick," Eagle said, "I told you. Damn it. I told you so." Eagle clenched both his fists, and Pam Neuman, Eagle's wife, clung to Eagle's arm tightly.

"I'm sorry, buddy. I truly am," I said, "I'd asked around earlier if there would be a storm coming, but nobody heard anything about one coming. I thought we'd be safe."

"Well, you thought wrong." Pam Neuman said, angrily.

Lisa said, "Nothing we can do about it now, Pam and Eagle. Let's wea-ther it out. Okay?"

Pam and Eagle shrugged with angry eyes. The rest of us nodded, agree-ably.

Lisa was right, as always. When she and I got shot last year in Mauston, she seemed to be the strong one. She always had an encouraging and posi-tive word. Just to make you feel at ease. What an angel. And this angel is mine. Yeah. I love her dearly. And I admit, I don't tell her enough.

When Bob's song came to an end, we applauded. Though we were still worried about the storm, we'd still enjoyed Bob's voice.

He briskly came to our table and grabbed his coat from the back of his stool, and swung it over his right shoulder. "I best to be leaving. With this storm brewing, I am not taking any chances." His eyes scanned toward us, and said, "I'm pleased to meet you, all of you. And, Nick. Please be-have yourself." He smiled at me oddly. "And don't be a stranger."

I nodded and shook his hand. "Be careful getting home, Bob," I said. As Bob turned to leave, I said, "Have a doctor check your middle finger, al- right?" Bob snorted. Then he turned and left for the curvy stairs, flipping the 'bird' at me.

Carina returned with our drinks. I tipped her deservingly. She smiled and went away with her blonde ponytail swaying back and forth as she walked to the bar for another customer.

Blake took the microphone to his lips, and said, *"Ladies and gentlemen . . .With the storm arriving soon, we just might have time for one more singer . . .Johnny B . . . . come on down . . . Johnny B. will be singing for us . . . . uh, 'Sweet low, Sweet Chariot'."*

We applauded to whoever Johnny B. was.

The time was nearing eight-thirty-five. The tornado siren blared loudly.

Over, and over, and over, again. The walls seemed to shake violently. The plate window was shaking worse than before. Some people were beginning to panic. Suddenly, the lights were flashing constantly . . . Off and on . . . On and off . . . And on, again. But dimly.

Blake hurriedly took his Karaoke equipment and broke it down as fast as he could. Clint, Eagle and I assisted Blake.

Johnny B., unfortunately, couldn't finish his song. The loudspeakers were crackling too much. But we applauded him just the same.

Clint was calm about the storm coming. He just puffed on his big cigar and drunk his Scotch. He took in the dilemma, as if this occurred on an ev-ery day basis.

I gulped my Red Lager down. Damn . . . . That was good.

Chapter Twenty-Seven

THE TORNADO SIRENS blew louder than ever now. The hotel's lights flashed every several seconds. The Down Under crowd panic has increased. At 8:45 Belle came rushing down the long and curvy stairwell, and quickly ordered two bottles of red wine to take back upstairs in Harold's Lounge.

She ran the length of the bar, running toward the swimming pool area, and stood between Mr. Ugly and a flight attendant from Midwest Airlines. She got Kim's attention and ordered the two bottles of red wine. While she waited, Belle admired Mr. Ugly's tie. "Nice tie, sir." Belle said.

Mr. Ugly maybe thought he was god-gift to women. He decided to get very friendly with Belle. Too friendly.

"Buzz-off, creep. All I said I loved your Elvis tie. I didn't say I love you.

You, idiot. And the answer is still no. How dare you ask me to go to your room. Besides, I'm a happily married woman. Behave yourself, or I'll call security . . . Bastard."

Kim returned with the two bottles of red wine. Kim stretched over the bar and handed them to Belle. And Kim said, "Having problems with him?" She pointed her chin to Mr. Ugly.

"Hell, no, Kim. I took care of it. Thank-you."

Kim nodded and waited on another customer.

Just as Belle grabbed the bottles of wine from the bar, and went through the back way, through the glass doubled doors, past the swimming pool area, the hotel went pitch black. The EXIT sign lights remained on. But the flood lights in the stairwells and hallways failed to power 'On'.

Now in complete darkness, Belle had tried to find her way back to Har-old's Lounge. Suddenly, she was pushed from behind, almost falling down on her face on the hallway carpet. She heard someone running past her.

Belle was just about to take a step, after regaining balance, when she was pushed again. A voice spoke. Maybe a female's voice. But Belle wasn't too positive about that. "Excuse me . . . sorry . . . Are you all right?" The voice said. It sounded foreign. Maybe Hispanic. Belle wasn't positive of that either.

"Yeah . . . Yeah," Belle said, as she leaned against the wall for support. "I am all right. Be careful next time." But the female foreigner disappeared into the darkness before she heard Belle's advise.

Belle regained her composure, and crept blindly toward Harold's Lounge with the two bottles of red wine. Unbroken . . . Luckily.

Belle's wristwatch, which glowed in the darkness, read: 9:03 P.M.

The wind was howling madly. The hotel seemed to be teetering. Shaking.

The crowd was hissing at the storm, and at other customers. I didn't know who or what was angrier. The crowd of people, or the wind?

At 9:10 P.M., the screaming mob descended to Down Under for shelter.

Security Personnel manned the curvy stairwell from the main lobby. Some security officer's were posted upstairs near Down Under's entrance, while others guided the convention personnel to safety. The Down Under Lounge was the lowest level you could go for safety. It was used as a 'Fall-Out Shel- ter'.

Approximately 220 people would have been able to squeeze comfortably, but the mob had increased over its capacity. There was not enough security personnel to control the flow of scared, angry, anxious people. They just pushed and squeezed, squeezed and pushed, until they felt like sardines with no way out.

Drinking glasses were shattering, people screaming for help, tables being pushed over, low and high chairs crashing to the floor. The sounds of voices made me think of either, the Summer Festival crowd, or a barroom brawl . . . .

Well, after I thought about that . . . . What is the difference?

Suddenly, the ceiling and surrounding lights began to flicker again. Dim . . . Dimmer . . . . Dimmest . . . Blackout . . . .

The back-up generator was slow in generating. By the time the generator powered-up, it was approximately 9:35 P.M.

The lights gleamed brightly once again, but only after when the lights fli-ckered slowly, minute by minute. The people were relieved.

There were still screaming and cries for help near the center of the lou-nge. A few laid injured with tables and chairs resting over their bodies. Sev- eral others were bleeding, but not serious enough to be rushed to the hospit- al. Thank God.

Chapter Twenty-Eight

SECURITY PERSONNEL STILL manned the stairwell. But the rear exits near the pool was unguarded. Some of the frightened people had tried to leave through the unguarded exit. But a observant security officer yelled from the stairwell and over the heads of the mob, and ordered them not to leave.

At this moment, Blake's baritone voice yelled out through cupped hands.

"A tornado has touched down in our parking lot . . . . Please refrain from exiting this lounge . . . I repeat . . . A tornado has touched down in our parking lot . . . Which parking lot, we don't know at this time . . . Please stay put. This is for everyone's safety . . . We'll let you know when it's announced All Clear."

Blake's authoritative tone had calmed the screams and argumentative voices. The crowd relaxed, or tried to relax and be more calm. Most of them were smart. Some were just plain stupid.

Through the upstairs thick glass-enclosed stairwell, flashing blue and red lights from the emergency vehicles, bounced off the walls and shot at the inky sky. Radios from the local and county officials, were crackling from a distance.

The yellow trucks from the electric company were blending in with the black and white, and red emergency vehicles.

The wind was strongly blowing, but slightly diminished. But not much.

The rain and hail had subsided.

Blake and his security team had announced that the south end of the hotel was destroyed from the violent sweeping tornado. The Baton Rouge Hall was no longer there where it stood an hour ago. The Grand Ballroom located on the eastside of the hotel was totally wiped out. The east and south parking lot were buckled upward shooting toward the sky.

The earth had become the sight of a war-zone.

"No fatalities at this time," Blake yelled out, still with cupped hands cir- cling his mouth.

Trees and electrical lines were battered and cut from their lives and lying across over-turned cars, buses, SUV's, campers, and some houses. The en- tire area was roped off with official yellow tape . . . . POLICE . . . DO NOT CROSS.

Police, firefighters and paramedics were searching for possible bodies among the de-bris. Helicopters were heard hovering the disaster scene.

The television, above the bar, televised the rubble closely, zooming in and scanning, scanning and zooming. As the cameras fixed on the damage, the over-populated Down-Under lounge took in a glimpse of the parking lot on T.V., and had wondered if their vehicles were among the overturned and damaged twisted metal.

So far, everyone was counted for. So far, no fatalities. So far, no major injuries . . . . So far . . . .

The Presidential Wing, French Quarters and International Wing went un- touched. Amazingly so. The New Orleans Hall, which was centered within the hotels structure, also went untouched.

The intersection of Howell and Layton Avenue, an eight block radius, and in addition to the Grand Milwaukee Hotel's parking lot, were shut down tighter than a drum. No one could go anywhere. For how long . . . ? It was any ones guess.

No entrance. No exits. The crowd were still in a frenzy . . . Frenzy . . . hell, hair-raising panic.

But nothing that anyone could do, but wait it out.

Chapter Twenty-Nine

"WHAT THE FUCK?" A terrified female's voice scream came from the 'J'—styled bar near the rear exit. "Call security," She screamed again. "Immediately . . . Now!" She ordered Mr. Zombie, again to call security. But he stood and stared blankly at her. His lack of co-operation caused her to push him a-side. "Hell, I'll do it myself . . . Get out of my way."

She grabbed the house phone receiver from the wall, which was directly dispatched to Blake's Dee-Jay booth . . . .

"Blake, this is Kim at the bar. Come quickly. Please."

As soon as Blake hung-up, he grabbed his walkie-talkie that was clipped to his wide black belt, raised the radio carefully to his lips, and spoke into it, aggressively.

"Security-Two . . . This is Security-One . . . Come in." Blake said.

"Security-Two, Go."

"Report to the Down-Under bar. Kim needs help . . . I'm pushed up against my Dee-Jay booth and surrounded by the mob of angry people. I'll get there as soon as possible . . . Ten-Four?" Blake messaged out.

A male voice appeared over the receiver again.

"Ten-Four . . . I'm on my way."

Blake with radio in hand, pushed through the sardined-like crowd with ease. I noticed a well-dressed male figure descending from the curvy stair-well also with a radio in his hand. He too, had to push and shove his way through the very stressful and angry crowd. But, since he was closer to the bar then Blake, the male figure was appointed. Lucky him.

Blake wore a black cowboy hat, black western shirt with some fancy stitch around the flap of its pockets, black Levi's and black cowboy boots. The highly pointed ones you can buy at 'Boots 'R' Us'. His dark, shouldered length hair was evenly trimmed around his ears and laid smoothly across his black western shirt. He made me think of Hop-Along-Cassidy, but lacking silvery-white hair.

From where we were sitting, I could hear Blake saying; "Excuse me, Ex- cuse me, please . . . Let me through, please . . . Thank-you . . . Sorry. But I did not mean to step on your toes. Sorry again."

After a few moments had elapsed, Blake yelled once again with cupped hands.

"Don't anyone move," he yelled to the crowd. A voice somewhere in the crowd yelled back to him.

"Where in the fuck'n hell are we suppose to go, ... Idiot." Some angry male voice said.

Blake ignored the asinine remark, and returned to face Kim. After a few more minutes had elapsed, he waved toward our direction. With confusion,

I pointed to my chest, questionably. Blake nodded and pointed with his fore-finger at us, then gestured us to come to the bar.

Lisa, Clint, Eagle and his wife Pam, and myself, had pushed against the wall of people and forced our way through. Pam the singer and Johnny B. had stayed behind and en-joyed their drinks.

By the time we'd arrived at the bar where Blake and his team of security stood waiting, we must have stepped on half of the population's toes and feet, and whatever else. The crowd was very angry. Oh well.

"Watch where you're going, asshole."; . . . ."Ouch! Damn you! . . . Moth-a' Fuck-a'." We must've said *"Sorry"* more than dozen times. Whew!

As we approached Blake and his team, Blake had his hands on his hips, and was smiling.

"You made it through without being killed, huh?" Blake said, still grin-ning.

"Welcome to Down-Under, pal." A security officer said.

Lisa slapped Blake's left shoulder, lovingly. But Pam and Eagle just gave him a mean look. Clint just shrugged. And I said, "Very funny, partner."

"The reason I had asked you here, people," Blake's eyes shifted to each and every one of us, "is because my team and myself need your detecting expertise in a matter that just came up."

We stood stiffly among the angry mob and listened to what Blake had to say to us.

After he'd spoke, and laid heavy instructions and demands on our fearless team, he said to me.

"You and I will be working together, side by side on this case. O-kay, Nick?"

I nodded. "Whatever you say, boss."

Then his eyes shifted over to my cohorts, one by one.

"Pam . . . Lisa; you take the Presidential Wing . . . . Eagle . . . Clint; you take the French Quarters." Then he turned and focused on me.

"And finally, Nick, you and I will take the International Wing."

Lisa said, "What are we looking for, again? I couldn't hear everything that was said with all the background noise and all."

Blake said, "Kim's rare coin collection. A person or persons grabbed her coins from the counter underneath the bar. My security team will be posted here and ask questions, while we do our thing. We believe the coins were taken after the lights went out around nine p.m., or so." Blake glanced at his Harley-Davidson watch. "Time now is ten-o-five. Whoever took them can- not get far. The entire perimeter is shut down and guarded by the local and county authorities."

We all nodded. And did what we do best . . . . Investigate.

Chapter Thirty

P AM AND LISA strolled up and down the northwest end of the hotel struc-ture look-ing into trash bins, bathroom stalls, dark hidden corners and other dark secluded places.

The Presidential Wing consists of rooms that were numbered from 1100 through 1300.

"We don't even have a passkey to look into the rooms, Lisa. How would we know if the thief or thieves are in one of them?" Pam inhaled deeply.

"This is so ridiculous." Pam shook her head in disgust.

"Just keep your ears open for anything. We'll listen with our ears against each door. And maybe we'll be able to hear conversation. Who knows, the perps might be bragging about their findings."

Pam shrugged. "Okay. You're the trained detective."

The French Quarters were designed as a 'T'-shape. The room numbers ranged from 4100-4500 and located on the West end of the hotel. And main-ly used for flight atten-dants and pilots of various airlines.

"There are over four-hundred rooms we have to check. Also keep a close eye on the missing coins, Clint. How are we going to check and keep a look- out on all these rooms when there is only the two of us patrolling the area?"

Eagle said, as they were turning doorknobs and leaning into the cherrywood framed doors.

"Patience, my friend, patience." Clint said, grinning.

"Patience is a virtue, huh? Is that what you're saying, Clint?"

"Yep. That's what I'm saying. We'll be here for a long while. Time is all we have."

As Clint and Eagle listened and observed, observed and listened, Clint had noticed there weren't any surveillance cameras in the hallways. Probab-ly didn't matter. Clint thought. It was too dark to see anything anyway.

❯ ❮

The International Wing had been used for foreign travelers. As far as my knowledge goes, it was strictly utilized for VIP's and foreign business asso-ciates. Maybe salesper-sons', consultants for foreign trade, or maybe even for rare coin collectors. Now that's a thought. Umm.

"Blake, why in the hell did Kim bring rare coins with her to work? It does not make any sense, whatsoever." I said.

"Good question, Nick, very good question. But my security team probab-ly will find that out. My radio has been quiet since we started this long walk to nowhere. But I expect some information very soon."

I nodded.

The time was 12:15 A.M. Still nothing.

The only thing Blake and I had observed near room 5109 was a house-keepers cleaning cart. Maybe it was abandoned because of the tornado warn-ings. And the housekeeper sought shelter. But we had no idea who was using it for the night. And why was it still resting here near room 5109? After all, the tornado had past more than an hour ago. The housekeeper, I would think, would want to finish her cleaning and go home. Maybe she was too stressed out, and stayed with the crowd at Down-Under . . . Maybe.

Turning to Blake, I asked, "Don't you have a master passkey for these rooms?"

Blake said, "On a normal day, yeah. But I wasn't scheduled to work security tonight."

"How about your security team. Would they have a passkey on their per-son?"

"They should. Yes. But we just can't walk in anyone's room without the guests permission."

I nodded again. "Maybe we should start knocking on doors, Blake. What do you think of that?"

Blake agreed.

As Blake and I stood in front of Room 5114, and Blake's knuckles was just about to make contact with the heavy cherrywood door, his radio crackl-ed.

"Security-Two . . . calling Security-One . . . come in please . . ."

❯ ❮

"Lisa, are you okay? What's wrong?" Pam said, concernedly.

"Maybe nothing." Lisa wasn't very convincing.

"Come on, Lisa. Something is wrong. I have known you too long to hide something from me."

Lisa and Pam stood in the intersection of the hallway in the Presidential Wing, facing each other. Lisa nodded in agreement.

"Okay. You're right, Pam. Something is nagging at me."

"What?"

Pam and Lisa started down the hallway again maintaining their search for the stolen rare coins.

"You know that bartender who's working with Kim?" Lisa said.

"The beast. That one?"

"Yeah. However you want to describe him. That's the one." Lisa said.

"Yeah, go ahead, I'm listening."

"Well . . . He really bother's me. And I just can't shake it."

Pam silently listened.

"I think I know him from somewhere. But I can't place him. I just cannot put my finger on it."

"Well, whoever he is sure left an impact on you. Hasn't it?" Said Pam.

"Yeah. It sure has." Lisa shrugged. "Let's forget him for now. We were told to find the rare coins. So let's focus on that."

"Okay, Lisa. Whatever you say."

"Well, Clint. Here we are on the top and last floor. And still nothing. What now? Do we backtrack and start from the top and work our way back down?"

"Not a bad idea, Eagle. We are heading back down anyway. We might as well. Let's do it, just in case we'd overlooked something."

Clint lit his fresh cigar and smiled. And Eagle smoothed his dark brown hair with his right hand and re-adjusted his short-curled ponytail, pulling it tightly into the brown rubber-band.

Backtracking they went.

"This is Security-One . . . What do you have?" Blake said.

"We might have something of interest. Can you report back to Down-under . . . . Please"

"Ten-Four." Blake ended the transmission.

We marched downstairs, passed the swimming pool, and entered through the glass-doubled-doors that lead into Down-Under.

The angry mob had dwindled to approximately thirty people.

Nice and quiet. Whew.

We noticed security had Dena, Carina, and Belle encircled with Milwau-kee police of-ficers. Blake seemed to be shocked. His jaw hung loosely downward, and his eyes frozen in place.

He glared at Security-Two for a brief moment, then, Blake gestured with his forefinger, curled and pointing to himself, suggesting Security-Two re- port front and center.

Security-Two approached Blake, head hanging down, as if he knew pun- ishment was on the agenda. Blake pulled him aside near the glass-doubled doors where Blake had entered.

"What the fuck are the police doing here?" Blake whispered firmly. "This is hotel busi- ness. It's an internal incident. We could have taken care of the theft of the coins without outside help. You better have a damn good explan-ation for this."

He stared down at the tiled flooring, then, raised his head, squinting into Blake's eyes. "Well . . . uh . . . Dena . . . uh . . . Carina and Belle were asked to take a polygraph test. And they got violent with us. So we called the police."

"Damn it, Hank. You could not handle three females on your own? You had to get the police involved?" Blake's expression was furious and tight.

"Sorry, sir. But Dena and Carina weren't the real problem. They finally agreed to the polygraph. It was Belle who remained stubborn and unincorp-erative. She's a character, that Belle."

Blake shook his head and looked at the floor, chewing on his lower lip.

His eyes focused on me.

"Nick, you're friends with Belle, right?"

I nodded.

"Maybe you can talk some sense into her and explain how important the polygraph is. I'll deal with the Milwaukee's finest."

Blake returned his focus on Hank. "Anyone else you questioned?"

Hank inhaled deeply and released it up in the air, blowing a strand of hair away from his eyes.

"Yeah. I questioned a guy named a Mr. Perry Madass."

"Mad-Ass? As it sounds?" Blake chuckled.

"No, sir. His last name is pronounced Madass . . . (Muh-daz)."

Blake chuckled again. But quietly. As he quietly chuckled, he slowly lift-ed his black cowboy hat from his head, slicked his hair back, set it back on his head. "Madass . . . Muh-daz . . . Ha . . . Ha . . . Funny."

Chapter Thirty-One

THE TWO-HUNDRED SOMETHING people were free to leave and go back to their rooms. Or stay for a drink or two.

As logic has it, the most possible suspects were maybe four, maybe five.

Or maybe even six. The information the security team, mainly Hank had col-lected, again, logically speaking, were the customers sitting or standing clos- est to the glass-doubled doors near the swimming pool area when the lights went out.

Once through the glass doors, the suspect or suspects could have gone anywhere. Such as: Harold's Lounge, men's or/and woman's bathrooms, or maybe even all the way up to the fifth floor of the French Quarters.

But, most predominately, the International Wing. That one was the clos-est of all the wings combined.

Could a person or persons steal the rare coins, do what they have to do to hide them in a secure place, and still have time to return to the Down-Under

Lounge, unaware to the public?

This is what we need to find out.

Belle was sitting with Dena and Carina at the end of the bar that was clo-sest to the curvy stairwell. All were sipping different soft drinks through a plastic straw. I wouldn't have been surprised if the drinks were laced with alcohol. Release the tension that was building up.

As I approached the three lovely ladies, I had glanced up toward the long twenty-five stairs, curvy and glassed-enclosed stairwell. Greg, the room-service employee, was being escorted down the stairs by security. And he wasn't smiling. Two security officers were a few steps behind Greg.

As Greg took his last step from the carpeted stairs and touched the tiled flooring, I said, astonished, "You're a suspect, too?"

He just shrugged and looked confused as the rest of us. He continued to be escorted to a small round table where splinters of broken glass laid spark-ly from the bright light above him. You can hear the crunching of broken glass being pushed into the red carpet from under their feet.

The two security officers picked up three overturned chairs and set them near the closest small round table. The three sat around the table with Greg in between the two officers. They were scrutinizing Greg hard, leaving him nervously uncomfortable. Can't say I blamed him.

I turned away from Greg and his escorts and pulled a high stool away from the highly glossed bar and pulled myself up and sat next to Dena on her right. I'd positioned myself so I could view all three females comfortably.

Carina had sat in the middle of Dena and Belle and drunk their drinks.

A few moments later, Clint, Eagle, Lisa and Pam strolled downstairs and joined the rest of us. Lisa sat next to me on my right, looking confused and tired. She looked worse than ever now.

I was beginning to feel guilty coming to the Grand Milwaukee Hotel the way things had been unfolding.

Kim and her helper Mr. Zombie, (if you wanted to call him her helper), stood behind the cherry wood bar huddled together as Blake, Hank, Perry Madass, and the hotel's finest security team stood opposite of the J-styled bar. Clint, Eagle, and Pam stood in the background near the glass-doubled doors, which was near the swimming pool entrance. As they were standing there near the catering cart, Clint, Eagle, and Pam had snuck two Brats and a

Polish Sausage. Yummy . . . Yum . . . Yum.

Kim was explaining the theft incident while everyone close-by listened.

Eyes bounced from Kim to Mr. Zombie to Blake to Perry Madass to Blake's security team and to my three law-abiding cohorts who stole sausage and brats from the catering cart. Then back to Kim again.

"And that is why I had brought my coins to work." Kim explained. "I ne-eded to have them appraised." She paused, and took in a deep breath. "I want the mother-fucker who stole my coins. The coins go back three gener-ations, Blake."

Tears suddenly appeared from the corners of her eyes. Kim went to the other end of the bar, grabbed a bottle of something, poured herself a shot and downed it hard. Then she returned to the crowd of listeners with strong smell of whiskey on her breath.

"We'll find the bastards who did this, Kim. Guaranteed. I promise."

Blake grabbed a white napkin from the stainless steel catering cart and handed the soft material to Kim. She wiped her eyes free of tears and the smeared eye make-up.

"Thanks, Blake." Kim said, as she dabbed her eyes and face.

He nodded with a grin.

Blake couldn't help but gaze at Mr. Zombies white shirt several times while Kim had given her theft statement.

"Is that blood . . . ," Blake hesitated. "What's your name again? I don't think we've met."

"You talking to me, buster," Mr. Zombie said.

"Yeah . . . Yeah I'm talking to you. Who else has blood on their shirt?"

Zombie looked around and shrugged. His left eye twitched several times.

With a growling tone in his throat, as if he swallowed drywall, he said,

"Mr. Salmeno . . . Name is Salmeno."

"When did you become employed for the hotel, Mr. Salmeno?"

"Who wants to know?" Salmeno said, growling.

"Listen, asshole," Blake said, as he pointed his finger at Salmeno's face,

"You answer my question, or I'll detain you under suspicion. And just may-be have you fired. Got that?"

He nodded. He suddenly seemed co-operative. But reluctantly.

"What's the question again . . . Blake is it?" Salmeno said.

Blake nodded. "Yeah, that's right. I'm Blake. Now, the fucking question was, when did you start working here?"

"Oh yeah. That question."

"Yeah, you idiot. That question."

"I was hired March 1st. But didn't actually start work until the day after."

Salmeno said, leaning against the bar.

"That will be March 2nd." Blake said, also leaning against the bar. Blake's nose was just an inch away from Mr. Salmeno's nose.

"Bingo. Smart man . . . Really smart man."

Blake's eyes squinted hard. But his tone was even.

"If I hear anymore complaints about you, asshole, I just might forget that I'm a peaceful man."

"Is that a threat?" Mr. Salmeno's left eyebrow raised in an arch form, and his right eye squinted harder than Blake's.

"A fucking promise. I don't know who the fuck you think you are, but your unforgivable attitude stops here and now."

Blake's veins seemed to swell from his neck and forehead. But his bre-athing was controlled.

"Now, the blood on your shirt. How did that happen? And when?"

"I cut myself on broken glass this evening. It's my blood."

"Where's the cut?" Blake unfolded his upper body away from Salmeno.

"What do you mean? 'Where's the cut?' "

"Am I going to fast for you, Mr. Salmeno? Shall I slow down with the questions? What part of the question you don't comprehend? I'm a patient man, Mr. Salmeno, but it's wearing very thin by the second. Now, the cut. What part of your body was cut? Understand?"

"Oh." Suddenly, the light went on in his brain. "Oh. My finger." Salmeno lifted his forefinger above the bar and showed Blake.

"Pretty band-aid, Mr. Salmeno . . . Tweety-Bird. You have a sense of child-ish humor, at least. Do you like Bugs Bunny, too?"

"Shut-up, Blake." Salmeno's fists were clenched. But Blake ignored the intimidation.

"I won't shut-up. Not until I'm through with you."

"You want me to take off the bandage, Mr. Blake, sir? Do you need to see the cut?"

"Cockiness won't put you on my friendly list. And, no," Blake said, "I do not need to see the cut. Let's just hope you don't have AIDS."

Mr. Salmeno grunted. Maybe he even snorted. PIG!

Chapter Thirty-Two

LISA'S EARS HAD perked when she'd heard Salmeno's name. She thought about it for a moment, but still it didn't ring any bell's with her. She just couldn't help but stare at Salmeno again.

But this time Mr. Salmeno didn't notice Lisa's piercing eyes on him. He was too damn busy talking to Blake.

A flash-back appeared in Lisa's brain, but faded quickly. She shook her head. "Damn it." Lisa muttered. "Damn . . . Damn . . . Damn it, anyway."

Kim walked toward Lisa and startled her.

"What's up with you, Lisa. You look like you had just seen a ghost."

Lisa just shook her head.

"Do you want a stiff drink?" Kim said, half-smiling.

"Yeah. That'll be great. Thanks. A triple shot of vodka and a little tonic. No lime."

Kim nodded and went. She returned quickly and set the drink in front of Lisa. As Lisa took in a few gulps, she cocked her pretty head toward Perry Madass. Something was different about him.

Another headache, darn it. Something's missing from Perry. She scrut-inized him from head to toe.

Was it his personal appearance? Or the way he sat? What was it? What's so damn dif-ferent about him? Lisa gulped her drink again.

❯❯ ❮❮

"Belle, tell me your story and why you refuse a polygraph test." I said

While Belle contemplated deeply, Dean and Carina had softened to the idea, but they were reluctant to do so.

Carina said, "I really don't understand the reasoning behind it, Nick, but if I have to take a lie-test, I will. I just didn't like the way the security officer approached me with the idea."

"How did he approach you, Carina?" I asked.

"He treated me like a criminal. Very demanding, you know."

"Hank? Was it Hank who treated you like a criminal?"

She nodded sadly. "Yeah. Yeah. Hank."

"He was just doing his job, Carina." I said.

"But did he have to come on so strongly? He made me feel so small and worthless. You know, like shit."

I nodded, trying to understand the situation.

"I agree with you, Carina," Dena jumped in. "He treated me like it was racial. I'm dark-skinned, so automatically I'm guilty, right? If Hank had asked instead demanded, I wouldn't have gotten so irate with him. I apolo- gized for that. But I will take the poly- graph test if I have to. I like working here. I'll take it just to prove to him I'm innocent."

"Okay. Fine. That's great. Thank-you, ladies. It's well appreciated. Kim, I'm sure, will even appreciate it."

"Why Kim," Said Carina. "What does she have to do with this?"

"Everything." I said.

"What does that mean, Nick . . . ? 'Everything'?" Dena said.

"She is the victim here. It was her coins stolen. And since you and Kim are co-workers, she'll feel even safer knowing that you are innocent. It will make you three working to- gether more comfortable." I took in a sip of my beer.

"Oh. Yeah. I see what you mean, Nick." Dena said.

Carina nodded, agreeably.

The time was two-thirty, Friday morning. The wind had calmed down to a slight breeze. The thick gray clouds had broken into thin—feathered—like clouds. And the half-moon was brightly glowing through the picture win-dow.

The blue and red lights were still flashing and bouncing off the hotel walls. Police ra- dios were still crackling with information. And it looks like were stuck here the duration of the weekend. Damn.

Chapter Thirty-Three

Down-Under had been turned into an interrogation center now. The bar had been closed to the public for over an hour, but drinks were still being served to the interrogators and suspects. Very nice.

We were all tired, but we wanted this investigation to end quickly. De-tectives never sleep.

Belle still was sticking to her guns. NO LIE DETECTOR TEST!

"You know where to put that, buddy. And if you don't know, well, let me tell you. Up your funky-ass. I do not care if you and I are friends, Nick. No reflection on you. But I'm not taking any fucking detector test. They can fire me if they want. I really don't care. At my age, I truly need the rest."

"But, Belle, if you refuse, it would only show guilt." I said.

"Fuck-you." Belle said, as she slid off her barstool and stammered away.

But she couldn't go too far with all exits being secured. I hope she realized she was caged as much as we were.

One hell of a week-end.

"What's this I hear about Juanita Alverez?" Kim said.

"She's missing. No one has seen her since the tornado sirens had gone off." Hank said.

"Who is Juanita Alverez?" Clint asked.

"She's a housekeeper for the hotel." Blake said.

Pam said "Well, maybe she got scared and went home just before the tor-nado." Pam Neuman put her arm around Eagle's waistline and hugged him tightly.

Pam the singer spoke, "No, I don't think so. I'd seen her at the bar just before nine, or little after nine. I'm not too sure. But I really don't think she went home. I remember seeing her 'cause I had to brush by her to get a Brat for myself and a sausage for Johnny B. I am positive."

"How do you know Juanita?" Eagle asked.

"Well, damn, Eagle. I'd been coming here for hellava long time. I know just about everybody here. Except Al-Freak-O here." She pointed her in-dex finger at Mr. Salmeno. He grunted and growled at the same time. Ama-zing. Blake had looked at him, as if he was thinking. *"I dare you, bastard. Make a move on Pam the singer, I'll kill you."*

Suddenly, Lisa stepped down from her stool and staggered carefully to—ward Mr. Madass and studied his appearance. As she was walking toward Madass and maintained her balance, she turned her head left and glared at Mr. Salmeno.

Another flash-back.

But it disappeared as fast as it came. Lisa shook it off and refocused on Mr. Madass.

Now Lisa stood with her right hand on the back of Madass's stool to keep herself from falling. Mr. Madass turned his head away from CNN News and faced Lisa square into her face. Madass was squinting severely.

"Well, hell-o, sweet thing." Mr. Madass had a difficult time focusing his eyes on Lisa. He even had difficulty seeing the television, which was only four feet above the bar.

"You're squinting, Perry. Why don't you put your glasses back on?"

Madass was silent.

He ignored Lisa's suggestion. Then Madass turned and faced the televis—ion once again, squinting.

As Perry focused on CNN News, Lisa scrutinized him closely. Lisa de- tected, even though she was intoxicated, she detected his flashy tie print of

Elvis Presley missing, too.

Blake, and Pam the singer, and Johnny B. noticed Lisa standing and stud-ying Perry.

"Isn't she dating Nick, Blake?" Johnny B. asked.

"Yeah. I noticed that, too. Why is she flirting with Mr. Madass?"

"I don't think she is flirting, guys," Pam the singer said. "She's detecting. And even I should have noticed it myself."

"Notice what, Pam?" Johnny B. asked.

"His tie and glasses. He isn't wearing them."

"Am I missing something here, Pam?" Blake said.

"Blake, think about it," Pam the singer said. "If your eyes were bothering you really that bad, and you had prescription glasses, wouldn't you be wear-ing them? Look how he's squinting his eyes."

"Yeah. You might be right." Blake said.

"I know I'm right, Blake."

"So, why isn't he wearing them?" Johnny B. said. Blake and Pam ignored his question.

"Blake," Pam the singer said. "I do not want to tell you how to do your job, but shouldn't you go over to Madass and just be a little inquisitive?"

Blake nodded and walked several steps toward Perry and stood on his right side, look-ing over his shoulder.

Blake bluntly asked, "Perry, where are your Clark Kent glasses?"

"Yeah, Perry," Lisa quickly stepped in. "Where are your ugly, unstylish, fucking glasses? And while we're at it, where is your flashy Elvis tie?"

Perry's head went left and right and left again. His eyes bouncing from Lisa to Blake, Then back to Lisa. He leaned back in the stool and crossed his woman-like scrawny arms over his scrawny chest.

"Well, Lisa. I guess I lost them."

"Your tie, too?" Blake said, glaring at Perry.

Perry took in a very needed deep breath, and swallowed hard.

Turning to Blake, Perry said, "Well, Blake, I guess I lost that, too." Perry's eyes squinted so severely, it seemed to change his facial features into Orient-like profile.

"Where were you when the lights went out, Mr. Madass?" Johnny B. couldn't resist getting involved.

Perry did a forty-five degree turn in his stool and squinted and stared squarely at Johnny B.

"What is this . . . Some kind of joke? Okay, funny guy. I'll play along with your silliness. I was in the frigging dark . . . HA . . . HA!" Perry laughed, nervously.

Blake, Johnny B., and Pam the singer couldn't hold back their wide grins, that turned into laughter. Then Lisa joined in.

I went over to the laughter and stood behind Lisa and hugged her from behind. I whispered softly into her ear. "What's so funny? Let me in on the joke."

Kim returned from serving drinks to Dena and Carina, and stood near the counter where her coins used to be.

"You guys are having a time of your fucking lives. Laughing and joking.

What about my damn coins? Is anyone looking for them? Blake. What the fuck is going on here?" Kim said, furiously.

"We're just trying to figure out where Perry's glasses and tie disappeared to. He claims he lost them. But how could he lose them if he was sitting here all along. He claims he didn't go anywhere." Hank said, hoping to put out Kim's fury.

Kim said, "So, *who* cares about his glasses and tie? What does that have to do with my missing coins anyway?"

Johnny B. said, "Maybe, while the lights were out, he made wild love to some crazy and wild woman for half-an-hour, as he was sitting here in the darkness."

"Funny," Perry said. "Ver-r-ry funny."

Additionally, Nick said, "And the wild and crazy woman walked off with Perry's items."

"Cut the crap," Kim said angrily. "We have a missing housekeeper and a missing case of coins, *rare coins*, I might add, and all we are doing is crack-ing funnies at Perry."

Perry suddenly spoke, "How stupid can you detectives be. The answer to Kim's missing coins, is what Kim just got done saying. Jeez. Detectives . . . . . .

. . . . you are not." Perry turned and faced the bar and gulped his drink.

"What did I just say, Perry?" Kim leaned over the bar with arms crossed, and glared at Perry for a moment. Perry's eyes squinted again.

"Missing coins . . . uh . . . Missing housekeeper? You find what's her name, Alverez, ..." Perry was cut short.

"Ah. So you think the housekeeper took them, do you?" Kim said.

"Well, yeah. Isn't that logical." Perry bounced his dark brown eyes from every gazing eye's on him.

"You may have a point," Blake said. "But you *do not* know Miss Juanita Alverez like we do, Perry."

"What do you mean by that?" Perry said.

"She worked here for many years. Her record is so clean you can eat off of it . . . Nice try, Perry. Nice try." Blake said, grinning.

Kim had agreed with Blake.

Perry said, "So where is your Miss Alverez, Mr. Blake. Miss Kim? Huh?

Tell me that?" If Perry continues with his cockiness, either Blake or Kim will kick his ass. Madly.

Chapter Thirty-Four

PERRY SAID, "You find her, and I'll bet my last dollar you'll find Kim's coins."

The lounge filled with silence. No one spoke for a time. Security, Blake, and Kim just gazed at Perry, waiting for the right moment to shut him up. It wouldn't be pleasant.

I turned my head left, and briefly studied Mr. Salmeno. He stood in sil-ence and drunk his red wine. He just listened to the conversation. Just as well. No one trusted his opin-ion, anyway.

"Yeah," Kim said, still leaning over the bar, "And also find your glasses and tie, too, I assume." Kim's expression turned for the worst. Her face be-came so tight, I thought it might explode.

"Fuck you, you . . . you wimp," Kim was on a role. (Watch out) . . . ."I have known Juanita for a long time. And she wouldn't have stolen my coins . . . Boy! If you had your tie on right now, Wimpy, I'd . . . I'd strangle you with it." Kim leaned closer to Perry . . . Nose to nose. "Don't come here and condemn my friend. You don't even know her. Bastard."

Kim had her whiskey glass in her right hand. Without warning, the brown liquid substance was streaming down Perry's bony face. Madass didn't even know what hit him. Kim's eyes scanned Perry's shirt. Up and down . . . Down and up. With Perry's face still frozen in place, the shocked look, Kim asked Perry.

"Perry, this shirt you're wearing . . . uh . . . wasn't the same shirt you wore when I had opened up at four in the afternoon. You had on a solid white shirt with blue pinstripes. Now you are wearing a chicken-yellow shirt with init-ials *PM* . . . What gives, Perry?"

Kim's fists, on top of bar, clenched tightly. Her knuckles were white with bright red blotches.

Perry sat quietly, still in shock. But angry dark eyes pierced Kim's eyes.

And Kim's angry eyes pierced Perry's eyes. It was a staring contest.

Oh Boy!

Perry had the audacity to say, "I still think Miss Alverez took the coins, you fucking people. Why blame me.?"

Like a streak of lightening, shooting across the sky, Kim's right arm with clenched fist shot across the bar and planted a wallop of a punch on Perry's whiskey-stained face. Fist-to-face contact was so powerful, Perry found him-self sprawled out on the linoleum floor with the stool splintering in more than dozen pieces.

Perry, half-dazed, looked up around him. Shaking his head, trying to stop the bells ringing in his head, blood sprayed from his nose and mouth, re- decorating the black and white linoleum with fine dots of red.

We all glared at Kim in amazement. We were stunned. Blake and his Se- curity team weren't sure what to do. They didn't know if detaining Kim for assault on Perry was in order, or applaud her.

Well, anyway, she wasn't detained.

❯❯ ❮❮

Greg, Belle, Dena, Carina and Greg's security escorts ran to the commo-tion of shat-tering sound.

Greg said, looking down at Perry's bloody face, "Great piece of work, Kim. You re-arranged his face so well, he almost looks handsome." Greg gave Kim a high-five.

Everyone broke into laughter, except Perry and Mr. Salmeno. But it did curb the thick tension in the air. Then Perry yelled something about suing the hotel and Kim. But no-body seemed to care about what Perry had to say.

As we were standing over Perry, another security officer, tall with a dark crew-cut, ran down the long, curvy stairwell leading from the upstairs lobby, into the Down-Under lounge practically skipping two stairs at a time, ran up to Blake, brushing past the mini-mized crowd. Mr. Crew-cut came to a sud-den halt, nose to nose with Blake.

"What do you have that's so urgent, Scott?" Blake said, still glancing at Perry's lanky form.

"I . . . I . . . found . . ."

"Catch your breath, Scott. Just take it easy." Hank said.

Scott nodded with his right hand over his heart. Gasping.

After a few moments of gasping, Scott finally got an extra wind. Leaning against the curve of the bar, Scott explained his findings.

"I found Miss Alverez's coat still hanging in the employee's lounge. If she left the build-ing, she left with nothing. Even her black purse was found hanging over her coat on a wooden hanger.

"Furthermore, Blake," Scott continuing, "She didn't even punch-out on the clock. So, she must still be in the hotel somewhere. You agree?"

Blake nodding, agreeably, put his left hand on Scott's right shoulder.

"Yes, I agree. Great work, Scott, great detective work."

Scott had a widely grin. I believed he blushed slightly, too.

Blake pulled Perry up from the floor by his sport-jacket lapels, trying to avoid contact with Perry's blood. He put his right hand in his right rear black jean pocket and pulled out something shiny and silvery.

Blake, then said, "Perry Madass, you are here detained under suspicion."

Blake adjusted the heavy metal object and slapped it on Perry's wrist.

"Why the hell are you hand-cuffing me?" Perry looked a-fright.

"I just informed you . . . Under suspicion. Understand?"

"What suspicion?"

Blake turned Perry around aggressively and completed hand-cuffing Mr. Perry Madass wrists behind his back.

"You cannot explain your change in appearance, the hasty accusation a- gainst Miss Alverez. And you knew exactly where Kim had laid her case of coins. Not too far from where you were sitting. It was an easy reach for you,

Perry.

"Now Juanita is missing. If you are involved in her disappearance in any fucking way, Mr. Madass, may God help you."

Then Blake pushed him ahead and through the glass-doubled doors, past the swimming pool, and to the security office they went.

We just stood there looking through the glass doors, drinking our drinks, and watched them disappear down the hallway and around the corner. Rais- ing my glass, I said out loud, "Salute."

Chapter Thirty-Five

I T WAS MARCH 10th, 1997, Friday morning; 10 A.M.

The security office was evenly squared with freshly painted gray cinder- block walls. The office was windowless. No view, whatsoever. I scanned my environment and got acquainted with my surroundings.

On the far end wall, to my right, ten spiked nails were heavily pounded into the gray cinder-block wall. Evenly spaced. From the spiked nails were clipboards. One for each thick nail.

On the clipboards were 8" by 11" sized forms. Black and white lettering.

Bold-typed. Forms included; *LOSS PREVENTION, INVENTORY, AND RE-QUISITIONS.* The remaining clipboards had black and white photos (some were in color) of side and front shots. Mug shots, I presumed. Some of the photos were sent from Milwaukee Police Department.

To my left were several gray filing cabinets with Mr. Coffee pot, and old doughnuts resting on top. Next to the filing cabinets, a bubbler with blue and white spigot. Dixie Cups stacked ten high on top of the bubbler. The con—tents in the bubbler was three-quarters full.

The rest of the office was non-descriptive. Just light and dark gray blend-ed together.

Blake said to me, "I would've offered you doughnuts and coffee, but as you see, Nick," Blake pointed toward Mr. Coffee and doughnuts, "coffee is cold and doughnuts hard. With the power lines down and all, no electricity.

Even the bubbler isn't working. Water's warm."

So we made do. The back-up generator lasted only twelve hours before it shut itself down. Not enough *Umph.*

So here we were in a flashlight setting with cold coffee, and two-day-old doughnuts. Marvelous.

The weather was chilly and 45 degrees with overcast. The emergency crew were still cleaning up the mess. But, still no serious injuries or fatal-ities . . . So far . . . .

Blake sat behind his gray metal desk in his gray metal chair. Two other gray-leathered chairs were directly in front of Blake's desk. The two chairs were used for detainees. Like the one Perry was sitting in. Hand-cuffed.

Mr. Madass still looked a-fright. Now, both his eyes were swollen half closed, and had a camouflaged band-aid over his nose. He was still lacking eye glasses. He squinted a lot, but you wouldn't have noticed it. The swollen eyes squinted permanently . . . at least, until the swollen went down.

Hank sat in the other gray chair next to Perry on his left. And Scott lean-ed against the gray wall near the bubbler near the right side of Blake's desk, filing his fingernails evenly.

I stood behind Hank and Perry, casual-like, with hands in my pocket, no-ticing Blake and his men were still wearing the same clothes they had on yesterday. I had pity on them. But I did not have pity on Perry. Scumbag.

I had taken a shower, changed clothes, and ate a hearty bowl of Wheaties before I reported to Blake's security office. And I smelled good, too.

When I had left our guest room, Lisa was snoring away the hours. She needn't to be with me at this particular time. We both had felt her job was done for now. Until further notice.

Lisa had volunteered to search for Juanita Alverez the housekeeper, but Blake had enough help from his own men. Blake appreciated her asking, but considering her intoxicated condition, he had to decline.

"The flight attendant who was sitting near me, well, maybe she had taken the coins, Mr. Blake." Perry's voice squeaked. Maybe from the band-aid be-ing to tight on the bridge of his nose.

"Yeah, right," Hank said. "That's bullshit."

"Well. How convenient for her. She steals the rare coins, takes them to her room, then, when the time comes for her to leave on her flight some-where, and of course, we know we won't see her and her crew for a few long months. And in the meantime, she's getting her beauty sleep, while I wile away the hours with you trying to convince you and your playmates I'm innocent." Perry stretched the syllables on 'innocent'.

"Enough of your babbling, Mr. Madass." Blake raised his tone a few notches. "I have heard just about enough out of you. My patience is running very thin. Now, where did you hide the damn coins?"

"What makes you think I took them. Huh?"

"Answer my question. Damn it." Blake was extremely frustrated and way beyond sleep. He took his big right hand, smoothing his fine trimmed beard, and thought deeply.

Silence was so heavy in the average gray office, I was expecting the cin-derblock walls to crumble under its weight. I'd walked a few feet toward the water fountain, clinched a Dixie Cup, placed it under the blue spigot, tapped it until the warm water filled my cup. I sipped. Yuk.

I grabbed a hard, but dried apple turnover, and bit into it. Yuk, again. A rock would've been tastier. The water didn't fill my emptiness, nor the apple turnover. I was still hungry . . . no, starving was the word for the way I felt.

I needed to lose weight, anyway.

Perry broke the silence. "I'll take you to my room, Blake. Have your men tear it apart. I really don't care. I'm telling you, you won't find anything in there. You'll be wasting your time. But just to satisfy you and your merry men, I'm giving you my full co-operation. So, whaddya say?"

"Un-handcuff me and let's take a stroll." Perry seemed restless and anx-ious to leave. Squirming and jumping in his seat.

Hank said, "I guess we should have thought of that a long time ago. Just too damn tired, I guess."

Perry remarked. "Yeah, Hank. Justify your mistakes. That always seems to work."

"What room are you in, Perry?" Blake said.

Scott was still silent, still filing his fingernails and still leaning against the cinderblock wall.

"I thought you guys knew my room number. Boy. This security, as you call yourselves, is very slow."

"If you haven't noticed, Perry, ole' pal, the power is out. Which means the computers are down."

"Oh. Yeah. Right. Duh . . . me."

"Well . . . What is your room number?" Blake asked impatiently.

"Uh . . . let me see, now . . . ."Perry set his free hand up to his mouth and tap-ped his fine-lined lips with his forefinger, gazing up through the darkness.

"Oh, yeah. I remember now. YUK . . . YUK." He tried to do an impression of 'Goofey', but failed. "Room 5109."

"Get real, Mr. Madass," Blake said. "I'm almost positive I'd helped a wo- man carry her luggage to that room the other day."

"Well, you are mistaken, Mr. Blake, mistaken, royally. I had that room for a week now. Impossible . . . Just impossible. By the way, is she good-look- ing?"

"Okay, smart-ass. Have it your way. Let's go." Blake said, getting up from his chair. "We're wasting time."

Blake stood, then, walked around his desk pulling the 'cuff' key from his shirt pocket, and un-handcuffed Perry. Perry rubbed his wrists gently a few times. We were all expecting Perry to start swinging at any one of us. But it did not happen. Mr. Madass probably knew he would have been dead before he hit the floor.

Blake clinched the dry-cell-operated-flashlight from the top of his desk with his right hand, and we followed him to Room 5109.

The International Wing . . . By golly.

Chapter Thirty-Six

IT WAS NEARLY noon when we arrived at Room 5109. We had to walk by Room 5114. Upon our passing, I observed Perry picking up step and stealing a quick glance at the door of Room 5114. Why? I thought.

I was a few steps behind Perry. As I passed Room 5114, I had studied the same location as Perry had. But there wasn't anything of interest . . . To me anyway. Nothing there that impressed me. Nothing. But complete darkness.

Blake said, as we approached Room 5109, "If this is your room, Perry, I must assume you have a key. Right?" He looked at Perry expecting him to say *no* or something like; *"I lost it."* But to Blake's surprise, Perry displayed the plastic room key, slid it into its slot, and quickly pulled it up and out.

The green light glowed against the darkened hallway on the lock mechan-ism, indicating the key unlocked the door to Room 5109. Mrs. Johnston's room? Questionable at this point.

Gently, Perry pushed the door handle downward and the door opened.

Another surprise . . . A happily plumped woman in a cotton bathrobe, don-ned in pink curlers and pink slippers, 'Eeeked' with fright.

"Sorry, Mrs. Johnston, wrong room." Blake said, closing the door.

The housekeeper's cleaning cart was still parked near Room 5109. Just resting there against the off-white hallway wall. I'd remembered seeing the clothed-material cart last-night. Could it belong to Juanita Alverez?

Blake had his mouth half opened, as if he was about to say something. He suddenly closed it. Then, he turned around and faced the door to 5109. And knocked. Tapping three times. "Security." He announced.

The door opened slightly from the door frame with the security bar still a-ttached to the inside of the Mahogany door. Through the crack of the door, all we could see of Mrs. Johnston was a rounded face covered in facial cream and two pink curlers on each side of her gray hair.

"Sorry to bother you again, ma'am. But this man claims this room is his for a week." Blake pulled Perry into view so Mrs. Johnston could scrutinize the bastard. "Do you recognize him, ma'am?"

"No, Sir. Never seen him before in my entire life." She shook her head so rapidly I thought she might spray everything: wall-to-door-to-us with her fa-cial cream.

"Thank you, ma'am," Blake said softly. "Sorry to have bothered you."

She closed the door gently until the lock mechanism clicked into place.

Turning to Perry, Blake slammed him against the hallway wall.

"Okay, Perry . . ." He pushed Perry against the wall again near the house-keepers cart, resting his hand, arm extended, up against the wall, obstructing any attempt of Perry's escape. Hank stood on Perry's right side, while Scott stood on his left. I stood behind Blake and scanned the dark hallway.

The light of the flashlight was on Mr. Madass's bony and bruised face, causing his facial structure to protrude. Spooky. Further down the long hall-way were two exit signs above the stairwells, which gave us some lighting. But too dim to see anything.

Perry's head bounced off the wall, as Blake released Perry's slick black hair from his clinched fist.

"Talk, Mr. Madass . . . ." Blake pronounced Perry's last name as it was spelled.

"It's MUH-DAZ," Perry bellowed. "My name is pronounced . . . Muhdaz."

"Whatever. I what the fucking truth, Mr. Mu . . . Mu . . . uh . . . Awe, forget it."

Blake waved his hand in the air.

"Whatever, Perry. I want the truth. The pass key. Where did you get Mrs. Johnston's pass key from?" Blake's fist was clinched tight, and shaped like a sledge hammer.

"The front desk. A week ago." Perry's Adam's Apple went up and down several times. Hard.

"You lying sack a' shit." Hank said, gazing in Mr.Madass's dark eyes.

Still remaining silent, Scott just leaned against the wall, but ready for action.

Suddenly, the generator came to life and hummed again. The hall lights blasted with brightness. It took a few minutes for our eyes to adjust to the sudden rays of light. Perry stole the chance to escape. Stupid man. With no time wasted, Blake clinched his fist around Mr. Madass's collar, and pinned him against the wall again, handcuffing him yet again. Hands behind his back.

"Blake," I said, pointing to the cleaning cart. "Do you think this belongs to Juanita?"

"It might. Wasn't the cart parked here last night, Nick?"

"Yep."

In the background, from the stairwell, we'd heard male voices speaking softly. Within minutes, several security officers who were searching for Alv-erez, appeared around the corner near Room 5110.

"Anything, guys?" Blake asked.

"Not yet. Nothing. Na'da. But this is our last floor, Blake. We searched everywhere, but here." A short, five-five, my guess, male with healthy thick groomed blond hair, donned in a blue Blazier and gray dress slacks, leaned against the corner of the hallway near Room 5110. Arms folded across his burly chest.

The other two security officers were dressed identical to Security Officer Blondie, leaning against the banister.

"Okay, Joe. We checked this room already," Blake said, pointing over his shoulder toward Room 5109.

Joe said, still leaning against the corner wall. "Then we have only these three rooms to attend to. Right, Blake?"

Nodding, Blake said, "Yeah. Rooms 5110, 5112, and 5114. Did you find any trace of the rare coins, Joe?"

Shaking his head, once to the left, and once to the right . . ."Nope. And if we *do not* find Miss Alverez and the coins up here on this floor, we are S-O-L."

We all nodded, agreeably. Except Mr. Perry Madass.

Chapter Thirty-Seven

THE TORNADO CLEAN-UP was on its last phase. The vehicles in the parking lot of the hotel that were damaged were towed away. The fallen trees and branches were sawed, scooped up, and hauled away.

The utility lines were re-connected. And the clean-up of the hotel's park-ing lot laid heavily on the hotel's maintenance crew's to-do-list.

The time: Two-sixteen P.M . . . . Friday afternoon.

Clint, Lisa, Eagle and Pam Neuman found me standing inside the Room 5110 with Blake and his security team, as they searched the 12x12 for the rare coins.

And, of course, Juanita Alverez.

Clint had told me the bad news.

"My Ford SUV was massively damaged. It'll take a week . . . uh . . . maybe two weeks before CarStar will be able to repair it. But the good news, they'll give me a loaner for as long as I need it."

"Great, Clint. But how are you able to get the loaner?" I said, as we step-ped out of the room into the hallway.

"No problem. They're going to drop it off here today or tomorrow."

"That's just great, buddy. But just in case CarStar drops off a compact, I will be renting a car of my own. With my long legs, I'll probably need all the space I can get."

"That's fine, Nick. Just bill it to our agency."

I nodded, then, turned to Lisa. "How are you doing with all that had been happening, honey?"

"Okay, I guess. I just might have to forget about that awful bartender who works Down-Under, whatever his name is. You know, Nick, I truly believe his name is *Not* Salmeno. I know that pig from somewhere. I just cannot, for the life of me, figure it out. I have other important issues I have to con-tend with, anyway."

"Yeah. I know you do." I said, hugging her tightly against my chest.

"You do know, don't you." We hugged, as if there were no tomorrow.

"BLAKE! BLAKE!" A male voice bellowed with excitement. "I think I found something of interest."

Blake side-stepped and kneeled down between two doubled-beds next to the male screamer, rummaging through a large plastic bag.

"Who do you think owns these clothes, Blake?"

Blake peeked over from the edge of the bed and noticed Lisa and me hug- ging in the doorway of Room 5110.

"Nick, Lisa, come here."

We released ourselves from each other, and knelt next to Blake in hidden view. Scott and Hank held Perry at bay near the mahogany desk. Perry strug- gled to get away. But Hank and Scott would not allow such a thing.

Blake laid the clothes neatly and evenly on the sapphire carpet. The in-ventory had begun. (1silk-gray tie . . . 1 buttoned down white shirt from a well known store, and 1 white crew-neck T-shirt). But the gray tie, white button down shirt, and the T-shirt had an additional color to it. Not bright red . . . Not blood red, but a rusted-copper color, which appeared to be dried blood. The substance was splattered throughout the shirts and tie.

Blake peeked over the edge of the bed again and stared angrily at Perry.

"Is this your room, Mr. Madass?"

"No . . . No . . . No. Across the hall . . . That's my room, uh, 5109. My room is 5109 . . . 5109 . . . You hear me. Not this room." Perry was squirming wildly. It seemed to me Mr. Perry Madass was in the midst of a nervous breakdown.

He was fighting like a girl, kicking at Scott and Hank aimlessly. He could not do too much damage. The handcuffs were probably doing more damage to Perry's wrists than afflicting pain to Scott and Hank. Hank then tackled Mr. Madass to the floor and sat on his buttocks.

While Blake and Lisa and one of the security officers were involved with the bloody clothing I decided to do my own investigation. I asked Perry pol-itely where he had got-ten the pass key to Room 5109. Of course, he lied to me, which I expected out of him.

Then I'd asked Hank to search Perry's pockets for the pass key to 5109.

Hank looked up at me, as if I told him there wasn't a Santa Claus. Hank had looked over toward Blake. Blake nodded, but with a doubtful expression.

Hank obeyed Blake's gesture. He found the pass key in Perry's left coat pocket and handed it to me. I thanked him, smilingly. Hank shrugged and continued to sit on Perry's backside, while Scott filed his fingernails yet a-gain. I walked out into the hallway, shut-ting the door behind me, locking it.

I turned, faced 5110's door, inserted Pass Key 5109 Hank had given me from Perry's coat pocket, into its lock mechanism, then pulled it up and out.

I was surprised . . . no, not surprised, but relieved. My intuition, gut feeling, and de-tective wit were still operating at top level.

After the glow from the small green dot shot into my eyes from the heavy silvery lock mechanism, indicating its lock release, I pushed downward on the horizontal handle, and the door opened wide with five pair of shocking eyes gawking at me. It would've been six shocking eyes gawking at me, but

Mr. Perry Madass was too busy kissing the sapphire-colored carpeting.

"Blake," I said, smiling, "You have your man." My eyes pointing toward

Perry's sprawled-out body. "Do what you want with him."

"What about Miss Juanita Alverez?" Blake said.

All eyes were on me now, as I walked and bent down next to Blake, han-ding him the pass key.

"Turn it over, Blake," I said. "You'll see writing on it. It's blurred. You can make it out, can't you?"

He turned it over, studied the writing carefully, and nodded.

"Yes, Nick. I can make it out just perfectly." Blake stood and casually strolled toward Perry's stretched-out scrawny body, knelt down beside him.

And without saying a word, Blake went into Perry's rear pants pocket, and clinched on his thick, alligator-woven wallet. Opening the wallet, Blake thu-mbed through it, and there he found another pass-key. He slid it out, then, threw the wallet next to Perry's swollen face. He walked out of the room, turning left. He stopped one room over, faced Room 5112. He slid the plastic pass key into its heavy lock mechanism, and pulled it out. No green light. Nothing.

But between the walls, we'd heard voices yelling. "Who's there . . ." Who is there . . . . . . ? What do you want?"

We also heard Blake's voice, calmly saying: "Sorry. I'm with the hotel security. I am just testing your door lock. It seems to be working just fine. I am sorry to had bothered you."

Blake continued to the next room. The very last room. Which was 5114.

He did the same motion like the last room. But this time, the green light appeared brightly. By this time, Lisa, Hank, Scott, the screaming male, two other security officers, Clint, Eagle and Pam Neuman and myself were semi-circled in the hallway between rooms 5110 and 5114. We probably had looked like the 'Welcoming Committee'.

The door to Room 5114 was pushed open with Blake's pointed black boot. He went in and was swallowed up within the 12x12 sized guest-room.

The semi-circled bunch moved in closer, but couldn't see squat. Na'da.

Lisa and I were in the lead of the crowd, so Lisa and I took advantage of the situation and allowed ourselves in.

Suddenly a loud, squeaking voice appeared from Room 5110. It was Mr.

Perry Madass. "Oh . . . no . . . Oh . . . no . . . no . . . no." His yell turned into weeping.

Like a little boy whose toy was taken away. We ignored the boyish sound.

Lisa and I continued to approach Room 5114. I peeked into the room be- fore Lisa. She stood partially bent over my right shoulder to take a peek her-self. But I didn't en-courage it. Nick Edwards, the protector.

I realize I shouldn't be protective, or overly-protective of Lisa. Well, after all, she is a detective. And we do crime scenes, such as this one. But I still did not want her to see what was lying on the hotel bed, while I was with her anyway.

The bullet hole in the corpse's forehead was extremely clean. The exit wound was not as clean. Needless to say, it was messy. The hand grip to the Smith & Wesson, .38Cal, laid loosely in the victims right hand.

Suicide . . . ? Maybe . . . Maybe not.

Lisa looked down near her right foot. She kneeled and picked up a black frame, which appeared to be from a pair of eyeglasses. Her right foot moved slightly on the carpet. Then, the crunch of broken glass . . . Lens to be exact.

Was Lisa and Blake thinking what I was thinking . . . ?

Things do not always appear as they seem . . . Now, do they?

Hank returned to 5110 and looked down at Perry's rolling tears. Which was soaked into the sapphire carpet. Perry tried to look up at Hank, but it was too difficult. Being on your stomach, well, let's just say, it wasn't easy.

"Guess what we found in your room, Perry?" Hank said. "And it isn't very pretty, either."

"I keep telling you guys my room number is 5109. Why don't you be-lieve me? Huh?"

"Okay, Mr. Madass. I don't have time to argue with you. I'll leave that up to the local officials. Now, don't go anywhere. Are you comfy?" Hank said, as he exited the room. Perry just squirmed and rattled the handcuffs.

Chapter Thirty-Eight

ENTERING ROOM 5114, Scott carried a soft black velvet bag with white en-twined cords. The drawstrings were tightly shut and the bag hanging loosely in his right hand.

Everyone in the room eyed Scott in wonder, except Blake. He was lean-ing over the corpse, trying not to touch anything. Scott came to a halt along

Blake's right side, dangling the black velvet bag in front of Blake's curious eyes.

"What do we have here, Scott?" Blake said, as he was setting the phone piece back into its cradle.

"See for yourself." Scott handed the mysterious bag to Blake gently.

Blake, then walked a few feet to the matching double-bed, which was near the un-draped window, opening the velvet material carefully. Blake sat sideways on the corner of the bed. He tilted and shook the bag carefully until the last item laid comfortably on the floral bedspread.

The bag was heavy before, now Blake new why.

The rare coins had dated back to the 1700's. They were protected with heavy oak-wood frames, and a thick window-glass, and wrapped in durable plastic. There must've been over a dozen coins of history here. I thought. To be sure the bag was empty, Blake shook it yet again. A clear plastic bag slid out and revealed two pure white soft gloves. Used for handling, I pre-sumed.

Looking up at Scott, Blake asked, "Where did you find these?"

"Would you believe right under our noses," Scott grinned.

"Where?" Hank asked.

"In the housekeepers cleaning cart. Right outside of Room 5109. It was buried under-neath all the sheets and pillowcases."

"Fine work. Job well done." Hank patted Scott on his right shoulder, and smiled widely. "Blake had called the police, so they will be here very soon. I suggest we exit this room before we contaminate anymore evidence."

We all agreed. And walked out single file.

Blake had posted several security officers in front of Room 5110 and 5114, protecting the crime scene until the MPD and Homicide Detectives ar-rived.

Blake, Scott and Hank strolled with Madass, who was still handcuffed, to the security office. He was heavily guarded until the police came and off-ically arrested him.

Chapter Thirty-Nine

TIME WAS FIVE-TWENTY-THREE P.M. Friday afternoon. March 10th 1997.
Blake and his security officers accompanied the police, the detectives, and the coroner. The police photographers were taking pictures of Room's 5110 and 5114. The Forensics was busy dusting for fingerprints. The media was encouraged to wait outside or wait downstairs in the lobby. They chose the lobby. Warmer.

Blake and Homicide Detective Aldrich stood outside of Room 5114, Mr. Perry Madass's room, discussing the incident.

"Are you sure this wasn't a simple suicide?" Blake asked.

"The look of things," Aldrich gazed into the room, "I do not think so."

"What's the evidence?" Blake asked.

"The angle of the wound. Very little evidence of powder burns on her forehead. That tells me the gun was fired from a distance. Not too close to her head. Also we found a letter opener on the carpet near the corner of the night stand with blood splatter. I wouldn't be surprised if we find her finger-prints on it, which will, of course, tell me she was trying to defend herself. The Forensics found a spent round in a picture painting above the bed we'd found her on. It matches the .38S&W. It would be my guess the gun will be registered to a Mr. Perry Madass."

Blake thought deeply, staring up at the ceiling.

"What?" Aldrich said.

"Well. That just about explains everything, Detective. I think you have your man. Good luck."

Detective Aldrich took a few steps, then, turned. "Blake . . . Madass . . . what kind of name is that anyway?"

"A weird one. But it's pronounced MUH-DAZ."

Aldrich chuckled silently. Then he said, "Okay, Blake. We'll take it from here. By the way, where is the prisoner?"

"In the security office, downstairs, handcuffed. I'll take you to him."

Blake and Det. Aldrich went downstairs leaving behind his two security officers guarding the two rooms.

Kim was serving drinks to all the concerned at Down-Under.

"The first round is on me." Kim said. "I want to thank you all for your support and honesty. If it wasn't for Blake, Lisa, Clint, Eagle and his wife Pam, and of course my special friend Nick, I wouldn't have gotten my rare coins back. But, please . . . please, let's not forget another friend and co-work-er Juanita Alverez. We are all saddened by her needless death.

"May Perry Madass rot in *HELL* forever. Raise your glasses ladies and gentlemen." Kim said, as tears streamed her cheeks.

We did

I yelled, "SALUTE"!

After partying all night, Friday night, Lisa, Clint, Eagle and Pam Neuman and I decided to stay until Sunday, March 12th. We needed a good-night rest.

Saturday was the day to recuperate.

I felt guilty partying Friday night, being the fact Juanita Alverez was murdered. But everybody else was having a good time *who knew her*. So.

Since I didn't know her at all, why did I feel so guilty? I couldn't answer the question honestly. So I partied with them. Did I have fun? Maybe. I was too intoxicated to remember.

The hotel's ballroom and Baton Rouge Hall was nothing but a big dark hole. Debris of bricks and brick dust. Diamonds of broken glass had glittered in the dawn of light. Steel frame doors, hanging from hinges, were swinging in the cool breeze. Water-soaked carpet and interior walls were all that re-mained.

Wedding plans cancelled. Saint Patrick's Day party ripped from the res-ervations book. Hopes of memories shattered.

I guess it's true. 'It's *not nice* to fool Mother Nature.'

But Mother Nature had sure fooled us.

Who would ever think a tornado would ever sweep through the City of Milwaukee.

As I was thinking about that, a tornado touched down nearly thirty years ago near this same area. But the damage wasn't so excessive.

Thank God.

Chapter Forty

CLINT'S LOANER FROM CarStar arrived Saturday, just as I figured. A Com-pact. So, as planned, I rented myself a luxurious Ford Marquis. Roomy.

We said our good-byes to everyone. Shook hands and took in hugs, as well. Some kisses, too. We were on the road by ten A.M., Sunday morning.

Needless to say, because of the inconvenience and the disaster, our rooms were paid for by the Grand Milwaukee Hotel. Included were our meals and drinks. It seemed to be a vacation. It was anything but . . .

Clint, Eagle and Pam Nueman led the way to Chicago in his Compact Honda CX. We turned right leaving the hotel, headed south on Howell Ave-nue. Then, we turned right again at the next stoplight near Super-8 motel on Grange Avenue and veered left to I-94. The large green rectangle sign stated

TO: CHICAGO. We veered and changed lanes merging with Sunday's traf-fic. Which was very light and maneuverable.

Yesterday, Clint had made reservations at the Holiday Inn, in Downtown Chicago. Two rooms and five people. Umm. I wondered how that was going to work. I was hoping Eagle and his wife Pam would share the room with Clint. I might sound selfish when I say this, but Lisa and I hadn't made love in several days. We need to be alone. Being what she had been through, I had still hoped she would be in the mood. It was doubtful, but I remained hopeful.

The Milwaukee Journal's Sunday paper had been read this morning by Lisa and me. Perry Madass had told police he was innocent. The only thing he confessed to was the fling with Juanita Alverez for the week during his stay at the hotel. But he did not kill her, or steal the rare coins.

Perry stated he was a professional appraiser of rare coins, and he would not do such a thing, especially steal from his own clients.

But the evidence against Mr. Perry Madass didn't look promising. Not-hing was in his favor.

≫ ≪

We were only twenty minutes out of Milwaukee and passing through Oak Creek Township. Upon our passing, on our right side of the 'I', American Appliance store of Oak Creek were flashing their marquee brightly. 'SEVEN DAY SALE . . . COMPUTERS . . . T.V.'S . . . RANGES . . . REFRIGERATORS'.

Yeah . . . Right. I'll buy ten of them tomorrow.

Lisa and I sat quiet for those twenty minutes. Just after we had passed the appliance store's advertisement, Lisa questioned the stolen coins.

"Who do you think stole the coins, honey?" Lisa said, looking straight a-head.

"I really don't know, sweets. Who do you think?" I drummed the steering wheel with my fingers.

"Perry could be fabricating to the police."

"Even the fling with Miss Alverez?" I kept my eyes forward.

"Sure," Lisa said positively. "This is only a theory, but it's possible, espe-cially after speaking with Belle."

"Oh." I said.

"Yeah. She told me she was heading back toward Harold's Lounge when the lights went out. When she was in the hallway she said she was pushed hard and almost causing her to fall down. But she had regained her balance.

"The person who'd pushed her had to be a big woman, or a strong man. I believe she had told me, after she had regained her balance, another person had shoved her, again, causing her to lose her balance. Belle was positive it was a woman with foreign accent."

"What did the foreign woman say?" I asked.

"The foreign voice apologized and had asked if Belle was alright. Belle truly believes it was Juanita Alverez. The sounds of it, to me anyway, Miss Alverez probably was chasing the person who had stolen the coins, and she tried to stop him."

"Meaning Perry, our boy." I said glancing over at Lisa.

"Yep." Lisa finally looked up at me. "I also believe Perry went to his room, 5114, which was only two minutes . . . tops, from Down-Under Lounge.

Perry shut the door and tried to hide the coins somewhere in his room. Are you with me, Nick?"

"Um..Um..Yep."

"Okay. But Juanita, being a close friend of Kim's, was not going a locked door stop her. She took out her master pass-key . . . Being a housekeeper, she had to have one, obviously. So she pulled out her pass-key, slid the plastic key into the lock, pulled it out quickly, green light comes on . . . She's in. Perry becomes startled. I have to assume he was toting a weapon, in this case, a .38S&W".

"What makes you assume that, Lisa?"

"Well, I'm sure he carries a lot of money on him. And if not money, a lot of valuable coins. Right?"

I nodded.

"Al-right-ty, then. He had to protect himself and his valuables. So, there-fore, he was toting a weapon. I'm getting off track here, but Kim told me a- nother coin appraiser quoted her 5,000 dollars for her rare coins. But Kim believed the coins were worth more than that. So Kim needed a second opinion.

"Coincidently, Perry was staying in the International Wing for a Foreign

Coin Convention. Sometime throughout his stay, Kim must had strike up a conversation with Mr. Madass pertaining to her coins."

"Honey," I said, "I think I know where you are going with this."

"You do, do ya', Mr. Smarty pants. But if you do know where I'm going with this, and you finish my theory, don't forget I still own it."

"Okay. It's a deal," I smiled. "Things just got out of hand and Juanita had threatened Perry she was going to report him to security or just tell Kim he had her coins. He pulls out a gun from somewhere, maybe the desk drawer, and shoots her point-blank. He panics. Then takes her master key, changes his shirt, undershirt and tie, finds a room empty using the master key to let himself in, which was Room 5110, and hides his clothing in a bag, and tosses them underneath the bed.

"But what I can't figure out, why not hide the coins in the same room with his bloody clothes." I said, focusing on the highway.

"Don't you see, Nick. Perry hid the coins in Juanta's cleaning cart to make it look like she stole the coins."

"Great theory, sweets," Patting her on her left knee, I winked at her. "I like it, but can we prove it?"

"Nope. We can't." Lisa said. She refocused on the windshield, eyes front, facing the rear of Clint's Honda. "And corpse's don't talk."

I nodded. Still on I-94 toward Chicago, I was thinking how much fun I had planned to have with Lisa and the gang at the Grand Milwaukee Hotel.

Damn.

Chapter Forty-One

WE WERE QUIET for a time taking in the scenery. Today was slightly warm-er that yesterday. The temperature was hitting fifty-five degrees, sun peeking through the edge of some thick cloud, and the majority of blue sky was seen for miles. Very pleasant.

Traffic flowed freely, as we drove in the far right lane.

We were into our travels about an hour now when Lisa jerked her pretty little head at me. She was pale-faced with trembling lips.

"Nick. Turn the car around and go back to Milwaukee. Quickly . . . Hurry."

I glanced at Lisa. My jaw hanging downward, and eyes bulging. Almost ready to pop out. "Why? What's wrong?"

"DO IT!," She bellowed. "I'll explain later."

As I searched the next exit to turn around, Lisa was on her cell phone cal-ling Clint. I noticed Clint's break-lights glowing readily. Lisa told Clint to continue to Chicago . . . We'll catch up to you later . . . Don't know how much later, but we'll be there. Clint's break-lights went off and sped forward. Lisa clicked the 'OFF' button on her cell phone. Phone went silent.

We found an exit, Russell Road, not to far from Wisconsin/Illinois State-line. We turned around heading back to Milwaukee, '94' North/Northwest.

The time nearing 11:40 A.M., when we'd crossed over into Wisconsin.

The big brown wooden sign on the roadside had words chiseled artistic-ally. It read: 'WELCOME TO WISCONSIN' . . . But in our case, the sign should have read: 'WELCOME BACK TO WISCONSIN . . . MISSED US . . . HUH?'

➤ ◄

As we passed Kenosha's exit, Lisa breathed in a lot of air. Exhaled calm-ly. Her pinkish facial color returned slowly.

"I remember who he is, Nick. I remember. Thank God."

She rummaged through her black leather purse and pulled out a small art- icle clip-ping from some old newspaper. The article wasn't fresh. Yellowish stains and torn edges had accompanied it.

"Remember who?" I said.

"Salmeno. I have an article of him from 1985 when he and his big brother Ruby was being released from prison. It's been twelve years ago this month since their release. Matter of fact, this Wednesday coming up will be their twelfth year anniversary of being freed from Joliet Prison."

I thought about that for a minute or so.

"That'll be the fifteenth. Three days from now." I said, my eyes still fo-cused on the 'I'.

"Un-uh. That's correct. I sure would like to find out why he is in Wiscon-sin. Better yet, what the hell he's doing in Milwaukee?" Lisa said.

I wasn't paying any mind to my speed, 'til Lisa brought it to my atten-tion.

"We're in a hurry, Nick, but you need to slow down. You're driving way too fast." She leaned over to her left, eyeing the speedometer. "Ninety miles an hour! Jeez. Slow down."

"Oops." I quickly glanced in my rear view mirror for any State Troopers. I didn't see any. Whew. I slowly lifted my right foot from the gas pedal until the needle came down to sixty miles an hour.

I said, "Didn't you tell me earlier this Salmeno guy's name was Bales-teri?"

"I did. And it is Balesteri. He must be working at the hotel under assumed name. His real name is Rudy Balesteri."

"I wonder where his brother Ruby is hiding out at." I said.

"Good question, Tex. Very good question."

"Chicago?"

"Maybe. Maybe not."

We drove some distance in silence, as Lisa continued to study the article and photo-shot of Rudy. In the photo Rudy had a scar on his left side of his face identical to 'Salmeno'. His eyes were also hollow, zombie-like, as 'Salmeno'.

The age of Rudy's photo was twelve years young. In the photo his hair was totally jet black. His age ranged from early to mid-thirties. The photo was snapped in black and white. But it was him. Positively. Now, in reality, he's slightly heavier and gray pushing through his jet black hair.

I wanted to stomp on the accelerator and hit 100 miles an hour, but Rudy wasn't worth a ticket, or a terrific collision. So I played it smart and safe. I maintained speed of sixty mph.

Lisa clinched and pulled her cell-phone from her purse again. Punched in Clint's number.

"Clint, Lisa. When you arrive in Chicago look up a Sergeant Peter Dill-man, District Five. Ask him to start searching for anything on Ruby and Rudy Balesteri . . . Any rap-sheet that might go back as far as 1985. That was the year they were released from prison. The date; March 15th, 1985, to be exact."

"Okay. Sure. But, what's going on? You didn't explain anything earlier."

"Yeah. I know. Sorry. I just realized who that man was who was bartend-ing at Down-Under."

"Yeah. Who?" The cell phone began to crackle with static.

"Can you hear me, Clint?" Lisa said, frowning.

"Yeah. But barely. Go ahead."

"Rudy Balesteri, he's in Milwaukee, and it smells like trouble. I, I mean, Nick and I want him. We're going after him and get to the bottom of things, such as, my parents death. And why he murdered them."

"Do you truly believe Balesteri's killed your parents?" Clint said.

"Damn straight, Clint. You better believe they did. I want them dead. Just like the way my parents died." Lisa face became very tight and red.

"Easy, Lisa. Easy. We just can't blow them up."

"You want to make a bet, Clint." But, before Clint responded, Lisa clicked the 'OFF' button.

I just looked at Lisa, and sucked in a lot of air. Suddenly, the cell phone rang. It rang a few more rings before Lisa decided to answer it. She probably knew it was Clint.

"Yeah." Lisa said.

"Let me talk to Nick. NOW!"

"Clint wants to talk to you, Nick." She handed me the phone.

"Nick, here."

"Damn it, Nick. Talk some sense into her . . . Okay?"

"Sure."

Click.

I could use a cigarette and a keg of beer right about now. I thought.

Turning to Lisa, I said, "Lisa, I never, ever, seen you like this before. You be all right?"

"Yeah, I'll be just fantastic when Rudy and Ruby are six feet under. And I'll be dancing on their graves. Yes. Yes, then I'll be all right."

Lisa lit two cigarettes. I hoped one was for me. It was. Now, the keg of beer.

I gave Lisa my fine grin and tapped her on her left knee with my right hand. Silence set in yet again.

Sometimes silence is good for the soul. Meaning, Lisa and I. We can just sit for hours and feel each others emotions and thoughts. Kinda' scary . . . but nice.

But I got used to it . . . Lisa did, too.

Chapter Forty-Two

WE ARRIVED AT the Grand Milwaukee Hotel at one P.M. Lisa and I weren't too sure if we should check-in and get a room or wait to see how the day went. This might take a day. Then, again, maybe not. We let that thought lin-ger in the air.

Lisa stood near the sliding doors, while I walked over to the front desk. A woman and a man from the other side of the front desk, both tall with brown hair, and both had the young look, were conversing deeply among them-selves when I had approached the desk. They both ignored my appearance. I wondered if I was invisible. Two, maybe three minutes had elapsed when they finally realized I was there pulling funny faces. They looked up at me, as my smile faded into a straight line across my lips.

Finally the brown-haired woman walked away from her co-worker. I was face to face looking at a warm smile she had given me. A smile practiced in time.

"Yes. May I help you?" She fluttered her brown eyes at me. Luckily for the woman, who seemed to be flirting with me, that Lisa's back was toward us. The temperament Lisa had at this particular moment, and if she had seen flirting from this woman, I would have bet my life that Lisa would have put the desk clerk into the floor.

"Yes, ma'am. This is very urgent. I need to speak to Blake in security as soon as possible."

"Sorry, sir. But Blake worked a lot of hours the last couple of days. So he went home already. Poor man. He was so exhausted from the tornado incid-ent and some investiga-tion he was working on."

"Yes, ma'am, I know. I was aiding him in the investigation." I said.

"Oh. And who are you?"

"My name is Nick Edwards. A private investigator. And that woman over there smoking a cigarette," I nodded toward the sliding door. "she's also a PI. If we are unable to get hold of Blake, maybe we have more luck speaking with Hank or Scott. Are they available?"

"Well, no, not hardly, sir. You see, security normally works the night shift. But I could call maintenance. Sometimes they do security when need-ed."

"I guess. But Blake is the person I *really* need to speak with. But, if main-tenance is it, I guess I'll talk to whoever you have available in that depart-ment."

She nodded with a flirtatious smile. She picked up the phone and dialed three or four numbers. Then, she dialed seven other numbers. Dialing the maintenance pager, I pre-sumed. She set the phone gently into its cradle. She had glanced at me with that elegant smile again, but didn't flutter her dark eyelashes. My guess, she didn't want two black eyes.

"We'll just wait for him to answer my page, sir. You may have a seat, if you like." She pointed toward a loveseat facing a non-burning fireplace.

"No, thank-you. I'll stand over there by my partner."

She nodded agreeably. "Okay. Fine." Then she turned toward a male guest who just approached her as I was strolling toward Lisa.

Lisa and I stood near the automatic sliding glass doors inside the lobby and lit our cigarettes.

The time was slipping away. It seemed for a long while, but in reality it was only ten minutes before a man in a light striped-blue shirt and navy work pants approached the front desk. His name was Robert Johnson.

The elegant smiled-woman spoke to him softly. Then her eyes met Lisa's and mine. Robert followed her eyes. He nodded and stepped away from the desk slapping it a few times, as if he needed a sudden push toward us. He came up to us and smiled gracefully.

"My name is Robert. I'm with the Hotel Maintenance Team."

"I'm happy for you, Robert." He gave me a not-so-happy look. But he didn't say anything.

I introduced Lisa and myself.

"Want to step outside so we can talk." Robert said.

"Sure." Lisa and I nodded. We stepped out and away from people traffic.

Robert lit a non-filtered cigarette . . . inhaled . . . exhaled slowly letting the gray smoke stream from his nostrils expertly.

What's his next trick, I thought.

"What's up, Nick and Lisa?" Robert let his cigarette hang from the left side of his lip. From the wind, some smoke blew in his nose. He took in a deep breath, and choked. Lisa and I smiled silently.

I said, "Were you here during the tornado?"

Robert said, "Hell, no. Thank God. I had several days off. My first day back."

"Then you probably don't know anything about what's been happening as of late." I said.

"Like what?" Robert said. Lisa stepped in and took off her dark sunglass-ses and gazed in Robert's eyes.

Lisa said, "You have a man working here who is a felon. We saw him working down-stairs bartending several nights ago. His name is Rudy Balest-eri. The name he's using here is Mr. Salmeno. So, Mr. Robert..uh . . ."

"Johnson. Robert Johnson." Robert added.

"So, Mr. Robert Johnson, what do you know about this?"

"Salmeno. Yes. Yes, Phil or Philip. He prefers Phil, though. A felon you say. I do not think so. I am positive the CEO would have caught that during his background check. You have to have a very clean record to work here. I should know. Before I was hired I had a misdemeanor. A DUI. And that was it. I almost didn't get hired for that reason. But the CEO's decision was wav-ered."

"I'm happy for you, again, Robert." I said. If Robert heard me, he didn't let on.

Lisa said. "Who is your CEO?"

Robert hesitated for a moment. "Why? I do not want to seem uncoopera-tive, but I don't see the point giving out his name to you."

"It's important. Either you tell us, or we just have to use other means. You'll be saving us a lot of time if you tell us." Lisa gave Robert a hard long hard stare.

Robert thought a few moments longer. But he softened.

"Okay. His name is Mr. Masano. And if he isn't available, his assistant, Tonya will be happy to assist."

"Masano's first name." I said.

"Elvis. Elvis Masano." Robert's expression tightened. Any wrinkles he had on his face, disappeared.

"Tonya's last name." Lisa said.

"I rather not reveal hers. If Elvis wants to inform you of her name, so be it."

"Are they available now?" Lisa asked.

"No. They're both in a meeting."

"How long?" I said.

Looking at his Mickey Mouse watch, Robert said, "Four o' clock." He took in a long pull from his non-filtered cigarette and blew the bluish smoke into the cool air. " I got to get back to work. Anything else?" Robert said.

"Yeah. Where is Mr. Masano's office?" Lisa asked.

"Why?"

Lisa and I just stared at him, aggressively. No need to answer his ques-tion. Just stared.

"Okay. Okay. Around the corner from the front desk, straight down the hallway. You can't miss it. On the door it'll say *CHIEF EXECUTIVE OF-FICER*."

"Thanks." Lisa and I said.

"Sure. Good luck." We shook hands. Then, departed.

I turned to Lisa. "This might be more difficult than we'd thought, honey."

"Yeah. Let's get a room." She smiled lovingly.

"My thoughts exactly." I smiled agreeably.

Chapter Forty-Three

AFTER LISA AND I checked into our room in the 'Travelers' section of the hotel, we showered together, then made love madly. She's a tigress, and I am loving it . Making love to Lisa is the most breathtaking experience I had ever had. Her soft silky hands and fingers were a natural. When she touches me . . . WOW! Her lips are sweeter than wine. And when she looks at me with her bedroom blue eyes, her sensual observation of my body, it reaches deep into my soul. IT IS PARADISE.

We showered again, but separately. If we had showered together, again, we'll never get any work done.

The time was 3:12 P.M. Lisa and I dried, dressed and went downstairs to Harold's Lounge. The hammering, drilling, and the sounds of electric saws were heard as we approached the lobby to Harold's.

The carpenters were in the process boarding up the damaged section from the evil tornado. The thick layers of plywood divided the Grand Ballroom, which wasn't a ballroom any longer, from Harold's Lounge. So, the lounge was still open to the public. How nice.

As we walked through the archway into Harold's beautiful setting, Lisa and I were in awe. Exquisite, hardwood tables and booths. A two-tone Pers-ian rug with red border and light gray in the center that covered the entire flooring. Crystal Chandelier hanging evenly and centered, brightening up the establishment. The damaging tornado didn't seem to have any effect in here.

Amazing.

Bob the bartender was leaning against the wine storage cabinets as we approached the bar. He was looking at nothing. Business was extremely slow. Naturally and obviously. The post-tornado had kept guests inside their rooms, and outsiders away.

When we climbed onto our stools, Bob had this surprise expression. A happy sort of face.

"Well, well. Welcome back. Or didn't you guys leave yet?"

"Yeah, Bob. We left this morning," I said, "But something came up. So here we are again."

He nodded, expressionless.

"See you weathered the storm, huh, Bob?" Lisa said.

"Boy. I say. I was glad I left when I did Thursday night. What are two you having?"

Lisa ordered a glass of red wine.

"You, Nick?" Bob asked.

"A bottle of MGD with a tall glass." I said.

Bob went and came back and set the drinks in front of us expertly. As always.

I sipped my beer from my glass. As I did so, I'd noticed Bob was flirting with my girl-friend Lisa. I think he liked her. He wasn't bashful.

Lisa sipped her wine slowly. Bob leaned against the wine cabinet again. It was directly across from us. Close enough where we could converse.

"Bob. Do you know a Phil Salmeno?" I asked.

Lisa took the clipping from her purse and showed it to Bob.

"Yeah. I know him. He's an asshole."

Lisa and I nodded readily.

"Is he working today?" Lisa said.

"Nope. Belle will be here working 'til Monday. And Down-Under will be open on Tuesday. Down-Under is usually closed on Mondays."

"So, is Phil working Tuesday night?" Lisa asked.

"Yep. That will be the fourteenth. I believe he starts at six P.M."

Time was 4:15 P.M. Lisa and I was on our second round of drinks when we heard Bob say, "Hi, Elvis . . . Tonia." They both nodded quietly.

Elvis stood six feet and slender build. His hair was dark and short with ripple of waves. His skin was slightly on the dark side. Spanish, my guess. His profile made me think of Elvis Presley.

Elvis Masano wore a tan three piece suit with a stripped tie, white over tan. The pow-dered-blue shirt had a button-down collar with gold cuff-links pushing through the coat sleeves.

Tonia had a long dark-haired ponytail with a green rubber-band holding the hair in its place. Her black-framed glasses were thin with dark brown eyes hiding behind the lens. She was pleasant to look at. Her smile was wide with thick lips.

Her pants suit was dark in color with a white frilly blouse tucked smooth-ly around her waistline. She was medium height. Another guess, she could be Puerto Rican. She was young and bubbly.

They sat on the left of us several stools down. They both ordered coffee.

I looked at Lisa, then leaned closer to her right ear.

"Do you want to ask them about Rudy Balesteri, or should I?" I said.

"Let's both ask."

We slid off our stools and stood behind Tonia and Elvis for a few seconds as they took in some coffee. With his cup in his hand, Elvis turned around and faced Lisa.

"Yes, may I help you, ma'am?" Elvis scrutinized Lisa for a long moment.

"Yes. If I can have a minute from your busy schedule."

Tonia turned around and faced me. I was smiling at her. She returned the favor, but remained silent.

"Sure. But just for a minute."

"Thanks." Lisa said. She showed the clipping to Elvis of Rudy Balesteri.

But even before Lisa could ask her needed question, Elvis's mouth opened wide, and gazed at the photo wide-eyed. Stunned.

"Do you know this man, Mr. Masano?" Lisa asked.

Elvis sat quietly for a time, as if his mind was searching for the right words to spill from his mouth. Lisa asked the question again, just to be sure he un-derstood the ques-tion. Then, suddenly, his lips quivered some words.

"No . . . No," shaking his head several times, as if a fly was in his ear. "I do not think so. Never saw him before. Nope." Elvis returned facing the bar drinking his java. It seemed to me he was shutting down the conversation.

Tonia leaned over Elvis's back and took a gander. "Let me see the picture for a second." After ten seconds elapsed, her dark brown eyes grew to be the size of saucers. She opened her mouth slightly. Then shut it. Then she moved back onto her stool and nervously glanced at Elvis.

"Maybe we should return to the office, huh, Mr. Masano?"

"Yeah. You're right. Lots of paperwork to catch up with. He turned to Lisa with a shrewd grin.

"Sorry, ma'am we couldn't be of more help."

Looking at Tonia, she said, "So you didn't recognize him, either. Right?"

"No. Sorry."

They slid from their stools and went. Bob leaned over the bar slightly and watched them disappear around the corner of the bar's archway. He looked at us point blank.

"They're lying to both of you. They know that character. Elvis is the one who had hired Phil Salmeno."

"Thanks, Bob." We said.

He nodded. "Sure. Anytime, Nick . . . Lisa."

We paid our bill and gave Bob a five dollar tip. He smiled as we returned to our room.

Chapter Forty-Four

THE TIME WAS six P.M. Lisa and I ordered in. We called room service. While we waited for our evening meal to arrive, we snuggled on the double-sized bed and watched the 6 o' clock news.

The Channel-4 newscasters were announcing the tragedy of several series of storms and tornadoes that swept through the two states of Wisconsin and Minnesota.

There was a sixty-second shot of the Grand Milwaukee Hotel, the Heli-Cam scanned across the entire structure of the hotel and its parking lots.

"Thank God no one was killed in that furious tornado," said the anchor-man. "Since we're talking about tragedies, unfortunately, there was a death at the Grand Milwaukee Hotel, but unrelated to the tornado that had touched down Thursday night. However, there appeared to be a shooting, but details unclear at this time. But what we do know is a man named Perry Madass . . ."

Suddenly, a wide grin came over the anchormans lips. He had pronounc-ed Perry's last name incorrectly. He tried to refrain from laughing, which he succeeded from doing so. He found his composure, and continued . . . .

"The shooter confessed to the killing of a Miss Juanita Alverez. A lovers quarrel is our understanding . . ." A snap-shot appeared on screen of Juanita Alverez. Her features; long dark-hair, almost jet-black, a well-rounded face and a model of a smile with bright evenly teeth, mid-to-late twenties, and very beautiful dark brown eyes. The anchorman continued.

"She was well-liked by all of her friends and co-workers at the hotel, and very dedi-cated to her job. But most unfortunate, she was engaged to be mar-ried next month . . . How very sad . . . ." Then they went to the weather.

"What do you think of that crap, Nick?" I had my right arm under Lisa's shoulders and Lisa had her head on my chest. She didn't look up at me.

"Perry and Juanita's love affair?"

"Yeah."

"I'm sure he's lying."

"Me, too," Lisa said, nodding into my chest.

A knocked appeared on our door. It was room service. I got up and answered it.

"Hey, Greg, what's happen-en'" I said.

Greg was a jovial and smiling type-of-a-guy. He's of African-American Heritage, small in height, but built solid. Hair close to his head, and always had a smile. He had experience in bartending in several locations of the State of Wisconsin, and hotel management. Well educated, and friendly.

He walked in with a silvery cart, a two-shelf-er, with also silvery trays and a wine bucket full of ice. On the trays was our meal covered with heavy lids. As Greg lifted the heavy lids, and displayed a great steak, the steam rose with a blast of succulent aroma. Mm . . . . Yum.

Before Greg had left the room and after I'd tipped him, I asked him about the other night.

"Why did security suspect you, Greg?"

"Well, I told security I was serving food when the lights went out and I heard a noise shortly after . . ."

"What kind of noise?"

"Male and female voices yelling . . ."

"About what?"

Greg shrugged. "I don't know. The storm was too loud to hear much."

"Were you serving meals in the International Wing at that particular time, Greg?"

"Yep, Room 5112. I was in the room serving the guests when suddenly I heard a pop. The guests did to. We thought the noise was thunder, or lighten-ing. Well, anyway, after I had reported back to the kitchen, in the dark, mind you, security was waiting for me and told me I was a possible suspect. I was so flabbergasted, I wanted to punch that security officer right in the snout.

"Well, of course, I decided against that idea right quick. So I went along with being detained. You know what I'm saying, Nick?" I nodded. "Once I was taken downstairs to Down-Under, and I saw other employees being que-stioned, I didn't take it so offensively then."

"So, was that it?" I said.

"Yeah. That was enough for me." Greg hesitated before he stepped into the hallway. "What do you think of this crazy weather we've been having?"

"Craz-zy." I said, grinningly.

"You know, Nick, I'm from Alabama. And I thought Alabama had unpre-dictable weather. I love Alabama, don't get me wrong, Nick, but I feel safer here in Wisconsin. You know what I mean, Nick?"

I nodded. And Greg departed.

"Holiday Inn, Ray speaking, may I help you?"

"Yes, you may. I'm looking for Clint Douglas. Has he checked in yet?"

"Douglas?" Either Ray was hard of hearing, or he needed confirmation.

"Yes. Douglas . . . First name Clint."

"Wait a minute, sir. I'll be right back, as I will check this out for you."

"Thanks." I said.

A few minutes had elapsed. While I was waiting, I eyed Lisa lying on the double-bed with her legs stretched, legs crossed. A lot of thigh was exposed from below the seam of the hotel's white bathrobe. Her face was buried in a mystery/thriller novel. And she was very engrossed in her reading.

"Are you absorbing the beauty of my legs, horny, ah, I mean, honey?" Without even uncovering her face from Alfred Hitchcock Mystery novel, she knew what I was doing.

"How do you do that, Blondie?"

"Do what?" Lisa put the book down on her bare legs and looked at me.

"How did you know I was looking at your sexy bare legs? I could have been absorbing the perfect form of your breast."

"Yeah, you could've. But my breast is covered."

"Good point." Ray's voice returned into the phone's earpiece, and Lisa returned to Hitchcock. And I still wasn't any wiser how Lisa knew I was ab- sorbing the looks of her legs. She's psychic?

"Yes, sir. Mr. Douglas checked in this afternoon. Shall I ring his room for you, sir?"

"Please. Thanks again." I said, politely.

"Sure. Wait another minute while I ring his room, sir. May I ask who's calling?"

"Mr. Nick Edwards."

"Thank you, sir." He put me on hold, and music of Mozart pleasantly played in my right ear. I only waited fifteen seconds. And on the fourth ring, Clint answered. His voice sounded as if I had awakened him.

"Hey, buddy. Nick, here. Did I wake you?"

"Well, yeah. But that's okay. I needed to get my body up anyway. What time is it, Nick?" I guess Holiday Inn failed to supply the room with a clock.

I thought. I glanced over to the digital clock on the blonde nightstand next to my side of the bed.

"Eight P.M." I said.

"Eight? Wow. I must've been terribly tired." Yawn. "What's up?"

"I was just wondering if you made contact with Sgt. Dillman yet."

"Lieutenant. He got promoted a while back."

"Oh. Yeah. I forgot."

"No. I didn't make contact with Dillman, but I did talk to the 'Comish'."

"What's the commissioner's name?" I lit a cigarette and set it in the clear crystal ashtray. I found a BIC pen on the nightstand, opened the drawer, and pulled out a note pad. I was ready to write.

"Commissioner Robert Michlen . . . M-I-C-H-L-E-N."

"Got it. Thanks. So what does he have to say, Clint?"

"Not much. But he did say the case was never closed on Don and Katie

Murray. The department is still keeping their eyes and ears open. And keep-ing the faith. You just don't know about these things. Someone just might come forward with information about their mysterious death."

"Yeah. You're right. Is that it? Case was never closed?"

"No. Get this. The 'Comish' said Rudy's brother got blown-up back in 1987. A bomb malfunctioned. He's dead."

"Obviously. When you say 'Rudy's brother', Rudy's brother, as in Ruby Balesteri?"

"Yep. You got it, Nick." Another yawn, but wasn't as long as the first yawn.

"Was Rudy involved in the bombing?"

"Maybe. But no evidence of that."

"Location of the bombing?"

"Park Plaza Hotel. It isn't too far from here where we're located."

"Peachy. Did the 'Comish' give you a reason why?"

"About the bombing?"

"Uh-huh." I said. I puffed my last puff of cigarette and smashed it in the crystal ashtray.

"He didn't know. But Dillman might. I have to call him the first thing in the morning."

"Did he know when the bombing occurred, ah, date and time, I mean?" I said.

"He couldn't remember off-hand. Dillman would know that, too. I would imagine." Clint said. He seemed to be waking up now.

"Okay, Clint. Thanks. Let me know if anything unravels."

"You bet." I heard a straining noise over the phone.

"What's that weird noise I'm hearing, Clint?"

"Either it's my stretching, or Eagle and Pam are at it again. They've been going at it since we settled in."

"Damn," I said. "Horny son-a-va-bitches, aren't they?"

"Yep." We disconnected our conversation.

Chapter Forty-Five

I LOOKED AT LISA with an expression she knew all too well.

"Ah, you have information you're dying to tell me, Huh? What is it?" Lisa said.

"Well, I guess you can start dancing now."

"Wha . . . ? What is that suppose to mean?"

"Remember you were saying earlier you wanted the Balesteri brothers die the same way your parents had died. And you would dance on their graves."

"Yeah. I remember."

"Well, Ruby died in an explosion at Park Plaza Hotel in 1987. I believe he was planting a bomb and it malfunctioned."

Lisa looked up and stared at the ceiling for a long while. Her hands ges-tured pray-ing hands. "Thank-you God. One down. One to go." Lisa jumped out from the bed and danced an unfamiliar dance. A Lisa Special, I guess.

I said. "Tomorrow Clint will call Dillman and try to get more information on the bombing."

Lisa stopped dancing, or whatever she was doing, then went to the ice bucket, grabbed the bottle of Rose', and drank from the bottle. She released the bottle from her lips and took in a few breaths. She said, "I'll drink to that sonavabitch, uh, Ruby Balesteri." She took in another pull of wine with some of it drooling from the corner of her mouth. Then wiped her mouth with the back of her hand and gazed at me for a moment.

"Join me in a celebration drink, honey."

I clinched the wine glasses, one in each hand, and held them in front of her breast while she'd poured the wine. I tilted my glass toward Lisa's, and we clinked. We sipped. After feeling warm and oozy from the wine, we cud-dled each other in bed, and slowly made love.

➤ ◄

It was a cool Sunday evening and the rain slanted against the hotels' lobby window. The North-Westward wind, vibrated the marquee, which read: 48 degrees in neon lights. As Lisa and I walked in Harold's Lounge, the temperature was even cooler, and empty, except for Belle and Kim.

Since the lounge was as quiet as a funeral home, and no customers, Belle and Kim amused themselves. Belle was reading a Kellerman thriller: *Stalker* and Kim was in the midst of a crossword puzzle.

Both were leaning against the 'Z' shaped bar.

We slid our butts on the bar stools.

Looking at us, Kim strained her dark brown eyes against the dim lighting.

"When did you two return from Chicago?" Kim said, still squinting.

"We never made it to the windy city." I said.

"Something came up," Lisa said. "So here we are."

"Where are your friends?" Belle asked, closing the thriller novel and set-ting it aside on the bar.

"They continued to Chicago, while Lisa and I will be doing business here." I said.

Kim set our drinks in front of us, which we didn't even order. Kim went by memory. We said thanks. Kim smiled.

"So, what business you two involved in now?" Belle asked.

"Before we answer your question," Lisa said. "How well do you know Elvis and Tonia?" Lisa's eyes shifted back and forth to the two females.

Kim, still leaning against the bar, said, "Not too well, I guess. How about you, Belle?"

"Same-o. Same-o." Belle shrugged.

"Did you ever notice anything suspicious about Elvis and Tonia in the last week or so?" Asked Lisa.

"Like what?" Belle and Kim said variously.

"Like talking privately to Phil more than usual." I said. I sipped my beer. Set it down in front of me, and kept my right hand clinching to it.

"Yes," Kim said. "I remember such an occasion. On out most busiest night, Karaoke night, we were working Down-Under when Elvis pulled Phil Sameno aside for a long while, leaving me with impatient customers. I was furious.

"When Mr. Sameno returned after twenty minutes, or so later, I asked the asshole what was so important Elvis had to pull you away at the most crucial time. Do you know what the fucker said to me?"

Lisa and I shook our heads.

"He said to me; 'Fuck your-self. It isn't your damn business, bitch'. Can you believe that jack-ass. And Elvis didn't do anything about it, either. You know, Nick, I've been working here hell of a long time, and I don't need that kind of treatment from anyone.

"I do not know what is going on here, but, I hope you and Lisa will find out." Her right index finger and thumb barely touched. "I am this close of quitting . . . This close." Her right hand shook with emphasis.

"What night was that?" I asked. Lisa's glass was empty. Belle went and re-filled it. Lisa was happy. Belle resumed her position at the bar. Listening.

"Thursday night. The 2nd of March. It's one of our busiest nights."

"That was his first day on the job as a bartender, wasn't it?"

Lisa said.

"Yeah, I guess," Belle said. "What's with the questions?"

"We would rather not say at the moment, 'til we have more information

TrainTipCudahy Public Library Patron "He said to me; 'Fuck your-self. It isn't your damn business, bitch'. Can you believe that jack-ass. And Elvis, of all people, didn't do anything about it, either. You know, Nick, I've been working here hell of a long time, and I don't need that kind of treatment from anyone.

"I do not know what is going on here, but I hope you and Lisa will find out." Kim squeezed some dusty air between her forefinger and thumb. "I am this close of quitting . . . This close, I tell ya'." Her right hand shook with em-phasis.

"What night was that?" I asked. Lisa's glass was empty. Belle went and re-filled the glass. Lisa was happy. Belle resumed her position at the bar.

And listened.

"Thursday night. The 2nd of March. It's one of our busiest nights."

"That was his first day on the job as a bartender, wasn't it?"

Lisa said.

"Yeah, I guess it was come to think of it." Belle said. "What's with the questions?"

"We would rather not say for the moment 'til we have more information. No reason to stir something up, if there isn't anything to stir up." I said.

Kim and Belle looked at each other and shrugged.

We finished our drinks and thanked them for the information. Lisa and I decided to take a stroll around the undamaged structure of the hotel. Since the tornado, the hotel almost seemed deserted.

We walked here and there: through the gift shop, in and out of the game room, and finally we found ourselves in front of the hotel, under the long green canopy, holding hands and watching the early spring rain fall around us.

Chapter Forty-Six

WE WERE SITTING in matching gold wing chairs in the hotel lobby. My face buried in the *Journal* with Lisa sitting next to me. We patiently waited for Elvis and Tonia report to work. Time: 8 A.M. Lisa had a magazine. I believe it read: *Newsweek*. But she was most clever than I gave her credit for. She'd cut out two small holes in the magazine for her blue eyes to see through. At this time, Lisa had her nose into the magazine, gazing. Boy. What a real detective.

Quarter past the hour came and went. Nothing. Half past the hour, still nothing. I had read the comics three times and the Metro section four times.

Boring.

Lisa was flipping through the two-holed pages over and over again. She yawned. Another, bor-r-r-ing.

Eight-forty-five A.M., Elvis and Tonia walked past us from behind and swiftly disappeared into the narrow hallway and entered their office. On the door the sign read: *Chief Executive Officer.*

The door closed softly and clicked shut. Then, another click. Double-locked. Interesting. Lisa and I looked at each other and shrugged. We went back to our boring reading material and waited again.

By ten A.M., Lisa and I couldn't sit and wait any longer. We stood and strolled the narrow hallway with our reading material in hand. We faced the heavy mahogany door. Leaning into it, we pressed our ears firmly in the center of the door, listening carefully for any peculiar noises or conversation.

People walked to and fro and stared at us. We just smiled and waved. They didn't wave back.

Other people with children rushed swiftly past us and took a double-take.

Again we smiled and waved. And again, the passing people didn't wave. Friendly hotel.

Finally, at 10:30 A.M., we heard Elvis on the speaker phone talking loudly to Rudy/Phil. What Lisa and I gathered from the conversation was frustration and anger.

The conversation with Rudy/Phil didn't seem to go very well. Elvis angry voice turned up a notch. Or I should say several notches.

"You better be ready . . . you, sonavabitch. The tornado damage was not enough insurance coverage. Be ready, or else, Rudy."

Then silence.

But before the silence we'd heard, or we thought we heard a heavy object crashing to the floor; Maybe, the phone, maybe, the floor lamp. Or, maybe Elvis fainted from anxiety.

Chapter Forty-Seven

AT ELEVEN A.M., Harold's Lounge had opened for lunch. Carina, a cock-tail waitress, and Dena the bartender watched us as we walked in. As eve-ryone else, they were surprised to see us, too.

"So, you're back here on business, huh?" Dena said.

"What sort of business, Nick?" Carina asked.

"Detective business," I said.

Lisa said. "How would you two ladies like to make extra cash?"

Dena said. "What do we have to do?" Dena and Carina looked at each other with huge smiles.

"Keep your eyes and ears open for anything unusual. I don't care what it is. As long as you see or hear things Phil or Tonia, and even Elvis might be involved in."

"What are you and Nick expecting them to do?" Carina said.

"We're not sure, yet. But the three are acting mighty peculiar. And we want to know why. Okay?" Lisa said with a half grin.

"Yeah, sure. Okay." Dena said as she wiped the bar and some ashtrays.

Carina nodded. "This is more exciting than being a waitress."

We all nodded at each other. Lisa pulled out two fifty-dollar bills. Then, handed one to Dena, the other to Carina.

"This is your advance payment. Any substantial information you two give us, you'll get more money just like that. Okay?" Lisa said.

Nodding with a smile, they both thanked her gratefully.

"You want anything to drink, Lisa and Nick?" Dena asked.

We shook our heads. "No." Lisa and I said in unison. I said, "Not now. Maybe later. We have to keep our wits about ourselves at the moment."

Again Dena nodded

We left and did some detecting.

❯❯ ❮❮

In the lobby, near Down-Under Club, facing the narrow hallway to the CEO's office, Lisa was back in the gold wing chair with her two-holed magazine. Waiting and hopefully succeeding that Tonia or/and Elvis come out from their office.

The time was approaching two-twenty-six P.M. Monday afternoon. As she was deeply involved in her surveillance, I was patrolling the Grand Mil- waukee hotel's interior and exterior. And hopefully so, bump into Phil/Rudy doing anything he shouldn't been doing. Whatever that might be.

I was informed by one of the employees of the hotel Rudy was staying in one of the guest rooms. Which I was told by another employee, was against hotel policy for any employee to rent a room. I find that rather odd. Um.

My guess, Elvis had a hand in the arrangement.

As I completed the perimeter patrol of the hotel, and walked through the automatic sliding glass doubled-doors of the lobby, I heard my name being paged. I noticed Lisa had her nose in the magazine. She didn't notice me en-ter the lobby, or even hear my name announced over the PA system. I non- chalantly walked to the front desk and introduced myself to the flirty clerk I had spoken to before.

She nodded to the red phone in the corner of the desk, near the glass slid-ing doors. She couldn't resist. She fluttered her eyelashes at me and gave me a flirty smile. Two people can play that game. So I winked at her as I walked around the outer side of the horseshoe-shaped desk.

I noticed the light flashing on the red phone. I punched the white-flashing button, leaned against the curve of the huge desk and picked up the bright red handset. I put it to my right ear. A male voice was on the other end.

"Yeah," I said.

"Nick?" The voice said.

"Yeah," Again I said. It was Clint.

"I finally made contact with Dillman."

"Yeah."

I shifted my body and faced Lisa. Or should I say . . . magazine.

"Can you talk, Nick?"

"You talk. I listen." I said.

"Oh, yeah. Okay. Got'cha. Well, anyway, Dillman gave me some inter-esting scoop on the 1987 bombing that occurred at the Park Plaza here in Chicago."

"Do tell," I said.

"The Park Plaza Hotel was in deep financial debt. Some big wig from the hotel had hired the Balesteri Brothers to blow it up for insurance purposes.

According to the *Tribune* the explosion was set to go off at three-fifteen in the morning on March 15th."

"Interesting," I said, still staring at Lisa-slash-magazine.

"Yes it is. And listen to this, Nick. In 1989, another bombing, which ex-ploded suc-cessfully, happened at three-fifteen in the afternoon, on March fif- teenth. A company named Pullman Standard. Also in financial trouble. Now, we do not know if Rudy was involved. No evidence of that.

"Here's another bombing you should know about, Nick."

"Yeah, lay it on me, buddy."

"Howard Johnson, Waukegan, Illinois, blew up in 1991. And, do you know what date that occurred on?"

"March fifteenth?"

"Bingo . . ."

"At three-fifteen." I said confidently.

"Yeah, right. In the A.M."

"Anymore?" I asked.

"Lots . . . 1993 . . . International Harvester . . . North Chicago . . . March 15th, at 3:15 P.M . . . 1995 . . . John Deer . . . Highland Park, Illinois. Bombed. March fif- teenth, at 3:15 A.M. All were financially drained. See the pattern, Nick?"

"Yep," I said quietly.

"But no arrests or convictions. Not even sure if Rudy was involved in those, either. But anonymous witness believed she recognized Rudy at the John Deer site the night before. But un-confirmed."

"Anything else you want to add, Clint?" I said.

"Nope. But you and Lisa have to be careful. Something is brewing. I can smell it, Nick."

"Sure, Clint. We'll be careful. That goes for you, Eagle and Pam, too."

"You bet. Give Lisa my best."

"Will do," I said.

"Bye."

"Bye," I said. We disconnected.

Chapter Forty-Eight

I N THE CORRIDOR of the hotel a magazine stand had a small white sign in red letters which read: "FREE . . . TAKE ONE". So I did.

A classic 1957 Chevy was featured and enlarged on its front cover. I clinched it, swung it under my armpit and strolled over and sat next to Lisa.

I took the auto magazine from my armpit, opened it, and buried my face in the black and white-typed pages, as if I was reading.

Nick Edwards the bookworm.

Talking into the magazine, I asked Lisa, "Anything?"

"Na'da." Lisa said, also buried into her magazine.

"Is that the same magazine," I said. "you had earlier, or is that a collect-able?"

"If this was a collectable I wouldn't have cut two little holes in it, smart ass." She said, as she peeked at me through the little holes of the magazine.

"How about you? Anything?" Lisa said.

I couldn't see her face or eyes. But if I did, she probably was either smil-ing, or flapping her tongue at me. I had hoped for smiling.

I said, "Maybe. I took a walk around the hotel *where* I could walk. The south side of the parking lot near the hotel's ballroom is still roped off as ex-pected. So my perimeter patrol was extremely limited. Almost cut in half."

"So, in other words, nothing." Lisa said. She probably had a grin, but I could not see it.

"Boy. I trained you well, Detective." I said. I grinned. But Lisa didn't see my loving grin.

"Sssh. Hush-up, you," Lisa whispered. "You want to blow my cover?"

"I must admit, you are even cute *behind* the cover of Newsweek." I said.

"What are you trying to do? Pick me up, cowboy?" Lisa said, jokingly. "I am not easy, I want you to know."

"Ah. But only with me." I said.

"Ah," Lisa said mockingly. "You think you know me, don't you?"

"I do." I said.

"Do not, I repeat, do not be overly confident. I just might bust your bubble, cowboy."

"You can bust my bubble anytime, sweetheart."

"Bogey, you are not." Lisa said softly.

"Okay, pretty lady. This pilgrim wants to get to know you a little better. What do you say, little lady. Is it a date?" I said.

"Your John Wayne impression needs improving, too, but better than Mr. Bogarts'."

"Well? Is it a date? Ah, uh. Ah, uh." I said, still trying my impression of Mr. Wayne.

"How about now, hot pants?" Lisa muttered.

"HERE? NOW?"

"Sshh, you. Of course not. Not here, bozo. Meet me in my room in an hour."

"Hour?" I questioned. "How long does it take you undress?"

"Okay . . . Okay. Twenty minutes."

"Okay. Twenty minutes. That is more like it." I said. My eyes were get-ting cross-eyed staring at the magazine too long. I need a break. I was sure Lisa needed a break, too.

Lisa stood and went. After thinking about the twenty minutes, waiting, well, I couldn't. I stood and went, too.

Chapter Forty-Nine

AFTER OUR MID-AFTERNOON delight, we showered, brushed our teeth, and I shaved. After doing all that, I walked to the window and sat at the tiny round cherry-wood table, while Lisa was touching-up her beautiful face.

The second floor window had showered us with a semi-good view. Noth-ing to brag about, but it was something to pass the time away.

Our room overlooked the north-end parking lot. My view for today; dark wet road on Layton Avenue with a misty rain running down on the rooms' window somewhat blur-ring my vision.

Burger King was sitting on Layton Avenues' edge, directly across the parking lot in front of me. To my left, McDonald's was constructed evenly with Burger King. And on my right, Dunk'n Donuts. Anything you wanted was right here for your eating pleasure.

Across Layton Avenue, direct opposite side of Burger King; Perkins Family Restaurant. I'd heard the food there was good. We'll try it sometime.

Maybe tonight.

Lisa was still in the bathroom. Now, she was blow-drying her shoulder length blond hair. The humming from the blow-dryer seemed hypnotic. My mind was wandering. It focused on Rudy Balesteri. Then bounced to Miss Tonia, then, Mr. Elvis. What were they up to? Was the question came to mind. It wasn't the first time that question popped into my head. And prob-ably wouldn't be the last.

Whatever was stirring around us, probably was heading toward unhealthy territory. Maybe deadly. Where there's Rudy, there's trouble. Deadly, dead-ly trouble.

Now, Lisa and I have two mysteries to solve. One, we have to make Rudy confess to the killing of Lisa's parents, Don and Katie Murray. Two, find out why Rudy was in Milwaukee . . . and why Grand Milwaukee Hotel.

Lisa's blow-dryer went silent. She walked out of the bathroom and came toward me with nothing on, except her black laced bra with a pink bow cent-ered between the two cups, and black panties to match. She completed her final touches to her hair and sat on my lap in the armless wooden chair. Her back was facing the window. Her blue eyes shadowed from the late after-noon semi-darkness. She gazed into my eyes happily.

"I love you," She said.

"Ditto." She gave me a clown-frown sort of look.

"Ditto? Why 'ditto'? Can't you say the words, the three lovely words . . . *I Love You.*"

I shrugged with my eyes on hers. "You know, honey, I love you. You're the best that ever happened to me."

"So, why is it so hard for you to tell me, bucko?"

Bucko, I thought. Where did that come from?

Her strong arms embraced my neck, and her shapely tan legs dangling over my lap, swinging slightly. Her height was five-foot-six and her weight, approximately 120-130 pounds. She reminded me of a little school girl sit-ting on Santa's lap asking for her fa-vorite toy.

I didn't mind at all being her Santa Claus. Nope. Not at all.

"Let me explain my feeling on *Love.*" She nodded and listened intently.

"The word 'love' shouldn't be used lightly," I said, still gazing into her beautiful blue eyes. "I always feel love for you, sweets, but if I say 'I Love You' every time you want me to, then it's just a word floating away in thin air, meaningless. Not going anywhere spe-cial. And you are special to me.

"I admit, I do not tell you enough. And I'm sorry about that . . ."

Lisa put her soft forefinger to my lips and hushed me.

"Tex, Love means never have to say you're sorry."

"I believe, what you just said, Lisa, was from some movie I'd seen when I was a teen-ager. I think it was 'Love Story' with Ryan O' Neal and Ali Mc-Graw. But I'm not sure at the moment. Do you remember that, honey?"

"My daddy always said that. I heard it from him." Lisa said with sad eyes.

"Oh." I held Lisa as tight as I could. I wanted us to remain in this position forever. I just didn't want to forget this precious moment of emotional feel-ings pouring out be-tween us. It's so beautiful and breathtaking.

I then whispered into her ear. "I love you." She hugged me so tightly. Tears flowed down her rosy cheeks and made contact with my face, get-ting my cheek wet. We sat in that position for, how long . . . well, for a very long time.

Chapter Fifty

"Yes, Carina," I said. "I'll tell her when she awakes from her slumber. By the way, is Kim working tonight?"

"No. She went to Juanita Alverez funeral. I would have went myself, but I was needed here at the hotel. I didn't know Juanita that well, anyway."

"Such a horrible scene, died so young, and for what? This whole crazy episode just makes me sick."

"Yeah, Nick, you are so right. It tears me apart, too. Well, Nick, I got to get back to work. Now, be sure Lisa gets my message. Okay?"

"You bet, Carina. Thanks again. Lisa will surely be pleased with your findings."

"Hope it helps?" Carina said.

"I'm sure it will, Carina . . . Bye."

"Good-bye."

I didn't even have my hand from the handset, when the phone rang again.

I picked it up.

"Hello." I said.

"Mr. Edwards?"

"Yeah."

"Lieutenant Dillman . . . Fifth District . . . Chicago Police . . . Homicide."

"Oh. How are you doing, sir?" I said.

"I guess, all right. How's Lisa?" Dillman's voice was an even flowing sound of baritone. He probably was in his late fifties' . . . early sixties'.

"She's angry, sad, and bitter with her parents' death. But she is a strong little lady. I give her that."

"That she is," Dillman said. "She was always strong and determined. Is she there now? I like to speak with her."

"She's napping at the moment, sir. What do you have for us? Anything new?"

"She needs to be aware of possible evidence we have on Rudy killing her parents."

I said, "What do you have, Lieutenant?"

Dillman cleared his throat. "Excuse me, well, we found an envelope full of threatening letters during our investigation. They were dated over the period of ten years. They are boxed and secured in the evidence room now."

"What kinda' threats?"

"Nothing in particular. Just notes made out of paper clippings and pasted neatly on Xerox paper and mailed to the Murray's residence. All this took place while Rudy and Ruby Balesteri were in prison."

"What did the notes say exactly?"

"One note I remembered clearly, read: 'Watch your back, Detective Mur-ray . . . We know where you live . . . When we get out of this hell-hole, you are dead'."

"The stupid idiots actually signed the letters or notes?" I said. I sipped my cold coffee. Set it down on the table, near the window, pulled a cigarette from my pack, inserted it between my lips, and took in a long pull of smoke.

Ahhh.

"No, not exactly. It just had clippings of the letters; **BOSS BROTHERS** in big bold letters."

"Boss Brothers. Were there periods after each letter in 'BOSS'? "

I asked.

"Yeah. But I do not know what the acronym means in 'Boss'. Probably a made-up name Rudy and Ruby concocted."

"Ruby is dead . . . Right? You know, from the explosion. Was that confirm-ed, Lieutenant?"

"Yep. Definitely it was Ruby. No doubt about it, Mr. Edwards."

"Nick, sir. Call me Nick." There was silence for a short time. Then I said.

"I'm baffled on the dates of the explosions. All the bombings occurred on March 15th of different years. That goes for the time, too . . . 3:15 in the A.M.

Or 3:15 in the P.M. The sabotage occurred every couple years. What do you make of it, Lieutenant?" I said. I finished my coffee and smashed my cigar-ette into the small glass ashtray.

"My guess, that the date, March 15th, was the date they were sentenced and when released from prison. The time, again, my guess, it matches the month and the date of same. The third month of the year, the fifteenth day of the month. Anniversary date." Dillman explained.

"Logical, I guess."

"Well, it will be the twelfth anniversary this coming Wednesday."

"Yeah," I said, looking at the desk calendar. "March fifteenth."

"Yep. Rudy is up to something. And it won't be pretty, knowing Rudy." Dillman said.

"No it would not." I agreed. "Another bombing, maybe?"

"Maybe. Most likely." Again, Dillman cleared his throat. "Just keep your head low and your ass tucked in."

"Yeah, I was told that before. Do you know a Detective Cole, sir?"

"Not that I can remember. Why?"

"Well, he warned me of the same thing. Must be a Chicago Police thing."
I said.

"Maybe. Got to go, Nick. Good luck. And be safe. But if I were you and Lisa, I'll be snooping around for bombs in the Milwaukee area. Maybe even the hotel you're staying at. Be careful. I don't want anything to happen to Lisa, especially another bombing. Her parents were enough. Like I said, got to go. Talk to you later. And keep me posted."

"You bet."

On my end, I heard the dial tone.

Chapter Fifty-One

LISA WAS AWOKEN from the rapping on our room's door. Before I had ans-wered it, she quickly went into the bathroom. She gets embarrassed easily. Lisa is a very private person. Another reason I love her.

I had waited 'til she closed the bathroom door. When I opened the maho-gany door, I had a surprise waiting for me. A flying arm, with a hard fist attached to it, made contact with my square chin. I fell backward, catching and bracing myself against the desk.

He stood in the doorway rubbing his knuckles, his dark eyes penetrating into mine, then he said, "You stay away from me, or else I'll kill you and your lovely lady of a friend . . . Lisa Murray . . . You got that, asshole?"

I didn't answer. I just soaked in his piercing eyes. Then he turned sharply left and stomped toward the stairwell exit. The hallway quietness was re-placed with the slam-ming of the stairwell door. Then his footsteps finally faded away into nothing.

By the time Lisa came out of the bathroom, I was standing and closing the guest room door.

My chin throbbed, but no damage. I wiggled my jaw some. It didn't feel broken. My grandmother, bless her heart, could hit me much harder than he did. At least I know he cannot punch well. Lisa gazed at me with concern.

"What just happened here, Nick?"

"Obviously, word is out that you and I are asking questions about Rudy Balesteri, which is in our favor." I said, rubbing more jaw.

"In our favor . . . Whaddya' mean . . . in our favor?" Lisa expression tight-ened. Now, she had this look if she needed to punch me.

"Settle down, honey. Just settle down." I was beginning to talk funny. "No reason to be nervous."

"Nervous. *Who's* nervous? Hysterical is more the word. I am hysterical."

Lisa's blue eyes began to leak silvery liquid.

"Honey, don't worry." I gently rested my hands on her well-firmed shoulders, gesturing her to sit on the bed. She did.

"Calm down," I said. "This is part of detecting. We're bound to step on peo-ple's toes. It is a lot better than waiting around and surveying. Now the nut-shell is cracked wide open."

Lisa calmly said, "What do you mean by that, honey?"

I wiped her tears away with my index finger. She grinned.

"They are going to screw-up now. And when they do, you and I will be right there hav-ing the last laugh. I was hoping our sleuthing would've pissed someone off. We got them looking over their shoulder. And their nervous-ness will turn into clumsiness."

Looking at my swollen chin, Lisa said, "But it's you with the dark bluish—green bruise on your chin."

"Ah! But this is nothing. Remember last year how we both survived our gunshot wounds."

"Yeah, and you almost died."

"But I didn't." I wiped the last fallen tear from Lisa's worried face. I had leaned over and kissed her cheek gently. "The point is," I said, "We will sur-vive this. We'll get through this, just as long as we stick together."

Lisa nodded.

I said, "Just to be safe, we'll clean and load our weapons. It is time we protect ourselves."

But before I went to my suitcase to fetch my weapon, Lisa pulled me to-ward her.

"Nick, you didn't tell me who was at the door . . . Who punched you?"

"Elvis." I said.

"Elvis . . . ? Elvis Masano . . . ? The CEO?" Lisa's voice went up a notch.

"Yep. It was he."

I took a facial cloth from the bathroom rack, spread it open evenly on the counter-sink, and poured a few ice-cubes from the ice bucket onto the facial cloth and twisted it until it was shaped like an ice bag. I then firmly pressed it against my throbbing chin.

OUCH!

Chapter Fifty-Two

IT WAS LATE Monday evening nearly ten-thirty P.M . . . (still March 13th), my beloved Lisa and me were sitting at the round table, near the window, with the red curtains drawn and the hanging lamp brightly shining over us as we cleaned our weapons.

She was eagle-eyeing through her barrel of her .38Cal snub-nose, when she said, "So, I guess I owe Carina another fifty buck-a-roos, huh?"

"Yep," I said, as I added my final touches on the firing pin of my Forty-Four Magnum. Then I laid the weapon down on the table next to me with a dull thud.

"And it seems we're on the right track," Lisa said, "as far as Lieutenant Dillman is concerned."

"Yep."

"I just do not understand why my daddy never told me about those threats he got in the mail from the Balesteri brothers."

I glared at Lisa, grimly.

"Come on, Lisa," I said, "You know darn well why your dad didn't tell you."

"Yeah, I guess. Call it denial. But you're right, Nick. I know my daddy didn't want to worry me. But, my daddy tells me everything. But, why not this?" Tears began to swell. I reached and touched her hand caressingly.

Silence.

The only sound in the room at the moment was lead and brass sliding into our weapons' chamber.

❦ ❦

Carina's alertness had helped us, Lisa and I, locate the exact wing and room Rudy was staying in. It had made her another fifty-dollars she didn't have before. She was happy, and so were we.

Eleven-thirty, Monday night, we waited around the corner two doors down from Rudy's room waiting for our cue.

Tonight, Lisa wore a long, black wig down to her well-firmed butt. A minty-green miniskirt (lotta' thigh), and a thin white blouse. She had on dark web nylons, white pearls and black high-heels with opened-heel.

But, her make-up was moderate.

For me, I donned a blue blazier jacket, light gray dress slacks, white shirt with buttoned-down collar, and a silk red and white-striped tie. My hair was dyed black (temporary dye) the one you buy in a can for Halloween. And my black shoes were highly spit-shined.

Blake gave me a hotel badge he found in his desk drawer. It clasped and hung evenly on my Blazier jacket near my heart. The badge was shiny, and easily to see. My glued-on black mustache had the suave and brilliant look of *Clark Gable*.

Our disguise was perfect for this thrilling evening.

11:40 P.M. Rudy's phone rang. He picked it up, spoke a few words, as Lisa and I stepped into the parking lot. Rudy's vehicle wasn't too far from his first floor guest room. Lisa and I walked and waited in the parking lot near Rudy's cream-colored Crown Victoria. When Rudy walked into the parking lot I had Lisa 'Spreading Eagle' against Rudy's sedan's grille.

Rudy, on cue, came running toward Lisa and me.

I said, "You Phil Salmeno?" Lisa was fighting with me. She was punch-ing, squirming, and struggling ferociously.

"Yeah. What's going on here?"

Lisa had her right hand into her black shiny purse, gripped her .38 caliber calmly. As calmly as she could muster.

I had my .44 Magnum in my shoulder holster under my right armpit. All clean, loaded, and ready to go. No worries. I was 'Hotel Security'. Rudy wouldn't expect a thing. Or would he? Let's think positive . . . Okay?

I thought.

I said, "I caught her tampering with your Crown Vic, tank for a car."

Lisa still struggled aggressively. What an actress. What a woman.

Rudy came in closer and stepped into the shadows of the yellow parking lot lights. Lisa broke free from my not-so-tight grip and ran toward Rudy.

I pulled my .44 from its holster. And Lisa pulled her .38 from her purse.

When she was close enough to Rudy, she kicked him in the groin with force.

He went down grabbing himself.

As I slowly and casually walked toward Lisa and our prey, gun at my left side, barrel downward, Lisa kicked Rudy in the face with her spiked high-heel. He fell on his right side groaning. He wasn't too sure of himself now. He did not know what to do, or think. Besides, he was still stunned from the forceful kick to his 'privates'.

"Okay, *Agent 99*," I said loudly, "Do you want to blow him away? I know you're itching to . . . Or shall I?" Rudy squirmed. His mouth wide open. Probably was going to shout *"SEEE-CUR-UH-TEEE . . . HELP ME"* Lisa did not care about that if he did. She was go-ing to blow him away for killing her parents. She kicked him again, but this time in the head. Damn. I thought. What a tough woman. Or was it just anger? All her anger built up inside her for twelve years, was coming out like a loaded cannon.

"You mother-fucker . . . You killed my parents." She had her legs spread out evenly, well-balanced. The hammer cocked, fully-back. Rudy squirmed again, more than before. He reminded me of a scared snake, which he was.

A snake, that is.

Lisa had the barrel pointed at Rudy's left temple. He tried to crawl away from my toughie companion, holding himself. But it seemed difficult to do.

Instead, he said, "What the fuck are you talking about, bitch." With that, I pulled him up by his coat lapels, his feet dragging the asphalt, then I cold-cocked him. Blood squirted from his nose and mouth.

I said, "That's the second time you called my woman a bitch." I punched him square in his face. When I released his lapels he hit the asphalt parking lot heavily.

"What the fuck going on here." His words muffled from the blood pour-ing into and from his mouth.

"You killed my parents . . . Remember. Do you remember Detective Don-ald Murray . . . Homicide Police . . . Chicago. You and your frigg'n brother Ruby, and Ruby is a sissy's name, I might add, blew up my parents car on my fuck'n graduation day. My mother was in that car. You killed my par-ents. And now you are going to pay big time, you . . . you bastard."

Lisa resumed her firm position . . . Leg spread evenly, gun pointed at Bale-steri's temple and hammer fully-cocked with both hands steadily on her .38 Chief Police Special.

We were hoping to scare Rudy to the point of confession. But it did not come. Instead, he screamed loudly from the deepest of his lungs and through his vocal chords.

"WE DID NOT KILL YOUR PARENTS . . ." His voice seemed to choke.

He gasped for air, and swallowed hard. His tone of his voice came out like a very angry and scared mouse.

" . . . We wanted to kill your father . . . *not* your mother . . . just your father, but some-one beat us to the punch . . . ."Again, he swallowed hard and gasped for the cool night air.

" . . . Your father," Rudy continued, "put a lot of people away in prison. He had made a lot of enemies." His breathing regained normality.

"My brother and me, you see, wanted to kill him . . . I wish we had. I wish it was us who'd blown him away. But if we were the ones to blow him away in that car, it would've been just him, and not your mother. Ruby and I just didn't operate that way. We hunt and find our enemies. But your mother was not our enemy, I repeat, NOT our enemy. Your father was.

"I am terribly sorry about your mother, but I am glad, no, I am joyously happy that your father is dead. He was just one big pain in our asses."

Lisa had kept her stance steady. But I noticed tears had swollen up in her blue eyes. She seemed to be lax and confused. Damn it. Rudy was getting her to his way of thinking. She's caving to his denial. He might be telling the truth about not killing her parents, but that would be discussed later. But now, Rudy had the control of the situation, and I didn't like that one frigg'n iota.

Rudy had gotten up with a slight struggle and reached for her gun. I pul-led my .44 from my shoulder holster, aimed, pulled the hair-trigger, and blasted his kneecap . . .

The pain of it all . . . Tooo . . . baaad . . . Tooo . . . fuck'n . . . baaad!

More blood stained the asphalt parking lot . . .

Better his than ours.

Chapter Fifty-Three

BLAKE, LISA AND I were sitting in the gray cinderblock security office. Everything was the same as before, except the lights were shining brightly. And the coffee and doughnuts were mighty fresh.

The time: 3:30 A.M., Tuesday.

Sitting behind his desk, Blake leaned back in his gray leathered, heavy metal chair. His gray and white Formica top for a desk, had nothing but fan-ned sheets of paper, neatly in front of him.

Today, Blake wore a preppy blue blazer, gray slacks with a very fine crease evenly pressed. His black leather shoes were highly shined. Very pro-fessional. His blazer was unbuttoned, and hung loosely, advertising his crisp white shirt and flowery tie. His thick hands laced over his flat stomach.

"So, you two think I should hire Carina on my security team, huh?" Blake said.

We both nodded. Lisa said, "If it wasn't for her sharpness and eagerness to help, Rudy would have probably had followed through with his bombing plans."

Blake nodded.

"Yeah," I said, "While he's laid up in County Hospital, we can now at least focus more on Elvis and Tonia."

Blake said, "Do you really think he had planted a bomb, somewhere, here in this hotel?"

"Yep," Lisa nodded. "Somewhere, but where, we just don't know."

I said, "We might just have to shake-up Elvis and Tonia for the location of the bomb . . . Or bombs."

"What evidence do you two have that there is a bomb, or bombs?" Blake looked at me, then returned and laid his eyes back on Lisa, bringing his body forward toward his desk.

"The M.O . . . The pattern." Lisa said.

"What M.O.? What pattern?" With confusion and doubt, he'd crossed his legs on top of his desk and took a quick glance at Lisa's legs.

If we weren't friends, I would've pulled his chair out from under him. But I behaved. Blake can look, but do not touch.

"Unless you check the CEO's ledger, the answer to your question would not be accurate." I said.

"What do you think I would find?" Blake asked.

"If the hotel's ledger is balanced to a 'T'," Lisa said, "then, nothing to worry about. If the ledger proves otherwise, you know, a major debt, expect disaster."

"A bomb." Blake stated.

"Yes, Blake . . . A bomb. Or, again, bombs." Lisa said, crossing her legs. Blake caught a glimpse of thigh again. Then he looked at me.

"Nick, do you think there is a bomb, too?"

"I do."

"And you think the bomb, or bombs would be set to explode at three-fif-teen in the afternoon." Blake had his chin resting on his knuckles.

"You bet," Lisa said, "Wednesday . . . uh . . . Wednesday afternoon."

"Tomorrow afternoon . . . March 15th, just to be accurate."

I said.

We looked at each other for a long time.

Silence. Then we nodded agreeably.

"Okay," Blake said, "I'll check Elvis's ledger. But, for the record," His eyes bounced from Lisa to me, back to Lisa, "our conversation stays in this God-forsaken room. And, I'll have my men shadow Elvis and Tonia."

Lisa and I nodded.

We stood. Shook hands. Then we left.

Chapter Fifty-Four

"IF RUDY AND Ruby didn't murder my parents, then, who did?" Lisa sat opposite of me at the white-clothed table in the Courtyard Café. Which was attached to BJ's lounge in the Grand Milwaukee hotel.

The time: 9:15 A.M., Tuesday.

Our waitress had a face and smile of Ann Margaret, the Hollywood act-ress. But her hair was light brown, opposed to bright red of Ann Margaret's.

The name tag above her left shirt pocket, read; *MANAGER*. Understaffed, I guessed. She came to our table and poured our coffee.

Then she went.

"Very good question, honey. You know, we were focusing too much on the Balesteri brothers, we failed to think of other suspects likely to have a vendetta against them."

"Back to the ole' drawing-board, huh, Nick?" Lisa curled her lower lip. She set her gold-rimmed coffee cup carefully into the matching saucer near her right side, and sat back in her chair. Lisa looked exhausted and expressed disgust. "I was so positive the Balesteri brothers were the murderers."

Holding her hand across the table, I said, "We'll go to Chicago and check open records at Cook County Courthouse. Maybe the Commissioner will be so kind to give us his per-mission to search through your dad's cases, and check for any prominent suspects who were convicted and released around the time of your parents unfortunate death."

Lisa was silent for a time. She leaned forward with her breast caressing the edge of the tablecloth and took in some coffee. She set her coffee cup down, sat straight back in her chair again, and stared through the entrance-way, looking at nothing, just a blank gaze.

The manager returned to our table and poured us more coffee. She smiled from the corner of her left mouth, as her light blue eyes bounced from me to Lisa. "Is everything alright?" The manager asked.

I nodded and grinned slightly. Lisa didn't say or do anything. She didn't even look up at the manager. She continued to stare at the entranceway.

The manager turned and left shrugging her well-formed shoulders.

After the long extended silence and staring at nothing, Lisa finally spoke.

"Do you think," Lisa said her eyes planted on mine, "Do you think Rudy was too afraid to tell us the truth? Maybe Rudy and his brother actually did kill my parents. Maybe he was just probably saving his own ass by saying someone else was responsible for blowing up my parents' car."

"He was convincing." I said. I set my coffee cup down in front of me, and sat back, crossing my arms over my chest.

"So you believe him . . . Rudy. Why?" Her blue eyes were enlarged and big as saucers, as she scrutinized me.

"Yep. Sorry, babe, nothing personal. But, I will tell you this. If I find out he lied, and he did kill your parents, I will shoot his other kneecap clean off."

Lisa grinned. Then said, "You get-off shooting people, don't you, Nick?"

"Just certain ones, who deserves to be shot. If I shoot every person I do not like, I'll go bankrupt just on ammo alone. The economy is balanced, but not that balanced where I'd waste ammo just on anyone."

Lisa smiled widely. She lifted her cup, and took in some more coffee. Set it back in her saucer. Then she slid her arm across the table and rested her right hand on my left. We sat in silence, again, looking at each other very pleasantly.

Chapter Fifty-Five

Hank and I were on *Bomb Duty* this early Wednesday morning. The time was 6:07 A.M. March 15th. The big (bomb) day. If there were any at all.

Searching for explosives was not my idea of fun and excitement. I would rather be at the gym and be practicing my side-kicks and front-kicks. Maybe break some boards. Now that is fun and sporty. (Or love-making) . . .

Hank and I started on the north of the hotel. We knew the south-end did not need to be searched. The tornado did an expert job destroying that. But there were still plenty of places to search. Hank and I were trying our damn-est to be logical and figure out where a saboteur would hide a bomb that would cause the most damage.

The hotel's budget was six-digit-negative according to Blake's informa-tion. So the search was on for the bomb . . . or bombs. If Rudy maintained his MO, we needed to have the explosives defused before three—fifteen this afternoon.

Blake had Elvis report to work early. But Blake refused to tell Elvis why.

When Elvis arrived at five this morning, the front desk advised Elvis to meet Blake in his security office.

"Elvis," Blake said, "We have reason to believe you had hired Rudy Bal-esteri, or maybe you know him by Phil Salmeno, to blow-up this hotel."

Blake gazed heavily into Elvis's dark brown eyes.

Elvis was silent.

"How many bombs had been planted, Elvis, and where are they located?"

Blake said, clenching his fists.

Silence.

"There are over one-thousand guests in this hotel . . . Are you just going to risk their lives, just because you are way over the hotel's budget?"

Elvis remained silent. Blake's patience was wearing thin.

"The insurance company will not cough-up a single dollar when they find out it was sabotage."

Silence.

"I could have you and Phil/Rudy arrested on grounds of conspiracy and insurance fraud. Not mentioning, sabotage and endangering people's lives."

Blake pounded on his desk. "Damn it, Elvis! Talk to me . . . Please."

Elvis slowly moved his dark eyes toward Blake's face, squinting and sne-ering. But he remained silent.

Blake's unsuccessful interrogation with Elvis was interrupted by female screaming voices in the gray basement hallway. Blake rushed from his security office and came to a sudden halt a foot away from the office's thres-hold. Lisa was practically dragging Tonia by her arm across the gray base-ment floor. Elvis stayed in his chair, silently, while Blake helped Lisa with Tonia's violent rage.

"Blake," Lisa groaned. "Take Tonia . . . ugh . . . please . . . ugh . . . She's just too much for me to handle." Lisa, between heavy breathing, said. "Also, we need the hotel evacu-ated . . . the bomb squad . . . and the police here."

Still sitting, Elvis turned his body at Tonia, sideways, and gave her the devil-look.

"Sorry, Elvis. She made me confess. She threatened to shoot me if I did not talk."

"Bitch." That was all Elvis said. Then he returned facing Blake's desk.

Blake took Tonia and handcuffed her left wrist to Elvis's right wrist. Then he called the Metro Police, District-Two and Six. Bouncing his eyes from Tonia and Elvis, he dialed-up the Bomb Squad. He returned the hand-set back into its cradle, and faced Lisa.

"How many bombs, Lisa?" Blake smoothed his trimmed beard.

"Tonia believes Rudy told her and Elvis there were three. One in the French Quarters, and one in the Presidential Wing. She couldn't, or wouldn't confess to the third."

Blake turned to Elvis and Tonia.

"Well . . . Where's the third bomb and the exact location?" Blake started to pace around his office. But maintaining his eyes on Tonia and Elvis.

This time Tonia joined in with Elvis's silence.

Suddenly, Blake's radio crackled with information.

"Security-One . . . This is Security-Two . . . Come in."

"This is Security-One . . . Go Security-Two . . . Come in." Blake said.

"Nick and I are in the maintenance room near the French Quarter. There seems to be suspi-cious wiring connected to the flood-light timer of the French Quarter . . . Over."

"Okay, Security-Two. Excellent. Bomb Squad is on their way. Did you find anymore suspicious wiring? . . . Over."

"Negative. But we're still probing . . . Over."

"Check Presidential Wing's lighting system. Be advised, there was a bomb planted in that particular wing. The exact location, has not been determined, as of yet. Just be care-ful . . . . Over."

"10-4. Be advised, Security-One, the timer here at the French Quarter section is set for 3:15 this afternoon . . . Over."

"Ten-Four. Keep me posted, Security-Two . . . Ten-Four?"

"Ten-Four."

After the last transmission, Blake slid his two-way radio into his blazer's inside pocket. When he looked at Lisa, she was eyeing her wristwatch. Then he glanced at his watch. The time was eight A.M.

Seven hours and fifteen minutes remaining.

Would it be a *BOOM*? Or a DUD?

It remains to be seen . . . .

Chapter Fifty-Six

THE TIME WAS now 11:30 A.M. The second bomb was located and defused by the bomb squad. A great percentage of the hotel was evacuated and free from danger. The police, once again, roped-off the entire perimeter of the hotel, which included Dunk-n-Donuts, Burger King, and McDonald's. The orange bar-ricades were mounted along the curbs of Layton and Howell Avenue. And the hotel guests and outside customers had moved their vehicles as far as one mile, maybe, two miles away.

The only living soul on the premises were employed City, County, and Federal officials. The string of ambulances, paramedics, and fire trucks were parked along the outer edge of the parking lot on the avenues.

The famous pizza parlor next to the hotel decided it'll be safer if they had close for the day and send their people home. Smart.

Lisa, Blake, Hank, Scott and I were standing near the barricades on How-ell Avenue watching the Metro Police pull away and pass us as they drove off with Elvis and Tonia in the rear seat.

As Rudy was laid-up in the County Hospital, with a bullet wound in his knee, his legal rights were read to him by the arresting officer.

The third bomb was still ticking away, somewhere. The three musketeers remained silent; meaning, Elvis, Rudy, and Tonia . . . . Omerta . . . The Code of Silence.

Thinking about it . . . Was there a third bomb? Or were they playing us for fools?

Or, were there more than three bombs planted in the hotel to be activated at three-fifteen this afternoon?

Several hours from now, we'll know for sure.

Tick . . . Tick . . . Tick . . .

At one P.M., the sun was shooting warm haze of yellow rays on the earth. The sky was smiling blue, and cloudless. The wind had hugged itself into a slight breeze. It just wants to make you light up a camp-fire and roast marsh-mallows. But, under these circumstances, it just wasn't a good idea.

The remaining of the hotel employees had joined the outside spectators with anxiety. The crowd hissed and mumbled. And some spoke loudly and angrily.

I was standing in the middle, between Hank and Scott on my right, and Lisa and Blake on my left, just waiting for an explosion. But, if we had been lucky, the bomb squad officials would come out and announce . . ."ALL CLEAR!"

While waiting, for whatever came first, Lisa and Blake were involved in a heavy discussion, but whispering. Blake nodding, curling his lower lip, and Lisa shaking her right hand with her index finger pointing outward at Blake.

I glanced to my left and stepped in earshot of the secret conversation. Just to catch anything of interest.

" . . . . and that is why I think someone else is involved, Blake." Lisa said, paying me no mind. I felt like an outcast.

❯ ❮

The Grand Milwaukee Hotel was built over fifty years ago. Even with structure renovations over the years, it still was built solid with mason and it seemed to be securely built as of today. The hotel's structure was planted, and perfectly centered in its surrounding parking lot. And, about two, three, or maybe even four blocks away from the two main avenues; (Howell and Layton). So, if there were to be an explosion, either side of the avenues would be safe.

So one would think . . . .

But did we positively know the size of the explosives? Or, even had a slight idea what kind of bomb it was?

No. We did not. So with that in mind, the police had pushed the anxious and terrified crowd further across Howell and Layton.

Safe . . . Maybe.

The traffic was detoured further south on Howell Avenue, away from the hotel and west of Grange Avenue, and further west of Layton, and east of Van Norman street. Now, the streets and avenues were dead from traffic; no cars, buses, or trucks. Even the General Mitchell International Airport was shut down. No aircrafts, whatsoever. Except for Helicam's from the media, hovering, taking photos of all the excitement.

People biting their nails and hugging each other in fear, as if it was their last hug. Some probably were in such a frenzy, they probably were snorting cocaine. Or, even shooting up, and smoking pot and drinking alcohol on public sidewalks, while the police watched the hotel with their own anxiety.

❯ ❮

The bomb squad was still in the arms of danger . . . Maybe death. Then again, maybe nothing.

The time was still ticking away. Time doesn't stand still for anything. Or anyone.

180

The time now: 3:07 P.M., Wednesday, March 15th, 1997 . . . . Eight minutes away from a possible disaster. Most of the fearful crowd went home, or found a distant pub or lounge, and decided to observe the commotion on tel-evision.

The several media Heli-Cams was still in the sky, circling and circling, hovering and hovering.

Now, it was 3:08 P.M. The bomb squad still didn't come out and yell . . .

"ALL CLEAR." The chances that they will are slim. Maybe, they'll never yell those words again . . . *ALL CLEAR.* Ever . . . Never.

The time now: 3:09 and fifteen seconds. And still weren't any sign of the four brave men who went in courageously and tried to save so many lives.

And even the hotel.

But who's in there to save our four hero's from disaster? Would the fire-fighters and paramedics arrive in time to save them if disaster strikes? The tragic thought will remain to be seen.

At exactly 3:15 P.M. walls, windows, window frames, beds, dressers, carpeting, T.V. sets, bathtubs, sauna's . . . you name it . . . all destroyed in a flash of a second.

Was it possible our four brave men survived the blast? Let's hope so.

As the blast was occurring, the remaining crowd on Howell and Layton Avenue, turned away to prevent injuries to themselves, protecting their faces and their love ones from flying debris. Which included brick, metal, flying glass, and etcetera. The "*etcetera*" was an arm, and two left legs flying to- ward the terrified onlookers.

The International Wing, from the north end of the hotel, was nothing but a humongous hole. Just like the Grand Ballroom and Baton Rouge Hall that the tornado created a week ago.

The bright, red and shiny fire trucks glistened from the afternoon sun, as it sped to the disaster scene. The paramedics and ambulances followed suit.

In no time at all, the firefighters had the crime scene surrounded, hosing down the hungry flames, chasing the inferno's flames and destroying them into nothing.

Several hours later, the firefighters and paramedics *hope*, had turned into hopelessness. They came out of the smoldering building with no survivors.

May God Bless our bomb squad, firefighters, paramedics, and all of our police officers . . . from now 'til eternity.

We salute you all!

Chapter Fifty-Seven

THE ENTIRE NEIGHBORHOOD was shut down and in mourning. The sun had set in the west, and the moon had risen from the east. The stars were shining and twinkling brightly, as if winking at us.

The crowd had dispersed aimlessly with tears and heavy sobbing openly displayed.

From a distance, on Howell Avenue, Lisa, Blake, Scott, Hank, Belle, Bob the bartender, Greg, Dena, Carina, Kim and me, were standing among each other, watching the thick black smoke rise and flow across the community.

International Wing on the north end was so covered with dark thick smoke, you couldn't even see what damage had been done.

The flashing blue and red lights were bouncing off the hotel's structure and the spectators faces. Dozens of city and federal employees, dressed in suits, were walking around, assessing the damage, while others were hud-dled together discussing their fallen comrades.

Our friends and the rest of the hotel employees seemed totally lost and dazed. Tears had fallen from everyone. Lisa and I consoled everyone we had known who'd helped us in our investigation.

Now, as we huddled together, two dark shadows appeared, walking north from Howell Avenue. Once the dark figures were under the yellow, hazed street lights, we had recognized their faces.

"We came as fast as we could," Pam the singer said to the crowd. "I just received the call from my husband, Mark. He had informed me what had had happened. Is everyone okay?"

We nodded solemnly.

Johnny B. spoke, "I was on the other side of the bridge, I-794, when Pam called me on my cell phone." Johnny B. walked toward Blake resting his hand on his shoulder. "I am so, so, so, sorry, Blake. Thank God you and the rest are safe and sound. How did this hellish episode happen?"

"Sabotage, Johnny B. Lisa and Nick and I thought," Blake stared at the nightly stars, "we had all the saboteurs. But, obviously we hadn't. But three suspects were arrested. But there is a fourth one walking about. He or she actually had set the timing device for 3:15 this afternoon. We are working on that. It was totally an inside job. You can bet your bottom dollar, Johnny B."

Blake's eyes came down from the dark sky and gazed into Johnny B's shad-owed eyes. Johnny B. nodded.

"Who do you think, Blake?" Pam the singer said.

"Don't know for certain, Pam. But like I said, we're working on it."

Blake gestured toward Lisa with his right thumb. "Lisa, here, brought the idea of the fourth suspect to my attention. There might be more suspects be-fore this investigation is over."

I turned to Lisa. "How did you come up with that conclusion about a fourth suspect, honey?"

"I'll explain later, maybe on the way to Chicago." She stood on her tip-toes and kissed me softly on my left cheek.

I shrugged. Then I leaned over and kissed Lisa on her cute, tiny nose.

Before Lisa and I checked into another hotel, a motel, actually, which was down the street on Howell Avenue, we thanked Dena and Carina for their assistance. We shook hands and gave our hugs to everyone. Maybe we will meet again under better circumstances.

The motel we were staying at now wasn't as spacious and elegant as the Grand Milwaukee Hotel, well, before the explosion anyway.

No room service . . . No elevators . . . No music, or Karaoke. And, we were deeply saddened that there was not a sauna and swimming pool. It was just a room to relax and watch something boring on T.V.

I bought a six-pack of beer for myself, and Vodka and Tonic with several limes for Lisa. We made our drinks and sat up in bed with our backs against the headboard. Some Sci-Fi movie was on. I guess some monster was invad-ing Japan . . . ROAR!!

The time was nearly midnight when we decided to get some sleep. We had dumped the remaining pizza and lime in the trash, switched-off the T.V., and snuggled together the rest of the evening.

Long day ahead of us tomorrow.

Chapter Fifty-Eight

I T WAS THURSDAY morning, March 16th. The early morning clouds were promising rain. Lisa and I lied in bed, spooning affectionately. Facing Lisa's back, my left hand was draped over her left side. I couldn't resist. I started to caress her breasts while I kissed her soft, strong neck.

"Nick, honey, keep that up we just might have to pay the motel another day." Lisa was purring like a content kitten.

"Yep, I know." I said, still caressing her.

"You are not going to stop, are you?"

"Nope."

"What am I going to do with you, stud?"

"Satisfy my male animalism."

"And if I don't?" Her purring had seized.

"I might not be able to put my pants on."

"Oh." She was silent for a moment. Then, I felt something.

Lisa said, "Oh, I see . . . or should I say, I *feel* what you mean."

She rolled over and faced me. Then, she compensated my affection.

After my sexual animalism was satisfied, hoping Lisa's was too, we sat up in bed and I turned on T.V., remotely. We sipped our coffee. Then I turn-ed away from the television, planting my eyes on Lisa's left profile. She'd probably interested in some talk show.

Facing her left cheek, with her shoulder length hair disarrayed, I said,

"Honey, didn't you have something to tell me?"

Still facing T.V., she said, "Like what?"

"The other possible suspect, or suspects." Then she turned her blue eyes on mine.

"Oh, that. But if I remember correctly, my dear, I believe I said I will tell you on the way to Chicago."

"You're going to keep me waiting?"

"Yep. Sure am. But I thought you might've figured this thing out on your own." She took in some coffee.

"I didn't give it much thought," I said. Then I took in some coffee. I set my coffee cup down on the night stand, and continued. "I guess I was rely-ing on you to inform me."

"Oh. Am I detecting spoil-ism?"

" 'Spoilism' . . . . What is spoilism?"

She said bluntly. "You're fucking spoiled. Just because I am a detective now, you're depending on my detecting expertise, aren't you?"

"I've taught you very well, haven't I?"

"Yes. Yes you have. But I do not want you to give up your own detecting abilities. What I want you to do is analyze the situation, and think about the other possible suspect . . . or suspects.

"And when you have completed that task, then I want you to tell me what you have come up with. I just want to be certain you and I are on the same page . . . Ca-peesh?"

I thought about it for a minute or two.

"Okay, fair enough. Maybe I am spoiled. I'll give you my expert opinion on the other suspect . . . ."

"Or suspects," Lisa said, interrupting my words.

"Or suspects," I repeated. "when we arrive in Chicago."

With a sly grin, she said, "Fair enough."

We jumped out of bed. We showered. She prettied up her beautiful face, while I shaved, and brushed my teeth. Sharing the small bathroom at the same time could be hazardous to ones health. She poked me in the ribs, and I poked her in the left eye. With the bruise on my chin from Elvis Masano and the bruise on her left eye, we matched just perfectly. What a sleuthing team we are.

We'd carefully packed our clothes in our suitcases without hurting each other. Now, that's a good thing.

We inspected the room carefully. Just to be certain we had everything. I switched off the T.V., went to the front desk, and we checked out.

Chicago . . . Here we come.

Chapter Fifty-Nine

"A DOG?" WHAT KIND of a dog?" I said eyes focused on I-94.

"German Shepard. I already have an image what the canine should look like." Lisa's eyes gleamed with excitement.

"Oh?"

"Yeah. All black with a small patch of white on its throat."

"Male or female?" I asked.

Lisa had her forefinger on her lower lip, thinking. "Ah . . . female."

"Name?"

"I thought long and hard about the name if I had a female dog. I came up with Mariah."

"Oh, like the 'Wind.' "

"Yeah. Exactly. Her last name will be . . ."

"Murray?" I said with a grin.

"No, silly. Duchess . . ."

"Duchess, huh? Nice ring to it." I said.

Lisa went silent, thinking again.

"Yeah . . . Mariah Duchess. I like that." She said nodding to herself.

"Wish you luck, Lisa."

"Thanks. And when I'm on lengthy cases you can dog-sit."

"Thank you very much. And, if both of us are on lengthy cases together, who then?"

"Clint and Julia. Or maybe even Eagle and Pam."

"Did you ask them yet?"

"No. But I will."

"Wish you luck, again." I said.

"Thanks."

"You're welcome."

We were silent for a time.

The rain was light. And the wipers were set on intermittent. Chicago traf- fic was heavy, bumper to bumper.

From the corner of my right eye, I'd noticed Lisa gazing at me hard.

"See, Nick. If you didn't need your *male animalism* satisfied, we would have missed rush hour traffic." She crossed her arms over her well-shaped breasts, and turned her head toward the windshield. She found her self star-ring at a semi-trailers' break lights.

"Are you complaining?" I quickly glanced over to Lisa. She sat sternly in the passenger seat, eyes still glaring at the trailer in front of us.

"Me . . . Never." She continued to stare out the windshield, tapping her fingers on her crossed-arms, as if she was playing the trumpet.

I grinned.

Silence.

Eisenhower and Kennedy Expressways were always congested this time of day. Sometimes, even busier, if the Chicago Cubs or White Sox were playing. Now, when the Milwaukee Brewers play Chicago, now, that is a sight to see. Traffic galore. *Holy Cow!*

Lisa decided to nap. And this was a perfect time to think about the *other* suspect from the Grand Milwaukee Hotel, who might have been involved bombing the hotel's structure.

I reviewed the case over and over in my brain. I thought very deeply. But not too deeply, where I rear-end the vehicle in front of me.

The time: 4:15 P.M. The traffic was stop and go, bumper to bumper most of the way to Downtown Chicago's Holiday Inn.

By the time we'd arrived, I had figured out the fourth possible suspect.

Who? I didn't know at this particular time. But, I knew there had to be another person involved. I figured that much out, anyway.

Someone had to set the timers on that gloomy Wednesday morning of the explosion. The timers were set, probably between six and eight A.M.

The wires were already in place when Hank and I had checked the tim-ers around eight that morning. And the lights were set to go off at six that same morning. All three timers were set for the lights to come back on at three-fifteen P.M., on that *DARK* Wednesday afternoon, to detonate the ex- plosives.

But, by whom?

Rudy was in the County Hospital. Elvis and Tonia were heavily surveill-ed by the hotel security officers. So, who had excess to the maintenance rooms, besides security. Was it Robert, the Maintenance man . . . ? Umm.

Or one of the guests?

Chapter Sixty

THE PARKING STRUCTURE was right across the street from Holiday Inn, which was located on the edge of Downtown Chicago. As Lisa and I strolled across the catwalk/bridge, leading us to the hotel, we'd noticed the Chicago River still shimmering of green from Saint Patrick's Day.

With luggage in hand, Lisa and I walked through the glass-doubled doors of the hotel lobby. Clint, Eagle, and Pam awaited for our arrival near the front desk.

Eagle, with his right arm extended, hand opened, shook my hand. Then he said, "What took you two so long?"

I said, "Traffic."

Lisa said, "Sex." She spoke with a 'tude.

"Traffic."

"Sex."

"Okay . . . Okay," I said. "Sex and traffic. *You* know what I'm talking about, don't you, Eagle?"

Eagle really didn't want to be involved in our little disagreement, but he had a difficult time swallowing his words. So, he said, "Yep, sure do, buddy.

Sure do." He patted my shoulder and grinned. Lisa gave Eagle and I the devil-look. Then she shrugged and quickly walked over to Pam. Probably to get same gender comfort.

Clint's dark eyes bounced from Lisa to me several times. Then he said, "I made reservations at Genenalli's on Clark and Lake Street for eight tonight. Check in, Nick and Lisa and get settled. We'll meet you down here at seven-thirty near the elevators. We have less than two hours."

"Italian. Yum." I said.

"Hope you didn't mind, Lisa," Clint said. "We didn't know what time when you and Nick would have arrived, so we took the liberty to choose Ge-nenalli's."

"Fine. Just fine." Lisa gave me that certain look, like she was perturbed with me for making us late, and not being involved in choosing another rest-aurant. German food was more of Lisa's taste.

We checked into our room, freshened up, and unpacked, and changed in-to fresh clothing. As I was buttoning my bottom button on my shirt, Lisa had gently wrapped her loving arms around my waist. Her pretty blues gazed in-to my face. Then she said, "Sorry, Nick for being a total bitch."

"Bitch? I didn't notice." *Yeah . . . right.* I thought.

"Well, I am so sorry. I am just so upset . . . I was so positive Rudy was our man who'd killed my parents. It's like starting all over again."

"Don't worry about it, honey," I pulled her in closer to my chest. "We'll find those sonavabitches who'd killed your parents."

"Yeah, I know. But I didn't mean to be grumpy with you. Forgive me?"

"I understand. But there isn't anything to be forgiven for."

We hugged.

She pulled away slowly and stood in front of me at arms length with one hand on my shoulder.

"Did you complete the task I'd asked you to do . . . Umm?" Lisa grinned.

"The *other* suspect in Milwaukee?"

"Umm..Um."

"Yeah, matter of fact, I did. But the task wasn't much of a task. It was, how should I say, uh, quite simple, actually."

"What's *your* version, *Sherlock*?"

I told her.

"My thoughts, exactly," Lisa said. "But I didn't go as deep as you had. So you think it could be Robert, the maintenance guy? Interesting. Do you think Blake had suspected him?"

"I don't know. I'll call him later at his house."

"That's a plan." Lisa smiled widely. Then she gave me a soft kiss on my cheek.

Time was 7:25 P.M. when the shiny brass elevator doors slid open quiet-ly. Lisa and I glided across the mirrored-shiny floor, and found two match-ing wing chairs on the soft lavender carpet in the main lobby. We sat and waited for Clint, Pam, and Eagle.

Between the matching wing chairs sat a small round table. On the table was a current *Chicago Trib'*. It was open to the *Classifieds*. I briefly glanced at this particular *Ad*. It read: *Reward . . . Lost puppy . . . Less than a year old . . .*

. . . My gears in my brain began to turn rapidly. Yes, I thought. That would be a terrific idea. But would it work? One way to find out.

I slipped my silvery ball point pen and green covered-spiraled notepad from the inside pocket of my suit coat, and wrote a note to myself . . . *Call the Trib' Want Ads first thing in the morning.* I smiled, as I was returning my pad and pen into its pocket.

I was still smiling when Eagle, Pam, and Clint appeared in front of us.

I glanced at my watch. It was seven-thirty on the nose.

"What are you smiling about, Nick?" Eagle asked.

"I'll tell you guys later." The four looked at each other, shrugged.

"Okay, then," Pam said. "Let's go get a bite to eat."

We all agreed.

We shuffled through the revolving brass doors of the hotel onto the busy avenue of Downtown Chicago. We strolled leisurely up State Street, two long blocks. Then we turned left on Lake Street, and walked another two long blocks until we'd found ourselves facing Genenalli's on the corner of Clark & Lake Street.

We walked in.

We ordered, ate, drank, and discussed Lisa's case on the death of her parents.

We decided to split ourselves into several groups.

Eagle and Pam . . . Open Records.

Clint and Lisa . . . maybe Dillman . . . search in Lisa's father's old cases.

And me . . . Call the newspaper . . . Want Ads'

Clint put his drink down on his right, near the empty pie plate, then he turned to me.

"Wasn't there something you wanted to tell us, Nick? You were smiling in the hotels' lobby over an hour ago. What was that about?"

All eyes were on me now. So I told them my plan. After they listened in-tently, they seemed pleased and hopeful.

Chapter Sixty-One

TODAY IS MARCH 17th, Friday morning. I called the *Tribune* and placed my *ad*. It read: *Reward: 5,000 dollars offered for information on the death of a man and woman in a car bombing in Christian High School's parking lot twelve years ago on Graduation Day, May 18th, 1985. Call Mr. Nick Edwards, Holiday Inn, Chicago (on State Street).* I had placed the ad for one week.

While Clint and Lisa searched through her dad's old cases at the police department, and Eagle and Pam were at the County Court House probing open records, I ate at the Holiday Inn Lounge.

The waitress came, poured coffee and set a tall glass of iced-water in front of me. She took my order and went.

The weather was typical for Chicago. It was windy and extremely chilly. The temperature teetered between 40 and 45 degrees. Fog was rolling in from Lake Michigan, and Chicago River had noticeable vapors dancing over its tinted-green current.

The downtown crowd was bobbing up and down the streets, passing the restaurant's picture window with collars up and clenching their hats. The pe-ople who weren't wearing hats, had their hands deep in their pockets. And hair blowing wild. But, still no rain in the forecast. At least, that was what Channel-Seven, Meteorologist announced this morning.

The waitress returned with my orange juice and placed it on the right side of my sunny-side eggs, hash browns, and sausage, which was centered be-fore me. The plate of wheat toast with smeared butter was on my left. She smiled at me politely, did about-face, and went.

After I ate, paid my bill, and left a tip, I went to my room and called my pal Blake in Milwaukee.

"Good-morning, Nick. How's the gang?"

"So far, so good. The question is; how are you and the rest of my friends getting along without a job?"

"We'll get by. We'll collect unemployment for a while. And I will host

Karaoke elsewhere. And maybe do Dee-Jaying somewhere downtown."

"Least you have that. The reason I am calling, Blake, Lisa and I was wondering if you had figured out who the other suspect was."

"I am still working on that. Do you or Lisa have any idea?"

"We thought it might be Robert, your maintenance guy. We thought he might've came in early that Wednesday and reset the timers for three-fifteen that afternoon. But, he was only a guess. It might be someone else who had excess to the Maintenance Room."

"We're asking everyone. Especially Front Desk and Personnel Office if they had observed anyone suspicious, or if anyone came in early who wasn't scheduled."

"Well, good-luck, Blake. Just keep me posted." I had quickly given him the name of the hotel and our room number. "Keep us posted, and tell the gang we said "HI", okay?"

"Will do, Nick. Hope you find Lisa's parents' killers. You know, if I was you, I'll cement their feet and drop them into Lake Michigan."

"Now, that's a thought." We disconnected.

I sat on the corner of the bed and thought about Lisa's suggestion; She wanted me to move in with her after this case was over. I also thought about her dog, Mariah, the German Shepard. Jeez. I wondered if there would have been enough space left to walk around.

Two's a company. Three's a crowd.

I'll think about this some more. But for now, my thoughts were focusing on Sheryl's mother; Sandy Boehlis. I still need to go to Florida and find her.

Also, I need to find Sheryl's aunt and uncle who's somewhere in Orlando.

I need to take them in for their crimes. Justice has to be done. They broke a lot of laws and they should pay for them. Now, that should give me more time to think about moving in with Lisa, and her Wonder Dog, Mariah.

I really like my space . . . My freedom. I like the arrangements we have now. After thinking for a second or two, I remembered she does have an el-evator. It would be easier for my wounded knee. I had an operation on my right knee after getting shot last year, but it didn't heal quite right. Well, I'll think about that. But . . . My *freedom*? Tough decision.

What about Lisa's freedom, *her* space. Had she considered that? Both of our space and freedom had been important to us for a hell of a long time. Will we be able to adjust? Will we be able to get along? Or will we be fighting like cats and dogs. Dogs . . . ? Yeah . . . Mariah; The Wonder Dog.

Chapter Sixty-Two

LISA AND I were in a very deep sleep on a gloomy Saturday morning when the phone rang, disturbing the quiet air. I reached for the phone with my eyes half-open.

"Yeah."

"Mr. Edwards, you have a visitor in the lobby. Shall I send him up?" Said the Front Desk Agent.

"Who is it?" My mouth felt like a dozen muddy combat boots marching around in it.

"He says his name is Cole . . . Detective Cole from Fifth-District, CPD."

"What time is it anyway?" I said.

"Nine."

I looked over at Lisa for a moment. She seemed to be sleeping soundly.

"I'll come down and meet him in the hotel café. I'm not quite awake yet. Give me about twenty minutes. Okay?"

"Sure, Mr. Edwards. I'll tell him."

We disconnected.

I swung my long legs over the edge of the mattress and planted my feet firmly on the soft carpet and rubbed my hands over my face. I swaggered to the bathroom, turned the sink faucet on, splashing cold water on my face.

What did Cole want? And how did he know I was staying here? Ah. The newspaper ad. Did he have information of Lisa's parents?

That'll be great.

I quickly brushed my teeth, carelessly shaved, and got dressed. Then I kissed Lisa on her left cheek softly. She moaned slightly rolling on her left side, undisturbed.

Few minutes later, I found myself riding down slowly in the brass-coated elevator.

Still half-sleep, and not knowing what Cole had looked like, I asked the Front Desk Agent. He told me to look for a very tall bald-headed man, wear-ing a black windbreaker, white shirt, and black Levi's. I thanked him.

Cole was nothing I had imagined. (Nothing at all like Jack Webb).

As I was approaching the round table where he was sitting, he stood with his right hand out.

"Mr. Edwards, I presume."

I took his hand and we shook. "You presumed correctly, Detective Cole."

"The front desk gave me a great description of you. But he failed to tell me to look for a man with tissue on his face." He chuckled.

"Damn. I was in such a hurry to see you, I cut myself shaving." I peeled off the blotchy red tissue from my cut cheek and put it in my pocket. It would've been uncouth to set the bloody substance on the white table cloth.

"Good to see you are still alive and well." Cole said.

"Yeah, and the criminals hate me for it."

Cole chuckled again.

"What brings you here, Detective?"

"The ad in the paper, and also, I wanted to see what you look like."

He sipped some black coffee. With the cup in his hand, he asked, "How's the Boehlis case coming?"

"Fired." I took the coffee pot and poured me some.

"So what's this about a car bombing twelve years ago?"

"My girlfriend's father and mother was car bombed on her graduation day. We're here to find the bombers. Her father had worked in Homicide."

"Here? Chicago?" Cole was stunned. "I haven't heard anything about it."

Cole took a bite of his wheat toast, washed it down with black coffee and dabbed the corner of his left lower lip with a white cloth napkin.

"Yep. Right here in the *Windy City*. His name was Don Murray. And his wife's name was Katie. Lisa and my cohorts thought we had found our bom-ber in Milwaukee, Wisconsin."

"But no dice, huh?"

"No dice." I took the last wedge of my rye toast and smeared butter over it smoothly.

"Need help?" Cole asked.

"Maybe. Get all the help we can get."

"He's a fellow officer. We stick together through thick and thin. I will be more than happy to help. What do you have thus far?"

"Nothing. That's why I had put it in the classifieds. Hoping someone will turn up with information. So far, we don't have anything."

"Not to change the subject, Nick, but since you're fired from the Boehlis case, are you still planning to go to Florida?"

"Damn straight, I am, Detective. My investigation was not finished to my liking. I stay on a case until I get results."

"Determination. Gotta' respect that."

I grinned.

"I am also planning to go to the cemetery where Boehlis was buried, uh, I mean, sup-posedly buried. Actually, it is Clara Rueton's grave-site. Not Sandy's." I took in some more coffee.

"Where is this cemetery, Nick?"

"Cal-City Cemetery. It's right off Route 30 and Lincoln Highway."

"I'll come with you. That's my jurisdiction anyway. My department might want to exhume the corpse for verification."

"Great idea, Cole. I'll call Mr. and Mrs. Rueton. I'm positive they'll want their daughter to have a proper burial."

"Sure thing." Cole said, lifting the coffee pot at me. I nodded. He poured, and I took in a sip. Then he poured himself a cup.

"When are you going to the grave site?"

"Today." I said.

"Great. Timing couldn't be more perfect."

"I'll go to my room and tell Lisa."

"Is she your girlfriend?" Cole asked.

"Girlfriend, *and* Private Investigator. She's probably still sleeping. I'll leave her a note and meet you in the lobby. Okay."

"Sure. That's fine." Cole raised his coffee cup in agreement. I returned my two-fingered salute. Then I turned and left, leaving a few dollars on the table.

As I was approaching the elevators, and passing the desk agent, he caught my attention by sounding out my name.

"Oh, Mr. Edwards." He had a white business-sized envelope in his right hand, waving it in the air. "This just came for you."

I squinted, and wondered if my ad from the 'Trib' had been answered. He handed it to me. I thanked him politely. Then I leaned on the far corner of the curved desk, opening it carefully. I pulled out the white stationary. Un-folded it. And to my surprise, it read: YOUR DEAD!!! It was endorsed with familiar lettering . . . *B.O.S.S.* I read those letters before. No . . . I'd *heard* those letters from someone before, but whom? I thought. But at the moment my memory was playing tricks.

I pretended to be reading the note, but my eyes was actually roaming the huge lobby, carefully checking for anyone staring in my direction. Maybe, whoever had dropped the note off, waited to see who would have picked it up. And he or she was probably watching me this very second, just to see what I look like.

I asked the desk clerk who had delivered the letter.

"A teenage boy with long brown, maybe dark brown hair. And a *White Sox* baseball cap. Kinda' on the thin side." He shrugged.

I thanked him again. Scanning the lobby once again, my eyes failed to detect any kinda' thin, long brown, maybe dark brown hair with 'White Sox' baseball cap.

But I did notice two people. First one was male sitting in a gold satin wing chair reading the *First Edition* of the newspaper. His slip-on shoes was highly spit-shined. I couldn't see his face. But he had small hands. By the size of his slip-on shoes, I would say he wasn't very tall either. But his hands were manly hands; small, but not without age.

The second one was also male. He was leaning against the wall near the lobby's elevator's with arms crossed over his puny chest. He was also short. He had Italian sunglasses pulled down slightly over his beak-nose. Mr. Cool.

Dark, jet-black, wavy hair. And cut neatly. Handsomely dressed with a suit priced as a down payment on a new car. Very sharp. Neat-o.

I gathered the teenage boy was paid-off to deliver the envelope. I was set up. Imagine that.

Instead the elevator, I took the stairs, hoping someone would follow me. I walked upstairs slowly and listened for any noise. Nothing. I carefully open-ed the stairwell door leading into the hallway to my room. But I didn't see anyone loitering the hallway. Secured? Maybe. I unlocked, opened, and quietly closed the guest-room-door. I didn't want to disturb Lisa.

I quickly wrote a small note. Laid it neatly and noticeably on the small nightstand next to Lisa. I gently kissed her forehead. Tip-toeing out, I had closed the door quietly behind me. Then I looked up and down the hallway. Just to be sure no one was lurking. When it was safe, I went toward the stair-well door, and descended the stairs to the main lobby. Still no one was shadowing me.

In the lobby, I scanned for the two men I had seen earlier. Gone..? Least they weren't in the lobby. Maybe they were somewhere else. Watching . . . . Waiting.

As I was scanning the lobby, my eyes landed on Detective Cole, patiently waiting near the brass revolving doors with arms crossed and his right foot pasted against the wall. Our eyes made contact. He pushed himself away from the beige wall and went through the revolving doors. I fell in behind him.

As we stepped onto State Street from the revolving doors, I took another glance over my shoulder for any shadows. Still, no one. Just your normal people bobbing along to report to work or wherever they were going.

Coles' unmarked squad car was curbside. I got to the car first, but had to wait for Cole to open his drivers' door to pop the lock on the passengers' door. I opened it and slid in, taking one more glance for shadows.

Na'da'

The car squealed into traffic. Some idiot blew his horn at Cole. He just smiled and waved. But under his breath, he muttered *"Motherfucker."*

Few minutes had past when Cole decided to whistle some tunes. I didn't recognize any of the them. I sat quietly in deep thought. The endorsement on the note had bothered me deeply. My brain was forming a headache.

BOSS . . . BOSS . . . What did it mean? Who did I hear it from? Think, Nick. Think.

Cole took the expressway heading northwest to Cal-City. Then we exited on Lincoln Highway heading north. We went through four stoplights, turned right on Route-Thirty heading east. Quarter mile later Cole turned right. It took us right into Cal-City Cemetery. The temperature suddenly felt cooler.

Ten degrees cooler. Maybe more. I shivered. Spooky . . . !

The car took a few curves and some left and right turns.

"What section is it in, Nick?"

I told him. Then he pointed to the left. "There it is. Under the old oak tree."

Cole jammed the shift into park. We both got out in unison, leaving the doors wide open. We stood face to face with a falsified marble headstone. The headstone was engraved artistically. It read: *SANDY M. BOEHLIS . . .*

LOVING MOTHER . . . LOVING DAUGHTER . . . LOVING SISTER . . . REST IN PEACE . . . **1954-1977.**

The wind had picked up and had gotten colder. Mean spirits. I thought.

I put my collar up around my freezing neck, hands in my pockets. The bare oak tree branches rapidly shivered, forcing some branches to break and bris-kly crashing on the cold, hard ground.

Where I was standing, I looked as far as my eyes could see. Shockingly, the hard winds were only blowing around us. The remaining cemetery seem-ed calm.

Shivering, I said, "Sandy's family went all out, didn't they?"

"What do you mean?" Even though the wind was cold, Det. Cole seemed comfortable. Even his zipper to his windbreaker was unzipped and blowing in the wind, revealing his 9mm service weapon on his right hip. He didn't seem to care.

"The cover-up. Headstone and all."

"Oh, yeah, that. I see what you mean." We both stared at the dull gray headstone, shaking our heads in disbelief. Cole said, "Like I said earlier, I'll have the coffin exhumed and call Clara's parents and inform them . . ." He paused, then said to me, "Unless you want to call them, Nick."

"You can call. I'm fine with it."

He nodded.

≫ ≪

Returning to the Holiday Inn, it had finally occurred to me where I'd heard the acro-nym (*BOSS*). Dillman. Yeah, Lieutenant Dillman. But what did it mean?

The threatening letters sent to Lisa's father from Balesteri brothers had **BOSS** as an endorsement. My head was throbbing with pain.

Then I started thinking. *Who had sent the letter to the hotel?* It couldn't have been Rudy. He was in the Milwaukee County jail. Or the County Hos-pital. It could have been him. I thought again. Maybe he had called someone from Chicago. And this someone had read the ad.

Damn it. Everybody else was answering the ad, except the people it was intended for. Bah. This sucks. *I needed information . . . Damn it!*

I turned to Cole. I said, "Do you know what the letter's B-O-S-S is in ref—erence to?"

"Why?" We were a mile away from the hotel. The traffic was moderate on the express-way with several speeding cars flying past us. Cole's expres-sion tightened. "Look at those assholes speeding. Did you get their plate number, Nick. I surely didn't. They were going too fast."

"My answer exactly, Detective." He just shook his head in disgust.

"Sorry, Nick. But what was the question again?"

"Do you know what the letter's B-O-S-S is in reference to?" I repeated.

"Yeah I do. B.O.S.S. stands for Bomb Operations Special Service. It is run by the Balesteri family." He quickly turned his face at me, giving me a hard stare. Then he said, "Is this the case you and your friends on?"

I nodded. "Yep."

Cole's tense dark eyes was focused on the traffic. We were quiet for a second or two.

Cole said, "So what you're telling me, you're dealing with Balesteri, and you are *still alive?*"

"Not for long it seems." I said.

"Hooolllyy shit, Nick. I had run-ins with those bastards in the past. They *are not*, I repeat, *ARE NOT* to be fooled with."

"But we're not involved with them anymore, Detective." I said.

"But they might think you are."

"Word probably got out I had shot Rudy in the kneecap and flubbed his bombing operation in Milwaukee. That's what I'm thinking."

"YOU SHOT A BALESTERI . . . ! Damn. You best had killed him." Cole blew out some air. "I better stay with you and your cohorts until this shit blows over. My guess, it never will blow over. And I can't protect you and your friends forever. You best be careful, damn it."

"We will. And thanks for your help, Cole. I 'preciate it."

"Sure, kid. Is your girlfriend safe?"

"I surely hope so."

Abruptly, the unmarked pushed forward at a high rate of speed. The spe-edometer was reading; seventy-five and climbing. Then Cole leaned and clenched a red dome from under his seat, and quickly slamming it on top of the roof. It was flashing brightly. Vehicles were pulling over, left and right.

I tightened my seatbelt and held my breath. Lisa would've loved this kinda' ride. Years ago, she had raced with the pros. Speed was her middle name.

Flashing red and blue lights flashed at us when we'd approached the hotel's entrance. Ambulance, Paramedics, and Metro-Police vehicles had State Street blocked with orange cones and other emergency vehicles.

Cole had slammed his front tires up on the curb a block away from the hotel. Slamming it in park, we both jumped out in full stride and ran as fast as we could. I had noticed a silver gurney being rolled out with a black body bag strapped to it. So did Cole. Our legs and feet picked up momentum. Jumping over cones and other obstacles and pushing our way through curi-ous lookie-loos.

A uniformed police officer tried to halt us, but we kept right on running. But I did notice Cole's gold police shield swaying back and forth around his neck. The uniformed police got the hint. He let us go.

Approaching the gurney, Cole was yelling at the coroner between heavy breathes.

"Before . . . you take . . . the corpse, I would like . . . to see who it is. Okay?"

The female coroner expression tightened. "Who in the hell are you?" She looked beyond Cole's shoulder. "And who is he?" She said, pointing at me.

"He's with me. And I'm with Homicide. Detective Cole is my name."

"Any identification?" She said.

"My shield. Isn't that good enough?"

"What shield?"

I then realized Cole's gold shield was flat against his upper back. The chain attached to the shield was practically choking him. Taking the shield, I said, "We were galloping so fast, the shield had shifted." I let the gold shield fall on Cole's chest in view of the coroner.

"Okay. Now *that's* better." She grinned. She slowly unzipped the black body bag, revealing a disturbing sight. Cole leaned into the bag, as I peeked over his left shoulder. The corpse had a clean gun shot to the forehead. The face was old and leathery. Blood stains still clinging to his very fine and thin white hair. The corpse's face matched the color of his hair with purple shad-owing around his lips.

I exhaled aggressively to the point of choking. "Thank God the corpse wasn't Lisa."

"Or any of your other friends," Cole added.

"Yeah . . . Of course." I took in some more deep breaths.

We thanked the beautiful coroner. She nodded grinningly. Then we'd dashed for the hotels' revolving door. I was halted by Cole's strong hand, gripping my right shoulder.

"Let's not interfere with the detective's interview with Lisa and your other friends, Nick."

I reluctantly agreed.

The hotel's lobby was swarming with uniformed cops and plain-clothed detectives. The coroner was talking to some tall woman in a dark pants suit who was taking notes.

I was at the antsy point. I was just about to run toward Lisa to be with her when Cole grabbed my shoulder again.

"Calm down, kid. How long have you been a detective?"

I stared at Cole, confusingly. "Off and on for twenty years. Why?"

"You should know better not to interfere during an interview."

"Yeah, I do know better. But I had always worked alone. Never had a partner before that I care this much about."

"Just be patient, son."

"By the way, Cole, who was in the body bag?" I asked, my eyes remain-ing on Lisa.

"You don't know? But how could you. You're not from Chicago."

"So who was he?"

"Mr. Balesteri . . . Richard Balesteri . . . The top Mafia guy . . . The father to Rudy and Ruby Balesteri."

"You're shitting me, right?" I took my eyes off Lisa for a moment to gaze into Cole's eyes.

"I kid you not, Nick." His eyes were roaming the lobby and stairs for something. Or someone. Maybe a sniper pointing a gun at us.

"Who do you think shot him, Detective?"

"The look of things," He pointed toward Lisa and my friends, "My guess, either your friends are witnesses to the shooting, or one of your friends is the shooter."

"WHAT?" I said, loudly. I quickly covered my mouth realizing people were looking in our direction.

"Whoever shot Mr. Balesteri was a very damn good shooter. Right be-tween the eyes. Not bad . . . *Not bad at all.*"

I shook my head and decided to wait for the interview to be over. I want-ed to hold Lisa so badly, I could feel my knees shaking.

But Cole kept his big strong hand on my shoulder.

Still restraining me. Jeez.

Chapter Sixty-Three

"SO TELL ME, Lisa, what happened yesterday while Cole and I visited the cemetery?"

The day was Sunday, March 19th, Lisa had her head resting on my right shoulder and my arm around her well-framed body. She looked up at me with those baby-blues.

"If I told you once, I'd told you a-thousand-times."

"I know. I just like to hear it again. It's so amazing. By the way, where did you learn to shoot like that?"

"My daddy. Every weekend, since I was sixteen, my mother, daddy and I drove to our cabin in the woods. We took bottles, tin cans, and sometimes rotten apples that had fallen from our tree. And then we line them up on a fence-line, and a tree stump and start shooting. My daddy taught me how to breath properly, aim, and also how to hold the gun steady.

"My daddy once told me: 'Princess, a gun is like a dog. If you are afraid of it, it'll knock you down and bite you in the ass'. "

"Wise choice words." I said.

"Yep. Very wise man was he." Lisa smiled.

"So, back to your story, Lisa. How did you happen to shoot Rudy's and Ruby's father between the eyes?"

"You don't give up, do you?"

"Nope."

She took in a tiresome breath and told her story.

"Richard Balesteri, obviously thought our room was vacant. He didn't realize you had me sharing the room with you. He must've seen you leave the hotel thinking he had the room to himself.

"Well, when he jimmied the lock, and it opened, he didn't expect lil' ol' me lying on the bed pointing my trusty .38Cal. Police Special at him. Be-fore he even had the chance to aim his gun at me, I pulled the trigger, he fell backwards into the hallway, bouncing off the wall opposite of our room. And, then he slid down, like in slow motion, hitting the floor, butt first. His short legs sprawled out before him. I called the front desk to report a shoot-ing."

"You did good, honey, really good." Before I could hug her, she got up, and looked at me square in the face.

"GOOD? . . . . You said *Good?* It was great! With a capitol *G.*"

"Yes. Of course it was great. Great story, too." I pulled her down toward me. She let me hug her tightly.

She stared at the ceiling, and said, "But don't ask me to repeat it again and again and again. Got it?"

"I guess. How about if you record it? And, then I can play it in my cas-sette player in my car. Then I can listen to it anytime I want."

"No . . . No . . . No . . . No . . . No more. Now let's get out of bed and go down—stairs and have breakfast."

"Good idea," I said, "The last one to the bathroom is a rotten shooter."

We both jumped out of bed and dashed for it.

Lisa had me beat by her big toe.

≫ ≪

Clint, Pam, Eagle, Lisa and me had gathered around a table in the Holi-day Inn café for our late breakfast, trying to plan our Sunday.

My ad wasn't producing any action. Open records didn't sprout much needed informa-tion. And Lisa's father's old cases came to a screeching halt.

"Let's take a walk in the park near Lake Michigan, and feed the pigeons," Pam said.

"Pam, that's for old folks. Let's not push time." Eagle said.

"You have a better idea?" Pam said.

"I'm thinking. How about you, Nick? Do you have any ideas?" Eagle said.

"We could take a walk around the Art Museum." I said.

"What about the Field Museum?" Lisa piped up. "Or maybe even win-dow shopping." Lisa turned to Clint, "You, Clint?"

"Before I even think about recreation, Lisa, even you for that matter, I would be think-ing about heading back to Wisconsin, before all of us gets killed." We all stared blankly.

"Lisa just killed a top mafia guy. Don't you people think the mafia will be after us?" Clint argued.

"I *am not* leaving Chicago until I find out who killed my parents, Clint.

I am sorry. You guys came out here to help me. Let's not turn back now. But if you guys want to turn around and go back to Wisconsin, be my guest. But I am staying.

"Don't get me wrong," her eyes bounced at us, "I really appreciate all of your help. And we knew the danger before we came out here to investigate my parents death . . ."

"Hold on one minute, Lisa," Clint pointed his index finger, "Sure we meant to help you, but we didn't plan on you killing Mr. Richard Balesteri.

Our best bet is to cut our losses and vamoose out of here. Do you know where I am coming from?"

Nodding, Lisa turned to me silently. She was waiting for me to say some-thing. I did.

"Clint, you are absolutely correct. But if you and Pam and Eagle wants to call it quits, I'm sure Lisa will understand. But be advised, Clint, I am staying with Lisa and find the bastards, who in cold blood, mind you, murdered Lisa's parents."

Everyone was silent for a time. As the silence thickened, I observed an older man, maybe early sixties, standing in the doorway, which divided the hotel lobby and restau-rant's entrance, staring point blank in our direction.

He stood about five-five, or maybe five-six. Short, little twerp. I thought.

His hair thinned and gray. He wore a pair of old faded jeans and denim jack- et with a western shirt. His jacket was opened. I didn't notice if he was tot-ing a gun.

As the old man gracefully walked toward our table, Lisa looked up at him curiously as he passed by her. He came around behind me, slipping a 3 x 5 notepad paper, folded, and tucked it neatly under my saucer. Without a word, he walked away the way he came . . . Gracefully. Then he disappeared among the Sunday crowd . . . *Mystery Man.*

After he had left, I slid the white piece of paper out from under my saucer and un-folded it. Lisa looked on from my left, as Clint looked on from my right. Eagle and Pam leaned over the table gazing directly at me.

Everyone was silent.

I read the note to myself in silence. After reading the note, I refolded it and slipped it into my shirt pocket. I picked up my coffee cup with both hands and took in a few sips, finally realizing my friends were still eyeing me. I set the cup down gently and looked at Lisa and the others. Lisa's eyes were dancing in her head.

"Well. What is it, Nick. What did the note say?"

Everyone else held their gaze, waiting for Lisa's question to be answered.

Turning to Lisa, I said, "You and I have a date tomorrow at Toni's rest-aurant on Van Buren at noon, just you and me, and no one else. The note stated it was mighty important to be there. No cops. No one. The last few sentences were double-lined."

"What do you make of it, honey? Are we being set up for the kill 'cause what I had done to Richard Balesteri?" Lisa's throat seemed to clog with thickness. And she swal-lowed hard.

"Maybe. Maybe not." I took her hand, gently squeezing it. "Maybe we're being set up what I had done to Rudy. You know, shooting him in the knee-cap."

"Shall we follow you discreetly from a distance?" Clint said.

I shook my head.

"Maybe Detective Cole should be involved in this, just in case."

Eagle suggested.

Again, I shook my head. I turned to Lisa, gazing into her intensified eyes.

I knew right then, she was seeking my protection and support. I am her pro-tection, as she is mine. We'll protect each other. I thought.

On the flip side of the coin, maybe the timed meeting wasn't a set up for the kill. This could be the answer to my ad in the Tribune.

"Well," Clint said, half grinningly, "I guess we're not going back to Wisconsin for a while after all. Since that's the case, I suggest we hit a theater downtown and watch a good movie. We'll be in a warm environment with little walking involved."

"What's playing, Clint," Pam said.

"I don't know." He shrugged. "There has to be a good movie playing somewhere."

We all nodded agreeably.

Chapter Sixty-Four

AFTER TAKING CLINT'S 'good movie' advice, which wasn't a good movie after all, (that's my opinion) we returned to the hotel and sat in the lobby for a time. We didn't converse much. We just sat and studied people coming and going, observing anyone suspicious.

Whoever the short messenger *boy* was earlier, might return tonight with a change of plans. Maybe with an Uzi.

It could have very well been a set-up for tomorrow at Toni's restaurant.

Or maybe, just to make us think he'd spared us for twenty—four hours, and might come back tonight to blow us away . . . .

SURPRIZE! Pffft . . . *Pffft . . . Bang . . . Bang . . . You're dead . . . .*

So we all decided to pull guard duty for the evening. Except Lisa and Pam. Us men will take care of it and maintain our females' safety.

Our duty schedule went something like this:

Clint: 6 P.M thru 10 P.M.; Eagle: 10P.M. thru 2A.M.; Me: 2A.M. 'til . . . ?

Well, no action occurred on Clint's or Eagle's shift.

All I had were intoxicated bums who thought they were king studs, trying to get a room with easy and sleazy pick-ups. The front desk agent told them the hotel ran a re-spectable environment and won't tolerate prostitution on the premises.

Some were escorted out by security and other unwelcome guests left mig-hty kindly without incident.

I just sat, twirling my thumbs, minding my business, waiting or expecting security to toss me out for loitering.

But that didn't happen . . . I was happy.

By 8:45, my *waiting* tolerance expired on any expected action. So I trek-ked back to my room. After showering, shaving, changing duds, I woke up Lisa from her snoring expedition. She immediately jumped from bed, and proceeded to go into action . . . . Showered, did hair, and brushed her teeth, in a timely fashion, coming out sparkling and gleaming with brightness.

Approaching eleven-thirty, we were prepared for anything.

Monday was such a bright and sunny morning, Lisa and I decided to walk to Toni's restaurant on Van Buren.

As far we knew, our friends respected my wishes not to get involved in this *so-called* meeting.

As far as we knew, our obedient cohorts were still snuggled in their beds in la . . . la . . . land.

Though, periodically, Lisa and I did glance in the store's reflected win-dows, looking for our beloved friends, as well as our enemies . . . observing anyone suspiciously follow-ing us. But, so far, no one.

Every slow step we took, I thought it might be our last. We crossed over Madison Street with the lunch-hour crowd. Three more long blocks, we'd crossed over Jefferson Street. Horns blowing, whistles blowing, people yell- ing . . . cussing. *Such a beautiful morning now, wasn't it?*

But one traffic cop caught our attention. He had this rhythm and style to directing traf-fic. It was impressive. I wondered if he was taught that in the Police Academy.

We had Harrison Street to cross, yet. And, then, finally, *our* Van Buren.

Lisa and I turned right on Van Buren, still being observant for shadows.

Two humongous buildings later, we walked into Toni's, looking for Shorty, or just any-one who was expecting us. We didn't land our eyes on anyone, especially with an Uzi. That was a relief. But the restaurant was hopping with a lot of people. No shooting taking place here. I hope.

I flicked my wrist. My watch read 12:04. We were late, but not by much.

Lisa and I continued to patiently wait at the front entranceway. We scanned the interior again. Still, no Mr. Shorty. Were they that perfect and impatient, they had left the prem-ises? I really didn't think so. If they wanted us dead, they would have even waited until closing time. Shorty is here somewhere.

Suddenly, someone had grabbed our elbows. Lisa and I looked around, but didn't see anyone until we had lowered our eyes toward the floor.

The voice said, "Right this way, folks." Gracefully, walking between us,

Shorty escorted us by our elbows and keeping in step, though it was short baby steps.

Today, he was donned in professional attire, compared to yesterday's clo-thing. He wore a black suit, a crisp white shirt and a wide black tie. The black oxfords were gleam-ing with brightness. He made me think of a theatr-ical usher. I wondered if I should have tipped him.

Mr. Shorty rushed us to the far rear of the colorful restaurant, passing a large round table of eight chatty people, as if he knew where he was going.

Maybe a 'Reserved' table for three.

Then Lisa and I heard a sharp squeaky voice yell out, "Chic, over here."

To our surprise, another short man appeared. He was practically standing on the high stool smiling. How could he have seen Chic. Chic was so short, even the cockroaches had to over-looked him. Maybe just seeing Lisa and I,

Shorty # 2 just assumed Chic was with us. That could only mean one thing. Shorty # 2 knew what we had looked like. Which also means, they were spy-ing on us. Maybe they were shadowing us since the ad in the paper. Then, again, they just might be friends of Richard Balesteri.

Will we be shot dead right here in this crowded environment? Maybe. But I didn't think so. Too many witnesses.

Lisa quickly clenched my hand tightly as Chic stepped forward and shook Shorty # 2's hand. He was also dressed identical to Chic. Maybe they were Morticians. What a thought.

"How are you doing, Fritz?" Chic said.

"Fine." Lisa and I looked at each other and shrugged.

"I delivered as you wished." Chic said.

Again, Fritz said, "Fine."

Chic climbed on the high stool, literally.

Fritz gestured us to sit.

We did.

We all sat around the high round table, like one big happy family. I quickly scanned the interior, looking for any suspicious person with a gun. I didn't spot one. Not even two. Maybe we were safe after all. But my positive thoughts changed immediately. I glanced out this huge plate window, where we were sitting, and noticed several high-rise buildings. My dark negative thoughts kicked in.

Were there snipers on the high-rises? Maybe pointing high-powered, tele- scopic rifles directly at Lisa and me? We were sitting ducks. But I remained calm. And alert. I glanced at Lisa. She seemed calm. But I noticed dark wet stains under her armpits. And bead of sweat on her high forehead.

Suddenly, the waiter came to our table and set our plates in front of us. And glasses of red wine for all of us. Funny thing though, I didn't remember Lisa and I ordering any-thing. *Pre-planned?*

Our last dinner together? Might as well make the best of it. The steak and baked pota-toes were cooked to perfection. Just the way Lisa and I like it.

Who were these midgets? How long were they spying us? And how in the hell did they know Lisa and I ate our steaks medium-medium rare?

Lisa and I just sat there gazing at Chic and Fritz, as they played with their pasta, twirl-ing string of noodles around the expensive silverware. And drip-ping pasta sauce over the large spicy meatballs. I was expecting splattered sauce appear on their clean, crispy white shirt. But not these two clowns. They were experts. Well, why shouldn't they be? They were Italian, weren't they? They looked Italian. And they ate like an Italian, expertly.

Lisa and I shared glances again. And we shrugged again. Then we de-cided to join in eating. Lisa and I cut a small portion and taste-tested it. Then we swallowed a sip of wine. Lisa suddenly looked up at me. Was she read-ing my mind?

Our lips silently moved. Quietly, at each other, we formed the word from our lips. *"Poi . . . son."*

Was our food actually poisoned? Or was it the wine? Maybe both. A sil-ent death . . .

A few minutes had elapsed. Happily, we were still breathing air. Maybe this was a very slow death. These two clowns could very well be long gone before Lisa and I would collapse. Here? It could be right here as we sit. The street? Van Buren? Madison? Or, maybe even in the bathroom, heaving our guts out in the commode. Or, maybe die making love. What a way to go.

Ten more minutes had past . . . Come and gone . . . And still alive. This was a good thing. Didn't even feel woozy. I looked at Lisa. She seemed just fine to me, as if she just stepped out of the shower. She gleamed and seemed calm. This could be a very nice, wonderful date after all.

We were silent through the whole meal. We just grinned at each other between bites and sips.

Still no action. And we're still alive.

Finally, after Fritz took in his last bite of pasta, he looked up at me, then Lisa, back to me over the rim of his wine glass, holding it with both hands, and said, "I guess you two are wondering why the mysterious note, the mys-terious silence, and the mysterious meeting."

I shrugged, then gazed into Fritz's eyes, as Lisa shifted her eyes from Chic to Fritz, back to Chic. Then her eyes froze back on Fritz.

"Well, I will tell you," Fritz said, setting his glass down. He folded his hands and rested his chin. "The ad caught our attention Saturday morning. We were surprised, Chic and I. We thought the car bombing was long time forgotten. Seem like no one cared enough about Lisa Murray's parents. So we spied on you two for a few days. We weren't too sure who you were until later, Mr. Edwards.

"But when we heard the news on television about how Lisa killed Rich-ard Balesteri at the Holiday Inn, well, uh, that's when we'd figured she was with you investigating her parents death."

Lisa dropped her fork on her plate. The clinging from the fork to the plate caught the attention of patrons. They stared for a few seconds, and then went back to eating. "You know my parents?" Lisa's face went pale. Fritz raised his hand, waving her off.

"Let me finish, Lisa, uh, Miss Murray, just to be polite. I really do not know how to tell you this. But," Fritz hesitated, then turned to me. "Best if you hold her tight from falling from her chair, Mr. Edwards."

We *were* poisoned, I thought. Then my angry thoughts came out from my mouth.

"You poisoned our food, didn't you, you asshole." I said bluntly.

Shaking his head, Fritz said, "No . . . No . . . No. Nothing like that at all. But what I am about to tell you two, will be a great shock to Lisa. Maybe even you, too, Mr. Edwards."

Lisa piped in with fists clenched tightly, "*You* killed my parents, you fuc- king bastard. I should shoot you and the other midget sitting next to you."

Then Lisa grabbed for her purse. But Fritz had speed for a short person. He grabbed Lisa's arm forcibly, holding it tightly. Then I jumped over the table after Fritz, but Chic grabbed me.

"Calm down, Mr. Edwards. We understand you are upset. But it's not what it looks like. Trust me. Now, please, calm down, both of you." Chic's voice spoke evenly. No sign of nervousness. He continued. "It is very impor-tant Lisa's aware of her parent's death. Now, again, no more interruptions. Just let Fritz explain. Now, Mr. Edwards, hold Lisa as before. What you two are about to hear will shock the hell out of both of you. Now, promise, no more interruptions. Times a-wasting."

Lisa and I tried to calm ourselves, but reluctantly. But we did promise to behave. We gestured our heads, agreeably.

Fritz continued. "Lisa . . . Lisa . . . I am having a very difficult time with this.

But, I'll be blunt. Both of your parents are *alive*."

Lisa's mouth fell open wide and froze into place. Her face turned ghastly and ghostly white. I held her firmly just in case she fell over. Her voice had tightened. Speechless. Her mouth went cork dry. She just couldn't get those angry words out. But the next best thing, even to my surprise, but I should have expected it, she had raised her right hand, palm out, facing Fritz's face, and out of nowhere, she slapped him a good one, knocking him off his high stool.

Lisa said, *finally*, "This is *no* joke, bastard. What are you saying." Lisa had been look-ing down toward the floor where Fritz's small body frame had been lying, sprawled out against the plated window. He was rubbing his very red cheek.

"It's true, Miss Murray. Very true, what he is saying. What we're telling you is no bullshit." Chic said calmly. "On the day of your graduation, your dad hired me to bomb his car. He wanted Rudy and Ruby and their father think he was dead. Your parents were in deadly fear of them. Your dad told me and Fritz," Chic glanced down toward the floor at Fritz, then, his eyes bounced back to Lisa, "your mother had filed for a divorce. Katie, your mot-her, couldn't live in fear any longer. Your father couldn't live without your mother. If she divorced him his life would be over.

"So in order to save them from being blown up to kingdom come by Rudy and Ruby, and also save their marriage, he ordered me, and even paid me for blowing up his car. Everybody thought he was dead. And that's what he had wanted. And it worked. If your dad didn't do what he did, they would definitely been killed by the Balesteri family. "But, you need to know this, Lisa, there is no reflection on you. They both love you very much. They were watching you from a distance these past twelve years in disguise. Both are wearing a new profile; their names been changed, facial features; plastic surgery, you know, does wonders.

"Your dad's objective was to enjoy his retirement with you and your mother without looking over his shoulder every minute of his remaining life. He hopes, and your mother hopes you will understand. Now, with Rudy in jail, his father and brother dead, they both feel it's time to reveal themselves, come out of the closet, sort of speak, and to see you and be with you again.

"But one thing," Chic's small index finger went up, "for you to remember before we go and see them, plastic surgery, it changed their looks *big time*.

You won't be able to recognize them. Understand, Lisa? Mr. Edwards?"

We nodded.

Lisa was crying silently.

A small squeaky voice came from the direction of the floor, near Lisa's left arm.

"Is it safe to get up now?" Fritz said, trying to get up, still rubbing his bruised face.

Lisa nodded, wiping her tears away. She even extended her arm and help-ed him to his feet. Fritz briskly sat down, chug-a-lugging his red wine.

Forcing my laughter away from Fritz, and avoid embarrassment, I forced my words out, straining my vocal chords. I said, "How do Lisa and I know you two are telling the truth? How do we know you two clowns are not in it for the *big* five-grand, the reward money, and there *isn't* any Mr. and Mrs. Murray. You even said yourself they had plastic surgery. How would Lisa even recognize them? They just might be imposters. You do realize your story is far-fetched, don't you?" My eyes were bouncing back and forth like a tennis ball. My eyes finally zeroed in on Chic.

"Yes, we do realize that, Mr. Edwards," Chic said. "And it's quite under-standable why you doubt us. That is why Lisa's parents are here, right now."

Chic had this expression in his eyes which I didn't trust one iota. I had hop-ed Lisa didn't trust him, either.

"Here! In the restaurant? Right now!" Lisa nearly knocked her glass off the table. Her hands trembled fiercely, her lips quivered. Well, hell, her whole body was disco-ing. I held her close, calming her anxiety, or whatever her body was going through. Maybe a *nervous breakdown*? Hell, it had been twelve years of torture for her. Not able to see her parents. Now, is it over? Is Lisa and her parents back together again? If they are, it might not be the same. It *won't* be the same. I just hope they can work it out big time.

I also hope the 'mortician' brothers are telling the truth. Or there will be one big price to pay. And I'm not talking about the reward money, either.

"Yep," Fritz piped in. "They're sitting in our office in the far end of this building. Waiting. They are just as nervous as you are, Miss Murray."

"So, this is your restaurant. If this is your place," I said doubtfully, "then who is *TONI*?"

"Toni is our last name, actually, short for *Antonio*." Chic said happily.

"What's the relationship between you two?" I asked politely.

"We're brothers," Fritz said. "Can't you tell, Mr. Edwards?" Fritz shook his face very slowly, showing me his left and right profile.

"Obviously," I said.

Chic said, "Well, Lisa, uh, Miss Murray, are you ready to meet your parents?"

Lisa slowly nodded, holding back tears. She grabbed the designed red clothed-napkin, and wiped her tears. Then she blew her nose, returning it to her plate.

I suddenly jumped off my stool, and said, "I'm going with you, Lisa . . . ."

"That won't be necessary," Chic interrupted, "Or wise, Mr. Edwards."

"I AM GOING WITH HER," I loudly demanded.

"Sssh . . . . Sssh . . . . My customers are getting annoyed. Please, sir. Now sit down and have a drink on the house . . . Please." Chic calmly said. He took my elbow and guided me back onto my stool. I pulled my arm away. "The three should be alone and get re-reacquainted . . . No interference." Chic said.

I turned to Lisa, and said, "What do you want, honey?"

"I would love to have you meet my parents, sweetheart. But, maybe, just maybe Chic and Fritz are right about this. Under these certain circumstances, my parents and I should be alone."

I reluctantly nodded, agreeing with Lisa. But I didn't like it. I didn't like the situation one bit. I took in a few steps and squeezed Lisa hard. Then I glared into her eyes.

"If you are not back, uh, let's say in an hour, I'm coming in and get you."

"Sure. Okay. I'll agree to that." Lisa said, smilingly.

I stared at Chic and Fritz. They both nodded.

"Fair enough," Chic said.

"Fair enough," Fritz agreed.

Before Lisa and Chic left for his office, I had asked for identification from Chic and Fritz. Upon agreement, they laid their ID's on the white table cloth. I studied them carefully. The ID's were legit. I handed the ID's back to them. I turned to Chic, and said, pointing my index finger in the air. "One hour. Not a second longer. Ca-peesh?"

They both nodded again.

I tightly hugged Lisa's waistline, and gave her a hard kiss on her red lips.

And we whispered "I Love You". I patted her on her butt. Then they left for Chic's office. I ordered a beer. Fritz ordered wine.

We waited.

Chapter Sixty-Five

A s Fritz and I slowly drank our drinks I thought about everything that was said between Fritz and Chic. I was thinking I should have this all confirmed through Dillman. Well, after all, he was Lisa's father's best friend. He would know if Murray was processing toward a divorce. He would also know if Don Murray was planning on faking his own death. I took a sip of my beer, setting the glass down on the tablecloth, I had asked Fritz where were the bathrooms.

Giving me a strange expression, he said, "Toward the front doors. Make a right, near the telephone booth."

I gladly thanked him. I slid off from my high stool and went. But instead the restrooms, I slid open the antique phone booth doors, and sat, closing the doors for privacy. The ceiling light came on. You don't see phone booths like these anymore. Awesome.

I dialed up Dillman's office. On the fourth ring, a raspy voice appeared.

"Lieutenant Dillman, Homicide . . ."

"Lieutenant, Nick Edwards here. I have several questions to ask you. You have a minute?" My voice was rushed.

"Shoot."

"Was Don Murray and his wife pending divorce?"

"Not that I was aware of."

"Did Don ever mention to you about faking his death?"

"No. What's this about?" Dillman cleared his raspy throat.

"Lisa and I are at Toni's restaurant . . . with an 'I'. Its locale is Van Buren Street. The owners claim that the Murray's are alive and well. And in dis-guise. Lisa is supposedly meeting with her parents as we speak.

"Since the death of the father and son, and Rudy in jail, the Murray's now believe it is safe to come out of hiding. So, what can you tell me, Loo?"

"I say this is bull-shit. What's the owner's name?"

"Fritz and Chic Antonio. Do you know them? I believe their first names are nicknames. What do you think?"

"All I can tell you, Nick is they're ex-cons. Chic, yes, and you are correct on their first names. Don't have their actual birth names on file. Chic was convicted and sentenced in 1987 helping Ruby bomb Park Plaza Hotel. But Chic's sentence was reduced . . . Some plea bargaining crap . . ." He paused.

"Maybe you didn't know that, I don't know how you could . . . ."

"What?" I said, interrupting.

"Chic was an informant for Detective Murray. Most of the information passed down from Chic was legit. Murray got a lot of criminals off the street because of him.

"But, he also has connections with the Balesteri family. Chic is a con art-ist. And very sly. You and Lisa have to watch your back. What else did Chic say?"

"Murray had hired Chic to blow up his car to make it look like he got kil-led so Rudy and Ruby would believe he was dead. That was all planned just to have the brothers lay off Murray . . ."

"So Don and Katie could enjoy their time together without fear?" Dill-man said.

"Exactly." I said.

"Shit. If Murray's car was vacant, then I am a monkey's uncle."

"Why? What do you have, Loo?"

"The evidence we have is locked up in our evidence room. All of this shit was scattered over the high schools parking lot. If the mess didn't belong to the Murray's, who did they belong to?"

"My question exactly. Who did the evidence belong to? Where's the connection? And, yes, who was in that car?"

"Don and his wife Katie. I am positive."

"Positive . . . positive?"

"Well, Murray's gun and badge was found a few hundred feet away from the explo-sion." Dillman said.

"Don't take this wrong, Lieutenant, but that to me doesn't prove a posi-tive ID."

"Whaddya mean, Mr. Edwards?" His voice became stern.

I cleared my throat, and said, "His badge and gun could have been stored in his glove box, trunk, or even under the driver's seat."

"This is true, Nick. But knowing Don as I did, he carried his piece and badge every-where he went. I wouldn't doubt if he even took his service wea-pon to bed with him."

"Was his and his wife remains *positively* identified, Loo?" I asked with emphasis.

There was silence for a moment.

"Loo? Are you still there?"

"Yeah, I'm here. To your question, Nick, I have to say honestly, no, there wasn't any positive identification on the Murray's. We just assumed it was them. The threatening letters, the location. You know, right after Lisa's graduation ceremony, they were suppose to go to some fancy ballroom near downtown Chicago. The timing was perfect. Murray's go to their car. Lisa and her boyfriend were suppose to follow them.

"But, of course, Murray's left the high schools' auditorium immediately after the cer-emony. The car blew up while everyone, including Lisa and her boyfriend were still say-ing their good-byes to their colleagues. No witnesses.

Nothing."

"So the bottom line is someone was in that car. Maybe, not the Murray's. But some-body, or somebody's. Who got blown up, sir? Chic and Fritz claimed they were only hired to sabotage the car. Not kill Don and Katie."

"I don't know for sure. At this point, Nick, I don't know anything for cer—tain any-more. But if they are alive, Don would have contacted me by now. What has it been, twelve years? We were friends, Nick. Buddies. We're more like brothers. I don't believe he and his wife are alive."

"If I were you, Nick . . . I would get Lisa out of there . . . And quick!"

"Damn! I knew I should have listened to my instincts. Thanks, sir."

"You bet. And good luck." We hung up.

As I was stepping out, Fritz was leaning against the edge of the cherry-wood booth, listening to my conversation, no doubt.

With a calm voice, Fritz said, "Who were you talking to, buddy?"

Trying to retain my calm, I said, "Oooh, I really don't know."

"You're not getting cute on me, are ya'?"

"If you really need to know, I had to call my office and check my mes-sages. You do know I manage a business, don't you?"

"You were on the phone a very long time, buddy."

"Yeah, a lot of messages, you know. I've been away for awhile."

"Normal people listen to their messages, but I heard your voice talking to someone. Do you always talk to your answering machine?"

"So you don't buy my story. What can I say?" I said and shrugged.

"No, I don't buy your story. Let's go back to the table."

Walking back to our table, I looked down at Fritz, and said, "Why would it matter to you who I was talking to, Fritz, ol' man. That is, if you and Chic are on the up and up. What are you so paranoid about, huh?"

Fritz craned his neck, trying to look into my eyes. It was hopeless.

"Don't get cocky with me. If you called the cops . . ." Fritz let the sentence hang. He put his tiny hand on my lower back, and tried to shove me forward. "Let's go." He said. His *shove* was unsuccessful.

"And if I did call the cops?"

"You would be one sorry sucker. Maybe even a dead sucker."

"Why *not* the cops? What's the big deal anyway? What are you afraid of, Fritz?"

"It's not me or Chic. We had orders from Mr. Don Murray himself."

"What?" I said loudly.

"Shh . . . Shut up. We'll talk more when we arrive at the table. Okay?"

I shrugged. This isn't making any sense. I thought. We'd picked up our pace with angry faces gazing at us.

When we finally arrived at our table, I flicked my wrist. My watch told me I had fifteen minutes before I break down Chic's office door.

"Okay, Fritz. You don't have much time. So make it quick and explain about what you just said back there about Mr. Don Murray."

"Okay . . . here it goes. Murray faked his death, right?" I nodded. "Well, we know he didn't get his pension. And we also know, Miss Lisa Murray, his beloved daughter, received death insurance benefits. And, being a private detective, you should be aware of insurance fraud, and faking ones death. Correct?"

Again, I nodded. I knew where he was going with this, but I let him talk anyway.

"If the law ever finds out they're alive, Mr. and Mrs. Murray would serve a very long sentence in the slammer. Ca-peesh?"

I nodded, and said, "And Lisa will have to pay all the insurance money back to the government." Fritz nodded, agreeably.

"And *we*, Chic and me, will serve time, too. You wouldn't want that now, would you, Nick?" Fritz leaned over and pinched my right cheek. I jerked his hand away. He grinned. "Now do you understand 'no cops'?"

I didn't say anything. I just looked at my watch. Just waiting five more minutes to pass. Just five more minutes remaining before all hell will break loose.

I surveyed the restaurant from where I was sitting. Something was out of place. I couldn't place my finger on it. But something wasn't just quite right.

Most of the customers had left. That's normal. I scanned the place one more time. Something to do with the people. Being a ritzy place, customers usual-ly dress for this particular environment.

But something was off kilter. I studied the restaurant for the last time. I think I had spotted the imbalance. Unless these people I had spotted were blind, there wouldn't be any other reason to be wearing dark sunglasses in a dimmed light environment.

Maybe friends of Antonio's?

I glanced at my watch again. Time was up. I slid off my high stool and ran toward the rear near the kitchen with Fritz hot on my heels. His short legs had carried him quickly and with speed. The gap was closing inch by inch. As I went storming through the kitchen's swinging doors, an Italian man, maybe a chef, fell to the floor. Metal trays and lids clanged to the floor.

I had stopped briefly to check on the male chef, he seemed to be alright. I'd continued dashing through the kitchen, brushing against pots and pans hang-ing over a long stain-less steel counter. *More clanging noises.* The noise be-came deafening. Angry Italian voices, screaming, which I didn't under-stand. But the tone had a nice rhythm to it. I just kept on running. Another man dressed in a long white apron and a chef's hat came whistling around a corner carrying a huge bowl of salad. I didn't see him . . . And he didn't see me . . . . Another chef down, and more clanging noises. And many more angry Italian voices.

Fritz was yelling something. His voice was close behind me. I had block-ed out his tiny, squeaky voice. I didn't want to hear it. My pounding head was on Lisa. Hell with everyone else. Just get out of my way. *I am coming through.* I'd finally found the office. It reminded me of a small boxcar sit-ting by its lonesome in the corner. It had two small square windows; five feet apart from each other. Through the windows the office seemed dark. I didn't bother to knock.

I lifted my left leg, cocked it, and shot it forward. The wooden door flew open, shattering the diamond-shaped glass. Glass sprayed inside and outside of the boxcar-shaped office. The lock mechanism dangled by one screw.

Loud foreign voices were louder than ever now. Cussing. Though I didn't understand their language, I did understand angry words. And they were cus-sing up a storm. Maybe I should turn around and thank them for the steak we had. Maybe they'll shut-up for a minute and give me a smile.

Nah.

As I was fumbling for the light switch, I felt something wet, warm, and sticky on the wall. My hand slid down. That was when I had found the tog-gle switch. I flicked the toggle, office beaming brightly.

No Lisa . . . No Lisa's parents . . . . And no Chic.

All I had found was what was matching on my left hand.

Blood.

Everywhere . . . . Blood . . . On the white walls, the beige carpet, and on the mahogany desk . . . Everywhere.

The rear office door was ajar. I kicked it open, and I found myself staring into an alleyway. I ran outside, looking both ways. Up and down the alley-way. Nothing, but a trail of blood leading from Chic's office, and near a large green Dumpster. I jumped into it, searching frantically. Again, nothing.

As I jumped from the Dumpster, Fritz came running out. Timing couldn't have been more perfect. I jumped on top of him, pinning him underneath me. I started punching him. Left . . . Right . . . Left. He'd blocked some of my punches. But what did make contact to his face was well worth it. Blood had streamed from his nose and puny lips.

Suddenly, a strong grasp, came pounding on my right shoulder.

"Stop, Nick. You'll kill 'em." . . ."That's the idea," I said.

I turned around and looked up. It was Cole with a dark wig and dark sun-glasses. He pulled his handcuff out from his beltline, and proceeded to cuff Fritz. Then Cole said, "Don't touch anything." But he wasn't looking at me. He was looking inside Chic's bloody office. *Who was* inside he was yelling to? 'Don't touch anything'.

Three new faces appeared in the alleyway.

As Cole lifted Fritz from the dirty bloody ground, Fritz had yelled, "I want to talk to my lawyer." His knees were weak. And his dark pants was wet and stained from urine. Probably even shit his pants.

Cole turned to me, and said, "Hold this scumbag." He shoved Fritz at me.

I started to raise my fist at Fritz's ugly puss, when Cole turned and grabbed my swinging arm. "Don't you dare smack my prisoner, Nick. Better behave, man. Calm down. I have to make a few phone calls. Can I trust you with Mr. Scumbag?"

I shrugged. Then I nodded, "Yeah, sure."

Cole slipped a pair of latex gloves from his back pocket, slipped them on, and grabbed the phone.

The three new faces surrounded me in the alleyway, near the rear office door. They seemed to be dressed for Halloween. The three had funky sun-glasses and big noses, and ugly. Fritz began to squirm. I jerked the handcuffs once. Fritz suddenly became still.

The three *Mask*-a-teers slowly withdrew their rubber faces and wigs.

I should have been surprised, but wasn't.

Clint, Pam and Eagle circled my breathing space, and hugged me tightly.

Trying to calm me, Eagle said, "We'll find her, Nick. So God help us."

I nonchalantly punched Fritz in the solar plexus.

The office and kitchen were swarming with police officers; who were wearing dark blue uniforms and checkered saucer hats. There were plain—clothed detectives, Forensic Techs, and Police Photographers.

Lieutenant Dillman came in half-hour later with the County Medical Ex-aminer.

Dillman turned to the ME, and said, "Why are you here, doctor? There is no dead body here, sir. Just a lot of blood, and several severed fingers found in the office's wastebasket."

"Well, I guess the call came in so fast, and the caller was foreign, my people who had paged me, had misunderstood. Just out of curiosity, what'd happened, Loo?"

"Not much to tell yet. The only thing we'd determined; the blood was from a male. By the looks of the fingers, we believe it was an older man . . . uh . . . Maybe mid-sixties or so. A wedding band was still loosely hanging on the finger. Least we know he was married."

The ME listened silently.

Dillman continued, "The chef's witnessed a lot. Two tall men wearing dark long over-coats and dark brim hats forced their way in Chic's office. One chef informed our people he had witnessed the two men taping all the mouths with gray duct tape. He had peeked through the window for a time.

"Another chef had witnessed the cutting of the fingers. He believed the man had white hair and wore black frame glasses. The young blonde woman was slapped around a bit. And the older woman got the same treatment. But the older woman got slapped around longer and harder than the blonde.

"We were also informed some guy named Chic, one of the owners of the restaurant, was beaten to a pulp. But, what irks me, sir, with all the detailed information of what had happened here in the office, not one witness, not one chef, not one employee had noticed a get-away car. Damn it." Dillman pounded his right hand into his opened left palm.

Chapter Sixty-Six

"I WAS SUPPOSED TO protect her . . . Shit . . . . Shit . . . . Shit. Damn it anyway. I had felt that was a set up, but I went against my gut feeling, without any other plan in mind. Now she's missing, maybe even dead. The fucking mafia are mean son-a-va-bitches. They're relentless bastards. Lisa could be just about anywhere."

I was pacing up and down, down and up in our hotel room. Pam, Eagle and Clint just scrutinized me and keeping their mouth shut, letting me spill my anger out to them. Hell, what are friends for.

"Ease up, buddy. We'll find her. But it'll take time." Eagle said.

We don't have time," I screamed. " We got to find her . . . NOW!"

I paced the hotel carpet some more. Back and forth . . . Forth and back, I was thinking what to do. Where do we begin?

Eagle, Pam, and Clint continued to watch my every move, and very care-fully, too. What were they thinking I was going to do? Jump out the fucking window and *kill* my-self. I knew I was making them nervous. But this *never* had happened to me before. It's been a long time I had loved a woman. But when I do, she's taken away from me. *Fuck it.* I am going to *kick* some ass or asses royally. *I'm going to get my woman back!*

I'm usually a man of cool and calm. With cases involved other people's problems, I'm fine. I'm cool. Nerves of steel. But when it hits home . . . Man,

I just cannot think clearly.

I thought of drinking some beers. But I knew that wouldn't help my thinking. If I was on a drinking binge I just might get careless and shoot up the city. And shoot the first person I see who even resembles a criminal.

So I decided to drink coffee, and lots of it, too. I lit one cigarette after an-other. Man, I need a drink. But most of all, I needed to find Lisa.

"Let's get Dillman on the horn, Nick," Clint said, "And maybe Cole, too. They deal with the Chicago Mafia all the time. They'll know what to do."

"The FBI is already looking for Lisa and her so-called parents, whoever they are." I said. Turning to Clint, I said, "Yeah, you're right. Dillman is our best bet, Clint. But leave

Cole out of it. This isn't his jurisdiction. It's Dill-man's. And besides, Dillman is friends with Lisa and her parents. He'll take it more personal."

I pushed my hands through my frazzled blond hair. My hair felt like a scared porcupine, quills pointing straight up on ends. I felt a mess. I had looked it, too.

Pam piped in, "We don't know if Lisa's parents were even in Chic's of-fice. For all we know, it could have been a set up just to get Lisa in their of-fice, alone."

"According to the chef's and other witnesses there was an older man and woman with Chic and Lisa." Clint said.

"Yeah," Eagle spoke, "The chopped-off fingers had proven that of a man's, and the wedding band."

"With the fingers found, it will process through fingerprints, and come up with a positive ID." Clint said, happy with himself.

"And I know the wedding band didn't belong to Chic. He didn't wear one." I said.

"Do you always check a man's ring finger, Nick?" Eagle chuckled.

"You're a funny man, Eagle. But I am not in the mood. Sorry."

"I still believe Chic and Fritz were in it for the money. And this whole *God Bless it* situation is bogus." Pam said, angrily.

My eyes bounced around to my cohorts. "You're right, Pam. All of you are right. Putting that ad in the friggin' newspaper was supposed to help us find the killers. But it just made things more complicated." I said.

"We might have one murderer *now* . . . And that's Fritz." Eagle said. "They admitted bombing the Murray's car. And probably had lied about them fak-ing their death. They were probably in the car like Dillman said."

"Makes sense," Clint said. "Chic and Fritz are just covering their asses by exaggerating their story. They have a reputation being con-artists and very cunning."

"Yep. And they're very good at it, too." Pam said.

"I agree, Pam . . . Clint" I said. "But what bothers me is the fact several fin-gers were chopped—off. What is with that, anyway? And, if those two imposters were in on help-ing Chic and Fritz, why were his fingers dismem-bered? And, furthermore, why was the older woman slapped around like a rag doll?"

"And who in hell were those two men in overcoats?" Eagle asked.

Silence filled the room. We just thought about all the questions being tossed to and fro. But we didn't have any perfect answer. Clint broke the sil- ence.

"I'm calling Dillman," Clint said, as he reached for the phone. "Let's see what he can do for us."

We nodded in unison.

Chapter Sixty-Seven

CLINT SLAMMED THE phone down. Our nerves were so frazzled, we all jumped.

"He wasn't in." I stated.

"No. But as you know I had left a message."

I started pacing again, nervously thinking, when the phone rang. I made a dash for it.

"Hell-o," I said, catching my breath. My over-active heart had flipped a few beats when I heard the voice. "*Lisa, where are you?*" My cohorts had gathered around me, leaning in the phone and gazing at me with excitement.

"Are you alright?" I blurted.

"Yes . . . We're in some huge warehouse. I'm not positive of our location. We were blindfolded before we got in the car. But, the ride didn't seem to take too long from Toni's restaurant. It took maybe, five, no more than ten minutes.

"All I can tell you at this point, Nick, as far as my eyes can see, we are near railroad tracks. I think it might be the "L". Not positive . . . ."

"Where are you right now . . . Inside or outside of the warehouse?" I had brushed my hair with my fingers again, pacing, like a caged lion.

"Outside. I finally convinced the two creeps I had to go pee."

"Ah, good girl. The ol' 'gotta pee' trick."

"Yeah. But I *really had* to go, honey."

I didn't have anything to add to that, so I went to the next question.

"Can you see anything? Can you give me your exact location? Land-marks, uh, street signs, anything?"

"The railroad tracks . . ."

"Yeah . . . Yeah . . . Go ahead." I said, hurriedly.

"There's a big factory across the street with lights on. Maybe a welding place. I see sparks and flashes from where I am sitting, or squatting, I should say . . ."

I smiled. "Yeah . . . Keep going, sweetie. You're doing great."

" There's a very tall water tower, which is also across the street, and on the same side of the warehouse, an abandon gas station, or auto repair place. It's to dark to tell what it is . . ."

"What direction are you facing, Lisa?"

"Can't talk anymore . . . Someone's coming . . . Gotta go . . . Love you . . ."

"Love you . . . ." She hung up.

All faces were on me now . . . .

"Is she alright?" Pam said. She was gnawing on her thumbnail.

I shrugged, and said, "I guess. She sounded alright."

"What about the others?" Eagle asked. He gulped his glass of beer.

"She didn't say. She didn't have much time to talk." I said. Automatic—ally, my right hand went through my porcupine hair nervously.

"So where is she, Nick?" Clint said. He was the only calm person among us.

"Somewhere not too far from Toni's Restaurant. She was calling from a warehouse near railroad tracks . . . Probably the 'L' tracks. And maybe a weld-ing shop across the street. She also stated an abandon gas station or auto repair shop down the road from where she was squatting."

"Squatting?" Everyone said in harmony.

"Yes, squatting. I'll explain later. She also mentioned a tall water tower nearby. Across the street I believe she said. I couldn't get her to tell me what direction she was facing. Someone was coming toward her. We had to hang up quickly."

Now, with the information we had received, we were planning our run and rescue strategy. Silence had filled the smoky room.

Eagle shattered the silence.

"I got an idea." He snapped his thumb and index finger together. "Let's take the eleva-tor to the top floor. Maybe even to the rooftop. And maybe we can get a good view of her location up there. How about it, Nick?"

"Great idea!" I said. Then I turned to Clint and Pam, and said, "You two stay down here just in case Dillman calls."

"I'm your boss, remember?" Clint said, pointing to his burly chest.

"Please?" I grinned.

"Oh, well, since you'd begged. Now, go find Lisa."

Eagle and I grabbed two binoculars out of my gym bag and took the ele-vator up to the top floor. The door to the roof was tightly secured. But the top floor gave us enough view to work with. Thank God.

The darkness outside was overwhelming. But we made do. We scanned the dark streets of Downtown Chicago, hoping to find anything that Lisa had described. She said she wasn't too far from Toni's. So I searched for Toni's marquee. And hoping it was still open at this time of the night.

Eagle was searching for any tall water towers.

The reflection from the well-lit hallway wasn't doing us any favors. But we kept at it. I had one corner of the hallway picture window. And Eagle had the other corner.

"Hey, Nick!" Eagle's voice had carried to my ears from down the hall-way. "Come here. I think I located something."

I ran toward him, padding my feet against the red carpet.

As I was running toward him, he was down to the last word . . .

'Tower'.

"Well, I'll be damned. There isn't whole lot of towers around on this side of Chicago. Is there?' I said.

"Apparently, not." Eagle said.

"Anything else? I can't seem to see very well through the reflection."

Suddenly, from a distance, we heard clickety-clack . . . clickety-clack . . . ; coming at moderate speed; Steel to steel. Squeaky noises.

Living in Tomah, Wisconsin, we just don't hear these noises. But, Eagle and I figured it was the sound of a train.

If it was a freighter, it would blow a whistle a few times. This one didn't.

So, our next option was . . . It as to be an 'L' train. Like Lisa said.

Eagle and I had high-five each other.

Eagle said, "Down in front of the hotel is State Street, right?"

"Yep."

"Toni's restaurant is on Van Buren, right?"

"Yep."

"Then, with my calculations, I believe Lisa is about one mile from here."

"Great calculations, navigator. We'll give it a shot." I said, patting Eagle on the back.

Eagle smiled widely, and slicked his black hair over his ears and tugged on his stubby ponytail.

We padded back down to my room. Once down there, I quickly went into my gym bag, pulled out a Chicago map and laid it evenly across the stained square table, near the window. I found what I'd been looking for.

As I was circling the symbols of the railroad tracks in red, Eagle grabbed three weapons. A .357Mag, .44Mag and 9mm Glock, and loaded them ex-pertly.

I found State Street and Van Buren. I circled them in red. I had counted the following streets northward. I located Congress and Polk Street. I circled both of them in red. Close enough. I had marked a five-point star symbol at Lisa's possible location.

Pam and Clint had their noses in the yellow pages, scanning for any welding shop near Lisa's possible location. *Let your fingers do the walking.*

Talking aloud across the room, Clint said, "I found a welding shop on Congress. The company's name is *Sparky's* Welding, Inc. How sweet, huh?

Sparky."

We all chuckled. Eagle handed me the .357 and the Glock. He kept the forty-four magnum.

I grabbed the gym bag full of burglary tools, a few doubled-edge hunting knives and couple of dry cell type flashlights.

My eyes bounced from Clint to Pam. "Thanks for your help, guys. I real-ly appreciated it." They both nodded happily. Then my blue eyes landed on Eagle's tense face.

I said, "Come on, buddy . . . Let's kick some ass."

Eagle responded expectedly, "Alright . . . Kick ass—time . . . And it's about fucking time."

Before we had hit the door to the hallway, Eagle gave Pam an extended hard kiss. A strong bear hug followed.

"Please be careful, honey . . . You fighting animal you." Tears swelled up in Pam's and Eagle's eyes. They had hugged and kissed again.

Finally, we were gone.

Pam turned to Clint. "Are they going to be okay, Clint?"

"Yep. Remember last year when you were kidnapped?"

Nod.

"Do you remember how Nick had rescued you?"

Nod.

"Remember how Eagle and Nick kicked ass in the motel room in Sun Prairie, freeing you from that drug dealer from North Carolina?"

"Yeah, I do, just like it was yesterday." A grin materialized on her teary face.

"And don't forget, Pam. Nick and Eagle fought side by side in Desert Storm. They did just fine." Pam's eyes froze.

"What? Did I hit a nerve, Pam?"

"Well, maybe you didn't know . . ." She paused for a moment.

"Know what? Tell me." Clint said concernedly.

"Eagle got his right leg blown off over in Persian Gulf. He's wearing a synthetic leg." She paused again. Then said, "But I do get your point, Clint."

She put her right hand on his shoulder, and gazed into his eyes. "They will be just fine."

Clint nodded. "Yep."

Chapter Sixty-Eight

EAGLE AND I quick-stride out of the Holiday inn, crossing State Street, dodging a few speeding cars. Horns were blowing, middle fingers flipping us off and cuss words I couldn't understand . . . . Foreigners.

Our soles and heels echoed through the half-emptied parking structure.

I popped open the trunk to my rental and neatly stored the gym bag in the very deep trunk. I ran around to the driver side, got in, hurriedly unlocked the passenger door. Eagle barely was seated when I pumped the gas pedal. The passenger door slammed freely and forcefully.

We squealed through the structure, fish-tailing on State.

It was approaching midnight with light drizzle dancing on the windshield. The temperature was cool, the wind breezing from the east, making this a marvelous night for blood spill.

Eagle had his dark eyes peeled for landmarks I had circled in red on the map. We were on Congress now. Suddenly, Eagle spotted Sparky's Welding Shop. It was across the street from the warehouse exactly where Lisa had said it was. Good girl. I thought. Also a very tall water tower materialized on our left. And on our right, there was an abandon filling station. It was half—block from the warehouse. This was where we had parked. The drizzling rain had turned into a downpour. No thunder and no lightening. Just a great downpour.

The streets glistened of wetness. The pattering of heavy rain colliding with buildings, cars and asphalt, reminded me of Lisa and I running along some beach in our early meeting days. Which was only a few years ago. It was fun. Lisa was fun.

With our collars turned up and our baseball caps on backwards, we grab-bed our belongings from the trunk, closing the trunk quietly, crouching low and heading toward the warehouse, which I was hoping it was the correct one . . . The right location. But it seemed to be. I hoped.

There were lights on in the huge warehouse, but dimly showing through the 5 by 5 sized windows. That could be in our favor for now.

Eagle and I had split up. He circled one half of the warehouse, I the other.

Our plan was to meet in the middle, somewhere. I slowly walked, step by step, crouching. My eyes edging the window panes, until there were some clearance to observe the interior of the warehouse. I had peeked in every window carefully, straining my eye sight. But all I could see was wall to wall wooden skids, almost to ceiling level. I was still skeptical. Were we at the right location? . . . The correct warehouse? There weren't too many of warehouses on this side of downtown. This just has to be the right one.

Even though the downpour returned to a fine drizzle, the raindrops still found my eyes. Every few seconds I had to wipe away the moisture, slowing me down. Every second counted. No time to lose.

I had a crowbar in one hand and my 9mm Glock in the other. I had won-dered how far long Eagle had come. Were we even near completing out perimeter patrol? Here we are in a strange environment . . . No walkie-talkies, or hand radios. No cell phones. (Which I really don't believe in), but maybe I should. Eagle could be lying somewhere on the other side of this huge structure that's called a warehouse, bleeding to death. I came to the conclu-sion we were just plain nuts . . . No. Crazy's the word.

Walking and crouching a few more feet, I had stumbled onto something.

Making me lose my balance and fall to the muddy wet ground, in the pro-cess. It was hard for me to get up from the mud. But, luckily, there was a gray-painted door in front of me with a silvery handle. I stretched my right arm, grabbing for the slippery material. I had managed to get on my two feet and straightened my long two-hundred pound frame. I sought the wet ground and wondered what had made me fall. What did I slip on?

Bending over, I had found Lisa's cell phone. Amazingly so, it was still intact. She was probably right here, squatting, relieving herself when she'd called me. I had wondered if she left it here purposely, maybe as a clue. Or she was caught talking to me and dropped it while she was being whisk a-way somewhere. Maybe back into the warehouse. That would've been logi-cal, wouldn't it?

At least I know this was the correct location.

It's a good place to start.

But, my fear now was what if she was dragged to another locale?

I firmly pressed my right ear against the heavy steel door. Though I did not expect to hear anything through the solid steel material, I still had to try.

Silence.

As I was listening to *silence*, Eagle came around from the south side of the humongous structure, crouching. If he had bent any lower, he would've been waddling like a duck.

When he came in earshot, I whispered, "Anything, Eagle?"

He nodded. "Yeah, a shiny black Crown Vic is parked in the rear parking lot. I touched the hood of the limo, it was cold as a witches tit."

I grinned, and said, "That could be a very good sign the car didn't go anywhere. But with the cold rain . . ."

"Yeah, you're right. The coldness from the downpour could have cooled it down some-what. Can you hear anything?"

I shook my head. Eagle looked down at my hand. "What do you have there in your hand, Nick?"

"Lisa's cell phone. She must have dropped it accidentally, or she left us a clue." I paused. "Well, buddy, are you ready to go in and kick ass?"

"I was born ready," Eagle whispered.

I nodded happily. I clenched the slippery, cold and wet crowbar from the muddy ground, preparing myself to destroy the lock mechanism from the gray door, but Eagle was one step ahead of me. He pushed down the silvery handle with his sledge-hammer hand, and the door opened. We looked at each other, surprisingly, and shrugged. In unison, we said softly, "All right."

Eagle opened the door just enough where his 210 pound body could squeeze through the gap. He slid in easily. I followed, closing the door quiet-ly behind me. Eagle was on one side of the pathway, I was on the other, inching ourselves closer to the center of the cinderblock structure.

With our guns drawn, barrels pointing upward, we'd had listened for any sudden motion. Luckily, for now, the row of wooden skids were our shield, but not for long. Our shield of skids ended in the center of the ware-house floor. We continued to walk sideways, heel to toe, toe to heel. Care-fully and quietly. The warehouse was quiet. Extremely quiet for our concern.

Eagle whispered softly, "This might be a set-up, partner."

I agreed.

We came to the end of our comforting shield. Eagle took a peek to his right. I took a peek to my left. Eagle had observed an office, sort of. He tap-ped me on my shoulder. He pointed. Then I observed. At the far north end of the building, near the cinderblock wall, there were six metal folding chairs in a semi-circle. Within the semi-circle was a wooden folding table and placed dead center. Four of the six chairs were being occupied. But it was difficult to detect who they were. But my guess was; Lisa, Chic, and her so—called parents. But there was a large long gap between us, I wasn't positive. They could even have been *dummies* for all I know. A diversion? Maybe.

These *dummies* had their back toward us, and hands tied behind their backs with heavy rope.

The other two chairs were void. Maybe the two empty folding chairs had belonged to the two Mr. Overcoats. And maybe hiding somewhere in the darkness between the gaps of the wooden skids. Eagle and I tried to listen closely for abnormal breathing. But that was difficult, too.'Cause our breath-ing was the only thing we had heard.

But as my eyes focused on the four, whoever or whatever they were, I did observe a heavy blood-soaked towel wrapped around a left hand of one of the *dummies*. I couldn't be certain if he or she, or whatever, was breathing. But if they were dummies, dummies don't suck in oxygen anyway. The harder I had focused and studied the four objects, the more I had realized they were human. All four bodies had their heads slightly bowed, as if praying, sleeping, or worse scenario . . . dead.

From the corners of the high-stacked skids, Eagle and I surveyed the area. We still didn't see any movement of any kind. Whatsoever.

Yet.

With the cell-phone to my ear, I had tried to call Clint in the hotel. But without success. The front desk had informed me Clint had left with a man and a woman, meaning Pam. The man, hopefully, could be Lieutenant Dill-man. I said "Thanks" and we disconnected. If it was Dillman, this place will be crawling with cops very soon. One would hope.

Eagle and I knew we shouldn't waste anymore time. So with that thought in mind, we made a run toward the four bodies, expecting to be fired up on.

So far, no bang . . . bang. But we were alert for it.

Just as Eagle and I got closer, Eagle noticed a man on the very top of the skids, in a prone position, looking down at us with a long barrel, aiming carefully at our bodies, or our heads.

I craned my neck to my left, and to the top of the skids. There was anot-her man in a prone position, aiming just as carefully as his partner with a long barrel shotgun. We were set up for a crossfire. There was no place to shield our bodies. We were sitting ducks. So we ran. It's a lot better than sit- ting. We ran, crisscrossing, running and dodging. The bullets ricochet off the warehouse cement floor, near our heels, sending cement chips spinning through the smoky air. The gun smoke was tremendous. Eagle and I kept squeezing off rounds. Mr. Overcoats compensated. Splinters of wood from the skids were spitting at us as we ran closer to our goal . . . Rescue the four injured victims.

When I got close enough, I had recognized Lisa's profile. I released the crowbar I was unconsciously carrying in my right fist, dropping it to the ce-ment flooring, releasing clanging sounds. With my momentum of speed, I had clenched my right hand on the back of Lisa's chair, and slid her out of harms way. Eagle was still firing religiously on the perps.

When I had felt Lisa was safe from danger, I had turned toward my tar-get, kneeled, aimed upwardly and fired my 9mm Glock. My target jerked, dropping his shotgun to the warehouse's foundation, shattering the butt—housing in many pieces. Periodically, my eyes bounced from Lisa to Mr. Overcoat. Lisa seemed alright. But it was hard to deter-mine . . . She was still unconscious.

My eyes froze on my target for a moment. I had observed blood squirting from his left side. A perfect clean hole through his expensive overcoat, which matched the hole in his ribcage. He was moving slowly. If he rolled a few more inches to the edge of the wooden skid he was lying on, he would have met his Maker. So I'd helped the process along. I took aim, squeezed off a round, and the bullet found its target . . . Right between his brown saucer eyes. He became motionless. Permanently.

I checked Lisa again. Her eyes were fluttering, trying to stay open. But her eyes again had lied under her eyelids.

Shots were still being fired from behind me. I pivoted toward Eagle to see if he needed my assistance. That very second I had turned, I had witnessed Eagle's target's head being shot clean off from his broad shoulders. Blood had spilled over and dripped heavily to the gray cement floor. Smoke was pouring out from Eagle's .44 Mag. Spiraling and lingering in the thick air.

Eagle turned toward me, grinning widely, blowing on his smoking gun.

➸ ➴

Cutting the heavy rope with my doubled—edge hunting knife we heard sirens blaring from a distance. Hope they were coming for us, and not some other shoot-out. This is Chicago. Crime's committed every minute of every damn day in the *Windy City*. Marvelous . . . Just marvelous.

➸ ➴

Within seconds, from the time I heard the sirens wailing in the night, a line of cops, FBI, and paramedics stormed in fanning outward toward the center of the warehouse.

I pointed upward, and said, "They're up there, gentlemen. One on your left, and the other on your right . . . Dead."

Eagle and I side-stepped, so the paramedics can render First-Aid, CPR or whatever they needed to do. I quickly scanned the injured . . . .

Lisa seemed to be returning to reality . . . . Chic looked like he had been hit by a fast-speeding train . . . . Lisa's so-called father, Don, seemed to be on his last leg. And Lisa's so-called mother, Katie, was breathing heavily. Her ag-ing face was marred with deep dark bruises and swollen cheekbones and lower lip. Just like Lisa's bruises. But Katie's injuries seemed worse; maybe because of her age.

The sounds of more than a dozen officials, humming voices had echoed throughout the huge and bloody warehouse giving orders and asking ques-tions loudly to Eagle and me. Not speaking loudly deliberately, but the echoing caused it to be loud, like stuck in a tin can. At times I had wanted to cover my ears. But didn't.

As Eagle and I were giving our statements to the police, I glanced over the left shoulder of one of the officers and observed Dillman's expression, as his eyes bared down on Don and Katie Murray. When his sad and depressed eyes met mine, he had this look, I really couldn't describe, but it had seemed to me Dillman knew these two older couple. Then his gray-blue eyes spilled silvery liquid. He walked away, shaking his head lowly.

The paramedics lifted Lisa's dad on the gurney, covered and strapped him down and rolled him out into the wetness and dampness, lifting him into the rear of the ambulance. An IV tube was swaying with the wind so rapidly, the paramedics had to rush him into the ambulance before the IV had slipped out from Mr. Murray's veins.

Another trip, another victim; This time it was Chic who was wheeled out into the dampness and rushed into the rear of the ambulance. Then Katie Murray . . . . Lastly, Lisa was rolled out into the drizzling rain. By this time Lisa had retained her consciousness. But still dazed.

"What hospital?" I bellowed out to a female paramedic. She was of average height, blonde hair framed her round face with deep blue eyes . . . .concerned eyes . . . She said, "Ravenswood General. Do you know where the hospital is?"

I shook my head, and said, "No, but I'll follow you. Okay?"

She nodded, turned and ran to her emergency vehicle.

I was about to run to my car, but I was delayed by Clint.

"I am so sorry, buddy," Clint said. "She'll make it, you know."

I nodded with a short term grin.

Clint said, "I'll meet you there . . . later."

"Ravenswood General Hospital," I yelled, as I was running out to my car, which was still a half block away. The ambulance was already out of sight.

I guess I had to wing it.

Before I had left the warehouse, I turned and faced Eagle. Pam had her arms around him, bear-hug style, her head sunk into his brawn chest . . . . Cry- ing. I had noticed tears in his eyes, too.

Now, sitting in my rental with my wipers on intermittent, figuring out the direction to the hospital, I thought deeply . . . . This war isn't over by a long shot. You just don't mess around with the mafia . . . . Never . . . . Ever.

Bastards!

Chapter Sixty-Nine

I WAS NEAR LISA'S bedside in the ER as the Intern iced her swollen, beautiful face. The X-rays came back negative. No broken bones. Great! Just deep dark bruises circling her eyes and jaw line.

Not so great.

Lisa was released from ER to the second floor for her stay in the hospital.

The nurse wheeled her in expertly, and with concern.

"Miss Murray, your bed has been set up for you near the window. If you need anything, please press the NURSE button on the remote panel. The red button is for emergencies only." She said 'emergencies only' with emphasis.

Lisa nodded, and said, "Yes, ma'am, understood."

The nurse was middle-aged. Salt-pepper hair framed her oval and friend-ly features. Her teeth gleamed when she smiled. It seemed to be true teeth.

The nurse boosted Lisa on the edge of the bed and adjusted the bed to Lisa's liking. The mattress was angled at 45 degrees.

When the five-foot-four nurse was pleased with her work, she turned to us, and said, "Good-day. See you in a few hours, honey."

We nodded. Then she left, leaving the door open a crack.

Lisa and I were in middle of a conversation when the same nurse wheeled in Mrs. Katie Murray . . . Lisa's mother. After twelve years not being with her mother, or dad . . . This was so unbelievable. My eyes shifted from Katie to Lisa, back to Katie, then froze back to Lisa's. You could tell they were mot-her and daughter. No doubt about it.

The nice nurse did her routine with Katie.

Again, she was pleased with her perfected work. Again, she said Good-day . . . See you in a few hours . . . But this time she closed the door shut.

Lisa and her mother barely spoke to one another. Was the injuries too painful? Did they talk everything out in Chic's office? Or, could it be they were angry with each other? More so, Lisa. Lisa had the right to be angry at both of her parents. I know I would have . . . not being communicated those twelve years and not telling Lisa they were both alive.

≫ ≪

The cops didn't arrest Eagle or me, but there was a cop at the door all night. I stayed with Lisa and slept in the pale green leather chair, next to her bed, holding her hand.

Eagle, Pam and Clint would have stayed overnight also, but there wasn't enough room.

When we awoke early Wednesday morning a man in plain clothes was there from Chicago Police Department. Mrs. Murray was sitting up in bed, her left eye swollen completely shut and sipping on her apple juice from a big foam cup through a long straw from one corner of her not—so—swollen mouth.

Lisa's face was swollen and had two black eyes. The swelling was down a bit in her eyes. She could see out of them, but the lip was still very puffy and I could see the black thread from the stitches.

The same nurse earlier, came in and checked on Mrs. Murray first, then stepped over to observe Lisa's wounds.

To the nurse, Lisa said, "How's my daddy?"

The nurse's expression didn't look promising. She answered, "He is re-covering from surgery, honey. He lost a lot of blood. And he is very weak. But we think he will make it. But it's too early to say at this time. But I have to admit, honey, your dad seems to be a very strong-willed person."

Lisa nodded. Mrs. Murray tried to smile. But it was difficult. The nurse checked their charts that was hanging on the foot-end of the bed. Then she turned to the detective, "Don't ask too many questions. They both need their rest."

He smirked and nodded.

The middle-aged nurse gazed into the detective's eyes, and said, "I mean it. No more than fifteen minutes. They need their rest." The detective nodded agreeably. The nurse left leaving the heavy wooden door slightly ajar.

To the three of us, the detective said, "My name is Manex." He showed us his shield. "We'd like to know what happened." Lisa spoke. "It's a long story, sir."

"I have plenty of time," The tall red haired detective responded.

Lisa took in a very deep amount of air, exhaled, and said, "Okay, but where do I start . . . ?"

"From the beginning would be nice." Mr. Detective said, grinningly.

So the story went . . . .

"Twelve years ago, May 18th, 1985, on my graduation day, my daddy's car was bombed in the Christian High School's parking lot. I thought, as everyone else had, my mother and dad were in the car. But they weren't.

"They both went into hiding for their safety. You know, from the mafia, known as the Balesteri family. You see, my daddy was a Homicide Detec-tive for the Fifth District back in 1975. During that year he had arrested the Balesteri brothers; Rudy and Ruby for kill-ing my dad's partner and shooting and seriously wounding a uniformed cop.

"While in prison, the brothers had sent threatening messages, uh, letters to my parents' house. They both were planning to kill my dad when they were released from prison.

Two months later, after their release, my mom and dad were walking toward their car after the graduation ceremony. They were only about seventy-five feet away when their car had exploded.

"My mom and dad felt the shock wave, but the explosion didn't cause much injury. Well, it turned out Chic and Fritz Antonio had planted a bomb in the car . . . orders from Rudy's and Ruby's father, Richard Balesteri.

"The father knew his sons were planning to murder my dad, unclear a-bout my mother. Well, anyway, Richard Balesteri couldn't see them return-ing to prison. That was when he decided to hire the Antonio brothers to do the job.

"When my parents read in the paper that we were, meaning, Nick Ed-wards, which is my boyfriend and co-worker was seeking information about my parents death, and read also I shot and killed Richard Balesteri, they, my mother and father, decided to come out of hiding, and end this horror. When my parents entered the Holiday Inn where we were staying, somehow Chic and Fritz had recognized them.

"At that point and time, Chic and Fritz had kidnapped my parents at gun-point, took them to their restaurant, named Toni's Restaurant, near Van Buren, and locked them in Chic's office. Bound and gagged. Chic had later dropped off a note as we were eating in Holiday Inn's lounge. The note stated to meet him at his restaurant Monday noon. Nick and I didn't know what to think. So we met them at their restaurant shortly past noon that Monday, hoping they had information about my parents death.

"In a way, they had information. But it wasn't what I'd expected. Well, anyway, Chic and Fritz made us believe it was my dad's idea to have his own car blown-up and fake his death. Chic and his brother Fritz were really surprised to see my parents walk in the Holiday Inn lobby. Well, after all, they both thought my parents were killed in the bomb-ing. I can imagine them shitting in their pants when my parents strolled in the lobby." Lisa tried to smile, but it came out as a very small grin.

"But unknown to us, Nick and I, and everyone else, there were bodies in that car. But who?" Lisa shrugged. "At this point, no one really knows who was killed." Lisa took in another deep breath, and continued,

"Well, anyway, Chic got on the phone while me and my parents were in his office. He said, and I quote; 'Hey, Frankie, my man, we got a problem. A very big problem. Can you and your savvies come over and help me fix it?' I didn't think anything of it. I thought the problem was with his restaurant or something, but not us. I just have to learn not to be too trusting. Especially in my line of work.

"Within minutes, these two big men in overcoats and brim hats stormed in Chic's of-fice and scaring the shit out me. My parents seemed to expect some kind of trouble. They seemed to prepare themselves for something. But nothing like what had happened." Lisa paused a small moment. "Up until those apes barged in, I really believed there wasn't anything wrong. My par-ents were so calm about everything. I was convinced Chic really was friends of my dads. But, obviously, I was conned.

"I just was so happy to see my parents again. I was shocked, dazed, but thrilled all at the same moment. Everything happened so quickly. My head was spinning."

Detective Manex kept scribbling on his small notepad, flipping page after page, after page, one after another. At times, he had to shake his writing hand; writers cramp or the pen was running out of black ink. I really didn't know which. Lisa carefully inserted her straw in the corner of her stitched mouth, sip-ped her apple juice, then set the foam cup back down on her tray in front of her. She continued.

"I hadn't realized it then, but my parents knew something awful was go-ing down. My parents couldn't talk freely and tell me they both had been kidnapped and we were in danger. I also didn't realize they were such great actors. Being in hiding for twelve years probably had taught themselves that.

You know, how to be someone you're not." Lisa shrugged, sipped her juice and re-turned it to the stainless steel tray. The three of us just took in every word Lisa was say-ing. Suddenly, the heavy wooden door opened.

Lisa's nurse reappeared. All eyes gazed on her distorted expression.

"Detective, it is well over the time frame I'd given you. I said fifteen minutes." She glanced at her watch, and then said, "It's been thirty—five minutes already. How much longer, Detective, huh?"

"Not much longer, Nurse, uh . . ." He glanced down on her silvery name tag. And looked up again into her grayish-blue eyes and then said, "Nurse Whitaker. Ten more minutes at the most." Manex shifted his eyes to Lisa. "Right, Lisa?"

"Sure, right . . . Ten more minutes." Lisa said. Nurse Whitaker tapped her right foot on the waxed floor. To Manex, Nurse Whitaker said, "Okay. I am bending the rules here. But, okay . . . Ten more minutes. And that's it."

We nodded apologetically.

Nurse Whitaker did a 180 degree turn from her heels and went.

Lisa continued with her story . . . .

"Now, where was I? Oh yes, I remember. Well, as I was saying, my par-ents couldn't speak freely in front of Chic. He was with us the whole time.

As I was conversing and catching up on my parents welfare, these oversized animals, two of them, mind you, taped our mouths with gray duct tape. Our legs and hands were taped carelessly, but efficiently.

"We were slapped around. My mother more so than me. My father was punched a few dozen times. And Chic was punched, slapped, stomped and slammed senselessly. And before I could collect my thoughts, one of the bozo's took out a switchblade from his overcoat pocket. He picked up my father by his lapels, dragged him to Chic's desk and forced his left hand flat with his fingers overlapping the edge of the desk. With one quick motion of the blade, my dad's fingers, two I believe, were severed and dropped heav-ily into the wastebasket.

"Our screams were silent, of course. We just muffled the sounds from under our duct tape. But our tears and fearful expression spoke for itself. Blood squirted everywhere. Now, as for Chic, as beaten as he was, he had still remembered the deadline that Nick had given us. He whimpered to the two bastards that a private detective will be kicking our door down soon if we didn't return to the restaurant.

"So with that new information, these two men quickly blind—folded us, blood dripping from my dad's hand and all, they didn't really care, forcing us into the back alleyway, and pushing us into a waiting vehicle.

"As we were driving, I had counted in my head, as bad as it was pound-ing with pain, the minutes it took us from Point A to Point B. I tried to con-centrate on the sound of road noise, you know, if we drove on gravel, or paved asphalt or whatever. My concentration faded. I was trying so hard to listen to traffic noise. Even common noise we hear every day with our eyes wide-open. But I just couldn't focus or concentrate.

"Well, make a long story short . . . ."

"Please do, ma'am," Manex said, "We are almost out of minutes."

Lisa nodded, but continued.

"I finally had my first break. I had to use the bathroom. But there were no bathrooms available. So I went outside. Luckily, without my blindfold. And I still had my cell phone in my purse. I called the hotel, and spoke with Nick. I gave him some idea where we were. So Eagle and Nick came to our rescue." Lisa took in a very deep breath. "Well, that's it. That's all she wrote."

Manex looked up from his red notepad and said to Lisa. "You said some-thing about 'Eagle'. What Eagle? Or is that another long story?"

Lisa nodded.

"Okay, Lisa. We won't go there." Manex looked at me.

"Anything you want to add, Mr. Edwards?"

"Nope. Lisa had covered all bases, sir." Then his deep dark eyes landed on Katie. "You, ma'am? Anything else you remember?"

Her head went once to the left, then once to the right slowly. Silvery liquid streaming over her wounds.

"Sorry about re-hashing your dilemma, ladies, but . . . ." Det. Manex let his words hang. He nodded politely, closed his red cover to his notepad and slipped it into his inside coat pocket with his Bic pen. He turned to the door, reaching for the door handle, he hesitated. He turned again facing us. He said, "I am posting a uniformed officer as long as we need to. Just to be sure you two are safe." He tilted his big head forward and said goodbye.

We compensated his departure.

Then he went.

Chapter Seventy

LATER IN THE room, LT. Dillman stood near Katie's bed consoling her and caressing her hand, the one lacking the IV tubing. Katie felt heavy—hearted not telling Dillman of her and her husband's disappearance of those twelve years. She couldn't apologize enough.

To Katie, Dillman said, "You and Don were like family. Why didn't you tell me the truth? I would have protected your secret, Katie. What was really bothersome," Dillman paused, weighing his words carefully, "Maybe it is not my place to say, but Lisa . . . your own daughter. Why didn't you contact her?"

Katie eyes strayed from Dillman's. Her teary swollen eyes bounced from the walls, to the window, to the silent T.V. Her eyes finally found Dillman's hand resting on hers. Briefly, her eyes landed on the lieutenant's. All Katie could force out of her tired and weak body was a very slight shrug.

Lisa sustained her head toward the silent T.V., pretending to be interested in some talk show. I had observed Lisa's blue eyes beginning to swell with moisture and forcing down something hard in her throat. She didn't show any attempt to wipe her stream of liquid flowing down her bruised cheeks.

I sat silently and patiently, also pretending to be interested in some talk show.

Dillman realized this wasn't the time and place to discuss the Murray's dilemma. So, he kissed Katie's and Lisa's forehead, and shook my hand as he passed and left as politely as he could muster.

Silence filled the air. The tension was so thick you could cut it with an ax. It was too thick to cut with a knife.

I decided to leave mom and daughter alone with their deep—rooted thoughts. I went downstairs to the cafeteria to get some coffee, hoping they would talk about their indifferences.

Upon my return, I had found Lisa and her mother fast asleep. I grinned what I had observed. Lisa was curled up next to her mother in her bed, like two little children. I didn't have any need to disturb their sweet slumber. I turned toward the door when I heard my name called out. I pivoted toward the sound of my name, and Mrs. Murray, blinking her tired eyes at me, said,

"Please stay, Nick . . . Please?" Obviously, Mrs. Murray was a very light sleeper. Then Lisa awoke. With embarrassment all over Lisa's face, she stood quickly and fast-paced to her own bed.

I nodded to Katie and smiled at both of them.

So I stayed and stared at the silent television. Now it had a hair shampoo commercial. It didn't sustain my attention. As I was staring at this boring commercial, Lisa spoke and broke the heavy silence.

"The nurse came in after you left. She said the doctor wants us to stay another day for observation."

I nodded. "Good," I said. "What then? Is your mother staying in Chicago with us at the Holiday Inn?"

"Yes. She doesn't want to leave Chicago without my dad."

"But your dad will be here in the hospital for awhile. Is she staying that long?"

Lisa shrugged loosely, as if she was lacking strength.

"I guess. My mother has to do what she has to do. I'm thinking of staying here in Chicago 'til my daddy recovers."

I nodded encouragingly. "That's a great idea, Lisa. I will speak with Dill-man. Maybe he'll have an officer available to guard our hotel room." I paused, then, said breathing heavily outward, "Lisa, we're not out of the deep dark woods yet."

"Yes, honey. This I know." Lisa stretched for my hand with her free—IV hand. I gave my hand to her. We sat in silence watching the boob-tube for a long time. I leaned over Lisa's body, and took a peek at Katie. She was bre-athing evenly. Her chest went up and down calmly, slightly snoring from the left corner of her mouth. The snoring was so faint it didn't affect the mode of silence.

The silent air was comforting.

❧ ❧

It was a very late afternoon when Clint, Pam and Eagle walked in the room. Clint walked over to Lisa, leaned over, and gave her a kiss on her forehead. He stood and said, "It seems we found your parents killers, uh, would-be killers, Lisa. Dillman got Chic's and Fritz's confession in writing."

Clint paused, and took in a deep breath. He continued. "Here is a surprise for you people."

Our ears perked to the max.

Clint said, "Dillman believes the bodies that were found in your dad's car twelve years ago were auto thieves. He's speculating, of course, but he really thinks he's on the right path to success."

"Really," Lisa said. "I'll be damned. This could prove very interesting."

"Yes," Clint said. "Dillman will first check missing persons file that is dated back to May of 1985." Clint paused again. "Lieutenant Dillman will be charging Chic and Fritz with murder and attempted murder. There will be other charges filed against them. The DA is looking at conspiracy, and I be-lieve illegal use of explosives."

I said, "Those charges should put them in the slammer for the rest of their lives."

"I should say so," Eagle piped up. "I should say so."

Pam agreed, as we all had.

To me, Clint said, "And as for you, Nick, I wouldn't be punishing myself if I were you . . ."

"What do you mean?" I said.

"That ad in the newspaper, buddy, it wasn't a total mistake after all. It did force out the criminals we were pursuing."

"Yeah," I said. "But Lisa and her parents really paid a big price for it, though."

They nodded without speaking a word.

Chapter Seventy-One

TODAY IS THURSDAY, March 23rd; 12:20 P.M. when Lisa was officially released from Ravenswood General. The day was gloomy and drizzling lightly. It was an all day rain. While Lisa was packing her clothes and wait-ing for her doctor, I stood near the fourth floor window watching inflated, but colorful umbrellas, bobbing and meshing together on Ravenswood Ave-nue. I was expecting several umbrella collisions.

To me, with my back toward her, Lisa said, "My mother was ordered by her doctor to stay until after the weekend. He didn't promise anything, but she might be released Monday morning."

"Oh. Good," I said. I continued watching bobbing, colorful umbrellas.

"But that's not all. The doctor is concerned about her left eye. The swell-ing had wors-ened. His main concern she might lose her sight."

"Not good. Sorry." I walked away from the window and curled my arms around Lisa's waistline as she packed. She turned around and faced me, then heavily pressed her head against my chest. Crying.

We hugged each other firmly.

Lisa's mother awoke from her deep slumber. Her eyes blinked several times trying to clear sleep matter. Once her eyes had focused, she said, "Lisa, dear, are you leaving today?"

"Yes, Mom. I'm just waiting for my doctor to give me my prescription.
He should be here very soon."

Minutes later, Katie returned to her deep slumber, leaving Lisa finish her packing.

While Katie lied sleeping, Lisa kissed her mother's forehead softly. We went to visit her dad in ICU. The visit didn't last too long. Maybe fifteen minutes maximum. Don had his eyes open and staring at the ceiling. His IV tubes were entwined from the IV pouches to his right hand. The heart moni-tor was beeping irregularly. His breathing was shallow. His memory had thinly faded. His color in his cheeks was pasty white. He looked like a living ghost.

Lisa's visit hadn't registered in her dad's memory bank.

The shock was too tremendous for him. Seeing his fingers being chopped to pieces and discarded into a dirty wastebasket. Losing plentiful amount of blood. His memory was affected by it all.

Will Don Murray recover? Maybe, the nurse had said to Lisa. His dis-membered fingers? Were they salvageable? Yes the nurse had said. But she was doubtful about his memory. Her father's doctor will be the one to speak with on that matter Lisa was informed.

We thanked the nurse. Lisa turned to her daddy, kissed his cheek while squeezing his left hand. Lisa's teardrops fell near his eyebrow as she leaned over his paled face. She said softly, "I love you, daddy."

He didn't respond. His mind was elsewhere. If he had a mind . . . .

We turned and headed toward the long hallway back to the parking struc-ture with Lisa's arm around my waistline.

I helped her into the rental. I got in the driver's side. Inserted, turned the key and the six cylinders pumped quietly. Lisa dabbed her nose and eyes, wiping away dreadful and hurtful tears.

We returned to our hotel room. Undressed, turned on the TV and had lied in each others arms the remaining evening.

Turning her damaged, but still beautiful face, she said to me, "This is all my fault. If I wasn't so damned determined to find my parents killers, this wouldn't have ever happened."

I said, "But you didn't know, honey. Don't do this to yourself. If anyone is to blame it is me."

"You! Why you?"

"I'm the one with the crazy brilliant idea to put the ad in the paper."

"So," Lisa said. "But it helped to find the culprits . . . perps . . . murderers, or whatever you want to call those bastards. Didn't it?" Lisa turned away from me and stared at the TV, blankly. "This was what I had wanted. Somebody to take responsibility."

"It is nobody's fault. Not yours, not mine." I turned toward the TV and shared Lisa's blankness. "It's all part of the job . . . taking risks. I don't want to come off sounding cold or mean, honey. All I know is your parents didn't deserve this insane activity. And neither did you. So quit blaming yourself. Damn it. I love you very much, Lisa. I don't want you to go through the rest of your life you had done wrong. You didn't.

"What you did was only natural for a loving and caring daughter to do what you had done." I paused, and took in a deep breath. I grabbed Lisa's hand, and I said, "No more blaming yourself, please. Okay?"

She nodded. Her tiny nod didn't convince me.

Lisa said softly. "Only, if you don't blame yourself. Agreed?"

"It's a deal." Looking into each other's eyes, we squeezed each others hand, and shared a long hard kiss.

It was difficult not to make love to Lisa. I tried to maintain my manhood.

Considering her injuries, I had to settle just for a kiss and a few hugs. But she was worth waiting for. Least her lips returned to normal size. We sat in silence for a time with the TV muted, holding hands. I turned to Lisa, word-lessly. Her silent expression told me she was in a very deep thought mode. Miles, miles away. I know she'll tell me her very thoughts eventually. So I waited patiently.

The time had elapsed into thirty-minutes when her head turned to me and her lips carefully moved, weighing her words heavily.

She said, "Honey, sweetheart, I love you very much. What I am about to say to you, please don't think less of me, okay?"

I nodded lightly. "Of course not, honey. I love you, too."

"After all what I had been through . . . starting way back twelve years ago,

I decided to see a psychoanalyst. Maybe even a psychiatrist. All I know I have to see some professional. Seeing my parents alive was great, but very shocking to my emotions. I am so glad they're alive. But, now, I am having mixed emotions. I feel at times I could hate them for not contacting me, at least, telling me they were alive and well. I had lost twelve years of their lives. And they had lost twelve years of my life. I don't think we will ever get those lost years back."

Lisa was wringing her hands until her knuckles were white. Tears had fallen onto the sheets, creating a dark stain.

Still looking at me, she said, "Do you think I'm crazy if I commit myself to a professional counselor?"

I reached out to her wringing, white-knuckled hands and firmly squeeze-ed them. "I don't think you're crazy at all. I think it will be a wise choice, Lisa."

"Yeah, I do, too. As soon as we return to Tomah I'll look through the yel-low pages and do comparisons on a few psychoanalysts."

I leaned over and handed Lisa Kleenex tissues. We embraced each other gently. Still sitting up in bed, the television still muted, Channel-Seven news came on the screen. Lisa clenched the remote and clicked the 'OFF' button. No more news. No more bad news. No more sad news . . . Who needs it?

We just sat in bed, staring at nothing and listening to silence.

Chapter Seventy-Two

FRIDAY MORNING I called and asked Lt. Dillman if he would be able to post a uniformed officer at our door until things quieted down, or at least until Lisa and me returned to Wisconsin.

"See what I can do, Nick. Personally, I do not see a problem. But I have to clear it with the higher-ups. I'll get back with you on this. By the way, how's Lisa?"

"Disturbed." I said.

"She'll be alright, won't she?"

"We'll see. But it takes time to heal physically and emotionally. I am a positive person. And I think she'll pull through. She's sleeping at the mom-ent."

"That is what she needs right now, a lot of rest."

As we were talking on the phone, a hard knock on our hotel room door appeared.

"Hold on a minute, Loo, someone's knocking on the door."

I pulled my gun from its black leather holster that was lying next to my side of the bed on the cherry-wood night stand. I walked quietly to the door and peeked through the peep-hole, then I breathed lightly.

It was Clint, Pam and Eagle. Whew! I let them in shh-ing them as I point-ed to Lisa sleeping. They remained standing near the doorway, silently. I returned to the phone and continued my conversation with Dillman, placing my .38Cal. S&W back into its holster.

"It was only my friends at the door," I said.

"I gathered. 'Cause I didn't hear any gun shots. But I do have to get go-ing, though, Nick. I have another call coming in."

We hung up.

Turning my head toward my friends, patiently waiting at the doorway, I didn't notice this before, but their luggage was resting on the carpet near their feet.

"Leaving so soon?" I asked.

"Our job is done here," Clint said. "But you stay as long as needed. Just keep me posted on current events."

"Sure. But Lisa had mentioned to me she will be staying here until her parents recover. I won't' stay that long. I still have the Boehlis case I am working on. I'll probably stay until next Monday, though."

"Well, as I said, stay as long as you need to. Sheryl Boehlis can wait. Besides, you've been fired from that case."

"Yeah, I know. But I won't rest until justice is done."

"Yeah, of course. Mr. Justice himself."

I smiled modestly. We shook hands and I thanked Eagle and Pam for their courage and bravery.

"You bet, buddy," Eagle said, "Until next time, Nick."

"Until next time, Eagle . . . Pam." Pam stepped in closer and gave me a tight squeeze. She said, "Be careful, Nick. We love you."

"We love you, too."

The three sets of suitcases were lifted heavily, as if they had ton of bricks in them.

The trio turned and left, closing the heavy oak door quietly.

I went back to bed, snuggling against Lisa's sexy body.

Chapter Seventy-Three

L ISA AND I stayed low-key. For the remaining weekend we agreed to stay and eat in. Lisa kept in touch with the hospital, via phone. She gave them our hotel and room number just in case her parents had a relapse.

After thinking about what Clint had told me, I decided to take his advice and stay with Lisa and protect her from harm. Clint was right. Sheryl Boeh-lis can wait. I'll search for her mother some other time. Lisa needs me right now, which was far more important.

I guess any new cases arise Clint would handle them for me.

So I had thought . . . .

➤ ◄

The phone rang early Monday morning, nearing four A.M. It was March 27th. Lisa had scared awake thinking it was Ravenswood General Hospital. She grabbed the phone nervously, almost dropping the handset. Her voice cracked and she swallowed hard, barely getting the words through her dry lips.

"Hell-o, Lisa speaking, is everything all right?"

"No, damn it. Everything is not all right." Lisa's expression went into shock mode. The gruff-sounding voice on the other end of the line continu-ed. "I am looking for Private Investigator Nick Edwards. Is he there?"

Lisa seemed pale, as if she was on the verge of collapsing. But relieved the phone call wasn't for her. She paused and regained her composure. Turn-ing to the mouthpiece of the phone, she said, "Wait a minute, I'll wake him."

"Who is it?" I said.

"Don't know. He didn't say and I didn't ask. But he sounds very upset."

I gave Lisa a brief hug and a small kiss on her forehead. I slid my hands down from my tired-looking face, rubbed my bloodshot eyes, before answer-ing the fucking phone. I glanced at my watch. Jesus. It's four in the fucking morning. I took the handset from the nightstand, lifted it to my right ear, and grumbled. "Yeah, who is this?" I had this urge to cuss-out the caller, but I thought better of it.

"Art . . . Sheryl's boyfriend . . . She's missing, man . . . Fucking missing."

"Missing?" This got my half-shut eyes wide opened.

"Yeah . . . missing. I just got in from a sixteen day run, walked in and found this fucking note on the damn kitchen table. I called your office in Tomah. A Clint Douglas answered. He gave me your hotel and room num-ber. Sorry for calling so early in the morning, man, but I didn't know what else to do . . . Who to call?"

Ghost Buster's, I had thought to myself.

"Okay, go on." I said, wide awake now.

"The note said: 'Do not even bother to look for me . . . Bye.' And my gun is missing, too. Can you beat that, man?"

"Do you have any idea when she'd left, or even where she'd went?"

"I had to leave on a coast-to-coast run shortly after Sheryl's birthday. Which was March 9th. I left March 11th. I was on the road sixteen days as of today. She could have left to wherever, the same day I hit the road, or she could have left yesterday. I really don't know, man. This is really freaking me out."

"Give me your best wildest idea where she could have taken—off to, man. Guess."

Art was silent for a long moment. His gruff voice then returned to the phone. "My best fucking guess, she probably went to Florida searching for her crazy mother." Again, silence. When he had returned to the phone, I could tell he was holding back tears. "But my gun is missing, man. And two, maybe three full boxes of shells are gone, too."

"She could have been kidnapped . . ."

"What! No way. No . . . fucking . . . way, man . . ."

"Yes . . . Way. It is a great possibility the drug dealers finally found Sheryl.

You do know the inheritance Sheryl received from her mother and put in her trust fund, given to her by her aunt and uncle when she had turned eighteen, was stolen from the Chicago drug dealers. Remember? . . . . You just don't fuck with big time drug dealer's money."

"Yeah, I know that shit, man. But I do not think she was kidnapped."

"What makes you think otherwise, my man?" I said.

"I don't know. I just do." His voice was lacking dryness. He seemed much more calmer. For whatever reason, I couldn't fathom.

"Okay, okay, man," I said. "Let's just assume she had left on her own. Why would she leave you a not-so-warm note, and toting a gun . . . Oh, by the way , what kind of arsenal is she carrying?'

"A .357 Python." Art's voice seemed to have a slight braggart in it.

"Holy shit, man." I said. "Jesus Christ. Was she trained properly?"

"Yeah, you bet, man. She shoots really damn good too."

I grunted. "Alright, let's go back to the day you had left for your coast to coast run."

"Okay."

"Did she seem angry? Upset? Vigilant? . . . Any one of those?"

"Nope."

Liar, liar, pants on fire. I had thought. He answered without hesitation. Just too quickly for my concern.

"What shall I do, man? What shall I do?" Art cried out.

"Stay put. You don't go anywhere. Got that?"

"Yeah, okay."

"Good. I have to get dressed and shower, and all that shit. Then I have to go to my of-fice. Then I'll meet you at your apartment. I should be there sometime this afternoon."

"Yeah . . . Okay." He was too damn agreeable. And I didn't like it.

"Now . . . Stay put . . . Understand?"

"Yeah . . . Sure . . . Got it." We hung up.

I stared at the phone for a time. I thought. *He won't be there when I arrive at his place.* Damn it.

As I was setting the handset back into its cradle, Lisa turned to me and said, "Who was that, honey?" Lisa was wide awake now.

Sitting on the bed opposite of our bed with a small gap in between us, our knees were touching and I was getting excited. Calm down tiger, I reminded myself.

"Art. Sheryl's boyfriend."

"Boehlis?" Lisa's blue eyes widened. Her eyes were still awesomely beautiful even though she did have to black eyes encircling them. She had reminded me of a raccoon.

"Yep," I said. "She's missing and also toting his .357 Python. Art also in-formed me two or three boxes of ammo are missing."

Lisa's eyes had widened a few more centimeters. Her orbs were darkened and full of concerned expression.

"Sheryl isn't going to Florida to find her mother with open arms . . ."

I shook my head. "No. Open fire is on her devious mind."

Lisa nodded agreeably.

I said, "I really am beginning to hate Missing Person cases."

"Why?" Lisa's left hand reached out and squeezed my bare kneecap and did small circles around my scar with her forefinger where I had an opera-tion from a bullet wound last year.

"You just don't know if the person hires me to find their dearly beloved to be reunited, or to locate their lost loved ones to blow their friggn' brains out."

Again, Lisa nodded. "I agree, honey, but this case wasn't a Missing Per-sons. You were hired to find Sheryl's mother's killer. It just so happens we figured her mother to be alive and living in Tallahassee, Florida."

"And that is where Art and I believe she is headed, if not already there."
I said.

"You said something about a kidnapping. Do you really think she was?"
Lisa said, still making small circles on my right kneecap.

I shrugged and gazed into Lisa's concerned eyes. "That was the first thought that came into my mind. But I am leaning toward what Art said."

"Oh. What did he say?"

"He thinks Sheryl went to find her mother in Florida on her own accord. But the note she had written to Art was heartless."

"How did the note read?"

"Very hateful. The note said: 'Don't even bother to look for me . . . Bye.'

No; *I Love You* . . . No, *See You Soon* . . . No, *I Miss You* . . . No nothing. At first I thought she was coerced in writing the note by some crazy kidnapper or she wrote it that way to protect Art from any danger he might encounter, otherwise. But Art's gun is missing . . . ."

"And over sixty rounds of ammunition, don't forget." Lisa said, mindfully.

"Yeah, over sixty rounds of ammunition," I said, reminding myself.

"If she went to Florida over a week ago," Lisa leaned over to me, thoughtfully, "It might just be too late."

I agreed. I leaned closer to Lisa, almost nose to nose . . . lips to lips. I gazed into her eyes and said, "May I kiss you on your lips, or would it hurt too much?' She didn't answer. She just took my head into her hands and jerked my face into hers. We kissed hard until her lower lip was bleeding from her stitches. I tasted her blood and tried to pull back, afraid I was doing too much damage. But she held my head firmly. I didn't resist.

After the lengthy French kiss I went to the bathroom and retrieved a wet facecloth and handed it to Lisa. She dabbed her crimson lips, even though it was clotting, which was a good thing.

"Well, honey, I have to get ready to go to Tomah and Sparta to see Art . . . . Even though I think he'll be gone when I arrive there."

"So why go, Hot-Lips?"

I grinned widely, and said, "I don't want to take that chance, Crimson Joy."

She returned a smile. A smile that will last forever embedded in my mind.

"You'll be all right alone?" I said.

"I'm not really alone. I have the uniformed officer in front of the door in the hallway. And Dillman is a phone call away." She paused, then said to me, "But I would rather have you close and protect me, hot-tie."

"I bet you would, sexy. I bet you would."

Chapter Seventy-Four

SHORTLY AFTER SIX A.M. I had showered, shaved and brushed my teeth. I had my coffee mug filled with decaffeinated coffee, cream and sugar. As I was approaching the front revolving doors of the hotel, I snatched a few jelly donuts and a Boston Crème. My favorite. Complimentary breakfast. Sort of.

Lisa and I would have made love, but she was in too much pain. We just hugged each other for a long while. The electricity from her body energized me enough, where I was satisfied to get me through the long haul. I always miss her when I'm away from her. Though she had protection, I still had this guilt feeling deep inside my gut. As long as she was a private investigator, she never had been in danger to this extent. But I had to have faith she/we would get through this fucking mess.

I had about eight hours of driving time before I arrive in Tomah. There-fore, I had about eight hours thinking time.

First thought that went across my mind . . . .

What the hell happened before, even after, Art had left on his sixteen day run? Was Sheryl contemplating to go to Florida, searching for her mother?

Or was it randomly put into action? Maybe she was kidnapped? I won't rule that out, just yet. Was she gone the entire sixteen days . . . ? Just a week . . . ?

Maybe just two days? She could have left just before Art came home also.

When I arrive at Sheryl's apartment I'll do my search. Usually, but not always commonly in my favor, I find clues. Something should hit me in my face. Right? . . . Maybe not. Odds are not always grand.

I thought some more . . .

Was Art and me positively sure Sheryl went to Orlando? No, of course we weren't. How can we be sure of that? We couldn't. All we could, at this point, was guess. But it was very likely that was what she did.

Common sense . . . . So Florida it is.

Some of my wild thoughts told me she might even went to the firing range near Ft. McCoy, near Sparta, target practice. But that didn't even make any sense to me. It was too early in the morning for that. Duh.

Sheryl didn't even have inkling where her mother lived in Tallahassee . . .

Or did she? Maybe she found out something for her to take-off the way she did. Another thing flew across my mind . . .

Did she go by plane, or car? More likely, she drove. It would have been difficult to clear her toting .357 Python through Airport Security. And if even it wasn't a problem, there were delays to be considered. Long line at the airport; Search and Seizure and what not.

If Sheryl wasn't kidnapped, and she went on her own accord, she prob-ably was in dire need to get to Florida without any hesitation, or delays, whatsoever. So, my conclusion to that idea, she took here 1973 Gremlin to Florida. Where else could she have gone to?

Then there was the note to be considered.

What was *that* about anyway? No; 'Dear Art' . . . No; 'Love Always' . . . .

No; 'See you soon . . . miss you' . . . No . . . nothing. N-O-T-H-I-N-G . . . Na'da.

I had analyzed the note over and over again in my tired brain.

'Do not even bother looking for me . . . Bye!' Suicide? Was she really plan-ning to kill herself and fifty, or maybe sixty other people? This was sick.

Very sick.

She did snatch two or three full boxes of ammo. She had to have been thinking *Damage* in a very *big* way. On the other side of the coin, I might very well be jumping to conclu-sions. Right . . . ? Maybe . . . I was wrong before.

Was she planning on shooting everyone involved in her mother's disappear-ance, her death cover-up, for punishment? A good part of her family was al-ready deceased. Dead and buried: Sheryl's grandmother . . . Her mother's ex-boyfriend Mike, who was probably Sheryl's father. Also her godmother Clara Rueton. Dead . . . dead and buried.

Suddenly, like someone slapped me across the back of my head, sort of like a wake-up call, it hit me. Sheryl's aunt and uncle . . . I bet my PI license . . .

She's planning on killing her aunt and uncle for covering—up her mother's death-slash-disappearance, depriving her of her own mother's love. The lies her family had told her about her mother's supposed suicide. Sheryl had fin-ally snapped.

It is revenge time. Damn it.

I even had wondered if I should call Florida State Troopers and give them heads-up, sort of speak. They might have her in custody already. Or maybe even on a state to state highway speed chase this very moment.

These questions and my thoughts would be very difficult to satisfy now without any-thing in front of me to examine.

I pulled over at the next truck stop to get a decent breakfast. Thinking made me very hungry.

➤ ◄

By the time I arrived at my office, Clint had already left and I had several messages waiting on my answering machine. Two Cheater Cases, one tele- marketer, selling aluminum siding, and the big one, which I intuitively ex-pected.

Art had left a message he couldn't wait any longer. He took the liberty to adventure out on his own to Orlando, then to Tallahassee. But he stated he had left the front door key under the Welcome Mat. 'Make yourself at home'. How sweet. He had also said, 'Hope to see you in Florida some-where. Sorry. Then a click.

Another . . . *Damn it.*

I snatched Sheryl's file from my desk drawer, thumbed through it, be sure everything was in there I needed.

It was.

I set her file in my briefcase and wrote Clint a small note. *"I'll be in Florida, somewhere."* Then I drove crazily to Art's place in Sparta.

I had found the key exactly where Art said it would be. I let myself in and did a quick, but thorough search of the apartment.

I observed a week-old mail stacked on the kitchen table, unopened. I found the ad-dress to Sheryl's aunt's and uncle's house in Orlando.

Thanks to Art.

I had studied each Post Mark stamped in the corner of each envelope. Which had told me Sheryl was gone at least a week . . . Nick Edwards . . . The great sleuth.

The house was dusty, but orderly. I looked into her closets and bureau. The drawers were empty. Why wasn't I surprised? The closet, well the closet was really impossible to know much of anything. Unless I had known every stitch of clothing she had in there. She could have taken some hang-up clothes, but how many? I shrugged. Then I went into the bathroom. There were pantyhose and stinky facecloth and hand towels over the shower cur-tain rod.

I opened the medicine cabinet. I scanned it for a few seconds. Being sat-isfied, I shut it. I then looked under the bathroom sink. There was not anything there could tell me *anything.*

But what I didn't find could've been a clue. Sheryl's make-up bag.

Where ever she was going, or went, she planned to stay somewhere for a long while. But, then again, maybe someone wanted Art to think that. May-be *that* someone was the kidnapper. I still hadn't ruled that out.

I even searched Art's closet. I had found a double-barrel shotgun on the upper shelf up against the inner-closet-wall. Next to it, a box of cartridges.

Maybe Sheryl wasn't trained to handle a big gun yet. Maybe it was easier for her to carry a .357 Python. Next, I went into Sheryl's business office.

Her answering machine had 25 messages on it. Unheard. I played back a few: March thirteenth, Monday; *'This is Joan . . . appointment for Tuesday . . .*

March fourteenth . . . please call me back . . . Beep . . . . March fourteenth . . . *It's me again, Joan . . . Sheryl, did you forget about my calling yesterday for an appointment for today? . . . Please call me . . . please . . . This isn't like you . . . . Sheryl . . . . you know, ignoring my calls like this . . . Call me . . .* Beep . . . . March sixteenth, *Sheryl, this is Marge. Do you have an opening for tomorrow at ten A.M.? Please call. You have my number . . .* Beep . . . . And the messages went on and on and on . . . . .

The messages didn't tell me much. But it did leave a clue. A small clue. The messages clued me in that Sheryl was unable, or unavailable to answer her calls. But it didn't tell me where she went. I listened to all of her mess-ages. Not one call came from her aunt or uncle. No emergency call to come to Florida quickly. So, what was the big rush to go to Florida? That is if she went there. The gun . . . . The two or three boxes of ammuni-tion . . . . That really had bothered me.

I took in a very deep breath, collected my thoughts, and pondered.

My *Sherlock* instincts kicked in and told me she probably had gone to Florida. And she left either between the eleventh and thirteenth. Today is the twenty-seventh. She prob-ably had been gone for 14 to 16 days, so far.

Long trip.

I called the airport and booked a flight to Orlando. I lucked—out on the last flight out. Maybe I'll arrive to Orlando before Art would. He didn't act-ually tell me what transpor-tation he was taking. I probably shouldn't expect him to arrive until the 29th, Wednesday, if he went by car.

I boarded the plane on schedule. Florida, here I come.

The plane landed safely. I exhaled a lot of air of relief.

After buying myself a map of Florida, and rented a four door sedan, I was on the road to unfamiliar territory. Fun. Fun. Fun.

The expressway was quiet at this time of night. The travel time to the Nowak's house shouldn't have take me more than an hour from the airport. Well, it took me an hour and half. I got lost several times. It was hard to read a map and drive at the same time. Justifiable mistake.

I had finally reached my destination. The single lane road had been bum-py and treacherous. Enough potholes to create a golf course. The pitch dark-ness was not in my favor either.

Well, here I was at a very secluded and dark unfamiliar location. My eyes couldn't see a damn thing. But I knew I was near the Atlantic Ocean. I could smell the salty air. And I heard the rushing of choppy waves soaking up the beach-line. The light from the full moon shot down on the inky ocean and was riding the choppy waves, gleaming brightly. The house, a three-decker, stood alone on a private beach. Nice and rich . . . Fit for a king. Just to be positive with my location, I got out of my Ford sedan, walked to my trunk, popped it open and took my flashlight light out of my gym bag. Pointing it toward the three-decker, the heavy dry—cell—battery—operated flashlight beamed brightly on the address and its structure. The address was correct. Thank God. I didn't feel up to another rocky and bumpy ride in the dark.

I scanned my heavy-duty flashlight around the front of the house. Attach-ed to it was a two car garage. The overhead door was drawn up to the max. I stepped in closer for a peek-a-boo. No cars in the garage. No cars outside, parked on rippled sand. No Gremlin. And no Trans Am. But I didn't really expect Art's car to be here yet, anyway. But I did expect Sheryl's car. Sort of. But where were the Nowak's vehicles? No cars whatsoever. Odd.

The three-decker was highly polished with white brick and green trim-ming. The roof was peaked and pointed. And green. The off—white gravel walkway curved toward the front door from the pot-holed asphalt. But be-fore I went any further, I went back to my rental and donned my holster and .38Cal. S&W.

Safe and secure.

I flashed the light on my wristwatch. The time: 3:30 A.M.

With the ocean body behind me now, rushing and colliding against huge rocks, and with the gun in my left hand, I walked softly up to the front door. Gripping the brass door handle, I pushed down the latch quietly. Sound-lessly. The translucent-glass door opened freely. It wasn't locked. Trusting neighbors. Sweet.

I stepped in fumbling for the light switch near the door I had just walked through. Found it. I flicked it up, and the living room beamed with bright-ness. The house was totally quiet. Silence. Dead silence. Except for the sounds of the central air system hum-ming, grandfather clock ticking, and the vibration of the refrigerator down the hallway into the kitchen.

The décor in the living room told me these people had plenty of money. Maybe drug money. But that was my opinion . . . The house that drugs built.

The new plush matching furniture, which was solid white, was outlined along the dark paneled walls. In the center, in front of the plush white sofa, sat a glass-gold-trimmed coffee table. In the center of it were two crystal vases, centered evenly. In one of the vases were red and yellow roses. The other, white carnations. The flowers were wilted and drooped over the edges of the two crystal vases. The evaporated water left a dark film clinging to the guts of the well-designed crystal.

The art work above the mantel was very expensive. Artist; Rembrandt. There was an-other expensive and famous painting. And that one was located above the entertainment center, near the front door where I had come in. The

Artist; Da Vinci. Mona Lisa had this look about her . . . her smile, as if she was saying to me, *"You sly dog you . . . What took you so long?"* I compensated *HER* smile.

The highly-waxed oak flooring which was in the living room was also in the long hall-way. And that took me into the kitchen, past the dining room. The kitchen was elegant. Well, maybe it wasn't elegant, but very clean and spotless, except for dirty wine glasses and stuck-on food crusting against the chinaware in the stainless steel sink. I had noticed some green stuff forming around their edges too.

Everything was stainless steel. Even the refrigerator was stainless steel. It was like walking into a ritzy restaurant's kitchen. Or any respectable and clean restaurant for that matter.

My eyes fell to the kitchen's checkered—square floor. Black and white. My blue eyes had told me the Nowaks' had a dog. But by the sight of the dog dishes, their dog was far from being tiny. Probably they owned a Dober-man. Maybe even a Boxer. So with that observation, where was the dog? No sounds of barking. Did the Nowaks' go on vacation? And if they did, why was the front door unsecured? And the garage door wide opened?

But no cars in the garage. But then again, if they did go on vacation, why wouldn't they clean the dog dish? The dog food was so dried, you probably could have killed someone with the mound of raunchy food.

Suddenly, but I didn't understand where it was coming from, the smell, not strong, but strong enough where it had reached my nose and had almost made me puke. I sniffed like a bloodhound. I kept on sniffing until the staunch took me upstairs into the Master Bedroom.

That was when I saw it.

The bedroom door was ajar. I slowly opened it with my left running shoe.

I quickly jerked my right hand up to my nose and mouth, covering them. Automatic reflex.

Turning on the light, I almost let my dry bile up and out. I felt it coming up. The bloody crime scene was too unbearable to comprehend. I slammed down the light switch to the off position, and briskly, skipping two stairs at a time, went through the backyard screen door, heaving my dinner over the dewy, green grass.

Homicide Detective, I am not. Even though I investigate homicide cases, my stomach just wasn't prepared for what I had just witnessed.

I staggered to my car after breathing in a lot of fresh salty air. Suddenly, my left foot caught on something hard. I tripped, stumbled and fell. The flashlight went one way and I the other. I was in the dark once again. The beam of light was shooting across the lawn facing the rough edges of the ocean.

In the dark now, blindly stretching my left arm on my knees, I had come across something very hard. My left hand was slowly fingering the stiff hard object. The shape seemed to be of a head, but not human. Maybe it was a baby alligator. Maybe even a small crocodile. As my fingers did the scop-ing, the head-shape became very clear. But the smell was horrific. Like acid smell. I was shoeing away flies from my sweaty face. I felt bugs crawling all over my hands and arms. My shaking fingertips finally came in contact with a hole. Very hard and dry crusty hole. A huge hole.

I put my fingers to my nose. Just as I thought . . . Blood. Dry blood.

I pushed myself up and away and retrieved the flashlight from the wet grass, which was several feet from the stiffened object. I scanned the light in the direction of staunch, maggots and flies. And there it was. Half chewed furry canine. What was once a beautiful German Shepard, now lies nothing but bone, chewed up meat and some loose fur, and with no eyes. Its body being fed off by vultures. Maybe by other wild stray dogs. No doubt by her-ring gulls.

I got down on my haunches with the light shining over the corpse of—a –dog. I looked at its dog tags. Its name . . . *BOSSY*. I would have buried Bossy myself, but the two slugs were probably still in its skull. I didn't want to tamper with evidence.

The sad part of it was Bossy never had a chance to protect itself. The dog was still chained to the house.

Chapter Seventy-Five

I T WAS APRIL fourteenth. It had been over two weeks since my discovery of the bloody massacre at the Nowak's residence.

Art and I sat in the Orlando Sheriff's office of the Sheriff Headquarters building. It was made of white brick. The office was evenly squared. The walls were painted of one color. Gray. Even the furniture was gray. The gray Formica table where Art and I were sitting was centered on gray cemented flooring. Cabinets, Sheriff's desk and chair, all gray. Even the Sheriff's uniform was gray. Well, one thing that was in the Sheriff's favor, he was well-camouflaged. Blending in with the color gray, Art and I could barely detect he was there on the other side of the gray Formica top table, gazing at us with his deep dark brown eyes. If it wasn't for his deep dark Florida tan, we would have missed him completely.

Grayson was the Sheriff's name. He had handed me Sandy Boehlis's file.

A.K.A; Clarese Ruton . . . A name similar to Clara Rueton . . . Sheryl's God-mother. I was studying Sandy/Clarese past and present criminal report. And past and present photo shots. Sandy/Clarese had cut and died her hair. The hair in the photo was light-blonde. And cut short to the scalp. Mia Farrow style. Sandy's right arm and hand was scarred from battery acid. Thanks to her boyfriend Scott Selinski. That particular incident occurred in the year 1988, which explained why she wrote her daughter Sheryl with her left hand from 1988 to 1990. Major nerve damage. The arm and hand was useless.

In the year 1987, Sandy gave birth to twin girls. In 1990, Sandy/Clarese was arrested and convicted for murdering her twin daughters; Casey and Marcy Selinski. This also explained why Sheryl didn't receive anymore mail from her mother. Too busy serving time behind bars. And probably too embarrassed and ashamed. Or she could care less. The police report stated she poisoned the two with chemicals. Casey: With Chlorine Bleach, Marcy: Turpentine. According to the report, Sandy's neighbor, in Tallahassee, walked in freely, as she always did. Upon walking into Sandy's kitchen, the neighbor witnessed Sandy looking down on Marcy and Casey. She was sit- ting at the table. Casey and Marcy were on Sandy's lap. According to the witness Sandy had a blank look. No expression, whatsoever. Her neighbor thought Sandy was in shock. Seeing the evidence of chemical substance on the kitchen table and the two dead bodies on Sandy's lap, the neighbor did not hesitate. She ran home and called the County Sheriff.

I shifted my eyes, looking over the pages edge, observing Sheriff Gray-son staring at Art. If his eyes stared any harder, Grayson's eyes would have shot fire and melted Art's face.

I looked back down on the reports and continued my reading.

What I was about to read next explained a lot of things.

In late December of '96', around Christmas, Sandy Boehlis had escaped Tallahassee Prison. She'd been on the run since. Until now . . . .

Unaware to the police, until recently, Sandy had relatives living in Or-lando. So with that new information, the local, county and the state officials did a wide range search within the vicinity of Mr. and Mrs. Dale Nowak's residence . . .

It was fortunate for the officials that Art was available for identifying the bodies found in the Master Bedroom. I thought.

Art added to the Orlando Sheriff that the Nowak's were related to the fugitive. So the search was on . . . .

Less than a week later, the Deputy Sheriff had found Sandy Boehlis's body in a 1973 Gremlin; (who was the previous owner of the vehicle twenty years ago). How bizarre was that. The body was found propped up in the front passenger seat, one mile from the Nowak's residence, near the ocean, with a single bullet wound to her right temple. Using a similar weapon, bal-listics came back matching it to the *Python* as the weapon used.

The three bodies found in the Master Bedroom were Sheryl Boehlis, and Mr. and Mrs. Dale Nowak. Sheryl had a single slug wound to her right temple. Sheryl's uncle had ten holes in his body, which ranged from head to chest. Dale's wife had the same pattern. The four bodies together added up to twenty-two rounds spent.

Bossy, the German Shepard, found in the back yard, had two bullet holes through its brain. All were killed with the same gun. (.357 *Python*). Total of 24 rounds spent. That would have been approximately a full box of ammo . . . . . . thus far.

The ME estimated the death range to be around March 23, maybe 24.

That would've been three or four days before my arrival.

At this point and time, the weapon had not been located.

When I was done reading the report, Sheriff Grayson said, "Do you know what baffles me about this case, Mr. Edwards?"

I shook my head. "No, sir." Art just sat in his gray chair listening.

"What's so baffling about this case . . . ," Grayson looked over to Art again with that hard stare. I expected Art's head to go up in flames.

But didn't.

Though Grayson was talking to me, his deep dark brown eyes remained on Art. "The *Python* . . . . Where the hell is the *fucking murder* weapon. Please, someone tell me." Grayson's full attention went toward Art in a very big way. His growling voice went up a few notches. "Art, do you know where the fucking murder weapon might be?"

Art was stunned. He shook his head, nervously. "No, I don't . . . Sorry."

Grayson turned to me, his eyes still fuming. "The damn gun wasn't found at neither of the crime scenes, Mr. Edwards. Who shot who? Who was the first person to be shot? The last one to die? Does anyone know? Does any-one care? We've been searching for this fucking .357 over a week now."

His eyes were bouncing back and forth . . . Art, then back to me, several different times. Then his eyes had frozen on Art again.

What I had said just added to his fury. "Where are the two vehicles from the Nowak's garage, sir? Were those found yet?"

With his thick hand, Grayson pounded on the gray Formica top.

"Damn it, Mr. Edwards. Now, there's another thing. Where is the fuck-ing vehicles?"

"Chances are, sir," I said, "If the vehicles are located, just maybe, the murder weapon might be in one of them."

"Maybe. The way my luck has been going lately, fat chance that will hap-pen. But thank you for your optimism anyway, Mr. Edwards."

I nodded modestly.

Suddenly, the black phone rang.

When Grayson hung up the phone, his muscular body moved quickly. In a flash of a second, he was standing upright, slapping the table hard with his dark-tanned hand. He said, "Hot-damn. My luck is changing," Scrutinizing Art, Grayson said, "And as for you, kid" pointing his thick forefinger at Art, "That phone call just might save your funky ass."

Grayson turned to me and said, "Come on, Mr. Edwards, you too, kid. We're all taking a short trip to the Atlantic Ocean."

Chapter Seventy-Six

LISA AND I were decorating her parent's log cabin, which was in Kenosha, Wisconsin, the town where Lisa was taught to fire a gun when she was six-teen. Today was May twenty-seventh, Memorial Day weekend. This remark-able, gorgeous Saturday morning had brought us comfortable temperatures; ranging from 70 to 75 degrees. Ocean blue sky, and a light breeze. It was a very rare Memorial Day weekend. Usually we get hit with rain and gloom.

Lisa was in front, spacing the small, wooden-stick American Flags evenly along the sides of the Flagstone walkway, while I was pulling the last pull of rope, raising the American Flag up its flag pole. Old Glory was flapping and waving in the breeze proudly.

I smiled proudly.

I saluted it sharply. A few tears accumulated in the corner of my eyes.

I did a sharp about-face, and turned to Lisa. She was bending over nicely.

"Like the view, Blondie."

"Bet you do." I knew she was smiling, but I couldn't see it. I was too busy taken in by the well-rounded view.

Today Lisa wore plaid shorts, a white sleeveless blouse and running shoes. No socks. Her thick, blond hair was up in a ponytail. And as for me, I was wearing my usual; faded blue jeans, denim shirt with tails out over my buttocks. And white running shoes, lace-less. No socks.

"You know, honey," I said, still observing the sexy view, "I was really looking forward to Clint and Eagle being here for this Memorial Day."

Lisa unfolded her body, standing upright, gazing at me with her baby blues. "I know, sweet thing. But Clint and Eagle wanted to spend this day alone with their wives." Lisa paused, and said, "Clint was Viet Nam, wasn't he?"

"Yep. And as you well know, honey bun, Eagle and I were involved in Desert Shield/Desert Storm. What about your father?"

"Korean War vet." She smiled proudly.

"Still would've been a great time together if they came." I said, "We could've all went to the National Memorial Cemetery together and honor our troops who had served and died for our Country." I pulled Lisa to me, and kissed her on her sweaty forehead.

"Speaking about my father, he and my mother should be arriving late this afternoon, or early tomorrow morning. They both went to visit Lieutenant Dillman in Chicago and reconcile their friendship."

"How are your parents coming along, injury-wise?"

"Well, my daddy's fingers had been reconnected successfully. His mem-ory is vague. But okay. He lost twenty pounds. My mother's eye is patched.

But only for precautionary measures."

"Great!" I looked around the outside of the log cabin and pointed to it. "So, Lisa, this was your parent's hide-a-way for twelve years, huh?"

"Yes . . . Amazingly so. But true."

We were silent for a long while, hugging each other. I broke the silence.

"So, sweetie, how are your sessions with the psychoanalyst?"

"Okay. Slow. But okay. What about your case? How did it go with Art?"

"Sketchy. We looked into his whereabouts from his sixteen day run. His logbook proved to us he was in Orlando on March twenty-second, a day or two before the mas-sacre shootings. He had a load to be dropped off at the U.S. Naval Base. He could have killed Sheryl and the others. He had motive.

"The note tells us, Sheriff Grayson and me, that Sheryl probably broke up with Art. He could have gone bonkers and killed everyone, including Bossy, the German Shepard.

"My theory is he went for a quick visit at the Nowak's residence, and found Sheryl and her mother there. Remember I had told you Sandy had es-caped from Tallahassee Prison . . . ."

Lisa nodded. "What about Sheryl? Couldn't she have killed everyone, then shot her-self? Art, coming for a visit, had seen everyone dead. He could have taken the gun and maybe tossed it in the ocean."

"That was my first thought, Lisa. She also had motive. Her mother was found in the Gremlin with a hole in her right temple. She was angry with her mother for abandoning her, and pissed-off at her aunt and uncle for keeping it a secret of her mother's where-abouts for so long. But it was not proven if she had brought the murder weapon with her. Maybe Art brought it with him on his long haul. Long haul truck drivers carry some sort of wea-pon with them all the time.

"On the other hand, Sheryl could have brought the weapon with her for her mother's protection. Sheriff Grayson had checked the Nowak's phone bill. On the thirteenth of March, 2 A.M, Monday, a call was made to Sheryl's phone number. Now, ten days later from that phone call everyone was killed. If Sheryl was out to kill everyone, why wait ten, or eleven day's later. So with that idea in mind, it ruled out Sheryl. She probably went to Orlando to help her mother. Since her mother was on the run from the law, Sheryl had probably figured her mother needed some protection. Probably even run off with her mother and be fugitives together. With me so far, honey?"

Lisa nodded with deep concentration and processed all of my words care—fully and thoughtfully in her brilliant, detective mind.

"Sheryl was so excited to go see her mother, she packed speedily and left that morning. Answers the question why her answering machine was full of messages from the thirteenth . . ."

"But the Deputy Sheriff found the gun, though. What about that?"

Lisa asked inquisitively.

"Yes, my sweets, the gun was found near the body. The name belonging to the corpse was Sandy's boyfriend Scott Selinski. Now he also had a mo-tive, well, at least a motive for killing Sandy. After all, Sandy had murdered his twin daughters, Marcy and Casey, using lethal chemicals.

"Sandy was safer in prison." I grinned on that one. "He also could have gone bonkers and killed everyone on sight. Of all the suspects who had motive to kill, my best bet would've been Scott . . . ."

"Scott? Very interesting," Lisa said. "Wasn't he the one found on the bot-tom of the ocean floor?"

"Yes. In a car, BMW, with a hole in his forehead. I believe he had shot himself while driving at a high-rate of speed, losing control of the car, and plunging into the ocean. That was one of the vehicles missing from Dale's garage. The other vehicle belonging to his wife, we'd also thought was stol-en, was in the auto shop for repairs . . ."

"But there was another car found resting on the bottom of the ocean floor. Can you explain that, Lover boy?"

"Yes, you sexy thing you, I can explain that, and will. The car was a Ford Crown Victoria belonging to the driver and owner named Joey Galliano, the kingpin of Chicago drug dealers. Which I might add, had a slug wound in his throat from a Python. The bullet went through the driver's side wind-shield. It seemed Joey was chasing Scott at pretty close range, because the two cars were very close together resting on the ocean floor.

"Scott shoots Joey through the windshield while he was being chased. Joey loses control, plunging into the ocean. Scott kills himself, maybe a few short seconds later, shooting himself in the forehead. And both cars plunged simultaneously into the ocean.

"Maybe he was pissed at Scott for killing everyone. Now keep in mind, Joey Galliano was from Chicago. Grayson and I believe he dedicated him-self to find Sandy, Dale and Dale's wife for twenty years for stealing the drug money. And when he finally found them, they were all dead. Scott probably was just finishing off his shooting spree when Joey came into play. Joey had no way to get his money back now. Joey was pissed with a capitol 'P' . . . So the chase was on."

Lisa took in a very deep breath, shaking her head. "Great set of theories, Nicky baby. But was that all of it?"

"Yes, honey bunny. That's all of it." Grabbing her soft-touching hand, I said, "Let's go to the loft and make hot . . . passionate . . . crazy love before your parents come home."

"Thought you'll never ask," Lisa said happily.

Before entering the log cabin, we'd both turned around facing Old Glory flapping and waving in the breeze . . . . We saluted it proudly.

Salute everyone . . . !